WHEN SORROWS COME

SEANAN McGUIRE

WHEN SORROWS COME

AN OCTOBER DAYE NOVEL

DAW BOOKS, INC.

DONALD A. WOLLHEIM, FOUNDER

1745 Broadway, New York, NY 10019

ELIZABETH R. WOLLHEIM

SHEILA E. GILBERT

PUBLISHERS

www.dawbooks.com

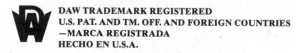

DAW TRADEMARK REGISTERED
U.S. PAT. AND TM. OFF. AND FOREIGN COUNTRIES
—MARCA REGISTRADA
HECHO EN U.S.A.

PRINTED IN THE U.S.A.

For Kayleigh.
Took us long enough, but now we're here.

ACKNOWLEDGMENTS

I know I say something like this almost every time, but I honestly can't believe we're finally here. After book after book of delaying the event we all knew was coming, I finally reached the wedding. And it only took me fifteen books! That feels like it should be enough to get me some sort of award.

Thank you all so much for still coming with me on these gloriously ridiculous adventures, as Toby demonstrates just how much trouble one protagonist can get into when given carte blanche to bleed all over everything. This is the second October Daye book to be composed and completed during a near-universal lockdown, and torturing her is much of what's been keeping me sane. I couldn't do that if you weren't here with me, and I am genuinely grateful.

My biggest thanks to everyone who's been here to help me keep my sanity intact during these trying times, including my D&D group (We blend! We really do!), the Machete Squad, the entire team at DAW Books, and my agent, Diana Fox, who has gone above and beyond the call of duty in beating this pivotal volume of Toby's adventures into shape. I couldn't have done it without her.

Thank you to my dearest, most darling and beloved Amy, who will be meeting me in the corn next October; to Vixy, who stands up against an onslaught of email with compassion and grace; to Crystal, who has been astonishingly graceful about her osmosis into our swarm of weirdoes; and to Dr. Gauley, for her incredible veterinary medical care. Thanks to everyone who has played Dungeons & Dragons with me during these days of awkward Zoom games and virtual dice, and to Chaz, whose well-timed assistance made my lifelong dream of owning my own Dance Dance Revolution machine come true. Thanks to Shawn and Jay and Tea, to

Margaret and Mars and a whole list of people, all of whom I adore utterly.

My editor, Sheila Gilbert, makes so many things possible, as does the patient work of Joshua Starr, who emails me to nag when I let things slip. Diana Fox has finally learned how to use Discord, while Chris McGrath's covers just get better and better. All my cats are doing well: Elsie, Thomas, and Megara all thrive on my being home constantly, and spend most of their time glued to my side, when not socializing our newest addition, Verity. Finally, thank you to my pit crew: Christopher Mangum, Tara O'Shea, and Kate Secor.

My soundtrack while writing *When Sorrows Come* consisted mostly of "Monument" by Keiino, the soundtrack to *Eurovision Song Contest: the Story of Fire Saga*, *The Horror and the Wild* by The Amazing Devil, *The Light* and *The Dark* by Delta Rae, endless live concert recordings of the Counting Crows, and the two new albums from Taylor Swift (I like *evermore* better than *folklore*, but both are lovely). Any errors in this book are entirely my own. The errors that aren't here are the ones that all these people helped me fix.

Now come with me. It's time to attend a wedding, and hope that everything goes smoothly. . . .

OCTOBER DAYE PRONUNCIATION GUIDE
THROUGH *WHEN SORROWS COME*

All pronunciations are given strictly phonetically. This only covers races explicitly named in the first fifteen books, omitting Undersea races not appearing or mentioned in the current volume.

Adhene: *aad-heene*. Plural is "Adhene."
Aes Sidhe: *eys shee*. Plural is "Aes Sidhe."
Afanc: *ah-fank*. Plural is "Afanc."
Annwn: *ah-noon*. No plural exists.
Arkan sonney: *are-can saw-ney*. Plural is "arkan sonney."
Bannick: *ban-nick*. Plural is "Bannicks."
Baobhan Sith: *baa-vaan shee*. Plural is "Baobhan Sith," diminutive is "Baobhan."
Barghest: *bar-guy-st*. Plural is "Barghests."
Blodynbryd: *blow-din-brid*. Plural is "Blodynbryds."
Cait Sidhe: *kay-th shee*. Plural is "Cait Sidhe."
Candela: *can-dee-la*. Plural is "Candela."
Coblynau: *cob-lee-now*. Plural is "Coblynau."
Cu Sidhe: *coo shee*. Plural is "Cu Sidhe."
Daoine Sidhe: *doon-ya shee*. Plural is "Daoine Sidhe," diminutive is "Daoine."
Djinn: *jin*. Plural is "Djinn."
Dóchas Sidhe: *doe-sh-as shee*. Plural is "Dóchas Sidhe."
Ellyllon: *el-lee-lawn*. Plural is "Ellyllons."
Folletti: *foe-let-tea*. Plural is "Folletti."
Gean-Cannah: *gee-ann can-na*. Plural is "Gean-Cannah."

Glastig: *glass-tig*. Plural is "Glastigs."
Gwragen: *guh-war-a-gen*. Plural is "Gwragen."
Hamadryad: *ha-ma-dry-add*. Plural is "Hamadryads."
Hippocampus: *hip-po-cam-pus*. Plural is "Hippocampi."
Kelpie: *kel-pee*. Plural is "Kelpies."
Kitsune: *kit-soo-nay*. Plural is "Kitsune."
Lamia: *lay-me-a*. Plural is "Lamia."
The Luidaeg: *the lou-sha-k*. No plural exists.
Manticore: *man-tee-core*. Plural is "Manticores."
Naiad: *nigh-add*. Plural is "Naiads."
Nixie: *nix-ee*. Plural is "Nixen."
Peri: *pear-ee*. Plural is "Peri."
Piskie: *piss-key*. Plural is "Piskies."
Puca: *puh-ca*. Plural is "Pucas."
Roane: *row-n*. Plural is "Roane."
Satyr: *say-tur*. Plural is "Satyrs."
Selkie: *sell-key*. Plural is "Selkies."
Shyi Shuai: *shh-yee shh-why*. Plural is "Shyi Shuai."
Silene: *sigh-lean*. Plural is "Silene."
Tuatha de Dannan: *tootha day danan*. Plural is "Tuatha de Dannan," diminutive is "Tuatha."
Tylwyth Teg: *till-with teeg*. Plural is "Tylwyth Teg," diminutive is "Tylwyth."
Urisk: *you-risk*. Plural is "Urisk."

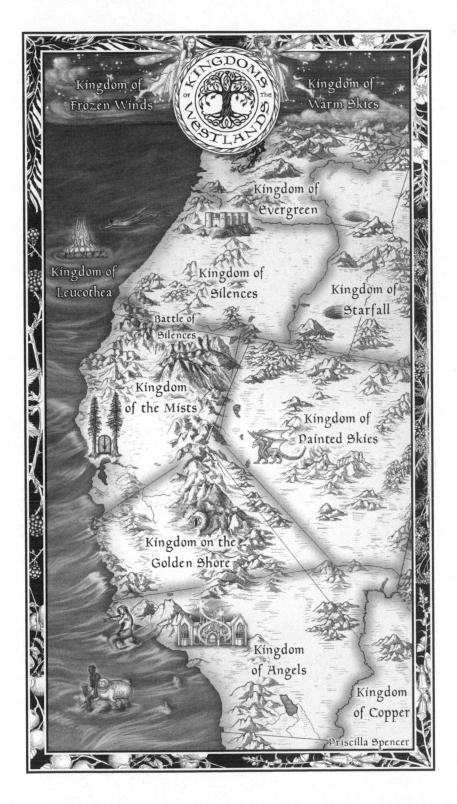

ONE

April 11th, 2015

When sorrows come, they come not single spies,
But in battalions.

—William Shakespeare, *Hamlet*.

IF SIX MONTHS AGO, you'd told me I would be the one to bring Oberon, King of all Faerie, home from his long exile, I would have laughed in your face. If you'd gone on to tell me I was going to declare myself a Torquill in all but blood, formally emancipate myself from my mother's line of descent, stand witness to a marriage which technically made Dianda Lorden my stepmother, and still be expected to spend time worrying about my wedding, I would have looked at you like you'd just grown a second head. Or possibly a third one.

Then again, if you'd tried to warn me I was even going to need to be concerned about any of those things happening—up to and including the wedding—I would have looked at you the same way. My life does not lend itself well to prognostication.

Thankfully for my ability to get out of bed in the evening, my sister-slash-Fetch, May, and my best friend, Stacy, figured out early on that I have slightly less than no idea what I'm doing when it comes to weddings. And because Stacy was the first person in my group of changeling hooligans to get married—only person so far, since Kerry prefers the "love 'em and leave 'em" model of relationship, and Julie's most recent serious boyfriend died—she was more than happy to step in and take over. May hasn't been married yet, although I expect her to propose to her live-in girlfriend, Jazz, as soon as I get my own marriage out of the way, but as a Fetch, her memory goes back much, much longer than a normal person's, and she remembers having been married at least a dozen times, as both the bride and groom.

Sometimes I think being May must be deeply confusing. And then I remember that being me is deeply confusing, and amend that to "being a person" is deeply confusing, and move on.

Anyway, between them, May and Stacy had seized control of all but the smallest details of the ceremony and were happily adrift in a sea of complicated plans and traditions I neither understood nor actually cared to understand. As long as they were willing to work with Tybalt on the parts he had strong opinions about, and I wound up married at the end of this, I was content.

All the parties involved seemed to find my inability to care about my own wedding somehow weird. I'd like to know when, precisely, I have done anything normally in my life. Most changelings can't even manage to get knighted, thanks to pureblood prejudices against anyone with a drop of mortal blood in our veins. Me, I got knighted, got counted—there's probably a better way of saying "was made a Countess and given a knowe of my own," but I don't know it—gave up the greater title in favor of returning to simple knighthood, became a Hero of the Realm, and somehow got engaged to a King of Cats while all that was going on. Weird is what we do around here. Weird is the only way we know how to *live*.

My name is October Daye. I'm still a changeling, even if my mortality is thinner than it used to be. I'm one of only two Dóchas Sidhe in the entire world, descended from Amandine the Liar, Firstborn daughter of Oberon and Janet Carter, and I'm the legal daughter of Simon Torquill. Something else has changed in the past six months: during her divorce, at which she was very much not a willing participant, Mom tried to say Simon couldn't leave her because Oberon was her father and she didn't want him to go.

Turns out the laws of fae divorce don't care if one of the parties is Firstborn. They only care whether all the children of the parties involved are old enough to declare which bloodline they want to officially be a part of going forward. Since Simon was married to my mother when I was born, he's considered my father in

Faerie, even though my actual father was human, which meant I was able to declare myself a Torquill and sever myself from my mother's family line forever. So now I'm a descendant of Oberon who's legally considered a child of Titania, and if that's not a headache happening in slow motion, I can't tell you what is.

Mom outing herself as a Firstborn has caused some changes in my life as well. She'd been passing herself off as Daoine Sidhe for centuries, leaving me looking like an underpowered descendent of Titania and not a perfectly normal descendent of Oberon. Not all the changes brought on by Mom's big announcement have been negative ones, although all of them have been annoying for one reason or another.

Most of the Firstborn have long since removed themselves from casual fae society, although I interact with enough of my aunts on a regular basis that it doesn't always feel that way to me. I don't tend to interact with my uncles—the only one of them I've met, I murdered. So there's that. Anyway, having access to one of the Firstborn is something most people, having never actually had it, would consider a good thing. So they want it. Because they're not particularly smart. And now that they know Mom's Firstborn, they assume they can somehow get it through me, even though I publicly repudiated her during the divorce.

This has resulted in a lot of "problems" in need of "solving" that, when I arrive at the place the problem supposedly occupies, have magically gone away and been replaced by a formal dinner party which mysteriously has a chair open for my bedraggled changeling ass, and a polite question about whether I have my mother on speed dial.

I have flipped off more nobles in the last six months than in my entire life previous, and that's saying something. My sister—lucky, awful August—is living Undersea in the Duchy of Saltmist with her father and staying fortunately clear of all the crap. The Undersea has a more pragmatic view of the Firstborn and tends to fight them rather than flirt with them. Probably smarter, in the long run.

One good thing about this development: I had been building a bit of a reputation as a king-breaker, due to a couple of acts of treason that really weren't entirely my fault, and it's unfair that people keep acting as if they were. A lot of borders had been closed to me unless Arden Windermere, the Queen in the Mists, got me special permission to travel. That includes the borders with our nearest neighbors: Silences, Painted Sands, and Golden Shore. I promised ages ago to take my squire to Disneyland, and not being allowed to drive through Golden Shore to get to Angels down in Southern California has made that a lot harder than it needed to be.

If monarchs are that much against being overthrown, they shouldn't do things that would make it seem like a good idea. The rot at the root isn't the revolution, it's the ruler who refuses to re-sign. King-breaking is a symptom of sickness, not the cause.

Anyway, it turns out that being able to travel freely because my mother's a terrible person is helpful with the whole "getting mar-ried" thing, since the High King of the Westlands, Aethlin Sollys, has claimed the right to host the wedding party. The only problem was that he's in Toronto, which is *several* Kingdoms away from California. Like, probably a dozen, even if we charted the route that crossed the fewest borders possible. Without Mom's selfish revelation, getting to my own wedding might have been impossible unless the High King wanted to make a royal decree—something he tries to avoid as much as he can, not wanting to offend the kings and queens serving under him. Part of avoiding king-breakers is, again, being smart enough to not encourage their development.

Luckily, with no one wanting to offend my mother by banning me from their demesne these days, I was finally in a position to draw a straight line across the continent, heedless of whose bound-aries ended where. It was a heady change, and I would probably have been pushing Tybalt to let me upgrade our Disneyland trip to Disney *World* if I hadn't been afraid he'd kill me for skipping out on having a proper honeymoon with just the two of us.

Finding out that I was allowed to travel again was enough to kick wedding prep, which had been ongoing at a slow, almost stately pace for quite some time, into high gear. I think everyone who actually knew me was afraid I'd do something or overthrow someone and get myself put back on home kingdom arrest before the wedding could take place. I couldn't entirely blame them for that. The more surprise dinner parties I get ambushed with, the more tempting it became to stab somebody who probably didn't entirely deserve it but was getting on my nerves enough to make it feel like a good idea at the time.

As I've already established, most steps in the planning process were taken out of my hands by the people smart enough to know that I cannot be trusted with an entire wedding, especially not my own. There were still a few decisions that needed my input, although none of them involved either the dress or the flowers, two things I was reasonably sure were usually the bride's responsibility. Tybalt was handling both, and questions about what he intended to do had a tendency to either result in Shakespearean profanity or actual feline hissing. My fiancé is Cait Sidhe, but he's normally better about keeping that from influencing his behavior.

Not that I minded. Honestly, it was kind of cute. It made me feel . . . it's difficult to explain how it made me feel when Tybalt relaxed enough in my presence to let his more animal traits show through. The first time I heard him purr, I thought I might die of joy on the spot.

Faerie isn't always the kindest place to live and, from what I understand, it never has been. We're all descendants of the same Three, but somewhere along the line we went from treating one another like one big family to making war whenever possible, setting up artificial hierarchies to determine who was better or more important than who. I'm not complaining about the fact that we figured out there were too many of us to all live like siblings—it would have made dating complicated, and marriage basically impossible—but there's literally no reason for any kind of fae to behave as if they're somehow better than any other. All our streams run from the same source, as it were.

There was a time, before Oberon's original disappearance—an event which fractured Faerie for centuries, and is still fracturing Faerie today, thanks to his continued refusal to tell anyone that he's back—when changelings were rare and almost feared. Sometimes the blending of fae and human blood can lead to people called merlins, mortal beings who can tap into immensely powerful faerie magic without any of the costs or limitations faced by true fae. There was a war. The purebloods lost. After that, they were a lot less inclined to go stepping out with the local human population, wanting to avoid another merlin uprising. And in the absence of changelings, they'd needed to find something else to hate.

I wasn't there, obviously. I was born in the 1950s, not the 1500s. But Tybalt is older than I am, and he remembers those days all too vividly. Without changelings, the other purebloods had turned a lot of their prejudices and smug judgments on the members of the fae community who carried clearly animal attributes—including the Cait Sidhe. They're still viewed as savage and uncouth even today, when there are changelings all over the place. Tybalt learned to suppress his feline side in order to be respected and treated like the king he is. Watching him learn that I wouldn't judge him when he let himself relax has been a joy and a gift that I'm grateful for every single night.

I'll be even more grateful when his adopted nephew, Raj, comes of age and is able to formally claim the throne of the local Court of Cats. Until that happens, Tybalt is technically still King of Dreaming Cats, his crown held in stewardship by Ginevra, a Princess of Cats and daughter of the King of Whispering Cats in Silences. His loyalties will remain at least partially divided between me and his people until Raj is mature enough to challenge him and win.

I honestly think Raj would win if he challenged Tybalt tomorrow; Tybalt would go easy on him, out of love and concern and the need to be rid of his position, and it would undermine Raj's entire rule. Raj knows it, too. That's why neither of them is pushing for the challenge to happen any faster than it needs to.

At least with Raj and his regent holding the Court, Tybalt has been freed to functionally move into my house. Even better, despite being older than the United States of America, which is something I do my best not to dwell on more than absolutely necessary, Tybalt doesn't hold with any of that puritanical human nonsense about a bride needing to be "pure" on her wedding day. Not that that ship hadn't sailed *long* before he proposed to me—and long before he and I were anything but enemies. I have a teenage daughter, Gillian, who lives with the Roane in Half Moon Bay, trying to figure out her place in Faerie without the specter of her deadbeat mother-turned-hero of the realm hanging over her.

My family life is a little complicated.

Of course, that doesn't make me special. For example, as we've been working on the guest list for the wedding itself—taking into account people like Arden, who would love to be there, but can't attend, due to the fact that it would leave her Kingdom without a queen in the event that one of our neighbors went "great, the king-breaker's out of town, let's use this opportunity to invade"—my squire has presented an unexpectedly massive problem.

Quentin has been with me for a little over five years, supposedly learning how to be a proper knight, which doesn't really make sense when looked at with an objective eye, since most of the time, I'm about as proper as a kick to the groin. Sir Etienne, who was responsible for the bulk of my training, gets this look of horrified dismay on his face whenever anyone reminds him that he trained me and now I'm a hero and isn't he proud? He is not proud—unless it's of the fact that I'm somehow still breathing. I never really grasped the courtly graces or knightly manners, and my sword fighting technique is basically "pretend it's a baseball bat and just keep swinging until the ball stops moving."

To be fair to Etienne, he's not the one who taught me how to swing a sword. That was my liege, Duke Sylvester Torquill, Simon's brother and Duke of Shadowed Hills. He was teaching me the rules of proper sword fighting when things got . . . complicated between us. We're currently not technically speaking to each other, mostly because his wife has decided I'm the enemy. The last time I saw either of them was at the formal court where they petitioned Queen Windermere for permission to wake their daughter, Rayseline, from her current state of elf-shot slumber.

The permission was denied, somewhat unexpectedly, by the Luidaeg, who's been showing up for court more often since her father came back. I assume it's because she's waiting to see whether Mom will follow up her "secretly Firstborn" bombshell by pointing out that Oberon is once more walking among us. But who knows for sure? The Luidaeg is old enough to have witnessed continental drift in real time, and the reasons she does things are sometimes difficult for people less long-lived to follow. I'm not even a baby to her. I'm barely a fetus. And if she wants Rayseline Torquill to sleep a little longer, that's what's going to happen.

Anyway, my squire has presented a surprising level of difficulty where my wedding is concerned, because he's part of an ancient system of free babysitting called "blind fosterage," wherein children who need to learn the customs of another kingdom or who are considered to be at high risk for assassination are sent off to spend some time being nameless and serving in someone else's court. It's an archaic tradition, but it keeps the kids busy and out from underfoot. And alive, which is sometimes the hardest part when you're talking about the children of titled nobility.

When Quentin's parents sent him away, they wanted to be absolutely sure no one would recognize him, which is why he wound up fostered to a relatively unremarkable Duchy on the other side of the continent from their home knowe. In Toronto. Because my squire, who can't remember to take his own damn clothes out of the dryer before they wrinkle, is actually the Crown Prince of the Westlands.

Yeah. I wasn't too thrilled either, when I first found out.

It might not have been such an issue now if his looks were different. When I first met him, he had hair the color of a dandelion that had just gone to seed, white-blond and fluffy, but as he's gotten older, his hair has gotten darker to match the hammered bronze color of his father's. He looks even more like both his parents put together, not less, and there's no way I can take him anywhere near Toronto without him being recognized. And that's a problem.

Everyone agrees that I can't get married without taking my squire, even Tybalt. It would be a massive insult, for one thing. It's also quite simply not going to happen. He's the son I never had, and while it may have taken me a while to admit that to myself, I love the kid too much to leave him out of something this important. Eventually, he'll have to return to Toronto and go back to Crown Princing around, instead of slumming it out here with me. Until that happens, though, he's family, and family doesn't get left behind.

He also can't come to Toronto with us. If he did, he'd be recognized immediately, and since part of the point of blind fosterage is keeping kids from being assassinated, telling the world where he is would be a bad thing. Even if "where he is" happens to be the upstairs bedroom of a known king-breaker.

We'd been experimenting with having Garm, one of Sylvester's other knights, cast an illusion to make Quentin look like someone else. Gwragen illusions are functionally unbreakable. Unfortunately, they need the caster to stay at least remotely nearby, and Garm and I have never had a close enough relationship for him to be particularly interested in attending my wedding. Honestly, I couldn't blame the guy for wanting to stay as far away as possible. He was pretty sure someone was going to wind up dead, and so was I, knowing my track record. So we needed to find another solution, and time was running out.

It was all enough to make my head hurt—and make me grateful that other people were handling most of the details.

It was early evening, and the house was quiet. Rare these days, but pleasant when it happens, as long as it doesn't last too long. I start getting twitchy when I don't know where my people are. Tybalt had gone to the Court of Cats shortly after he woke up, saying he needed to check in on Ginevra and make sure Raj wasn't making her pull out all her whiskers.

Jazz, May's live-in girlfriend, is a Raven-maid, one of the few truly diurnal types of fae. She'd been up for hours, spending most of them at her antique store on Telegraph Avenue, and May often left early to pick Jazz up from work.

For definitions of "pick up" that we all understand mean "meet at the store and then take the BART back from Berkeley." My Fetch doesn't drive, and we're all safer that way.

Quentin had been out since sometime after midnight the night before, having gone to spend the night with his boyfriend at Goldengreen. Dean Lorden is probably technically my brother now, which I try not to think about when I have a choice in the matter, but since my legal father married Dean's parents—both of them—I think that makes us family. And the tree gets more confusing, and the list of wedding invitations gets longer.

I rolled languidly out of bed, stretching my arms up over my head and enjoying the silence. Both my ancient half-Siamese cats cracked their eyes open to watch me go, but didn't stir themselves enough to get up, or even lift their heads. I leaned over to rub Cagney between the ears, and she favored me with a vast yawn.

"Good girls," I said fondly. Spike, our resident rose goblin, was off somewhere doing whatever it did when I stayed in bed too long for its tastes. Probably rooting around in the garden. It seems to like sleeping under the rosemary, and since it keeps the rats away, that's fine by me. None of us are sure how it keeps getting outside; the cats are indoor only, and we're careful about windows.

Not only to keep the cats from getting out. To keep any of the nasty surprises that proliferate in Faerie from getting *in*.

I made my way out of the room and into the hall, heading for the stairs. May always makes coffee, and sometimes waffles, before she goes off to meet Jazz. I don't get any benefits from caffeine these days—my system clears itself too quickly for most substances to have any effect—but I like the flavor. And Tybalt is forever pleading with me to eat more. I could start the night by making us both happy.

When I reached the kitchen, the hoped-for coffee was in the pot, a plate of something I suspected of being scones, if not waffles, was on the counter under a tea towel, and someone was talking in soft tones on the back porch. I stopped, turning toward the sound with narrowed eyes.

Call me paranoid, but since something usually *is* out to get me, I think I'm allowed.

I moved toward the door as quietly as I could, all but holding my breath as I strained to hear. Purebloods have sharper-than-human eyesight, and mine is pretty damn good, but most fae whose ears are just pointed, not furred or flexible, have human-level hearing. All I could make out was that one was higher than the other, and the higher voice was entirely unfamiliar.

People don't normally hang out on my porch talking without a good reason. I stopped, still straining to listen.

The deeper voiced person laughed, and I relaxed, because that voice, at least, I recognized. Dean had been coming around the house almost since we moved in, and his visits have only grown in frequency and length since he and Quentin officially started dating. I would have started making jokes about paying rent if anyone in the house had actually been paying for the dubious pleasure of living there. Thanks to a generous gift from Sylvester before he stopped acknowledging me, I own the place free and clear, with the exception of our yearly property taxes. I knew Dean's laugh.

The higher voiced person laughed in answer, and I frowned again. Why was Dean bringing a stranger around the house? It didn't make sense.

The easiest way to solve a mystery is to run straight toward it and knock it into as many pieces as possible. I shrugged, still frowning, and opened the door.

Dean was standing on the porch with his arms wrapped around a teenage boy I didn't recognize, kissing him like he thought the world was going to end as soon as he stopped. The boy had his fingers tangled in Dean's hair and was kissing him just as hungrily. I froze, staring at the pair of them. Neither one seemed to notice me standing there. I wouldn't have been able to slide a sheet of paper between them if I'd been inclined to try—and I wasn't so inclined. I was a lot more likely to slam the door and walk away.

The fae don't have a very strong attachment to a lot of human concepts about relationships. They've managed to creep into our culture, largely due to changelings like me, who come away from our mortal parents with lots of weird ideas, but that doesn't make them popular or widely adopted. Most nobles wind up in marriages with the potential for biological children because that's how you hold onto the throne your ancestors fought and possibly died to secure for your family line, but that's about where we stop putting restrictions on people.

The majority of fae, if asked to label themselves by modern human terms, will go with "bisexual," because the gender of their partners matters a lot less than the fact that everyone is there to have a good time. With shapeshifters and transformation magic and people who are literally trees for half the year running around, even "gender" can get a little bit vague and is rarely discussed outside of private conversations. Marriages may be two people, or three, or more—the largest stable marriage I've ever encountered was five people, all of them perfectly content with the arrangement.

It doesn't make much sense to me. I'm still human enough to be an absolute prude by fae standards, and I don't share. But as long as everyone's happy, or at least satisfied, Faerie doesn't care, and so I do my best not to care either.

But one thing Faerie *does* tend to be fairly strict about is loyalty. When the fae make promises, we expect them to be kept, and we don't handle it well when they're not. Dean and Quentin had never mentioned being in an open relationship to me, and we talked enough that I was sure I'd know if they were seeing other people.

My stepbrother was cheating on my squire on my own kitchen step, and I didn't know what to do about it.

The two of them pulled apart, and I found my voice, demanding stridently, "What the *hell* do you think you're doing?"

They turned to face me, Dean's eyes going wide as he realized they had an audience, the stranger's cheeks flushing a surprisingly vibrant red. He was paler even than my mother, almost the same shade as a sheet of paper, with dust-colored hair and brown eyes that managed to be a few shades lighter, like grimy cobwebs. His ears were sharply pointed, although not at an angle that would have betrayed Daoine Sidhe heritage. I breathed in, tasting the balance of his blood on the evening breeze.

Banshee, from one end to the other, with no traces of anything else.

"Sorry," said Dean. "We thought you'd be out."

"Oh, so you've done this before?"

The two of them exchanged a look, Dean's eyes getting even wider—if that was even possible—before the blood drained out of his cheeks. He whipped back around to face me.

"This isn't what you think," he said, words coming out in a staccato burst with no real space for breath between them.

"Really? Because what I think is that you want me to slap you upside the head before I call my father and tell him to tell your mother what you're doing."

The stranger burst out laughing. It was a high, musical sound, and when he spoke a moment later, it matched the bright tenor of his voice.

"I'm so sorry," he said. "We should have considered how this would look, but we really *didn't* think you'd be home."

I blinked at him.

"Talk faster," I suggested. "I don't have a very long temper right now."

"Isn't it the fuse that's normally measured in length?" asked the stranger. "You're the one who's supposed to be good at human idiom."

Dean was still pale, but stayed quiet, watching his new fling grill me. I scowled at both of them.

"Right now it's everything, so explain yourselves before I start stabbing."

"Fine, fine, but you have to let me mess with May when she gets home." The stranger held his hands up, palms toward me. "I know you want me to be able to come to the wedding without causing a major diplomatic incident, so I went to the Luidaeg and asked her if she could help me. I owe her a favor now, but this is permanent until she gives me the counteragent, so now I can come and see you get married like a good squire. I just have to be careful not to stub my toe and yell too loudly, or I could shatter all the crystal in Toronto."

I blinked. Slowly. Counted to ten and blinked again. "Quentin?"

He shrugged and lowered his hands, looking only faintly abashed. "Surprise?"

"Both of you get inside so I can kill you," I said and stepped out of the doorway, making room for them to pass me. Dean grabbed hold of his hand as soon as he lowered it, seeming to take some comfort in the contact. I was glad *someone* was taking comfort in the day.

Holding hands, they walked past me into the kitchen, and I closed the door behind them.

TWO

WITH THE DOOR SHUT and them safely trapped inside with me, the boys seemed to lose a little of their previous bravado. The one I suspected of being Quentin, despite being the wrong height, build, and bloodline, turned to look at me. He was still clinging to Dean's hand like a lifeline, and for the first time, he looked genuinely concerned.

Dean, on the other hand, looked like he was going to lose his most recent meal all over my kitchen floor. I favored him with a brief smile as I walked past them to the pile of baked goods May had left on the counter.

"I think these are scones," I said. "Anyone care to guess the flavor? May's been getting experimental recently. So it could be blueberry or plum or apple, but it could also be ham and raspberry or ginger and whatever the hell she's decided is a complementary flavor this week."

"Toby . . ." began the boy who might be Quentin.

"Nope," I said, with all the good cheer I could muster. It was a surprising amount. This was too ridiculous to be anything but abstractly funny. Either my squire had made an ill-advised deal with the sea witch for reasons I did not yet fully understand, or his boyfriend had discovered the single stupidest possible way to try to get out of the consequences of his own actions. And it didn't matter which was true because I was going to have a thrice-cursed scone before I dealt with it. "I just got up. Breakfast, then horrifying drama."

Always horrifying drama. In this house, horrifying drama is never a sometimes food.

I whisked the cloth off the pile of scones, revealing them to the rest of the kitchen. Even that seemed more dramatic than it necessarily had to be. The boys' impending revelation was infecting breakfast. The scones were pale pink, glittering with yellow sugar, and smelled like one of Luna's gardens. I picked one up and sniffed. It smelled sugary, tart, and floral all at once. I laughed.

"She made rose lemonade scones," I reported to the two boys. "Leave it to May to find a way to make even breakfast seem ominous. Either of you want a scone?"

"I'm good," said Dean.

"I'd love one," said the other boy.

"Here you go." I dropped the scone onto a plate and passed it to him before serving myself. May has long since figured out that the best way to get me to reliably eat is to keep food around the house, already cooked and ready to be shoved into my face. Scrambled eggs and bacon may be enjoyable, but they're not likely—that takes effort. Fresh-baked scones that someone else did all the work of preparing? I'll eat those. Same with coffee that someone else brewed. I may not get the pharmaceutical benefits of caffeine, but hydration is a good thing.

"October . . ." began Dean.

"Nope. Still fixing breakfast."

Both boys watched helplessly, the one who might be Quentin clutching his plate, as I prepared my coffee and carried it to the breakfast table, along with my own scones. I had taken two. Maybe that was greedy of me, but it's my house, and I was getting the distinct feeling this was going to be one of those nights where I didn't have a lot of time to sit down and eat.

The boy who was probably Quentin sat across from me, watching warily as I picked up a scone and took the first bite. He held his head like Quentin did, a little off-center, like he was expecting to need to tilt it in disapproval at my antics at any moment. And he had that Quentin-y look in his eyes, the one that implied I was about to do something absolutely appalling that would probably violate about a dozen rules of hospitality and nearly as many laws of Faerie, either written or unwritten.

The scone tasted like summertime perfume. I swallowed thoughtfully, and took a sip of coffee, lingering over the action. Let them squirm. If they'd done what they were claiming to have done, they deserved it.

Finally, I put my cup down and focused on the Banshee boy. "Prove you're my squire," I said.

"By the rose and the thorn, the root and the branch, I would need to have a death wish to pretend to be your squire when I'm not," he said. "I swear it on my magic, may it wither in my veins and stop my dancing if I lie."

"Nice, and suitably dire," I said approvingly. "But it proves nothing, especially since my squire, who is *smarter than an unnecessary bargain with the sea witch implies*, has magic that smells of steel and heather, while yours . . ." I breathed in deeply. "Yours smells of common gorse and vetiver. It's not even related."

He flinched a little. Apparently, that was more of a transformation than he'd been expecting. But this was the Luidaeg we were talking about here, and her magic is never just skin-deep. I took the opportunity to lean forward, breaking off another bite of scone. "So convince me," I said, popping it into my mouth.

"Your fiancé is a total nerd who tried to convince me you'd be fine with him dragging me to Silences for the weekend to watch a production of *Much Ado About Nothing*, and then he said that since back in Shakespeare's day 'nothing' was slang for female genitalia, it was the most appropriate play for a King of Cats on the verge of matrimony, since the title is actually *Making a Fuss About—*"

"Okay, you've met Tybalt," I said quickly, cutting him off. "And if you are Quentin Sollys, I have officially ruined the next King of the Westlands. Prove you know *me*."

He looked at me gravely, and said, "The first time I met you, I had been sent to carry a message from Duke Sylvester Torquill, which you summarily refused to hear, chiding me for my attempts to deliver it in the middle of a human neighborhood. I didn't know much about humans back then, so I believed you when you implied that someone might come along and . . . and overhear something that would betray the existence of Faerie to the mortal world. I was so worried I'd fail if I forced you to listen to me, by breaking one of the oldest rules, and that I'd fail if I didn't force you, because I'd be letting a Ducal message go unanswered." A note of frustrated misery crept into his tone. "I'd been in Shadowed Hills for almost a year. Everyone said the Duke was mad, but he'd been better since his wife and daughter came back, and then they all said it was only you who could move him to one of those black tempers, where he threw things and screamed, or tried to read secret messages in the cobwebs, or . . ."

His voice trailed off. I fought the urge to prod him to keep going. I'd been back for six years, and I still knew almost nothing of what it had been like to live with Sylvester while Luna, Rayseline, and I were all missing, presumed lost forever. People would only ever tell me that the Duke had lost his mind, or perhaps lost himself, in the tangled maze of bereavement and betrayal where he'd been abandoned. Etienne had been with him the whole time, and still couldn't speak of those years without paling and looking away. The general consensus seemed to be that I was better off for having been somewhere else.

And yet, Sylvester's temper and sense of right and wrong had been skewed enough these last few years that I sometimes felt like I needed to understand the man at his worst in order to figure out how to live with the person he was now.

The boy—Quentin, I couldn't pretend any longer that it wasn't Quentin—was looking down at the table, silent. I tapped the edge of my plate with one fingernail, filling the room with a sharp chime. He glanced up.

"Hey," I said. "I believe you."

Some of the tension left his shoulders.

I wasn't done. "I believe you have done something very stupid and very ill-considered, and I'm trying to decide how angry at you I am right now, so if you would please take a deep breath, tighten any necessary sphincters, and explain *exactly what the fuck it is you were thinking*, I *might* be less inclined to ground you until your own coronation!" My voice rose steadily throughout my little rant, until I was almost shouting by the end.

Quentin flinched again. "Um," he said.

"*Um*? That's what you have to say for yourself? *Um*? Oh, well, let's pack in it, folks, everything's fine, your parents aren't going to have me tried for treason after all!"

"Treason?" asked Dean.

I turned and glared at him. He quailed, apparently realizing that attracting my attention right now was a bad idea.

"Yes, Dean, treason," I said, forcing my voice to stay level. "I don't know how you do things in the Undersea, but here on the land, bargaining with one of the Firstborn to transform the Crown Prince into someone new, someone who has *no blood relation* to either the High King or the High Queen, who cannot possibly inherit the throne that is his by right of birth, is considered a little bit, I don't know, treasonous. Since I already have a reputation for king-breaking, which is entirely unfair and unearned—"

Quentin made a choked sound that might have been laughter. I shifted my glare briefly to him, and he quieted again.

"—but is definitely a factor of my life, I need to consider what it looks like when my squire goes off and pulls this sort of ridiculous stunt for no good reason whatsoever."

"But I *have* a good reason!" protested Quentin.

I narrowed my eyes at him. "And what could that good reason possibly be? And don't think I've forgotten that you still haven't told me the terms of your bargain with the Luidaeg. I'm about thirty seconds away from calling her and demanding she transfer your debts to me."

He blinked. "I don't really know how that would work . . ."

I put a hand over my face. "By Oberon's balls, I need you to tell me that you did *not* trade your firstborn child to the Luidaeg in exchange for the ability to attend my wedding."

"I didn't. And it's really weird hearing you swear by someone we've met. Even if he still hasn't really acknowledged that I exist, or talked to me, or anything like that."

I lowered my hand. "Noted. Tell me what you paid first, and then tell me why you thought this was a good idea." Dean made a sound of protest. I held up one finger, signaling him to silence, while continuing to glower at Quentin. "Now, please."

"I, um, I traded her my identity for a new one, and I get the counter-draught that gives my real face and everything else back after I see you get married. Which means I have to attend the wedding, and we both have to be alive when you take your vows. And it seemed like a good idea because . . ." He hesitated, swallowing hard. "Because you're my *mom*, Toby. I have a mother, I love her, but she stopped being there for me seven years ago, and it's been you almost the whole time since then. You're my knight and my responsible adult and my *mom*. I know someone's going to try to kill you at your own wedding! I've met you, I know how your life works, and you're my *mom*. I have to be there. I'm your squire. I'd be failing you completely if I wasn't there."

I stared at him, barely aware that my eyes had started to burn with unshed tears. Then I blinked and they were rolling down my cheeks, salt painting my lips and overwhelming the taste of lemon sugar. I put my coffee cup down again and leaned back in my chair, opening my arms.

That was all the invitation Quentin needed. He flung himself out of his own chair and into mine, sending me rocking back, although the counter was close enough that we didn't—quite—topple to the ground. He pressed his face into my shoulder as he slung his arms around my neck, and I closed my own arms around him, and held that boy as tight as I dared. I was still crying, a slow leak that felt almost insufficient for the moment. This should have been a huge, dramatic thing, all racking sobs and blood.

Maybe my standards are skewed.

So Quentin clung to me and cried, and Dean sat awkwardly, looking on without saying a word. He did eventually lean forward and steal the second scone off my plate, something I supposed was within his rights as my younger brother. I didn't say anything, just kept holding onto Quentin and breathing in the unfamiliar gorse and vetiver scent of his magic, which rolled off his skin like sharp perfume. It wasn't unpleasant. I hoped I wasn't going to have time to get used to it.

Although that *did* mean I'd need to get involved with the wedding planning, at least enough to make sure the actual date arrived as soon as possible. Dammit.

Quentin finally sniffled and let go, pulling back and gathering his wounded dignity around himself at the same time. It was such a ridiculously feline gesture that I snorted despite myself, and he blinked at me, a hint of hurt flashing through his eyes.

"No, sweetie, no, no," I said, reaching up to run my hand quickly over the surface of his hair. "I'm not laughing at you. I'm laughing at myself, and the situation. Sometimes I feel like I've ruined you."

"You could *never*," he protested. "I'm going to be a better king because of what I've learned from you. I'm going to make you so proud of me. I swear I am."

"I'm already proud of you," I said. "I've been proud of you since the day you demanded to be my squire if you had to be anyone's—and you did have to be someone's; there's no way you'd be able to hold the throne without a knighthood at your back. But no, you just looked so much like an offended cat for a second there that I realized when you do take the throne, you'll be taking it as someone who's spent way more time with the Cait Sidhe than is standard for one of our monarchs."

"Is that a bad thing?" asked Dean, who had finished my scone and apparently took the fact that we were no longer crying as permission to speak. I turned to face him. He shrugged. "I don't know a *lot* about land history, but I know from some of the things Dad and Marcia have said that there are people who look down on the shapeshifters and treat them like animals."

"It used to be a lot more acceptable to treat them badly, back before the purebloods had as many changelings to kick around as they do now," I said carefully. It's not that talking about Faerie's failings makes me uncomfortable. It's that I naturally approach them from a semi-mortal perspective and think most of them are incredibly stupid, which can be a problem. For all that Dean and Quentin were my family, they were also titled nobility. Dean already held his demesne. Quentin's would eventually include the entire continent. That made it important for me to put things as delicately as I could, while also telling them the truth.

We can only improve if we face the things we've done wrong. But if I was too blunt, anything I told them would just get contradicted by the rest of their adult advisors, and it would do nothing but make them trust me less.

Tybalt has never been entirely open with me about what it had been like for him in the centuries before I was born, and honestly, I've never pressed the issue too hard. The part of me that still thinks like a human doesn't like to dwell on the fact that I'm about to marry a man whose age is measured in triple digits, and the part of me that's fae is incensed and embarrassed by the fact that a vague disdain for "beasts" is still so culturally common that it flavored many of our early encounters.

No one likes to realize they've been an asshole. Even after they've been forgiven and learned to be better, it's a hard stone to swallow, and it weighs heavy in the stomach.

"But why?" asked Dean.

"Transformation magic flows through water," I said. "Titania did her best to position herself as Oberon's true queen, the one shining light of Faerie, and she wove her workings with flowers." Three roads to magic: water, blood, and flowers. They branch and braid and blend together, and none of us is untouched by at least one of them. People like me, who carry only one path in their veins, are rare. Oberon is my grandfather, and both my grandmother and my father are—were, in my father's case—humans. I got none of Titania's flowers or Maeve's water. My illusions are fragile things compared to someone even partially descended from Titania, and my blood yearns for the transformations that come so easily to my grandfather, making it easy for Maeve's water-workers to twist and change me, with or without my consent.

"So we don't like shapeshifters because they're descended from Maeve?" Dean asked, incredulous. "Mom's a shapeshifter, and Merrow are pure Titania. Not even Oberon was involved in making them."

"Yes, and Pete said her own siblings basically abandoned her for being too 'bestial' when they saw that she had fins and scales and shifted shapes as it suited her," I said. "When you're judging things on appearances, it doesn't always matter what's true. And Titania was big into encouraging her descendants to be assholes."

"Like Eira," said Quentin.

"Yes, like Eira. So you have one Queen of Faerie doing her best to destroy another, saying anything that's too animal is bad and tainted and wrong, and then you have Oberon, who's kinda part animal himself—the antlers were a surprise—but also super protean. He could make himself the perfect man for Titania. And that probably just fed into the story she was trying to tell. If being part-animal was bad, and the King unchallenged was only animalistic when he was with the Queen Titania wanted everyone to hate, it would be easy to shift the story to one where Maeve was corrupting him. You know how much the purebloods like to believe the easy answer."

Dean scowled. Quentin looked down, ashamed. I chucked him under the chin with one finger.

"Hey," I said. "You got so much better, bud. Don't think you didn't. You've learned to listen to the people around you, to see everyone as a vital part of Faerie, and to listen to the things we're trying to say. That's amazing. You've come so far."

"And all your friends are inappropriate by the standards of a true royal Court," said Dean. "We're going to cause diplomatic incidents when you have to go back to Toronto with your own face."

Quentin looked briefly, almost comically, alarmed. I managed not to laugh, but it was a near thing.

"He's not wrong. You're dating a mixed-blood whose mother likes to punch people in lieu of diplomacy, your best friend is a Cait Sidhe, your other best friend was born half-mortal and still lives with her human mother, and that's not saying anything about your relationship with my family, which is weird and messed-up at best, and that brings us nicely back to the part where your idea of a solution was going straight to the sea witch. I have *broken* you."

He had the good grace to look chagrined and was inhaling to speak when my phone rang. The screen flashed "unknown number," which could mean a robocaller, but was more likely to mean someone like Etienne, whose number didn't technically exist and hence didn't have a listing to display.

I gave the phone a baleful look. "You know, once upon a time, this would have been on the wall, not the table, and we'd all be asking each other if we were going to get that, and if you weren't the one who actually answered, you could pretend not to be home," I said in a neutral tone.

"Really?" asked Dean.

"Really."

"Huh." He looked dubious.

I sighed and answered the phone. "Hello, October Daye's phone, October speaking, I was just in the middle of an important family conversation, so if no one's dead or bleeding, please hang up and call back later."

"I think I'm partially responsible for your current family conversation," said the Luidaeg, sounding amused. "Hi."

I sat up straighter, managing not to drop the phone. "Luidaeg!"

"Yes, I think we established that a few seconds ago," she said. "I assume this conversation is about your boys."

"Yes. It is."

"Before you yell at me, Quentin may not have his majority yet, but he *is* an adult, and nothing about my geasa demands people have achieved their majority before I trade with them. Honestly, I think it was set to do the exact opposite. Nothing more harmful to do to a mother who's lost her children than to force her to treat cruelly with other people's little ones." Her voice turned bitter toward the end.

The Luidaeg is the first among the Firstborn, child of Oberon and Maeve, old enough to have seen most of history unfold in front of her, and to have forgotten more of it than the majority of us will ever know. And a long time ago, for reasons I've never pried too deeply into, Eira decided to destroy her. They were sisters. They could have been each other's greatest allies. Instead, Eira followed her mother, Titania, into hatred of Maeve's descendants, and orchestrated the slaughter of the Luidaeg's children and grandchildren, leaving their bodies flayed and broken on the shore while her chosen cat's-paws wore their flensed skins back to their own families like trophies.

The Luidaeg had survived the betrayal of her sister and the loss of her family. Honestly, she'd done better than anyone had any right to expect her to, not taking her revenge upon the families of the people who killed her children, not declaring war upon her sister's own descendants. As far as I've ever been able to determine, all she did was make a bargain with the children of the killers themselves, binding them to the skins of her dead descendants to create the Selkies, and then letting them go to the sea. She was more than merciful—she was kind.

Eira couldn't have that. She went to her own mother and convinced her, somehow, that the Luidaeg was plotting unspeakable revenge, and Titania set a geas on the grieving sea witch in order to protect her own daughter. From that day forward, the Luidaeg was forbidden to harm any descendant of Titania unless it was because they had voluntarily offered themselves to her as part of a bargain; she was unable to lie; and she was obligated to do anything within her not inconsiderable power to meet any request that was made of her. The only redeeming virtue of this terrible imposition upon her freedom was that she could set her own price, tailoring it to both the size of the request and how much she genuinely wanted—or didn't want—to help the person who was doing the asking.

I made a noncommittal noise. Giving Quentin a way to attend my wedding and asking only that he actually do so was incredibly kind for one of the Luidaeg's bargains. She could have asked for anything. She could have killed him on the spot—the only time her bindings will allow her to harm a child of Titania—and informed him that as one of the night-haunts, he'd be able to attend the whole thing unobserved. Either he'd worded his request very, very carefully, or she'd tied herself in knots to give him what he wanted at the absolute least personal cost to himself. Knowing their relationship, I was willing to bet on the latter.

Maybe I hadn't broken our next king. He had come to the Mists as a blind foster, and he'd go home as the beloved honorary nephew of one of Faerie's greatest remaining monsters. That was a pretty decent upgrade, no matter how you wanted to look at it.

"This is his second deal with me, in case you forgot."

"I didn't." His first deal had been for passage into Blind Michael's lands, before he'd been formally considered my squire. Blind Michael's hunt had taken Quentin's mortal girlfriend, Katie, intending to transform her into a horse for one of his new Riders. I had gone to get her and the rest of the stolen children back. Quentin had followed me. Not smart, but definitely heroic. The Luidaeg's price tag that time had been dismayingly similar to this one: come back with me, or don't come back at all.

"Then I don't understand the problem."

I pinched the bridge of my nose. "You knew I wasn't going to like this, or you would have warned me before you literally *turned my squire* into *someone else.*"

"That's true." She sounded almost cheerful now. "You don't like anything that messes with your remarkably staid way of looking at the world. I honestly don't quite understand it. You've been through enough bullshit at this point that I'd expect you to be a little bit more flexible, but whatever. I knew you were going to be pissed. I also knew that this was really important to him, and he was going to push me to do it no matter how expensive I said it was going to be, so I gave him the lowest price tag I possibly could."

"While also guaranteeing I was going to do what you wanted me to do." A lot of people have assumed my relative disinterest in the act of planning my own wedding means I don't actually *want* to get married. They're wrong. There is nothing in this world I currently want more. Tybalt needs to know I'm not going to leave him; I need to know that I'm putting down roots in truth and not just in theory. I need to hold his hands and tell him I'm going to stay.

I just don't care about all the ceremony that comes with it—or the giant target that me plus any major formal event will paint on my back. That's why I've been so happy to push all the planning off on the people who care more about it than I do. As long as at the end of all this, Tybalt is my husband in the eyes of the world the way he already is in my heart and I get to spend the rest of my life waking up to him, I'm happy.

"Yes," she said dryly. "Attend your own wedding."

I scoffed.

"I'm serious. I know you've tried to convince him to take you to the human courthouse, sign a piece of paper, and call that a marriage. I don't think you fully comprehend how monumental it is for a titled member of the Divided Courts—even a lowly one—to marry a King of Cats. I can't think of the last time that happened."

That was enough to make me pause, and turn my body slightly away from the table, where Quentin was in the process of pilfering the remains of my first scone. Why teenage boys think food tastes better if stolen from someone else's plate is something I will never understand. We only have one female member of the current teen horde, Chelsea, and she has better table manners than any of the boys, possibly due to being raised by a single mother who actually had the time to give a damn.

Nobody reasonable has the time for that. The Luidaeg continued: "This is a historic event, whether you want it to be or not. Cait Sidhe don't intermarry with the descendants of the rest of Faerie, or if they do, they choose the charmaids and the courtiers, never the higher nobility or the ones who would ever have the ear of a reigning monarch or get themselves labeled heroes of the realm. This marriage matters. The fact that you would happily throw something so pivotal away in favor of being able to wear blue jeans to the altar isn't just ridiculous, it's selfish. So yeah, maybe I took advantage of the fact that Quentin understands the situation better than you do, but can you honestly blame me? I need you at that ceremony. I need that ceremony to *happen*."

I blinked. "Why do you, in specific, need it? I don't follow."

"Oh, for my father's—no, that's it. For my father's sake, and the sake of my own descendants, who still shift from feet to fins as it suits them. You may be just a knight, *Sir* Daye, but you're a hero, a former Countess, the dearest advisor to the future High King of the Westlands, the daughter of the last of the Firstborn, and the woman who brought Oberon back to us, even if most people don't know it yet. For you to marry one of the shifting kind and take him to your bed and bower is to change the future of Faerie. If I have to use your squire's true face as the lever to get you to start taking responsibility for your life and what it means to the rest of us, I will. I won't feel bad about it for even a second, either, so you can swallow whatever nasty thing you were about to call me. You're going to wear a pretty dress, you're going to say whatever that Fetch of yours coaches you into saying, and you're going to have a proper state wedding if it kills you."

I blinked. "Um. Wow. That was a lot."

"Yes. Yes, it was."

"Are you done?"

The Luidaeg paused. "You know, I don't know. I didn't expect you to let me get through that whole thing."

"Do you feel better?"

"Yes, actually. I do."

I sighed. "Then it was worth it. Okay, look, I'm going to get married, I'm letting May and Stacy handle the details in part because I don't want to cock it up, which you know I'd do if I touched *anything*—"

Dean was snickering behind his hand, presumably because I'd said "cock." Sometimes surrounding myself with teenagers feels like a questionable life choice. I glared at him.

"—and I'll go to Toronto when they tell me it's time to go to Toronto. Is there a reason this had to happen *now*?"

To my surprise, the Luidaeg laughed. "Guess they figured this was how they were going to get you to show up. Well, if it works for them, it works for me. Tell May I'll be bringing two guests with me, even if her invitation only says plus one. Poppy's my date for the evening, and I'm not telling Dad he can't attend."

The phone clicked as the line went dead. I slowly lowered it, setting it back on the table before turning my attention to Quentin and Dean.

"All right," I said pleasantly. "Since the Luidaeg has decided to be vague, one of *you* can tell me why you're doing this now, without discussing it with me, and why things suddenly seem to be moving on a timetable."

The boys exchanged a nervous glance, taking hands once again, as if to ward off some terrible consequence of answering my question. Quentin then looked at the floor, leaving Dean to face me alone.

"Coward," I said fondly. "Dean?"

"I, um. I really don't think this is my place, and I'd like to be excused from this conversation, please."

"Nope," I said, with malevolent good cheer. "You went with him to the Luidaeg's, so you're just as responsible for his bad choices as he is."

Quentin looked up, taking a deep breath. "I had to do this right now if I wanted to come to the wedding, because we're leaving for Toronto tomorrow morning," he said, in a rush.

I blinked at him. "Oh," I said. "Is that all?"

THREE

MOVING AUTOMATICALLY, my whole body numb, I rose from the table and started for the door. My stomach grumbled, unconcerned by silly things like my apparently impending marriage. I paused at the counter to tuck two more rose lemonade scones into a napkin, carrying them with me out into the hall.

The scuffle of feet warned me I was being followed. I didn't stop or look around until I reached the stairs and had the banister firm and solid under my hand. Unlike everything else around me—faces, plans for my own future—it wasn't shifting, but seemed content to remain good, honest wood, giving me something to lean on.

"Yes?" I finally asked.

Quentin shifted his unfamiliar weight from foot to foot, more at ease with his own transformed body than I've ever been with any of mine. "Are you okay?" he asked, in a small voice.

"I don't know," I said. "Apparently, my entire family has been conspiring to abduct me to Canada because I can't be trusted to know the date of my own damn wedding. So I'm feeling a little left out and a little disrespected and a lot like I need to go lie down in my bed or stand in a hot shower until I stop wanting to stab you all."

"We don't heal the way you do," said Dean.

"Hence the restraint," I said, through gritted teeth.

"You said you didn't want to have anything to do with putting the wedding together," objected Quentin. "You said it, and you always tell us family doesn't lie to family, so that means you must have meant it!"

"That is a bullshit fortune cookie proverb that I have never uttered intentionally," I snapped. "Not unless I was drunk or woozy from blood loss. Try pulling the other one. Something I *did* say, and know for a fact I said, was 'just tell me what to wear and when to show up, and I'll be there.' Well, no one's told me what to wear, and as far as I'm concerned, dragging the date out of you in my kitchen doesn't count!"

I turned and stormed up the stairs, leaving them staring after me. Neither one followed, and I was briefly grateful for that. Then again, Quentin's been living with me for years, and Dean grew up dealing with his mother's temper. When Dianda Lorden wants a few minutes to cool off, the smart thing to do is to let her have it.

The upstairs hall was still cool, dark, and empty, undisturbed by the turmoil downstairs. I stalked along it to my room, slammed the door open, and stomped inside, throwing myself onto the bed like *I* was the petulant teenager and the boys were the supposed parental figures. Just like it had when I was actually a teen and my feelings were occasionally too big for my body, the sheer overdramatic impact of my body against the mattress made me feel a little bit better. Even though it crushed the scones.

The cats, bounced out of their slumber by physics, raised their heads, opened sleepy blue eyes, and blinked at me. Cagney got to her feet, moving to sniff at my hair, before pronouncing judgment in her creaky Siamese voice with a loud and imperious meow. I rolled onto my back, automatically starting to scratch her ears.

"It's your King I'm mad at," I informed her. "He's being a controlling jerk."

She butted her head against my hand. I sighed and kept petting. Cats are good that way. They'll care if you're unhappy, but they won't let it get in the way of the important things, like getting properly adored by their bipedal servants.

Sometimes I wonder if the Court of Cats, when in session, isn't just all the Cait Sidhe taking turns having thumbs and petting each other, since that seems to be most of what the average cat wants out of life. Cait Sidhe aren't animals. They still have a normal feline desire for cheek rubs and ear scritches, and enough dignity not to go looking for them when other people are around. That's probably not how they do things, but it's a way to think about a Court I'll never belong to or properly attend without focusing on the violence that's haunted it almost every time I've been allowed inside.

The Cait Sidhe live in harmony with their feline kin, which means they fight for dominance with claws and teeth, and no one with any sense gets in the way of one of those conflicts. I've felt Tybalt's claws myself. Scary stuff. So it's nice to think, sometimes, that there are beautiful aspects to their governance to go along with the terrible ones.

I sighed, watching Lacey roll over and start to groom her sister's head with long swipes of her tongue. Maybe I was being unreasonable. Quentin and the Luidaeg were right; I had abdicated almost all decision-making aspects of wedding planning—it was understandable that people might have thought I didn't care. But they were also wrong. I had specifically said to tell me where to show up and when, and maybe that had sounded flippant, but I *said* it, and I was supposed to be the bride. Wasn't it standard to at least ask the bride if she was free to attend the wedding?

What if I'd taken a job? What if Arden had sent me off to fight a monster or something? What if I'd decided to take advantage of my current freedom of movement and booked that trip to Disneyland after all? I had a car. I liked to drive. I could have been just about anywhere.

Of course, all parties involved knew me pretty well, and knew the chances of me voluntarily being away from home were slim to none. I like my house. I like the part where it's solid, and mine, and the roof doesn't leak, and the wards all answer to *me*. Before we'd effectively stopped speaking to each other, Sylvester used to devote a considerable amount of time to trying to convince me to move into the knowe in Shadowed Hills. He believed the place of the fae was—and is—in Faerie, and with most of deeper Faerie sealed at Oberon's order, what we have left is the Summerlands, where the knowes are anchored.

You know what they don't have in the Summerlands? Cable television. Until recently, they didn't have Internet, either, and only had sporadic phone service. No take-out Indian food. It's no wonder that when given the choice, most of the teenagers I've met have chosen to take up residence in one of my spare rooms.

He did have a point, though. The fae tend to thrive more in the Summerlands, purebloods especially, blossoming in the absence of the omnipresent iron that humans like to work into their designs. Even changelings need to spend a certain amount of time on the other side of the hills to maintain our equilibrium. We don't get sick or anything if we spend too long in the human world—and that's a good thing, given that I spent fourteen years as a koi fish in the Japanese Tea Gardens in Golden Gate Park—but we get . . . faded, in a way. We do better when we maintain a balance.

And none of that was enough to make me give up my home in San Francisco, the City by the Bay, land of mists and hills and twenty-four–hour convenience stores. I liked where I lived and I lived how I liked, and sometimes I still struggled a little with the fact that I'd started letting other people in, and that meant I needed to take them into account when making decisions.

It still would have been nice to be included enough to pack my own suitcase.

I sighed, rolling over and burying my face in my pillow. I was sulking. I knew that. I was wallowing in my own hurt feelings, and I needed to stop and get on with my night, especially if I was going to be leaving the Kingdom in the morning. Arden was one more name on the list of people who must have known my wedding date before I did, because there was no possible way for them to take me out of the Kingdom without telling the Queen I answered to.

My eyes snapped open as I rolled over again, pushing myself into a sitting position. Tybalt didn't like Sylvester. May liked him maybe too much—she had all my memories of a childhood in which he had been the only reliable parental figure, the only person who would bandage my skinned knees without concerns that I might be bleeding on his clothes, the only adult who seemed to reliably give a damn about my survival. Luna and Melly and Lily had all done their best, but they had also held back a little, perhaps out of respect to my mother's role as my actual mom, perhaps because they weren't sure what to do with me. Sylvester, though . . . Sylvester had always been there. He had taken care of me when no one else would.

It was Sylvester who had offered me the Changeling's Choice that brought me fully into Faerie, when my mother had been doing her best to turn me mortal and allow me to die in the course of a natural human lifespan. It was Sylvester who had dried my tears when I wept from missing my human father, who had told me he was sorry for the hurt, but that it was all right for me to miss him, to mourn the life I'd given away when I chose Faerie over the human world.

He hadn't told me, not for years, that because he was the one who offered me the Choice, he would have been the one to snap my neck if I'd chosen to be human rather than fae. The purebloods try to be kind when they deal with changeling children, even if many of them view us as little better than beasts, but their kindness has limits.

Tybalt *wouldn't* have told him. May might still have been too hurt to tell him. Simon would have to know—one more person for the list of people who'd been keeping secrets from me, which I hate, and who was going to have to make it up to me with apologies or cake or something else small but complicated—since he was legally my father and presumably had a part to play in the ceremony, but would Simon have called his brother?

I couldn't call Sylvester. He was always going to be my liege, but at the moment I was still semi-exiled from the Duchy that had always been my home, so calling him for anything other than an emergency would have pushed the bounds of propriety. I fumbled for my phone and dialed the only other number I could think of, flopping back onto the bed as I pressed the phone to my ear.

The phone rang. And rang. And rang again, until I started to worry about going to voicemail. Naturally, that was when it clicked and a harried female voice with the faintest faded lilt of an Irish accent said, "Bridget Ames' phone, Bess speaking, office hours ended *hours* ago, tell me why I'm not taking ten percent off your grade?"

I smiled to myself. "Hi, Bess. It's Toby."

Her tone shifted immediately, becoming warm with delight. "October! Is that daughter of mine bothering you again? She's supposed to be in the kitchen, getting the dishes to order after our supper, but I wouldn't put it past her to have run off to yours. She says you have faster Internet."

"We don't, really. April says Shadowed Hills is her masterwork, and we're still on San Francisco's municipal network. Chelsea just likes that we always have snacks." And she likes spending time with the boys. Not many people her age at Shadowed Hills.

Bridget is human. She lives in the knowe because her husband, Etienne, isn't. Neither is their daughter, Chelsea. Bridget didn't know she was sleeping with a Tuatha de Dannan when she started her original affair with Etienne; considering she's a folklore professor and still teaches at UC Berkeley despite living in the

Summerlands, that's probably a good thing. It would have been hard as hell for her as an academic to resist the urge to write research papers about her sex life.

The idea was amusing. I smiled again, closing my eyes. "Anyway, as far as I know, your teleporting troublemaker is still at home. The boys just got back from an errand, and Raj is off at the Court of Cats."

"Having a quiet night in, then?"

"Yeah, just me. Your husband around? I have a question for him." I could have asked Bridget, but I hadn't known her for nearly as long, and no matter how she answered, it wasn't going to irritate me as much as Etienne had the potential to do. I wasn't looking to make myself angry. I was trying to triangulate how angry I should be. There's a difference.

Honest, there's a difference.

"He's in the kitchen with Chels. I'll get him for you. Hold on a second."

"For you, anything."

There was a clatter as Bridget put the phone down. Having a cellphone inside a knowe is materially different from having a landline only in the absence of the cord. The magic April uses to make the signals work doesn't always cover the entire knowe, and sometimes calls drop, or become weirdly distorted, or jump from one phone to another—you can be having a conversation with one person and suddenly be connected to someone else in the knowe who just happened to be using the phone at the same time. It's messy. Leaving the phone somewhere that gets a stable signal is occasionally the only solution.

A minute passed, agonizingly slow in the dimness of my room. There was a scraping sound as the phone was lifted on the other end. "Hello?" said Etienne.

"Planning any upcoming trips?" I asked.

He sighed. "I told them it was a bad idea. I told them you would react poorly. I swear I did. Sometimes I feel as though the people who claim to care about you the most dearly have never actually met you."

"Uh-huh. And how long have you known?"

"My invitation arrived two weeks ago," he said.

Two weeks ago. I tried to think back, to remember if there had been any unusual secrecy or caginess, or if May had filled the kitchen inexplicably with pixies. Sometimes she baked cookies for them, but I couldn't remember anything out of the ordinary.

"Two weeks," I said flatly.

"October, I'm sorry they chose not to inform you."

"It's fine. I assume that if you've been invited, Sylvester knows?"

"Yes," said Etienne. "His Grace is aware."

He didn't say anything more. Neither did I, letting the silence stretch between us like an unbreaking thread, waiting him out. It sometimes seems like half of PI work is being quiet and letting other people incriminate themselves. For all his love of the rules and codes that a "proper knight" was meant to live by, Etienne was far less accustomed to holding his tongue when not in the presence of the nobility.

"He is not presently intending to attend," he said—not blurted, as each word sounded reluctant, but also like he simply couldn't stand the silence any longer.

I said nothing.

"Dammit, October, this wasn't my idea. I didn't make or execute the plan."

I sighed. "But you went along with it. You kept quiet when you knew it was going to upset me, and you went along with it."

To my surprise, he laughed.

I blinked. "This isn't funny."

"Yes, it is. I was your knight, October. I stood responsible for you as you went out of your way to upset, vex, bedevil, bother, and annoy absolutely everyone of any high position in the Mists. I used to wonder if you were using the peerage as a checklist of people to get on the wrong side of. It was my responsibility to teach you honor, comportment, and the courtly graces, and I failed and succeeded in equal measure because I crafted you into the most infuriating creature ever to walk in Faerie. And as it seemed your only goal was, at times, to vex those you felt took themselves too seriously, it seems only fitting that the same fate be visited upon you by those who love you as you are. You have a sister willing to arrange an entire wedding for your sake. You have a man who loves you. Let them love you as best as they know how. They only emulate what they admire."

The line went dead. I lowered the phone, staring at it for a moment before dropping it onto my chest and staring up at the ceiling. I didn't call back. There would have been no point.

He was right.

I had spent my childhood rebelling and running away from the establishment, whatever the hell *that* was supposed to mean. My mother had no title, but she *was* a landholder, and people had a dismaying tendency to defer to her, for reasons I had lacked the information to understand at the time. My not-quite-father figure was a Duke, and everyone around us either worked for him, swore fealty to him, or both. Thumbing my nose at the people in power had been a way to feel important, even though I wasn't. Even though I was just another changeling who would never amount to anything.

Only now I *was* the establishment. I spent time, socially, with kings and queens—was even going to marry one of them. I had been to various kingdoms, sometimes as a diplomat, sometimes as a hero. I *was* a hero. What I wasn't was particularly good about keeping my mouth shut when under pressure. Preventing me from knowing when the wedding was going to happen kept me from accidentally blurting it out in front of the wrong person or wrong pixie, who might carry the news back to any of the various people who had reason to wish me or Tybalt ill. This had been a smart way to do things.

I still didn't like it. I sighed and closed my eyes, letting the dimness of the room and the comfortable softness of my bed lull me into a light doze. Staying where I was sounded even better than a hot shower and was easier on the water bill. It wasn't a true slumber; my eyes snapped open as soon as the scent of musk and pennyroyal drifted through the air, marking Tybalt's arrival.

I didn't move or say anything, just lay there with my eyes open and my phone on my chest, fully clothed and barefoot, staring at the ceiling. There was a soft rustle as Tybalt made his way across the room to the bed. Like all cats, he could move in total silence when he wanted to—and often did. Like most people with sense and compassion, he understood that sometimes sneaking up on your fiancé the hero who usually has a knife with her is not the best possible idea.

"October? Are you awake?"

Upon reflection, I elected not to answer him and kept staring at the ceiling.

The mattress bent as he sat upon the edge, his weight pulling it downward. "I can hear you breathing. I know you're awake."

I rolled onto my side, propping myself up on one elbow. "Then why did you bother to ask?"

"It seemed polite." He looked at me solemnly. I looked back.

Even my residual irritation couldn't rob me of the ability to enjoy the view. Tybalt was not the most beautiful man I'd ever seen. I live more than half the time in Faerie these days, and we have entire *species* that have been bred like show dogs for the sole purpose of each generation being prettier than the one before it. That's sort of a joke but also maybe possibly not since I'm thinking specifically of the Daoine Sidhe. Their Firstborn is exactly the kind of woman who would command her descendants to choose their spouses purely on the basis of how attractive they thought the babies would be.

Cait Sidhe don't do things that way. Their beauty, when it arises, is entirely natural, the result of good choices and good genes. Tybalt is pale, thanks to living a primarily nocturnal life, with sharp, strong features and the lithe build of a runner or swimmer. He doesn't need to be a powerhouse, not when he can be fast enough to defeat most opponents without risking a hair on his own head. Plus, I like that I can get my arms around his shoulders without straining.

His hair is brown, more-or-less striped with black depending on his mood and how comfortable he is. Like most Cait Sidhe, he learned to suppress his more animal attributes when he was very young in order to be taken seriously. Most of the time, his feline heritage shows only in his pupils, which are oval and react strongly to the light, and in his incisors, which are larger than the human norm. No whiskers, no tail, no flexible ears.

It's like at some point we decided, "Hey, we're immortal magical beings who live in a world of rainbows and miracles. Let's all conform to the most boring standard we possibly can, okay?" It's no wonder the fae go to war at the drop of a hat. There's nothing else for us to do.

His eyes are green, rare for a human but common among the Cait Sidhe, and banded in different shades like the layers of a piece of malachite. I used to find his mouth cruel, before I got permission to start kissing it, and now I find it perfect. So no, he may not be the most beautiful man in the world, but he's the most beautiful to me.

He was clearly done with Court business for the night, having exchanged whatever he'd worn to visit Ginevra for a shirt advertising Shakespeare & Co. Books in Berkeley. Sometimes his endless dedication to Shakespeare in all clothing choices gets old, but it makes him happy, and it's not like I'm exactly vying for Faerie's best dressed over here.

"So," he said, with a small but audible sigh. "You know."

"That I'm apparently getting married tomorrow? Yeah, you could say that I know. You could also say that I'm unhappy about being left in the dark about the one thing I explicitly said I wanted to be informed of. I'll get over it. You may have to give me a little while, and some assurance that Kerry's already working on the cake, but I'll get over it."

"I know you dislike secrets—" he began.

I held up a hand to stop him. "A surprise birthday party is a secret. A surprise public proposal is a bad idea. A surprise wedding is an *affront*."

"You said all aspects were up to us," he said, pivoting to a slightly safer place in the conversation. "You said you had no opinions."

"I also said you should tell me where to be and trust me to be there," I said. "You sort of dropped the ball on that one."

He sighed. "I wanted to avoid a diplomatic incident if at all possible, by preventing the monarchs through whose territory we are to travel from sealing their borders—against either one of us."

I blinked. That was a wrinkle I hadn't considered.

Kings and Queens of Cats are territorial even by fae standards, and they don't coexist. Ginevra's father, Jolgeir, is the King of Cats in Portland, Oregon. When Raj takes his throne properly, she'll have to choose between going home and challenging her father to a fight—potentially to the death—or striking out to find a territory that doesn't currently have a ruler. Either way, she can't go home and return to the way her life was before she discovered she had a Queen's potential running in her blood.

To reach Toronto, Tybalt would have to pass through the territories of every Cait Sidhe monarch between here and there, and unlike the Kings and Queens of the Divided Courts, who would treat us like temporary, somewhat unwelcome guests, he could have been faced with challenges.

"I don't heal like you do, little fish," he said. "I would prefer not to come to your bower broken and bleeding and already half-dead.

I would offer you a poor wedding night if I did. Had word gotten out too soon of our planned nuptial date, the chances of someone deciding they had the time to assemble a challenge would have been higher than anyone wishes to take, myself included. This way, we will pass through like riders in the night, swift as anything and twice as difficult to catch or corner."

"How are we getting to Toronto?" I sat fully up, and politely didn't comment on the look of profound relief on Tybalt's face. Had he really been expecting me to sulk *that* hard? Well, maybe I would have, if not for Etienne slapping some sense into me. I can be petty when I want to be. I try my best to avoid the urge.

"Sir Etienne has agreed to the loan of his daughter for the greater distances," he said. "Otherwise, we will be depending on the kindness of each successive Kingdom to carry us along. The High King insists this is how he and his wife travel when the need strikes them, and that all his vassals will be obliging."

Somehow, I doubted they were going to be as obliging for a king-breaker and a King of Cats as they were for the High King and Queen of the Westlands, but that was a problem for the future. For tomorrow, apparently. "Okay. Do I need to pack?"

He blinked. "Is that all? My punishment for conspiracy is allowing you to select whatever horrors you desire from the black hole you refer to as a wardrobe?"

I reached over and socked him lightly in the shoulder. "Be nice, or I'll decide to be mad at you after all. My wardrobe doesn't contain any horrors."

The corner of his mouth twitched. "No. Merely bloodstains and suspicious slash marks."

"Is it my fault I have a very stab-able face?"

"Yes," he said dryly. "As it is not your face, but rather, your actions, which generally inspire the stabbing, I have to conclude that it is absolutely your own fault. I wish it weren't, as it means to accept you as you are is also to accept that you will occasionally come home covered in blood and act as if I'm being unreasonable for being upset about it, but I cannot change the world with wishing. I've tried many a time before, and almost always, getting what I wanted would only have made me less than the man I am."

"Almost always?" I asked.

"Yes." He smiled like the sunrise. "I wished you would marry me, and unless you inspire a level of stabbing that is awe-inspiring even for you, my Lady of Knives, in three days, my wish comes true."

"Three days? Not tomorrow?"

"Then Quentin did not actually 'mess up and tell you everything,' as he said over the phone," said Tybalt, sounding faintly annoyed. "We travel tomorrow. We leave at sunset and should be in Toronto by dinner. It would make me a monster to demand you cross a continent, enter a new demesne, and wed, all on the same night. We're to enjoy the hospitality of the High Court for a day," a twist of his mouth made it clear how much he was looking forward to *that*, "while final preparations are made, and you are afforded the opportunity to approve of those things as are not absolutely required and can yet be changed."

I raised an eyebrow. "Like what?"

"If you despise the cake for some reason, I'm sure Kerry would be delighted to commandeer the knowe kitchens and abuse the staff to make you something more to your immediate liking. Knowing her, she might actually view that as a gift, as it would save her from assisting with placement of the flowers. If you detest the flowers, I am afraid you'll have a longer negotiation on your hands for any changes; they have been selected according to their meaning, and to avoid any allergies or insults to the attendees. You would need to propose substitutions that would avoid causing a war."

I blinked very slowly. "This is way more complicated than I expected it to be."

"Yes, well." He shrugged. "I was honestly relieved when you elected to remove yourself from the process, as I was quite sure it would drive you to climbing the walls and repudiating the touch of man. As I very much enjoy touching you, I would prefer to avoid that unhappy future."

I snorted. Tybalt smiled.

"I am truly forgiven, if you are making such indecorous sounds in my presence once more."

"You're a jerk," I said mildly.

"Indeed, I am, for I am a cat, and what those of a more two-legged mindset view as 'jerkishness' is only feline, and only natural to me. But as you seem to be reasonably fond of such behavior, I do not regret my nature."

"I only like it from you," I said. "Because you're *my* jerk. Now tell me what happens tomorrow."

Tybalt read my tone as the invitation it was and shifted closer on the bed, plucking my phone from the mattress where it had fallen and setting it gingerly back on the bedside table. Despite April's growing fae-focused cell network, he had yet to start carrying his own cellphone, choosing instead to be difficult to reach and require us to go through convoluted message chains when we need to get hold of him. Tracking spells, pixies, and Spike's uncanny ability to find its people no matter where they go has made this slightly easier, but only slightly, and sometimes it's annoying.

Although it doesn't annoy me nearly as much as it does the boys. I skipped from 1995, when cellphones were new and strange, to 2009 in an instant. I'm used to a delay when I want to talk to someone. They really aren't. They're purebloods who will one day inherit kingdoms, but they're also children of the modern human world, as changeling as I am, in their own ways.

Tybalt slid his arms around me, shifting positions until my back was pressed against his chest and he was holding me. Nothing more complicated or suggestive than that. Just holding me. Sometimes that's the most wonderful thing in the whole world, having someone who wants to hold me for the sake of holding me, not because he thinks he might get something out of it later or because he thinks it's expected of him.

"Well," he said. "After you have packed up whatever horrors you choose to carry from your wardrobe—and pack for the assumption of a week away from home, if you would be so kind; Ginevra will be sending some of my subjects to feed Spike and the cats while we're away, and I've given them temporary keys to the wards to ensure nothing goes awry—we will proceed to Muir Woods, where we'll meet our traveling companions, and Arden will open our first gate."

"Arden has a range of about . . . I don't know, San Francisco to Portland is what, eight hundred miles? Where are we coming out?"

"We will be met by a detachment from the court of the Kingdom of Salted Skies, and from there, one of their courtiers will be able to take us another four hundred miles or so, to Highmountain."

"So Utah to Colorado?"

"I believe that's what the humans call those locations, yes." Tybalt rested his chin against the crown of my head—something only possible when we were both sitting or lying down—and continued, in a calm tone, reciting the list of jumps we'd be making across the continent, naming Kingdoms I knew only from my childhood geography lessons and Etienne's endless drills on courtly etiquette. I closed my eyes again, letting his voice soothe me.

Yes, this was worth it. Yes, this was why. They hadn't lied to me, just held back information until I actually needed it, and now we were going to get married, peacefully and with as little pomp and circumstance as possible. We were getting married.

This was going to work.

FOUR

"THIS ISN'T GOING TO WORK," I said, folding my arms as I looked from the small crowd that had formed on my driveway to my car, which persisted in being a VW Beetle and not something larger. Like, say, a bus.

Quentin, who still looked wrong to me, with his stranger's face and too-light hair, looked from the pile of our collective baggage to Raj and then offered, somewhat weakly, "Raj and Tybalt could be cats for the drive?"

"Oh, we *will* be," said Tybalt. "I have too much sense to trust my life to a motor vehicle while large enough to be flung through the windscreen."

"We could take the Shadow Roads," said May.

"Only if you're willing to leave your bags behind," said Raj. "Carrying a person through the shadows is hard enough. We aren't a luggage service."

Everyone turned to look at Tybalt. He put his hands up. "Don't expect miracles from me. It's not my job."

"It's mine, and this is a miracle that's not within my purview," I said. "Sorry. Even I can't fit four adults and three teenagers in a VW. I didn't go to clown college when I was young enough to listen to the lectures on distorting space for fun."

Someone in front of the house leaned on their horn, hard. I scowled, not bothering to turn around. We were in a residential neighborhood after dark, but we were also in San Francisco, within walking distance of the Castro District. If I insisted on silence after sunset, I'd be an asshole, not to mention a hypocrite, since it's not like the fae shut up as soon as we get out of bed.

I went back to surveying the unreasonable amount of stuff piled on my driveway. Even if everyone had been able to restrain themselves to a single bag, we would have had way too much for the car, and the only person with a single bag was Raj, who seemed to be intending to conjure all his clothing from a handful of feathers and dried leaves stuffed into a backpack. A good gig—if you had the illusion magic to make it work.

I know how to conjure a gown when I need it, but my illusions have never been amazing, or sturdy, unless I'm pissed when I weave them—and I'd rather not make plans for my own wedding that involve being angry for days at a time. Not when I was still having to fight the lingering urge to be annoyed at everyone *but* Tybalt, who had admitted to the "what if we just . . . don't tell her when the wedding is?" aspect of his harebrained scheme. It wouldn't have worked if the rest of them hadn't gone along with it.

The person who was blowing their horn honked again, longer this time, leaning on it like it was their job. I whipped around, ready to storm down to the sidewalk and inform whoever it was that we had kids living in this neighborhood, only to stop and blink at the edifying sight of Danny McReady, Bridge Troll and cab driver, parked in front of my house. There was a teenage girl sitting in his passenger seat, her dark hair pulled into pigtails and secured by what looked like strips of electrical tape. She leaned out the window, far enough that I was briefly worried she'd fall, and waved violently.

I blinked, hoping I didn't look too much like I was on the verge of having an actual stroke, and waved cautiously back.

"Who is it?" asked Quentin, whose view of the street was blocked by the corner of the house. For him, for the moment, the world still made sense. Must have been nice.

"It's Danny," I said. "He brought the Luidaeg."

I started walking toward the car before anyone could ask another question I didn't know the answer to. The Luidaeg stopped waving but didn't pull her torso back into the vehicle. Instead, she fluttered her eyelashes in an exaggerated manner. "Howdy, sailor," she said. "Going my way?"

"Technically true, since you've been on a ship with me, and you know I am," I said. "I have more people than I do vehicle."

"Not a problem anymore." She slapped the roof of Danny's car, causing him to grimace and make a deep rumbling noise that never quite rose to the level of actual words. He was smart enough not to argue with the sea witch, even when she was in her charming human teenager disguise. Smart man. "This puppy already had about a dozen expansion charms on it before I got in."

"Of course it did." Danny is eight feet tall and built like a civic park storage shed. One of the square concrete ones the kids break into during the winter when they need to get out of the rain. Without expansion charms, he would never have been able to wedge himself behind the wheel, much less navigate his car over speed bumps.

"Had to add a few extra so Dad's antlers would have the clearance they needed," she continued blithely.

I tried not to choke on my spit or stop breathing. Instead, I blinked hard and took a half-step back, asking, in a tone that was only somewhat strangled, "You mean he's really, uh, coming to the wedding with you? I mean, I know you can't lie, so you were telling the truth when you said you were going to invite him, but I didn't think he'd go along with it."

"Do *you* want to tell my father he's not allowed at your wedding?" She asked the question with a faintly abstract air, like she was discussing a possible change in the weather or a new fashion trend, not the idea of Oberon himself, King of all Faerie, attending my wedding.

"I—no, but I assumed he'd have something better to do with his time." Like literally anything. "And I'm pretty sure we're supposed to inform King Sollys before we bring another monarch into his territory."

"Oh, Toby. My delicate, rule-abiding little flower." She looked at me, and between one blink and the next, her eyes went from mossy green to solid black, and while I didn't actually see her teeth change shape, they suddenly seemed much sharper than they had been half a breath before. "All territories in Faerie, from the deepest water to the hottest volcano, belong to my father. He needs no permission to trespass there, for trespass is impossible for one who carries his name and place among us." She blinked again, and her eyes returned to a less alarming state as she smiled sweetly. "So it's going to be fine. You told May I was going to be bringing two guests like I asked, didn't you?"

"Um." To be honest, it had completely slipped my mind. The

fact that I was now comfortable enough with the sea witch to forget about direct requests probably wasn't a *good* thing, but that's where we were.

"Oh, whatever," said the Luidaeg, rolling her eyes. "It's not like she's going to argue with me."

Danny looked past her shoulder to me, mouthing "Help me," in an exaggerated fashion.

Right. This was another of those things where the ending was preordained; arguing about it would do nothing but make me look like a stubborn fool. I *am* stubborn, and I can be pretty foolish under the right circumstances, but this didn't need to be one of them. I took another step back, turning the motion into a pivot as I spun on the ball of my foot, so that I was once more facing the much less alarming group standing around my car.

They looked at me with plain and unconcealed curiosity. I took a deep breath, then clapped my hands together like I thought I was getting ready to lead some sort of spirit rally.

"Okay!" I said brightly. "Danny is going to give us all a ride to Muir Woods. Grab your bags and get in the car."

I didn't mention the fact that Oberon and Poppy were apparently already in the back. Instead, I looked hopefully to Tybalt.

"I don't want to boot Annie out of the front, and if it's just the two of us, we could take the shadows, couldn't we?"

He laughed. "I remember a time when avoiding the Shadow Roads was a thing you most deeply and devotedly cared about. Yes, provided the rest of our company does not object or feel abandoned, I will happily carry my bride to our carriage."

I looked over at the others, pleading silently. Quentin had gathered my bags in addition to his own, doing his duty as my squire, even if it made him walk a little awkwardly. I was probably the most lightly-packed bride in history, since I wasn't bringing my own dress, *or* any makeup. When I'd attempted to pack my own sad collection of brushes, May had come very close to slapping my hand before assuring me that she and Stacy had everything under control, and I didn't need to worry my pretty little head about a thing.

Since I didn't care about the process as long as I wound up married to Tybalt in the end, I had backed off again. Sometimes discretion is the better part of valor.

May shook her head and waved her hand dismissively.

"Go," she said. "Enjoy your endless run through the cold dark nothing with the man of your dreams, while the rest of us ride in a spacious cab that has things like windows we can roll up, a working heater, and yeah, I guess, the missing King of Faerie."

Jazz snorted, barely hiding the gesture behind her hand in time. I grinned.

Very few people actually know, for a fact, that Oberon is back from his long exile, and most of them were about to be in the car with him. The rest, well. I expected to see all but one of them at my wedding. August, my biological sister, technically knows Oberon is back, since her father's return home had depended upon that happy event, but I was more than reasonably sure she hadn't received an invitation to the wedding. As long as Simon didn't decide to bring her as his plus one, we'd be fine.

"Enjoy the ride," I said and turned to Tybalt, who spread his arms for me. I linked my hands behind his neck, not resisting as he swung me up into a surprisingly fitting bridal carry and took three long strides toward the shadows at the side of the house.

Every one of the deeper roads through Faerie has its own requirements—and its own costs. So far as I'm aware, only the Shadow Roads are still widely accessible. The Blodynbryd can reach the Rose Roads, but there are only two Blodynbryd left in the world as far as I know, so it's not like they can set up a bus service. All Cait Sidhe can access the shadows, when they want to, although how well they navigate them and how long they can stay inside them is tied to the same sliding scale of power as whatever it is that makes a kitten a Prince or Princess, and eventually a King or Queen. As San Francisco's King of Cats, Tybalt had been the living anchor of the Shadow Roads for decades, and when he set them aside, Raj would be right there to pick them up, keeping them accessible for the cats of their Kingdom. All the other roads might fall and be forgotten, but the Shadow Roads would endure as long as there were Cait Sidhe to run along them.

Tybalt stepped into the shadows, which parted for him like theater curtains, and we were plunged into a lightless, airless void, all heat and light replaced by the pounding of his heart and the thudding of his feet against the unseen ground. I curled into his arms, utterly helpless in this place where I would always be an intruder, no matter how many times I was invited, no matter how much he loved me.

Faerie keeps its secret places well-hidden when it can, and well-protected when it can't. The Shadow Roads would suffocate me if I dared to relax and stop holding my breath.

Or they'd try, anyway. Access to the shadows is a gift of the Cait Sidhe bloodline. Being basically impossible to kill, no matter how hard you try, is a gift of mine. I've drowned, been stabbed, bled to death, and—my personal favorite—fallen from such a great height that impact with the ground broke every bone in my body. And every time, I've gotten better. If Tybalt tripped and dropped me in the darkness, there was every chance I could stay lost there for decades, suffocating and then recovering, only to suffocate again without a chance to take a breath and start searching for my own exit.

Was it any wonder that when he carried me, I didn't struggle or try to get away? I've been dropped on the Shadow Roads once, when Raj's father, Samson, led a short-lived rebellion against Tybalt. Those few seconds ranked among the most terrifying things I've ever experienced, and that's saying a lot, given what else I've been through.

Now, though . . . now he carried me, the smell of musk and pennyroyal suffusing the . . . not air, because there was no air, but the space around us, so that they tickled my nose even as I held my breath to keep the cold from getting in. I could feel the ice forming in my hair, but his body was warm against my own, and his arms were tight, and I knew I was safe.

Just as my lungs began to truly ache from my refusal to take a breath, Tybalt tensed, and leapt, driving us out of the dark and back into the light . . . sort of. Gone was the eternal semi-twilight of a city after sundown, replaced by the much deeper natural dark that gathered among the redwoods of Muir Woods.

He set me on my feet and took a step away, breathing heavily. I coughed, leaning forward and putting my hands on my knees as I remembered how to breathe. It wasn't the easiest thing ever.

"Well, wasn't that better than a long drive with our merry band of fools?" I finally wheezed.

Tybalt laughed. His voice was still thready and strained, but he already sounded better. He straightened, offering a smile as he pushed his hair out of his eyes. There were no ice crystals on *him*. Someday, I'll figure out how the Shadow Roads manage to simply chill him, while they put me all the way through the deep freeze.

"If it grants me more time alone with you before our lives descend into chaos, it can only be of benefit to me," he said.

I snorted and straightened in turn, walking over to him. "Liar," I said.

He raised an eyebrow. "And why am I a liar?"

"As if there has ever been a time when our lives *haven't* descended into chaos." I offered him my hand. He took it, tucking it into the crook of his arm as he began leading me deeper into the wood.

It was early enough that the evening dew hadn't had time to settle, leaving the wooden paths constructed by the forestry department for tourist use dry and easy to walk along. I still focused on my steps as I thawed out, trying to concentrate on not taking a tumble and landing us both in one of the park's many rushing streams or piles of poison oak. The signs reminding tourists to stay on the path aren't only for the protection of the native plant life. Poison oak is one of those experiences I can absolutely do without, and healing fast does *not* protect me from topical allergens.

There's been less of it in Muir Woods since Arden came back, reopened her knowe, and turned the place into a hotspot of fae activity. There are no local Dryads yet—it takes time for their trees to sprout and grow—but Hamadryads, who have the ability to transfer their bond between home trees, have been moving into the redwoods, and Tylwyth Teg like our friend Walther have been encouraging the local plants to grow in ways more beneficial to the Court.

I guess this could sound like interference with a protected biosphere, and technically it sort of is, but encouraging native ferns and flowers to grow at the expense of the poison oak isn't the same as digging things up or poisoning their roots. Between the Hamadryads and the Tylwyth, I expected Muir Woods to be free of harmful plant life that wasn't somehow necessary to the animal inhabitants within the next ten years. And good riddance.

But right here, right now, it was still a good idea to be cautious. My eyesight isn't as good as Tybalt's, and so I let him lead the way, guiding us through the trees until globes of bobbing light began to appear in the branches overhead, glowing pale and lambent and filling the air with something very much like starlight. I hugged Tybalt's arm closer and kept walking, smiling as the chime of ringing bells announced the approach of the park's swarm of pixies.

They swirled around us only a few seconds later, a living storm of Christmas lights, red and blue and green and pink and orange and yellow. They rang frantically the whole time, making sure we noticed them. As if there had been any chance we wouldn't? I held out my hand, palm upward, and a few seconds later a pixie the color of a Blue Raspberry Jolly Rancher landed there, snapping her wings shut with a decisive chime.

I smiled at the diminutive figure. Most people view pixies as pests, but thanks to my tendency to get into trouble, I've had the opportunity to know them a little better. They're intelligent, family-oriented people who keep their tiny communities as safe and cohesive as they can in a world that's built to a scale much too big for them. Poppy, the Luidaeg's Aes Sidhe apprentice, was a pixie once, before she traded her innate magic to save Simon's life.

We don't do anything simply in this family. Never have, probably never will.

"Well met," I said, and the pixie chimed answer, inclining her head in greeting. Pixie voices are too high-pitched for people my size to understand although they can understand us well enough when they want to. I think sometimes they pretend we're too slow and our voices are too deep just to excuse ignoring the things we ask of them.

This one was, thankfully, in a more genial mood. She lifted her head and smiled at me, the expression almost imperceptible on her tiny, glowing face.

"Will you light our way to Arden?" I asked. The pixie nodded enthusiastically and launched herself back into the air, wings glowing even brighter than before. She rejoined the swarm, and they all swirled around us like a glittering windstorm before unwinding into a gleaming ribbon that pointed the way toward the knowe.

Tybalt smiled at me fondly. "I remember finding you arguing drunkenly with one of their cousins over . . . you know, I don't think I ever found out exactly what you were arguing over. The sort of thing which seems of immense importance to the inebriated, no doubt."

I sighed. "I miss being able to get drunk when I wanted to."

"I know, little fish. I also know that I would prefer you alive and sober to drunken and dead, and the very thing which prevents your drinking will keep your other choices from stealing you away from me like a thief in the midday sun." He put his hand over mine, squeezing my fingers briefly. "To every cloud, a silver lining; to every curtain call, an encore."

"Sometimes your optimism confuses the hell out of me," I said. "With everything you've been through, I'd expect a bit more bitterness."

Tybalt laughed. "I spent enough time very bitter indeed to understand that clinging to joy when I find it is the most essential thing in the world. Part of my coming to understand that is your fault, October. I realized quickly that if I dragged my feet with you, I would wind up weeping at your grave, and I have better things to do with my time."

I rolled my eyes. "It's a good thing you weren't born in the modern era. You would be the most obnoxious theater kid ever to get completely obsessed with whatever's hot on Broadway right now. And there's nothing sadder than a fae theater kid dreaming of Broadway lights." There's iron in the groundwater in the Kingdom of Oak and Ash. That's not a new thing, and the fae were able to scratch out a living there for a long while, but nothing lasts forever, even in Faerie, and as humanity built their great towers higher and higher, and the old cannonballs in the harbor rusted and polluted the shore more and more, it became obvious that anyone with an iron allergy needed to get out of there.

There are no purebloods or even strong changelings left in New York. Haven't been since before I was born. The ones who remain are the ones weak enough to handle iron and thrive in its presence, and those who don't want anything to do with Faerie.

I used to dream of running away to New York, back before I met Cliff and got knighted. After that, I dreamt of proving myself to Faerie, of earning the right to live a semi-human life and raise my children in peace.

I failed that time. I wasn't going to fail again.

Following the pixies had carried us through the main valley and up the side of a hill, where hikers and tourists who refused to stay on the path had aided erosion and the questing roots of the local trees in creating a ladder of sorts to the top of the rise. Those same hikers and disobedient tourists had doubtless been finding themselves less and less inclined to wander in recent days, repelled from the path they had helped to create by the anti-human charms Arden and her court were adroitly weaving through the trees. I could hear them whispering, if only distantly. They knew, in their unthinking way, that I was allowed to be here.

I felt a little bad about the fact that reawakening the knowe in Muir Woods was taking a part of a national forest away from the people who came to admire its beauty. Only a little bit, though. The knowe pre-dated the declaration of Muir Woods as protected territory; without fae magic making the loggers and gold-miners a little bit uncomfortable among the trees, they might have kept right on cutting until there was nothing left of the ancient redwoods but the memories of the people who'd been here before the Europeans came.

Maybe it's hypocritical of me, as someone descended from both European humans and fae, but I'm pretty sure coming to this continent and declaring it our "new world" was the worst thing any of us has ever been a participant in. And I sometimes wonder whether Oberon locking the fae out of the deeper realms and forcing us to jockey for space on Earth and in the Summerlands, after we'd been so long accustomed to infinite room to roam, didn't have something to do with the human push toward exploration. The fae got here first, following ocean tides and rumors, and the humans who'd been living with our presence for centuries came after us.

And we're here now; the damage is done. If we all decamped back to Europe tomorrow, if that were even possible, it wouldn't put things back the way they were before we crossed the ocean. The forest existed before the knowe; the park, with its endless stream of carefully lured tourists, did not. If Arden could protect the wildness that remained even a little bit with her charms, let her.

The knowe doors were standing open when we followed the pixies over the rise at the top of the hill, propped wide to show the impossible hall that extended from the middle of a towering redwood tree. Faerie's relationship to physics is often casual at best, and sometimes it consists of Faerie promising to call when physics knows it never will. A slender Glastig woman in royal livery stood to one side of the doors, leaning on her polearm perhaps slightly more than was strictly appropriate for someone who was supposedly on duty.

In contrast, the Tuatha de Dannan man across from her was standing at a level of attention that would have impressed even Etienne, normally the most rule-abiding person I know. This man

had dark hair that held highlights of improbable blackberry purple, and he wore the royal livery like he'd never voluntarily worn
anything else in his life, pride and contentment radiating quietly
off of him.

Neither of them seemed to notice our approach, the woman
being preoccupied with watching the pixies, the man staring appropriately and fixedly ahead on a straight line. That's why I've
always hated guard duty. We could make it all the way to doors of
the knowe before they knew they weren't alone.

Or we could have if I hadn't immediately stepped on a twig,
snapping it beneath my foot with a soft cracking sound. It wasn't
loud, as such things went. In the silence of the forest, it was a gun-
shot, and the reaction of the two sentries was immediate.

The woman, Lowri, shifted positions without straightening as
she turned to face us and smiled, her face framed by the shaggy
locks of her hair and the curving rise of her horns. Glastig are sort
of like Satyrs, only they got less of the sturdy solidity of goats, and
more of the finicky animal bits. They're also, technically, water
fae—in the old days, they supposedly hid their cloven hooves under
long skirts and sawed their horns off close to their skulls so they
could lure innocent people into ponds and drown them.

Before I learned how much time and energy Eira and her siblings had dedicated to demonizing the children of Maeve, I would
have believed a legend like that without question. Now I had to
wonder how many people the Glastig actually drowned, and how
many had been dumped on the riverbank for someone to find and
draw the logical conclusions about. It's hard to say, but there aren't
many Glastig left. Their numbers got thinned before the dawn of
the modern era, and the ones who are left are usually like Lowri,
selling their services to any noble court that will offer them a measure of protection.

I'd first met her in the service of the false Queen of the Mists,
the woman who'd taken Arden's crown and rightful place on the
throne after the death of our last King, Gilad Windermere. Unlike
most of the false Queen's followers, Lowri had been doing it for
protection and place, not because she believed any of the vile
things that woman said about changelings and the value of purebloods in our society. And when it became clear that the Queen
she served was no true monarch, Lowri had been happy to join our
ramshackle revolution and throw her lot in behind the true heir.

I liked her a lot. She was nice to talk to, told absolutely filthy jokes, and didn't take either herself or her job too seriously, although she was devoted to the monarchy. Which probably explained why she was on duty with the Crown Prince in the Mists, Nolan Windermere.

Nolan turned more slowly than she did, but his response was the same—a smile—although in his case, he did it without abandoning his rigidly proper posture. "My darling sister told me you'd be coming tonight," he said. "I suppose congratulations are in order, and I hope His Majesty won't take offense if I offer them first to Sir Daye?"

"Not at all," said Tybalt.

Older purebloods can seem like travelers stranded out of time to people as young as I am: they carry the memories and mannerisms of decades, even centuries, before I was born. In Nolan's case, that impression is accurate and very literal. He was elf-shot in the 1930s and spent roughly eighty years asleep before his sister arranged to have him woken before his hundred years were up. Maybe those last twenty years wouldn't have made much of a difference to someone who'd already slept through the creation of the Internet, the dawn of cellphones, and the entire computer revolution, but Arden had wanted her brother back, and as Queen in the Mists, she'd had the resources to make it happen. So she did.

Nolan has been adjusting slowly to this strange new century. Arden's been helping as much as she can, and her chatelaine, my honorary niece, Cassandra, has been doing her part. Cassie is a changeling, a grad student, and about as modern as they come. I'd be hard pressed to think of anyone better-suited to helping someone adapt to living in the present day.

When he offered me first congratulation, it wasn't to slight Tybalt. It was to reflect the etiquette as he had learned it, where the woman, if there was one, was the first to receive appreciation of her upcoming marriage. We confused the issue a bit, what with Tybalt being a King and me being a Knight rather than a Lady, but he was trying.

"In that case." Nolan bowed to me, so deeply it looked as if his forehead brushed his knees. "Congratulations on the occasion of your marriage, and may the blessings piled upon your house be so vast the roof is in danger of collapse before you can get the wedding party to safety."

I blinked. Then I looked to Lowri, who was barely managing to cover her expression of delighted amusement, and then to Tybalt, who just seemed pleased. Ah. So this was another pureblood thing, then, and not something I needed to worry about.

"Cool," I said. "And like, if the roof does fall in, we'll be sure to have a roofer on standby."

There was a long pause, during which I began to worry I had said something wrong or violated some ancient code of etiquette I lacked the context to understand. Then Nolan burst out laughing, loud and genuine, and I relaxed.

"You're marrying a spitfire, and I hope you'll enjoy her as much as both of you deserve," he said, clapping Tybalt hard on the shoulder. Tybalt bore the impact stoically, even looking somewhat pleased. I realized this might be the most positive contact he'd ever had with an acknowledged Crown Prince of the Divided Courts—Quentin didn't count. Even before I'd broken him, he'd been under blind fosterage and thus had no title to speak of. Thankfully.

I have no idea what the process of telling someone you have to refer to by title to wash the dishes looks like, and I honestly don't want to know.

Tybalt smiled. "I can promise you, I intend to do precisely that," he said, and clapped Nolan on the shoulder in turn.

That appeared to complete whatever archaic ritual of manly bonding they were playing out. Nolan straightened, almost but not quite returning to his ramrod stance, and said in a plummy, formal tone, "I congratulate you on the occasion of your marriage, Your Majesty, and for all that follows. May the Three who made us all bless your bridal bed with the rarest of rewards, and may your nights be fruitful and long."

"As you say," said Tybalt, and offered Nolan a shallow, almost shocking bow before starting for the open door. I blinked, then scurried after him.

Normally, I'm the one who goes striding through every open door without stopping to explain what I'm trying to accomplish, although I'm usually doing it bloody and heavily armed. This time, I was just trying to avoid mortally offending anyone before we even made it out of our home kingdom.

"Did the Crown Prince just say he hopes you get me pregnant?" I asked in a low voice. The knowe's entrance hall was long, paneled with carved wood panels that showed important moments in the kingdom's history. They had a tendency to change based on what was happening around them—that's one of the nice, if occasionally frustrating, things about knowes. They're alive, even if not everyone believes that, and at least somewhat self-aware, and that means that as long as they have the resources to do it, they can redecorate on a whim. Sometimes it's charming.

Other times, like tonight, it's an excuse to show me every major wedding, as judged by a building, ever to have happened in the kingdom. One nice thing about it: my acts of bone-stupid heroism featured less heavily than they usually did.

"It is a traditional blessing for a pureblood's wedding," said Tybalt. "You should expect far more interest in the condition of your womb and its potential contents than you are accustomed to in the next several days."

"No one asked Dianda about *her* womb," I grumbled.

"Ah, but when the Duchess Lorden took a second husband, she had already been a hundred years with her first, and borne him two sons, both fine and strong and suitable in the eyes of the land," said Tybalt. "Further, her wedding was something of a surprise to all assembled and should not form your basis for comparison to our own. If we had declared our intent to wed immediately on the heels of a divorce, and had the ceremony spontaneously performed by one of the Firstborn, we would have been permitted to skip over a great deal of the pomp and ceremony which is likely to attend us."

"You say 'likely' as if you didn't arrange the whole thing," I said. Tybalt shrugged but didn't contradict me. "And what, are Firstborn like Unitarian ministers? They're allowed to just say 'guess you're married now' and then you are?"

"That's a very crass way of putting it but, essentially, yes," said Tybalt.

I stared at him. "The Luidaeg has been *right here* this whole time," I said. "Why do we have to go to Toronto? All we had to do was tell her we wanted to be married and we could have been. Ages ago!"

"She knew of our engagement and did not volunteer. Does that not tell you something of the etiquette in play here? And I know she has informed you of the import of this occasion. She would no more have interfered with something that might improve the lot of her own descendants than she would have voluntarily moved away from the sea. In our case, the pomp and circumstance is the point."

Tybalt sighed and gave me a pained look. "As to why we must go to Toronto, we must go because we agreed to do so. To stand aside now would be to offer grave insult to the monarchy which dictates so much of your life, and always will. Moreover, as I am about to enter politically unusual waters—not uncharted, as Kings and Queens have stepped aside before, myself included—but strange, there will be some argument to be made that they have command over my actions as well once Raj takes the throne."

I knew Raj would never be comfortable telling the man who had raised him as uncle and regent what to do, but I hadn't considered that exiling himself from the Court of Cats could potentially put Tybalt under the control of the Divided Courts. I blinked, looking at the wood-paneled wall. We were walking past the carving depicting the marriage of Sylvester and Luna Torquill, him tall and proud, her wrapped in her stolen Kitsune skin and draped in roses. Seeing her like that made my eyes sting with the threat of tears I knew I wouldn't shed. I missed the Luna I'd grown up with, the one who loved me.

That Luna wasn't dead because she had never really existed at all. But she was gone, and she wasn't coming back.

"You're giving up so much more than I am," I said softly. "I know you're worried about offending the High King, but I can make it right with him if I have to. Are you sure you want to do this?" As the words left my mouth, I was briefly gripped with the terrible fear that Tybalt would suddenly agree with me and declare our marriage a bad idea, leaving me alone in the middle of the hall. And then High King Sollys really *would* have good reason to be mad at me, since his son and heir would never have his real face returned to him, and I would have to go back to the house by myself. It was an impossible, incredibly painful thought, and I had no one else to blame for it.

Thankfully for my nerves, Tybalt only laughed, low and soft, and put his hand over mine where it rested on his arm, squeezing lightly. "You don't escape me so easily, and if anyone's having regrets about this union, I assure you, I am not the one. Calm your concerns, little fish, and we'll be on our way soon enough."

We stopped outside the doors to Arden's receiving room. They were unattended, maybe because there were guards at the gate. We still hesitated a moment before I shrugged and knocked, the sound echoing through the hall. That was an effect of both acoustics and a clever amplification spell built into the wood itself. One more advantage to big old knowes: they're not only self-aware, but they've also had time for the people who care for them to layer and refine the magic that makes them good homes. It's a symbiotic relationship. They like to be lived in, and the people who live in them like to be comfortable.

There was a long enough pause to make me wonder whether the absence of guards was because Arden was elsewhere in the knowe when a voice shouted, "Come on in!"

So we did.

Having a queen who spent decades hiding in the human world, hired a changeling as her chatelaine, and hired a Cu Sidhe equally familiar with and comfortable in the human world as her seneschal means that in some ways, Arden runs a more casual court than most. We entered the receiving room to find her sprawled across her throne like it was a coffee shop easy chair, dressed in jeans and a well-worn green hoodie, flanked on the dais by two familiar figures. One of them was expected. The other was not.

We were in the presence of a queen, however informal she was being. That was her choice, and it shouldn't impact ours in the slightest. That didn't stop me from blurting, "Walther, what are *you* doing here?"

Walther Davies, alchemist and chemistry professor and once potential heir to the throne of the Kingdom of Silences, lifted his head and smiled, languid and smug as the cat who got the canary. And I'm marrying a cat. I know that expression pretty damn well.

"Coming to your wedding as the escort of Miss Cassandra Brown," he said, indicating Arden's chatelaine with a lazy wave of his hand. "If I honestly believed you had been in any way involved with sending out the wedding invitations, this is where I'd be offended at you for not thinking I ranked my own."

"And this is where I would remind you that bringing our own alchemist could be seen as an insult to the High Throne," said Tybalt mildly. "Be glad we embraced the modern concept of the 'plus one.' When I was young, no one who hadn't been thoroughly vetted and approved would have even been considered to be allowed within a hundred feet of a royal wedding, much less the disowned scion of a royal house."

Walther snorted. "I wasn't disowned, please. I forsook my claim to the throne. I offer about as much threat to the Sollys line as Cassandra does."

I made a noncommittal humming sound. High Queen Maida was born a changeling, daughter of a fae man and a human woman. She gave up her mortality in order to marry Crown Prince Aethlin, and that had eventually placed her at the head of a continent. No small trick, for someone mortal-born, and not something commonly known. But it made Walther's statement funnier than he probably intended it to be.

"Regardless, the High Queen herself agreed to the practice of including 'plus one' on the invitations," said Tybalt. "Bringing you ourselves would have been an offense. Bringing you as Cassandra's escort avoids insult, puts you close enough to call upon if the need arises, and is the tactically sensible choice."

"He's right, you know," said Arden. "I haven't been doing this as long as he has, or as long as the Sollys family has, and even I would blink if a visiting dignitary, invited or not, wanted to bring their own alchemist."

"You sent me to Silences," said Walther.

"Because you used to live there," said Arden. "That connection made your presence logical. Sending you literally anywhere else could be construed as an insult, and I'm not up for insulting random monarchs this week."

She snapped her fingers. The smell of redwood sap and blackberry flowers rose around her, along with a slight sparkle in the air, and she was gone, leaving her throne empty.

That's a trick not all Tuatha de Dannan can pull off. Most of the time, they use their teleportation magic to open doorways they can step through or allow other people to use. What Arden had just done was effectively open a doorway beneath herself to fall through, without doing any of the usual hand gestures or being able to see her destination. I raised an eyebrow, quietly impressed.

It was nice to have a queen who didn't actively want me dead. It was even nicer to see her starting to relax and blossom into the person she should have been able to be all along. I would never have tried to take her years in the human world away from her—they were too vital a piece of her identity, and they *mattered*—but I did enjoy seeing her become as casual about her magic as the rest of the nobles I'd known.

The smell of redwood sap wafted from behind us. I turned, and there was Arden, now wearing a floor-length blue velvet dress that hugged her figure as it plummeted toward her feet, the color calling the purple highlights to the surface of her hair. I nodded approvingly.

"When'd you learn the quick-change trick?" I asked. "You have an army of Hobs behind a screen somewhere?"

"Hush," she said. "It's an illusion, but you're not supposed to comment on it. I hope you'll be more polite while you're in Toronto."

"Doubtful," I said brightly.

"I wish I could come," she said. "I appreciated the invitation, even if we all knew I wouldn't be able to use it."

"It was the polite thing to do," said Tybalt gravely. I actually appreciated his reminding people that he'd been the one to put the guest list together. It might mean he got credit for things like sending Arden an invite—but he deserved that credit, as he'd done it, and I might well have gone "she can't attend, why make her sad by reminding her of that fact?" and just not sent the invitation at all. More, it meant people would view the more questionable guests, like the Luidaeg and the Crown Prince in the Mists, through the lens of a King of Cats, not the lens of a known king-breaker. It was better for everyone this way.

Honestly, it was.

Arden clapped her hands together like a classroom monitor trying to clear away chalk dust. "All right, where's the rest of your band of freaks and weirdoes? I'm ready to get this show on the road."

"Given traffic, probably halfway across the Golden Gate Bridge," I said. At her blink, I explained, "We had more people than we had comfortable room for in the car, so they're all riding with Danny, while Tybalt and I took the Shadow Roads. It'll probably be another twenty minutes before they get here."

". . . huh," she said, after a moment's pause. "You know, I've been locked up in this knowe long enough to forget traffic is a real thing, and not just something they invented for the movies to add dramatic tension to a moment that otherwise wouldn't have any. Twenty minutes, you say?"

"Plus however long it takes them to walk across the woods," I said.

"Right, right. Cassandra?"

"Yes, Your Highness?"

Arden made a face but didn't say anything. A knowe has to reach a certain size before a proper chatelaine is needed—Shadowed Hills doesn't have one, and I'm not sure the false Queen ever bothered—so when Cassandra took the job, there'd been no one standing ready to train her in what it entailed. But the Brown kids have always been resourceful, and she'd found a way to get her training, even if it was just from old books and talking to people like Etienne. She knew every rule and loophole of her position, including when it was appropriate to be irreverent and when it wasn't. Clearly, this was one of the "wasn't appropriate" moments.

"Please go to the gates and ask my brother to remove himself to the parking area," said Arden. "The rest of our guests will be arriving soon and should be allowed to skip the walk."

"Yes, Highness." Cassandra bounced to her feet, pausing only long enough to press a kiss to Walther's temple, then trotted toward the door, moving fast and purposefully.

Walther watched her go, not bothering to pretend he wasn't studying the way her butt moved in her reasonably tight trousers. When he realized I was watching, he shrugged, offering me a wry smile. I shook my head.

It doesn't come up as often as it used to, thankfully, but I spent fourteen years transformed into a koi fish and abandoned in the ponds at the Japanese Tea Garden in Golden Gate Park. That was the end of my attempt to play faerie bride and live a happy life in the mortal world; I had gone on a simple reconnaissance mission, tracking Simon Torquill in an effort to find out whether he'd been involved in the disappearances of Luna and Rayseline, and had found myself lost to the world for more than a decade. During that time, my own child had gone from a toddler who thought I hung the moon and stars to a teenager who believed I'd willingly abandoned her in order to run off and live a life of carefree childlessness.

Gillian hadn't been the only kid I abandoned, just the only one who actually belonged with me. Cassandra had been almost five years old when I went into the pond, and part of me still had trouble accepting her as a grown adult who had the absolute right to be romantically interested in my friends. Faerie makes age gaps complicated. When you're going to have forever, do you really care if one partner is twenty and the other is two hundred? I know that. I also know the age difference between me and Tybalt is much greater than the one between her and Walther, who's roughly my age. And it doesn't always help.

Other things that don't help: Stacy, my best friend since childhood, and Cassandra's mother, doesn't approve of her dating anyone at all, age-appropriate or no. According to Cassie, Stacy doesn't want any of her kids dating, which feels a little weird to me, since Cassandra, Karen, and Andrew are all old enough by human standards to be going out with other kids. Karen and Andrew are probably still a little young for anything more than holding hands and asking for rides to the movies, but there's no good reason their mother should react so negatively to the very idea.

I looked around. "Where's Madden?"

"I gave him the night off," said Arden. I blinked at her. She shrugged. "He wasn't invited to the wedding, and his boyfriend has been reminding him recently that working for a queen doesn't mean neglecting his home life."

"You know, that's the first thing I've heard either of you say to imply that Madden's boyfriend is fae." Madden is Cu Sidhe, one of the faerie dogs as Tybalt is one of the faerie cats, and he works at a café not far from the house, keeping roughly diurnal hours for the sake of the job that pays his bills, all so he can serve in the Queen's Court all night.

Arden pays her staff, having a better understanding of the economics of the modern world than most purebloods, thanks to having lived in it for such a long time, but Madden, like most Cu Sidhe, is loyal to a fault. He'll stay at that café until it closes or burns to the ground, whichever comes first.

"He's not," said Arden, and laughed at the expression on my face. "They're gay men living in the Castro District. Madden isn't breaking any rules when he tells Charles he works for a queen. Chuck just assumes my queenship is a little more socially granted and involves more pancake makeup."

Keeping Faerie secret from humanity is sometimes straightforward and sometimes really, really weird. I blinked several times before shaking my head and turning my attention to Walther.

"Were things this strange in Silences?" I asked.

He laughed. "I don't really know," he said. "I was still a princess when I was there, and they kept me and my sister pretty well insulated from the places where things got really weird."

I nodded. "Right."

Walther was never a girl, for all that people looked at him and assumed he was; he knew he was a boy from the time he was old enough to understand there was a difference between the two categories and that he was supposed to fall into the one most people didn't put him under. He'd still been a princess, with the rules and restrictions assigned to the role by our often archaic, surprisingly functional society. There was a reason he'd been so willing to repudiate his claim to the throne, rather than insisting on his rights as an exiled member of a fallen royal family, and a further reason he hadn't gone back to Silences when his parents retook the throne. He was happy here, with the people who loved him and did our best to understand him and had never once insisted he wear a fancy dress with lace frills to catch the eye of a neighboring prince.

"I took the advance crew through their portal about two hours ago," said Arden, attention on Tybalt. "By the time you get to Toronto, Stacy will have October's toilette laid out and ready for whatever's needed, and Kerry will be most of the way to finishing the cake."

"How many busloads of people are we sending to Canada?" I asked.

"Only three," said Tybalt, sounding slightly abashed. "The first, ours, and those who come later. It seemed more efficient to do it in multiple passes."

"'More efficient' is a phrase we use for car repairs and feeding hungry teenagers, not for getting guests to our wedding," I said.

"Too late now," he replied.

I made a scoffing sound and turned to Walther, silently pleading for backup. He shook his head instead, brushing his hands against his linen trousers.

"Sorry, Toby, but you abdicated this throne, you don't get to complain when the people you gave it to don't do things exactly the way you would have done them." He grinned as he walked over to us. "It'd be like me going back to Silences and complaining about the way Marlis is handling her duties as a princess of the court. It was my circus until I sold my shares, and now they're not my monkeys anymore."

"I hate you," I informed him.

"There's everybody's favorite hero of the realm." He kept smiling, intensely white teeth managing to make his eyes seem even more unrealistically blue. Being an alchemist meant he'd never needed to worry about whether his teeth were white enough. The eyes, in contrast, were all natural.

Many of the more similar types of fae can be distinguished by their eyes. Tylwyth Teg have eyes so blue they offend the sky, usually paired to very blonde hair. Before his hair darkened, Quentin could have passed as Tylwyth with a little extra illusion to brighten his irises. It was sort of a miracle that Walther didn't have more issues with his students falling in love with him—or maybe he did, and he just had ethics to balance the issues out. The only person I'd ever known him to be romantically involved with was Cassie, and she wasn't a chemistry major, keeping her safely out of his classes.

Think of the devil: Cassie came trotting back, surrounded by a fresh swirl of pixies. "Nolan is heading to the parking area to watch for your party," she informed me. "Lowri says she doesn't need backup. She can watch the door alone since, quote, 'Her Majesty has seen fit to invite all the troublemakers over at the same time, so there's no one left to ruin my night.' She was laughing when she said it, so I don't *think* it was intended as treason, but I can go order her to arrest herself, if you'd like."

"No, no, that's fine," said Arden, with an airy wave of her hand. "She's allowed to be a little disrespectful, as long as she's not doing it to my face. Queens who quash petty rebellion find themselves with much bigger problems on their hands."

"I should never have given you those etiquette books," said Cassandra, moving to stand next to Walther, who slid an arm around her shoulders.

Of all the things I would never have imagined when I was younger, standing with the Queen in the Mists, joking about the way the Kingdom was run, and not worrying that I was going to be arrested on trumped-up charges or have my clothing transformed into something I didn't want to wear would have been toward the top of the list. I had never realized how stressful it was to have my monarch despise me until the weight of it had been taken away.

I was contemplating the feeling when a glowing circle appeared in the air, accompanied by the scent of redwood needles and blackberry brandy, and our people started coming through. Quentin was first, still dragging my bags along with him, followed by May and Jazz, then Raj and Dean, and finally the Luidaeg and a nondescript man with short, goatish horns who could probably have passed for an ordinary Glastig.

I blinked. Normally, Oberon had antlers that would have put a stag to shame, only somewhat scaled down to account for the fact that he had a human's neck and cervical damage is not befitting for a King of Faerie. Normally, he was beautiful—terrible and forgettable in equal measure, a predator who drew and rejected the eye at the same time, like a glorious contradiction born to wear the crown. Now, he looked almost . . . normal. Almost like Officer Thornton, the human man he'd seemed to be until I told him that I was bringing him home and broke the ancient geas he had lain upon himself when he left us.

Still not sure how I feel about that. Both the fact that he had left us voluntarily—not compelled, like either of his queens—and the fact that I had been the one to bring him back, which was apparently the first step in some stupid-ass prophecy about my mother's descendants. My grandmother had been responsible for breaking Maeve's last Ride and seeing her lost to Faerie for five hundred years, if not forever, and now it was going to be my job to find her and bring her back. Bully for me.

I would have been less grumpy if the implication hadn't been that I was also going to be recovering Titania. Given my experiences with Eira, supposedly her favorite child, I was pretty sure she and I weren't going to get along, and I was tired of my enemies getting *harder* to punch as I got better at doing my job. Give me someone who's not immortal and infinitely powerful, please. As a treat.

Tybalt reached over and took my hand in his, squeezing tightly, before stepping forward. I followed. "Your Highness," he said to Arden, and offered her a shallow bow. "You have done our unworthy party a great kindness by offering to begin our journey. We are ready to depart."

He didn't thank her. Thanks are verboten in Faerie, basically taboo save under very narrow, very specific circumstances. Arden smiled understanding, and even as Nolan stepped through his portal and allowed it to collapse behind him, she turned away from us and lifted her hands, sketching a much wider gateway in the air. It glittered and sparked, and Cassandra watched raptly, apparently able to see something in the process that wasn't visible even to me.

A portal opened, wider than a door and taller than Danny, who hadn't come through from the parking lot. I couldn't blame him for not wanting to spend any more time in our company after being crammed into the car with this motley bunch of fools, and I didn't know if he'd even been invited to the wedding.

This was all very disorienting, and that was before the portal clarified into a splash of midnight sky spangled with diamond-bright stars, and a group of strangers standing on a brick promenade. "I can only hold this for a few minutes, so don't dawdle," said Arden, a touch of strain in her voice.

"Oh, we're quite done with dawdling," said Tybalt, and stepped through, pulling me with him.

The others followed, and we were off.

FIVE

"OCTOBER!"

Kerry's squeal was high, shrill, and almost jarring in this unfamiliar setting. It had taken us eight jumps, including one performed by Chelsea, who had joined us in Highmountain—her portal had exhausted her but carried us nearly two thousand miles in a single step—and now we were finally in Toronto, standing in the arrival hall of the royal knowe of the Westlands. Like Arden's knowe in Muir Woods, it had no name, because it didn't need one; when people said they were going to Court, they didn't have to specify. Not when they were this close to the royal knowe.

The space was familiar and strange at the same time. We had stepped through the final portal in upstate New York, and emerged into a palatial, echoing room with walls of polished curly maple, inlaid with panels shaped from the largest amethyst geodes I had ever seen, their raw crystal surfaces immaculate and glittering in the light that radiated from their cores before spreading to cover and obscure the ceiling. It felt simultaneously like we were standing in a forest and in a place that had been shaped by hand. The floor was polished amethyst, more smoothed than the crystals of the walls, but still clearly natural.

The room was big enough to host a ball, and the fact that they were using it for new arrivals implied things about the rest of the knowe that made me faintly uncomfortable. I looked to Quentin. He was staring raptly at the nearest geode, a look of heartbreaking youth and nostalgia on his face, and in that moment, I wanted nothing more than to gather him in my arms and tell him it was all going to be all right.

"Penny and I used to play floor hockey in here," he said, voice low enough not to carry. "In our socks, with an orange ball. I haven't thought about that orange ball in years . . ."

I put a hand on his shoulder. "It's always hard when you come home after a long time away."

It was going to be even harder for him, since he was coming home looking like a complete stranger, and he wouldn't be able to admit who he was to anyone without potentially getting both of us in serious trouble. "Allowed the Crown Prince to sell his face to the sea witch," not exactly in the big book of good knightly behavior.

Footsteps approached from the far side of the room, which was a neat trick, as there were no visible doors. They drew closer, and two of the vast wood panels peeled apart and swung seamlessly inward, revealing themselves to have been perfectly carved into the shape of two interlocking maple trees, complete with delicately pronged leaves. I swallowed several snarky comments about leaning too hard into the aesthetic. I was already insulting the crown by showing up in their knowe in jeans and a sweatshirt, with all my luggage. I didn't need to insult them out loud.

A woman walked through the opening, and the paneled trees swung shut again behind her. Even knowing they were there, they still vanished completely once they were closed. Maybe they only actually existed when they were open.

The woman drew closer, and I found myself looking away from her, unable to force my eyes to focus on her face, which was so impossibly lovely that it made me feel bad about myself even before I had taken in its details. How could I expect Tybalt to marry *me* when she existed? It didn't even matter if she was available. She was proof that women could be so infinitely more than I was that she made me extraneous to any needs my lover could possibly have had.

Describing her is literally beyond my capacity because she was too beautiful, and it crossed a line into the kind of beauty the mind is not fully meant to comprehend. Her skin was a few shades darker than the polished maple around her; her hair was a dark, glacial blue, almost as if it had somehow been scooped from some body of living water, and it fell to her waist in a cascade of curls, unbound and effortless. Her ears were pointed, and her fingers were long, and that was where my eyes refused to sully her any further with their attention, turning resolutely and irresistibly away.

"Nessa," murmured Quentin, voice low, intended for my ears only. "She's my father's seneschal, and one of the Gwragedd Annwn."

A lake maiden? That explained the beauty. Gwragedd Annwn are meant to be seen at a distance great enough to blunt the impact of their appearance, which can be literally deadly if they're not careful. Indeed, as she drew closer, Nessa wove her fingers through the air the way I always did when I was casting a human illusion and pulled a veil of nothingness down over herself. There was a brief sensation, like a soap bubble being popped, and I was suddenly able to look at her without the almost irresistible urge to look away.

To be honest, I had always expected the Gwragedd Annwn to be . . . more. That degree of aversion could come from particularly pretty Daoine Sidhe when they went without any masks at all. I'll get better when I give up the last of my humanity, but for now, occasionally being unable to look at someone seems like a small price to pay.

She was still beautiful, and her hair was still impossibly blue, but she didn't hurt my heart by existing anymore. She had blunted herself somehow, making herself comprehensible in the same way Oberon made himself ordinary, not an illusion so much as it was a reduction, a necessary lessening to fit within the limitations of this world.

"Hello," she said, and her accent was pure Nova Scotian, thick as maple frosting and just as delicious. "Welcome to the seat of the Westlands. We've been expecting you. In the name of His Royal Majesty, High King Aethlin Sollys, and his honored consort, High Queen Maida Sollys, it is my honor to extend to you the hospitality of this house for the customary seven days as we host and house your nuptials."

Her gaze fell on the Luidaeg, drawn there by whatever force guides terrible mistakes and misassumptions. She smiled, and it was a lovely thing, despite the illusion that brought her down to the level of the rest of us. "Sir Daye, I presume?"

Quentin stiffened beside me, his body going rigid under my

hand. So something about that greeting—casual and friendly as it was—didn't sit right with him. Well, it didn't sit right with me either, mostly because I didn't feel like watching the Luidaeg commit murder in the royal knowe of the Westlands.

"What was your first clue, the fact that I'm wearing electrical tape in my hair like some sort of fashion-deficient mortal teenager, or the absence of a bra?" The Luidaeg sounded as startled as I felt.

Nessa kept smiling in the face of such obvious rudeness, her gaze flickering to Oberon, who loomed next to the Luidaeg like some sort of marble obelisk doing a poor job of pretending to be a fae man of indeterminate bloodline, the horns on his forehead implying that he was probably some sort of Satyr or Glastig cross. One thing was for sure: he was no Cait Sidhe.

Nessa tried anyway. "King Tybalt?" she ventured. "We are very grateful to you for accepting Queen Maida's offer to hold your wedding here."

That was when Kerry's squeal split the air and saved us all from a situation that could easily have gone from embarrassing and faintly humorous to horrific in an instant, judging by the looks on Tybalt's and the Luidaeg's faces. Oberon, for his part, looked more politely baffled than anything else. He wasn't going to carpet the room with the little Gwragedd Annwn's entrails. That was good. At this rate, there was going to be a line.

Pretty much our entire group turned toward the sound of Kerry's jubilant yell. She had appeared through another of those puzzle-piece doors on the opposite side of the room. She bounced to her toes and waved vigorously, then launched herself in our direction like a friendly, chubby, hug-seeking missile.

May stepped forward to take the first hit like the sister-slash-Fetch-slash maid of honor she was, wrapping her arms around the barreling Kerry and allowing the momentum of the impact to spin them halfway around, Kerry's feet actually leaving the floor in the process. Nessa blinked, bemused, as May laughed.

"Wrong Daye!" she chided, letting Kerry go. "Not the bride!"

"There are no bad Dayes in this week," said Kerry, and launched herself at me.

She had bled off some speed in her little dance with May, and the impact didn't spin me around, just knocked me back a step. As always, Kerry was short, solid, and as much pure muscle as she was fat. Like most Hobs, she had long since decided the best way to approach the world was head-on with a smile on her pretty, round-cheeked face.

Her hair was a wild cascade of dark brown curls streaked liberally with white—a sign that she'd been baking, not of age, since she's as much a changeling as I am and still looks like she's in her mid-twenties. She's probably more of a changeling than I am at this point, after everything I've done to change the balance of my own blood. Kerry is still half and half, the way she was born, daughter of a Hob mother and a human father Kerry never knew and never particularly wanted to. She made her choice, and she's always been happy with it.

Not much of one for second thoughts and regrets, our Kerry.

"I told you I'd bake your wedding cake one day, and wait until you see it, you're going to swoon and sigh and tell that brute of a man you *think* you're marrying that you're terribly, heartbreakingly sorry for his loss, but you have to marry the cake instead," she said, barely pausing to catch her breath. "The sugar work *alone* should get me knighted."

"Being knighted is more trouble than it's worth, believe me," I said, laughing. Quentin sighed and nodded his agreement. His own knighthood was still a few years off, but he had already more than learned the cost of it.

"Then I'll take a nice little barony somewhere, especially if it comes with a nice little baron to keep my bed warm at night." Kerry leered, the expression rendered almost comic by her obvious affability, then whirled toward May, who was standing next to Jazz and watching our interplay with amusement. "And you! Second Daye extension! I'll have you remember that I promised to bake your wedding cake as well and give me the chance to show how incredibly deep the well of my skills extends sooner than later!"

May blinked. Jazz leaned around her, a polite smile on her face.

"Am I also allowed to leave my potential spouse for a cake?" she asked.

"You, I like," said Kerry. "You'll have a bride's cake of your own. It's a foolish custom when you're paying for it, but when you have a master baker offering their labor for free, you may as well have as many cakes as you can squeeze out of the kitchen. Which reminds me, the kitchen is gearing up for dinner, and Stacy's asked me to tell you she'll need at least twenty minutes to deal with," she waved her hands vaguely in the direction of my torso, "all of this. That means you're on the clock!"

Then she was off again, pausing only long enough to kiss Chelsea loudly on the cheek before she was heading back to the door she'd entered through, a cheerful whirlwind that left a cloud of flour in her wake.

I looked to Tybalt. "I thought you said I'd have a chance to object to the cake."

He shrugged apologetically and spread his hands. "That's between you and Kerry."

Meaning that, no, there wouldn't be a chance to object to the cake. Oh, well. I should have expected that. I turned, in silent unison with everyone else, to Nessa. She grimaced before forcing a smile, clearly trying to recover her dignity.

"Not Sir Daye, then?" she asked of the Luidaeg, who laughed.

"Not in the slightest, although we *are* related," she said. Since she was still projecting humanity with the focused determination only the Firstborn can seem to manage, the impression she was giving was that she was a cousin from the fae side of my family who had just decided to take the Tuatha express across North America out of nothing more than familial loyalty.

"Oh," said Nessa, sounding baffled. Then: "I am so sorry, miss. I intended no insult, to any of you."

"None is taken," said Tybalt. "I, the actual groom to be, apologize for allowing it to go on so long. It was uncouth of us not to correct you immediately and spare you this embarrassment. Now, I presume you were sent to escort us to our quarters for the duration?"

"Of course, of course," said Nessa, clapping her hands together in what looked very much like relief. "If you would all do me the favor of following me?"

"Sure thing," I said and, when she started moving, fell in easily behind her. Tybalt stayed close by my side, and Quentin stayed at my heels. I glanced back at him. He hadn't said a word since Nessa got close enough to hear him, which seemed a little odd, since his voice had changed along with the rest of him. It wasn't like she was going to hear him speak and go, "You're the Crown Prince!" and accuse us all of treason.

So far as I'm aware, hearing through illusions is not a power possessed by any corner of Faerie. Seeing through illusions is, for pureblooded Cait Sidhe, and smelling through illusions certainly is, but hearing? Not so much. And this wasn't an illusion, anyway. This was a total transformation, binding to the bottom of his bones, and it wasn't going to break so easily.

I still reached back and gave his shoulder a reassuring squeeze, earning myself a grateful look. Whatever was bothering him, it was *really* bothering him.

Nessa led us back through the widest of the puzzle-piece doors, into a long hallway as paneled in maple and amethyst as the first had been. Catching my confusion at the aesthetic, she gave me a tour guide's practiced, polished smile, and said, "Ontario is famous for our maple trees, which are an emblem of Canada the world over, and of course, amethyst is our provincial stone. When the royal seat of the Westlands was being settled upon, it came down to a question between the Kingdoms of Maple or Ash and Oak."

I hadn't heard the technical name of the Kingdom comprising most of Ontario in so long that it threw me for a second. The High Throne has been in Toronto for so many years that the Kingdom is almost forgotten, grouped in with the rest of the High King's holdings. "Guess we got lucky there, since we had to abandon Ash and Oak," I said.

"Yes, there were Roane among the Selkies of Beacon's Home when the choice was being made," said Nessa, with some pride in her voice. "My home Kingdom," she explained a moment later, in case her accent hadn't been indication enough. Beacon's Home is another of the Kingdoms counted among the High Throne's holdings, and it corresponds roughly with the Canadian province of Nova Scotia. One of the largest Selkie clans—now Roane colonies—is centered there.

"Good to know," I said neutrally.

"The Roane told the convocation debating the location of the ruling seat that Ash and Oak would be lost to rust and ruin within a generation, and war would follow if the seat had to be relocated once it had been established," she said smoothly. This was something she had practiced, whether in front of visitors or in her own mirror. Did Gwragedd Annwn use mirrors? The stories I'd heard said they could stun even themselves if they weren't careful.

But then, they would need to know what they looked like to cast the spells that allowed them to interact safely with the rest of us, so presumably, mirrors were involved somehow.

"We were very fortunate in that the monarchs attending the convocation, some of whom were already entangled with the on-going stirrings of revolution among the Colonies, agreed that placing the seat in their infant America was less essential than placing it in a location which would bring stability and prosperity to our new High Kingdom, and keep us from fighting a losing war against Europa when they sensed both weakness and wealth to be had. This continent had suffered enough from Europa's attentions. We deserved to be left alone to prosper or perish. It was due to the intervention of the Roane that we were able to open this knowe and dig its roots into the bedrock of the world, where they would never be sundered."

Quentin pulled a face. So we were getting a sterilized version of the ten-cent tour, and would get the rest of it later, when we were safely behind closed doors. Not a shock but, still, good to know.

"The Roane are good that way," said the Luidaeg, in a neutral tone.

"Yes, they were," said Nessa, clearly heedless of the danger she was putting herself in with that casual statement.

That seemed a little odd. She should have been up to date on everything that was happening within her liege's demesne. Or maybe my standards were skewed by the fact that things seemed to happen so quickly around me.

Not that my standards were what put that murderous expression on the Luidaeg's face. Maybe it wasn't nice to wander around the royal knowe of the Westlands with an undercover Firstborn, but since her father, the literal King of Faerie, was also with us, I was pretty sure we weren't breaking any laws, written or unwritten, which might indicate that hospitality demanded immediate disclosure. And the Luidaeg *had* accepted the hospitality of the house, if only through her silence, which meant she had to wait seven days before she'd be allowed to turn anyone inside-out for insulting her descendants.

Dean coughed. "I'm Count Dean Lorden of Goldengreen?" he said, somehow turning the statement of his identity into a question. Nessa gave him a polite look, like she was asking how that was relevant. "My mother is Duchess Dianda Lorden of Salt-mist?"

Nessa blinked. "Isn't that an Undersea Kingdom?" she asked.

Dean began to bristle. Before he could do much more than look annoyed, Raj stepped in, saying, "Duchess Lorden will be attending the wedding, and is a daughter of the Merrow, madame."

"Ah," said Nessa, still sounding bemused. "But the Count is, by all appearances, Daoine Sidhe."

Oh, this was potentially about to take a hard left turn into some seriously deep and dangerous waters, and one or more people might wind up badly hurt, hospitality or no. "The ducal consorts are Daoine Sidhe," I said hurriedly. "Dean takes after his father."

Nessa nodded. "I've heard such can happen," she said. "Well, it is a pleasure to make your acquaintance, young Count, and I am glad for all our sakes that you are here to witness such a grand historic event as the marriage of a King of Cats."

My gut twisted. Hearing my own wedding referred to as a "grand historic event" was never going to stop being upsetting.

"But, um, since I grew up in an Undersea demesne, I can say with some assurance that the Roane are absolutely still around," he said doggedly. "There are more of them than there used to be, even, since the Selkies fulfilled their bargain with the sea witch."

Nessa blinked. "Oh," she said faintly. "Well, I don't get home very often these days, or down to the coast. So I suppose I may have missed some soundings from the sea. My apologies if I've given offense to you, or to Saltmist."

It wasn't Dean she needed to be worried about, although the Luidaeg now looked merely annoyed, not murderous. It was a distinct improvement.

"Neither to me nor to my mother's holdings," said Dean, with the graceful precision of the born diplomat. He might only be a minor noble as such things were measured, but he had been raised to smooth over troubled waters—something that was probably much more essential in the Undersea, where going to war is practically the local hobby. They do slaughter the way land fae do unnecessary balls, or at least that's the impression they all try to project. Maybe it's all fluffy sea-lambs and tea parties when they aren't putting on a dangerous face.

I doubt it, though. Dianda Lorden is scary as hell when she wants to be.

Sweet Titania, I love that woman.

Nessa bobbed her head, less in agreement and more in evident relief that we were finally moving on from her possible faux pas.

"As I was saying, the debate over where to seat the High Kingdom had come down to Maple or Ash and Oak, and when the Roane spoke for Maple, the future was sealed. The first High King, long may his memory be a grace and a guidance, and never become a burden, felt it was important to show through the choices made in designing the knowe that we were proud as a people of where we had settled ourselves. That Canada was not 'second choice' to the Colonies, and we would do our best to live with this land, not hold ourselves superior to and apart from it."

"Does that mean there's a Tim Hortons in your banquet hall?" asked Raj dryly. "I can think of several among our number who would be relieved by such easy access to donuts."

Quentin glared daggers at him. Whether it was due to the implied insult to his childhood home or because he hadn't been the one to ask the question was less than clear.

"Unfortunately, no," said Nessa. "Although the High King might install one if he could get the fryers to work reliably on this side of the hill. The original designs that grace our halls were created by fae artisans, and as the knowe has expanded, it has incorporated their ideas and added a few embellishments of its own."

"So you believe the knowe is alive?" I asked.

"When you complain on Monday that you can't find a place in the library with decent light and on Tuesday a door that has always led to a rather nondescript storage closet opens on a library annex lit by glowing crystal spires, it's difficult not to credit the knowe with at least some small degree of personal agency," said Nessa gracefully.

The hall had been gently curving as we walked, and Nessa paused as it finally opened up like a fern, shooting off half a dozen halls in varying directions that would have seemed jumbled and contradictory had they not been so effortlessly organic. "Quarters have been arranged for the lot of you," she said, indicating the hall in front of us. "You may arrange yourselves as you wish. I had originally wanted to assign rooms, to be sure no one was slighted the honors due to their station, but the High Queen assured me that you would be happier seeing to your own needs."

"That'll be great," I started. "Just give us a little time to settle in, and—"

"But for the bride and groom, we have arranged a special suite," she said before I could get any further.

Oh, if they were planning to split us up, they were going to get a nasty surprise. I couldn't take my toys and go home, not with thousands of miles between us and California, but I could drag Tybalt and Quentin in front of a justice of the peace in Toronto as easily as I could in San Francisco, and Quentin only had to see me married, not see me married in his parents' knowe, to get the potion that would give his real face back.

"Meaning what, precisely?" asked Tybalt, before I could say anything and get us into trouble.

"You'll still be on the same hall as your party, you'll just be in a room specifically intended for you," she said reassuringly as she started down the hall. Lacking any better plans, we all followed her, some with more alacrity than others. May looked enthralled by the whole process of getting to what were effectively very fancy, very exclusive hotel rooms; Raj looked faintly amused, like this was nothing impressive; the Luidaeg and Oberon looked like tourists on their first trip to Disney World, when the Luidaeg wasn't glaring for one reason or another. Only Walther and Nolan looked entirely at ease, like this was neither impressive nor something they needed to make a show of disdaining.

That made sense. They had both grown up in regional equivalents of this place, and unless it had some pretty big tricks up its sleeve, it wasn't going to impress them much.

Nessa stopped at a door that looked like every other door in the hall, touching it lightly where the peephole would have been, if it had possessed one. The door seemed to sigh, which was impressive for a piece of architecture, and the doorknob turned, the door swinging inward to reveal a single room larger than the entire first floor of my house.

There was a bed big enough for most of us to have slept in at once, if we had been holding that kind of party. There was a sunken tub set into the floor, more than ten feet across and steaming gently. The walls were lined in bookshelves and velvet curtains, which wasn't quite enough to obscure the fact that more of those raw amethyst geodes peeped out from between the maple panels. It was like the owner's room at the largest bordello the world had ever known.

"I was told you would be bringing a squire," she said, and indicated one of the three smaller doors off the main room. "Squire's quarters are through here. There's also an en suite bathroom, and a small kitchen, if you're struck by the need to snack during the day. Only tell the icebox what you expect it to contain, and it will be present for you."

That was an interesting form of magic, one I'd have to poke at later at my leisure. "Your hospitality is a credit to your liege," I said solemnly, dredging the phrase out of the depths of my courtly education. From the startled but approving looks on both May and Tybalt's faces, I had gotten it right for once. "These quarters will be more than satisfactory for us. Will we be summoned for dinner?"

"Yes, as soon as the High King is ready for you," said Nessa. "I'll leave you to your preparations." And she was off, turning on her heel and striding off down the hall, moving with long, smooth strides, as effortless as a bubble floating over the surface of clear, cool water. When she was well clear of us, she snapped her fingers at the level of her cheek, and the sway of her hips became abruptly infinitely more compelling, making it almost impossible to look away.

"I've always pitied the Gwragedd Annwn," said the Luidaeg, voice low. "They're my sister's descendants. Black Annis was terrible to look upon, even for those of us who loved her more dearly than life itself, and so her children were so beautiful that they slew anyone who looked upon them without protections. Their children were less beautiful, thankfully, but still painful to behold. She used to say that anyone who thought beauty was a burden should try ugliness instead, and she handed out a lot of curses." She sighed heavily. "I miss her."

Oberon settled his hand on her shoulder. "I miss her, too," he said, and his words carried the weight of centuries of mourning for the lost, who might linger for a time among the night-haunts, but who would inevitably disappear forever.

"I need to talk to you," said Quentin, positioning himself in the doorway of the room I was going to be sharing with Tybalt.

I blinked at him. "Okay. Does it need to be in the hall for some reason?"

"No," he allowed, pulling the suitcases into the chamber to allow me to follow him. I stopped once I was clear of the door, crossing my arms and looking levelly at my squire.

He glanced quickly around, as if reassuring himself that all the people in earshot were people he knew and trusted—and who knew who he really was—before he said, voice low and tight, "Something's wrong with Nessa. I don't know what it is, but she's not acting right."

"And you couldn't say anything before because you're supposed to be meeting her for the first time," I said. "I was wondering about the way they trained the courtiers here. Do you think she's dangerous?"

"I don't know. I'd like to hope not, but . . ." He shook his head. "This would be easier if I could talk to the High King."

"Lucky for you, I *can* talk to the High King," I said, and patted him on the shoulder. "I'll ask him what's up after dinner."

"Discreetly, please?"

"Am I ever anything other than discreet?"

Quentin snorted and started hauling my suitcases toward the bed. He was barely halfway there when the door to what would be his room burst open, disgorging a frantic Stacy.

"Mom!" exclaimed Cassandra.

"Can't talk, fashion emergency in progress," said Stacy, and kept running until she was close enough to grab my wrist and yank me into the room. She didn't stop there, continuing to drag me toward the squire's quarters, which she had apparently co-opted at some point.

Tybalt didn't try to grab me back or defend me. He actually laughed. Traitor. "Mistress Brown," he said, inclining his head to Stacy, who was wearing a floor-length linen dress the color of her name, albeit a delicate and flattering shade of same. It was trimmed in white so bright that any dentist would have envied it, with laces in the same color. Simple, elegant, and remarkably practical—just like Stacy herself.

"Sir Cat," she said, voice tightly clipped. "The rest of you need to be getting ready *now*," she snarled, before yanking me into her purloined dressing room and slamming the door.

Inside, the room looked like an explosion in a vintage clothing store. Dresses, corsets, undergarments, and accessories covered every surface of what had been a pleasant if not palatial chamber suited for your ordinary squire—and this answered the question, quite handily, of whether Nessa had been aware that I was going to be bringing the Crown Prince with me; she would have made it nicer if she'd known it was going to be Quentin—turning it into a closet-slash-dressing room.

Apparently taking my shellshocked expression as criticism, Stacy scoffed.

"Quentin was going to be sneaking off to his boyfriend's room as soon as the lights went down for the day and you know it," she said dismissively. "At least this way he doesn't have to sneak back in to get his toothbrush."

I opened my mouth to argue, paused, and closed it again, shrugging. She was right. There was no real point in pretending she wasn't. "When did you get here?" I asked.

"Long enough ago to know how important it is that we get you ready and presentable ASAP. Kerry could only promise me twenty minutes." Stacy grabbed the bottom of my shirt and tugged. "Off with this abysmal rag. Quick now, and we'll see if you can't keep your bra."

I blinked at her as I pulled my shirt off over my head, leaving my stick-straight hair ruffled and jutting up in all directions, like I'd gotten overly amorous with a light socket. Then I scowled. "I'm *keeping* my bra."

"One nice thing about pureblood fashion grinding to a halt somewhere around the start of World War I, most of the dresses I have here either come with built-in stays or have matching corsets," said Stacy serenely, taking a step back and eyeing me thoughtfully. I lowered my arms, forcing myself to keep them by my sides. If I tried to cover myself, she'd just yank my hands down and snap at me for getting in her way, and it wasn't like I had anything she hadn't seen before. We'd been getting naked around each other since we were skinny-dipping in the pond between Shadowed Hills and my mother's knowe.

"Hmm," she said finally. "You know, your mother did you no favors with your coloring."

"Um, thanks?" I said.

"Not your fault, I know, but she could have given you more pigment than your average baby bird," she said. "I've seen your wedding dress, so we don't want to go with anything too light, but if we go too strong, we can wash you out easy."

I resisted the urge to ask her what I was going to be wearing to my wedding. Knowing Stacy, she wouldn't tell me anyway.

After almost a minute of studying me, she nodded decisively, said, "Lose the bra," and stomped over to the door, wrenching it open and shouting, "She's wearing the black ombre," into the room

before slamming the door again and returning her attention to me.
I hadn't moved, and her eyes narrowed at the sight of my bra.

"You asked me to be your lady's maid for the duration of this
trip," she said. "I distinctly remember a two pm phone call where
you wailed about how you thought Tybalt was going to make you
do something big and fancy and you had no idea how to do your
hair. Do you remember that?"

"I do," I said slowly. "But that doesn't mean you have to dress
me the whole time we're here."

Stacy looked at me flatly, her expression saying several unflat-
tering things about my intelligence. "Bra, off, now," she said.

I removed my bra.

"Good girl." She dug her hands into the pile of undergarments,
digging down through the pile of fabric and lacings, until she produced a lightweight corset in a modern enough style that I was sure
it wasn't meant to be seen. My suspicions were confirmed a second
later when she beckoned me forward, and said, "Let's get you
laced up."

"Yes, ma'am." Fighting wasn't going to do me any good. Stacy
has been one of my best friends since childhood—she held the title
unchallenged until May came along and had taken her sudden
rival with the impeccable good grace I loved about her. She knew
where all my buttons were, and how best to push them, since she'd
been there when many of them were being installed. Fighting with
her was never as easy, or as successful, as I wanted it to be.

She had taken her demotion from the assumed position of maid
of honor to head bridesmaid with incredibly good grace—one of
the only decisions I'd made myself, which may have helped. She'd
always expected to stand beside me for whatever nightmare of a
ceremony I would put together when left to my own devices, and
to smile through a puce bridesmaid's dress while we served pizza
at the reception. This was a demotion and a reprieve at the same
time.

She bustled around me, pulling the pieces of the corset into
place before starting to draw the laces tight. I smiled down at her,
feeling suddenly, overwhelmingly fond. "Hey," I said.

"What?" Stacy didn't lift her head, focused on getting the knots
to lay just right so they wouldn't show under whatever confection
of a dress she was planning to slide me into. Stacy's illusions have
always been stronger than mine, despite being a thin-blooded

changeling; whatever she inherited from her Barrow Wight ancestors doesn't fight against flower magic the same way my mother's blood does.

Despite that, she's never been a fan of enchanting or creating dresses out of raw materials. It's considered a basic hearth trick that every changeling should master, and she *can* do it, but she prefers real things that can't be accidentally destroyed by the wrong counterspell. One incident at Julie's twelfth birthday party, and she'd rather haul what looked like half of Nordstrom to Canada than risk dressing me in feathers and cobwebs.

It's endearing, if weird. "I love you a lot," I said.

She did glance up at that, startled, before she turned her attention back to my laces. "Yeah, well, let's see if you still love me when I finish your makeup," she said. "You're going to get a mascara wand to the eye."

I did. Twice. I also got a cloud of assorted cosmetic powders in my nose, causing me to sneeze while she was zipping me into my dress, muttering under her breath about how any purebloods who didn't like the modernity of zippers in the royal knowe could bite her, and then she was behind me, yanking my hair into compliance with brisk, rough efficiency that made me yelp several times.

I was sure at least one of them was audible in the chamber outside, but Tybalt did not appear to save me. Traitor.

When Stacy was finally done, she stepped back, her own hair in sweaty disarray, and planted her hands on her hips, looking me frankly up and down. "You'll do," she said. "Now get out."

"Do I get to look in a mirror?"

"Eyes are reflective. Go let Tybalt look at you." She pointed to the door. "If you make the High King wait, I think that's technically treason, and if I'm the reason you're late, I'm as treasonous as you are. People have died for less. Go. Get out."

I got out. Stumbling through the door back into the main chamber with no real sense of what I was wearing, save that it was one-shouldered and sleeveless and long enough to cover my feet, and the distinct sense that Stacy would send me to the High King naked if I forced her hand.

Tybalt was sitting on the loveseat across from the squire's room, a book in his hands, idly turning pages without seeming to really look at their contents. Stacy slammed the door behind me. Tybalt looked up.

He had been busy while I was getting changed, trading his traveling clothes for a pair of black leather pants that made his ass look amazing and were going to look even more amazing on my floor later in the morning, when I peeled them off of him. His shirt was probably better called a blouse. It started a deep shade of orchid purple at the shoulders, trending paler as it descended, until it turned white just above his waist. It was tucked in and belted, so I couldn't see what color the bottom was. Clear, maybe. Clear would have been perfectly fine by me.

I swallowed. It didn't help. "Um," I managed. "Wow."

"I was about to say similar," he said, setting his book aside and rising. "You look . . ."

"Stacy dressed me," I said needlessly. "I don't even know what I'm wearing."

He walked over to me, placing his hands on my shoulders, and turned me to face the hot tub. The wall beyond it was mirrored, because, of course, it was. The local nobles apparently got up to some kinky shit when they were visiting the High King.

My impressions of the way the dress fit were correct; it was fastened over one shoulder with an asymmetric neckline, hugging the line of my body until it reached my hips, where it broadened out into a flowing skirt. The fabric was uniformly black to my hips, where it began to show flashes of purple, red, and pale pink. Those colors became more dominant as the skirt continued to descend, until my entire lower body was the color of a bruised orchid. My hair was braided along the sides, fastened with pins shaped like orchid blossoms, and gathered into a twist at the back of my head. Stacy had managed to give it body somehow, making it look less like someone had used a ruler to style it.

I had no jewelry, and in this dress, I didn't need it. My only adornment was the knife belted at my hip. Over the dress at Stacy's insistence, to make it easier to take away if it turned out that even heroes weren't allowed to go armed into the company of the High King.

"You look amazing," said Tybalt, voice low, and kissed my cheek. "Now, we should be going. Nessa came to the door a few minutes ago, and I assured her that you were almost ready. If this is how Stacy thinks you should be dressed at all times, do you think we could employ her to live in the guest room and clothe you nightly?"

"Something's not quite right about that woman," I muttered, before returning to the matter at hand and raising my voice back to normal levels. "We both know that if we weren't in the high knowe of the Westlands, someone would put a stab wound in this thing before we had a chance to make it to dinner," I said, letting him guide me toward the door. "Is everyone coming to dinner?"

"I think they were concerned about causing offense to someone important by inviting only members of our party, so yes, we are all to dine with the High King and High Queen of your Divided Courts tonight. All save Stacy and Kerry, who have, I believe, pled preoccupation with addressing the disaster of your life as a reason they are unable to attend."

"Cheaters," I murmured.

"Quite." He opened the door, revealing the hall, where Nessa was waiting with the rest of our group. True to Stacy's prediction, Quentin was standing with Dean, the two boys holding hands as if they had nothing else left to cling to in the world. Chelsea and Raj stood nearby, Chelsea behind the pair, Raj in front, clearly protecting their friends. Interesting.

Everyone had changed for dinner. Everyone, that is, except for the Luidaeg, who was still wearing her customary overalls, hair taped into ponytails. I raised an eyebrow at her. She smirked.

"You clean up well enough," she said. "Shall we?"

"Yeah, let's go," I agreed, and she started down the hall, leaving the rest of us—Nessa included—to follow after her. Nessa looked anxious about the whole thing, clearly believing she was meant to be in the lead, and to be fair, she probably was. But the Luidaeg just as clearly knew where we were going. "Have you been here before?" I asked, pitching my voice low.

She laughed, bright and musical and delighted. "I attended the convocation where they decided to put the thing in Maples," she said. "Who do you think convinced the Roane it would be safe for them to leave Beacon's Home long enough to come and tell the land folk what to do with themselves? There were four of them in the kingdom, a family, living together at the edge of the sea, terrified of things they couldn't quite predict or see coming. But they were kind, and they wanted to help. Archibald and Sarah were close descendants of mine—I knew their parents, and their grandparents had been my own children, although they had different fathers, thankfully. That's part of why it's so important your

Firstborn stay a little bit to the side of Faerie. You would all be horrified to learn how closely your forebears were related to one another."

"Fae genetics are weird," I said, trying to keep my voice neutral. She was right.

Everyone knows Faerie began with the Three, that Oberon, Maeve, and Titania had created us all, one way or another, in some combination or other with one another. No one, seemingly not even the Firstborn, knows where they came from in the first place, but Maeve and Titania have always been referred to as sisters, making our family tree, morphologically diverse as it is, more like a family branch.

Maybe a family arrow. Something long and straight and capable of flying very far because there was nothing to slow it down.

Faerie's history is riddled with secret human ancestors, mortal outcrosses who have been politely concealed from society by the use of hope chests to turn the resulting children into purebloods and allow them to carry on the family line. Without the hope chests, we would never have been able to build the numbers to create a society, much less to thrive, and most of us cope by never thinking about it. Siblings don't marry each other, but cousins do, because cousins have to. If you want to continue your descendant line, you don't have a choice.

If we went far enough back along the branch, we'd probably find a point where Tybalt and I were related, since at least one of the Cait Sidhe Firstborn was descended from Oberon. For obvious reasons, made stronger by my own human upbringing, I had no interest in doing the research necessary to prove it.

The Luidaeg reached over and patted my hand, clearly reading the distress in my expression. "Sorry," she said, and while her tone was sarcastic, I knew her meaning was sincere. That's the only good thing about talking to someone who's been geased to be literally incapable of telling a lie. "I know you're still human enough not to like to talk about these things. But Archibald and Sarah were good people, and when I asked them to speak for Maples, they agreed. Packed up their children and traveled to the convocation to give their testimony."

I blinked at her. "Why did you get involved?"

"The Gwragedd Annwn was right when she said the Roane predicted war if we seated the High Kingdom in Ash and Oak," said the Luidaeg. "I had already seen it in my own twists of the tide, and I knew that when the iron rose from the harbor and had the land for its pleasures, the Kingdom as we knew it would fall. If that had been allowed to happen after seating the High Kingdom there, all the lesser Kingdoms would have believed they had the right to challenge for the throne. Not just in the Westlands—Europa would have joined the fray, and possibly the North Kingdom and Aztalan. Those last two weren't certain. The others were. The Shallcross family held the throne of Ash and Oak."

"I remember King Shallcross," said Tybalt thoughtfully. "Daoine Sidhe. Unpleasant fellow. Did he ever marry?"

"Yes, Queen Vesper was by his side for the last thirty years of his rule," said Quentin. "She was also Daoine Sidhe, of no known family line."

"He deserved her," said the Luidaeg. "I never met the woman, but from what I understand, his bride was as callous and self-absorbed as he was."

"They wed after I left, then," said Tybalt.

"You got out a good fifty years before the calamity." The Luidaeg looked like she was on the verge of saying more, but that was when Nessa finally tired of letting us lead and shoved her way between us, turning around so that she was walking backward like a tour guide as she smiled beatifically, if tensely, at the Luidaeg.

"It's a great honor that you're all to be allowed to dine with the royal family tonight," she said, in a bright, cheery, somewhat strained voice. "As some of you have clearly mortal heritage, it's possible you don't know the etiquette appropriate to the occasion. Please do not speak to the High King or Queen unless spoken to directly; you may address servants, but should refrain from doing so whenever possible, to make things simpler."

"Should we also refrain from looking directly at anyone who might outrank us?" asked the Luidaeg, tone dry.

Her failure to tell Nessa her name was starting to feel a little mean. Still, something about Nessa was bothering me, and Quentin said she wasn't acting like herself, and if this was keeping the Luidaeg happy, I wasn't going to say anything. When dealing with someone as old as the Luidaeg, it's generally a good idea to let them have their fun. Oberon was causing a lot less trouble. He was still walking quietly along with the group, looking at everything with the same calm serenity. He wasn't even what I would have called particularly wide-eyed; he wasn't gawking, just looking at his surroundings. All this had been built since his disappearance.

I wondered, not entirely idly, whether he approved of the things we'd done while he was gone. If he didn't, there was probably going to be some kind of a reckoning soon, and the thought of trying to protect the people I cared about from someone whose power was exponentially greater than the Luidaeg's was horrific enough to not be worth dwelling on.

And anyway, we had reached a door that actually did us the courtesy of looking like a door, albeit a massive, ornate one of carved maple inlaid with amethyst panels. These were smooth, polished pieces, almost as clear as colored glass, allowing us to see movement in the room beyond.

"Welcome to the Grand Court of Maples," said Nessa, and spread her hands wide. The doors swung open, revealing a room massive enough to make the entrance hall seem small.

The floor was polished amethyst, balanced by the raw amethyst ceiling. Crystals jutted down like stalactites, glowing from within with a soft light that somehow managed to not be purple, defying all logic and sense in the process. There were no corners, the room having been constructed in the round, and tall tables sketched out the circumference of the space. They weren't pressed to the wall, instead being set far enough out to both allow a generous amount of space for seating and to let the servers pass freely behind the diners. Every seat was occupied, save for a table that had clearly been left open for our use.

We could have put every member of Arden's Court *and* everyone who regularly attended the Court at Shadowed Hills at those tables and not come close to filling them entirely. The enormity of this venue was beginning to press down on me, becoming almost overwhelming.

Tybalt's hand settled on my shoulder in what would probably look like a proprietary gesture to anyone who didn't know me well enough to see how close my flight or fight response was to kicking in. Neither bolting from the room nor swaggering up to the High King and saying something inappropriate was going to serve me well right now, and I was grateful for Tybalt's intervention, even as I lightly resented the need for it.

Emotions can be contradictory, is what I'm saying.

More tables split the center of the room, preventing it from looking quite so much like a cruise ship buffet. These were long, straight tables that looked like they'd been hewed from ancient trees, each of them as big around as one of the great coastal redwoods, polished and sanded and stained but not painted in any way. It should have been rustic. It should have been charming. It wasn't. It was like something out of *Beowulf*, ancient and imposing, and I didn't belong here.

Nessa walked with smooth assurance down the center of the room, following a path between the tables, which were spaced wide enough to let us all follow her without bumping into any of the army of servers who moved between them with trays and baskets in their hands. The diners stopped their dining as we passed, turning to watch us with eager, calculating eyes. They were taking our measure with every step, and many of them were finding us wanting.

Too many teenagers, for one thing; it's not common for people to visit royal courts with an entire high school in attendance. I could see how intently they were studying the boys: Quentin, who seemed to be trying to disappear into Dean, Dean, who was defending his boyfriend as well as he could with the relatively slight outline of his body, and Raj, who was meeting their measuring stares with an imperious gaze of his own, daring them to say a single word about a Prince of Cats walking among them. They were looking for something, I realized. They were looking for their Crown Prince.

Of course. Even if no one here knew that Quentin Sollys was living in blind fosterage in the Mists, the people who commonly attended this Court had to know what age he'd be, and they'd have a decent guess at what he'd look like now. Every visitor important enough to get a dinner invitation had to be subject to a certain degree of scrutiny.

Nessa stopped when she reached the front of the room. "I am honored to present Sir October Daye, Knight of Lost Words, sworn to Shadowed Hills and carrying the banner in the Mists, and her consort to be, King Tybalt of the Court of Dreaming Cats," she said, in a clear, carrying voice. Then she faltered, finally appearing to realize that she'd never bothered to ask for anyone else's names, and said, "Along with their company, who have traveled here from the Mists to receive the grace and glory of your presence, and the joy of dining in your hall."

High Queen Maida was pressing a napkin to her lips like she thought she could contain her laughter through sheer force of refusing to let it out. High King Aethlin, on the other hand, was emulating his subjects in the way he scanned our party, making me suddenly, fiercely glad that Quentin had been foolhardy enough to trade his face for anonymity. If anyone had even suspected he might be with me, the way the High King was looking at us would have been more than enough to give the game away.

"Nice place," I said, breaking about twenty rules of etiquette and sending a titter spreading through the hall. None of the courtiers were gauche enough to laugh openly, of course, but their snickers and half-swallowed chuckles added up.

Tybalt removed his hand from my shoulder. Our approaches to nobles of the Divided Courts were similar: aggressive irreverence, bordering on disrespect. But he knew I could get away with more than he could here.

"We're quite fond of it," said Maida, lowering her napkin and smiling at me. "It is a pleasure to see you again, Sir Daye. We apologize for the difficulty of traveling here."

"Pretty sure even being nobility doesn't put you in charge of distance, and we took the Tuatha express the whole way." I waved a hand, indicating Chelsea and Nolan. "Easy as pie."

Chelsea raised a hand in the shyest of waves. For all her bluster and bravado in adapting to her life in Faerie, she was still a teenage girl who had only discovered how deep and complicated the strange roots of her immortal heritage went three years ago. She and the High Queen had more in common than she knew; they had both been born half human, although Maida's blood had been adjusted by a hope chest, while Chelsea's had been changed by yours truly.

And it wasn't like I could tell her. The High Queen's origins were a closely-guarded secret, extending even to her own Court. She wore cosmetic illusions when she went out in public, like now, to conceal the smallpox scars on one side of her face, left from a time before she'd been transformed. No one would guess, looking at her now, that she had come from anything but the purest Daoine Sidhe bloodline. She had hair the color of molten silver, falling around her shoulders in finely styled waves that looked less like hair and more like the consequences of pyroclastic flow. Her eyes were the color of blue topaz, and her features were delicately sculpted—not due to any illusions, just due to the gifts of her father's side of the family.

But she had given up her mother's side for the man beside her, who looked so much like an adult version of Quentin that it made my chest ache a little, because the boy who called me "Mom" and cried in my arms wasn't my son, not really, not ever. He was theirs, and when he became the mirror to this man, he would do it in their presence, far away from me. Seeing High King Aethlin here, in his natural environment, really drove home the fact that this was going to be Quentin one day, and there was nothing I could do to stop it.

Plus it was probably treason to even wish that I could try.

Maida nodded to Chelsea, acknowledging her, then blinked at the sight of Nolan. His mismatched eyes were striking, and an attribute he shared with his sister, the Queen in the Mists. He smiled roguishly back at her, inclining his head. She nudged Aethlin with her elbow.

"Nessa," said the High King, after a startled pause. "Were you intending to announce the rest of Sir Daye's company, or are we expected to introduce ourselves to our own guests?"

"I didn't think you'd insist on meeting a visiting knight's entire retinue," said Nessa, clearly flustered. Poor Gwragedd Annwn. We were throwing everything off for her.

Then again, she *was* the High King's seneschal, and this was a fairly severe breach of etiquette. I frowned, all the "something is wrong here" warning bells that had been ringing quietly in the back of my head starting to go off like sirens and combining with Quentin's warning to form one truly unpleasant conclusion.

Blundering into trouble isn't my superpower, but it might as well be.

Nessa was clearly wearing an illusion, but we knew that; she needed one to deal with the rest of us without doing damage through her mere presence. Expecting one of the Gwragedd Annwn to walk around without an illusion on was like expecting Raj to give in to Chelsea's occasional pleas that he attend something called "an anime convention" with no human disguise and as many feline attributes as he could sustain while remaining bipedal. I still eyed her thoughtfully, eyes slightly narrowed as I waited to see how she recovered from this fumble.

"You have my apologies, Your Highness," she said finally.

"There were so many of them, all arriving at the same time, that I did not get their names. It was an oversight, and one which I can rectify if given a moment—"

"Doing something now doesn't rectify leaving it undone in the past," said Aethlin, frowning now. His tone was sonorous, and for all that I avoid the company of Kings as much as possible—the Cait Sidhe kind excepted—I could hear the warning in it. However long this woman had been serving his family, her service was conditional on continuing to please him. And he was not pleased.

Faerie doesn't quite run on the feudal system, at least not according to Bridget, who is both a human academic and Irish and actually made a study of the true feudal system at one time. We run on a cheap copy, emulated when it was new and cool, but modified to suit the needs of a people who live forever and whose basic needs can be as varied as "basically human," "must sleep for six months of the year or wither," or "sets themselves on fire every night." There's no one-size-fits-all for us, and the purebloods who first decided on our system of titles and loyalties were smart enough to recognize that even as they mimicked an essentially unfair means of governance. A seneschal who defied a mortal king might find themselves imprisoned or beheaded.

Nessa was unlikely to face any consequences beyond dismissal. But people who aspire to be the seneschal of a king usually plan to do it for centuries, and if Quentin remembered her, she had already been here for at least a decade. She would have no concept of what came next, because doing that kind of long-range planning was ridiculous. The world could end in nuclear fire before it was time for Quentin to inherit and send her peacefully into a pampered retirement with the rest of the old King's Court.

Stepping in was a necessity, if only for the sake of the seneschal. "We're a bit much," I said politely. "Both independently and as a group. May I present His Royal Highness, Crown Prince Nolan Windermere in the Mists."

Nolan bowed, as formal and precise as if the etiquette had been completely without flaw and this was exactly the way a prince should always be introduced. "Your Majesties," he said. "I am grateful for your hospitality and will carry word of your exquisite courtesy back to my sister, Queen Arden Windermere in the Mists."

"You were rather more unconscious the last time we saw you," said Maida, with a flicker of amusement.

"Yes," agreed Nolan. "My sister, who is a very wise and very stubborn woman, and an excellent queen to her people, arranged to have me wake as soon as was permissible, that I might stand witness to her reign and to the bright restoration of our family's Kingdom."

"You do her proud," said Aethlin.

"My sister's chatelaine also travels with me," said Nolan. "Mistress Cassandra Brown in the Mists."

"Hi," said Cassie, with a small wave. "I, uh, feel like there's a lot of etiquette here that literally nothing in my life has ever come close to preparing me for, but it's an honor to be here, and I'm looking forward to the wedding and stuff."

Maida cocked her head. "I'm afraid I don't recognize your bloodline, dear. Who claims you?"

"Um, my boss is Queen Windermere, and my graduate advisor is Professor Weinstein, and my parents are Mitch and Stacy Brown, and Toby's sort of my aunt, which is why they asked me to come to their wedding, and please I would like to stop talking now."

"Oh, to hell with this," snapped the Luidaeg, and shoved her way to the front of the group, leaving Oberon behind as she pushed her way between me and Tybalt. Apparently his "hidden in plain sight" trick meant they were intending to keep his presence unannounced as long as possible.

Maybe that was why Nessa hadn't thought to get everyone's names, something that really *was* a shameful breach of etiquette. Any half-trained courtier knows you announce guests in the presence of a king and queen, and most of the available monarchs aren't even the high kind. But if Oberon was projecting a "don't notice, don't ask questions" spell somehow, it might have stopped her from realizing she hadn't asked certain essential questions at all.

The Luidaeg stood there in silence for a moment, an apparently human teenager facing down the two most powerful seated monarchs on the continent. Then she curtsied, so deeply it seemed like her forehead would have to brush against the floor.

Her hair, always an inky black, suddenly seemed to be dripping ink, or maybe tar, onto the straps of her overall and down her exposed arms. It soaked through the fabric of her overalls, gathering at her feet and on her hands, and when she straightened up again, it fell away, leaving her wearing a purple-black medieval gown with a subtle pattern of tentacles worked all through the fabric. It was striking, although not as striking as some of the dresses I'd seen her conjure for herself, improbable things made of the living, surging ocean.

"I am Antigone of Albany, called the Luidaeg by those in this modern world who know me," she said, and her voice was soft, but it carried to every corner of the hall. She kept her eyes on the High King as she spoke, eyes solid black and slightly narrowed. "My party was offered hospitality but not asked to prove ourselves— and believe me when I say that any party I choose to claim belongs to me, and you should be *grateful* for our presence."

The hush that had begun when she chose to speak endured past her speech, as every eye in the room stared at her. Stared at *her*, I realized, the obvious danger, the thing that needed to be monitored at all costs. No one was looking at the nondescript man behind her, who could have been a changeling or could have been something simpler, but either way lacked her aura of palpable, radiant menace. She had, simply by flashing her fangs, become the most dangerous thing in the room.

If King Aethlin had been holding a fork, he would have dropped it. As it was, he pressed his hands flat against the table and inclined his head, managing to give the impression that he was bowing fully and formally without moving out of his seat. It might have been more polite to rise. Judging by the faint shaking in his shoulders, I wasn't entirely sure he *could*.

"Milady sea witch," he said, infusing the Luidaeg's most common nom de plume with all the respect he would have put into her proper name. "We were not made aware that you were coming."

"As if I was going to miss the wedding of my favorite niece? Please." She studied her fingernails, which gleamed razor-sharp in the light. "You've been to the Kingdom I currently call home. You should have guessed I'd be here. Can we call off this charade? You know who we are. You invited us. Standing on ceremony means you're never on solid ground, and I'm hungry."

"I . . ." High King Aethlin stopped, catching himself. "Of course. My apologies, milady. I should have anticipated you and been prepared with proper honors." He snapped his fingers, pointing at a nearby server. The man jumped and scurried over, beckoning for the Luidaeg to follow him to the table that had been left open for our use.

She went without argument, having clearly decided that playing along would get her to dinner faster, and the others followed her, either inured to doing her bidding by long exposure or unwilling to take the risk of upsetting her. I stayed where I was. The Luidaeg isn't as murderous as she likes to make herself out to be, and I wanted to keep an eye on Nessa.

The High King's seneschal was also standing her ground, looking faintly lost as her charges wandered off to take their seats and place their drink orders. The servers had pitchers of water, beer, and what looked like apple cider, as well as bottles of both red and white wine. It was all a bit like preparing to dine in a very strangely themed restaurant.

"Did you require something further, Sir Daye?" asked Maida.

I held up a hand—another line crossed into irredeemable rudeness—and said, "I don't know yet. Highness, is it some sort of horrific insult to the crown if I use blood magic in your presence?" Quentin had asked me to do this discreetly. With as many missteps as Nessa had made during this brief introduction, I wasn't sure I could wait.

She looked startled as she sat back in her chair. "Insult, no, but confuse, absolutely. What is so dire that you would need to call upon the *blood* in a royal knowe?"

Flower magic is illusion, and common enough that no one bats an eye when it's used in the presence of kings and queens. Water magic is transformation, and perhaps the most common thing I've seen used *by* kings and queens. Blood magic, though . . . blood magic is magic itself. The more I learn about it, the more I resent the fact that the magic that flows from Oberon has somehow been coopted as the primary gift of the Daoine Sidhe, who belong so unquestionably to Titania.

With blood magic, a spell can be made or unmade, gifts can be shared across bloodlines, and heritages can be unraveled like skeins of yarn woven from silence and secrecy. All we have to do is breathe them in. With the diners carefully kept at a distance from the high table, and the High King and Queen both known quantities, this was the closest thing I was likely to get to being alone with Nessa.

"Tell you in a second," I said, and closed my eyes. I breathed in, tasting the heritage of the people around me. It's a small enough act of blood magic that it doesn't require anyone to actually be, you know, *bleeding*, which means it's something I've always been good at, even back when powering a spell with blood felt weighty and portentous, something to be done only under the direst of circumstances.

Yes, there was a time when my blood stayed mostly inside my body, where Tybalt assures me it belongs. How things have changed.

Aethlin and Maida were close enough to register: pure Daoine Sidhe from side to side. Whoever had held the hope chest that removed Maida's mortality had done an excellent job. The people to either side of them also registered; Tuatha de Dannan and Puca, respectively.

But no Gwragedd Annwn anywhere. Something else, something I couldn't identify, but that was subtly, delicately *wrong*. It was like going into the toy aisle of a department store, looking for a Barbie, and finding nothing but third-party knockoffs, their faces indefinably wrong, their hair a few cents cheaper and almost the exact color and texture of straw. A copy, in other words, something pretending to be Gwragedd Annwn.

Pretending very, very well. I opened my eyes, turning back to the High King, and smiled politely. "I appreciate your tolerance of my little habits," I said. "I do have another question to ask you, however, if you would indulge me?"

Aethlin frowned. "What do you need?"

"Can you please produce your seneschal? If the copy is this pleasant to speak with, I would like to meet the real one."

SIX

A HORRIFIED GASP went through the room. Aethlin half-rose, apparently thinking better of it before he could get fully to his feet, and planted his hands flat against the table again. "Are you insinuating something, Sir Daye?" he asked.

"Nope." I was being a jerk in a royal court again. I was finally back in my element, even if I was doing it in a dress way too fancy for the activity. "I'm not insinuating anything. I'm stating, blatantly, that whoever this woman is," I pointed to the woman I still thought of as Nessa, for lack of anything better to call her, "she is not your seneschal. She's not Gwragedd Annwn. She's faking it well enough that I can't actually tell you what she *is*, but she's been an impostor since we got here."

Nessa looked at me with wide eyes, either horrified or doing an excellent job of pretending she was. "Nessa?" High Queen Maida sounded more confused than anything else. "Is Sir Daye correct?"

The false Nessa looked briefly bewildered, like she didn't know how to react to this. Then she lunged to the side, wrapping an arm around my neck and yanking me against her. I didn't resist. This was at least interesting, and I was sure the royal kitchens would make me a sandwich if dinner got canceled.

Something sharp pricked my right side, pressed hard enough to make it very clear that I was being held at knifepoint. I sighed. Maybe I was going to need two sandwiches.

High King Aethlin had finished rising as soon as not-actually-Nessa grabbed me. He was storming his way around the high table while several courtiers had appeared as if out of nowhere to get the queen to safety. Everyone seemed to be on the move, treating this as an unusual and frightening moment of chaos. I, on the other hand, was finally relaxed. We were back on familiar ground. Maybe the false Nessa was an early wedding gift, designed to make me feel more comfortable.

No. Tybalt might be willing to do a lot of things to soothe my jangled nerves, but nothing that involved the possibility of me getting hurt. We're still sorting out the limits of my accelerated healing. There was no way he'd put himself in the position of being the reason we discovered my limits.

"You don't want to do that," I said.

"Speak for yourself," snarled the woman who I now felt safe saying was distinctly not Nessa. Louder, she shouted, "Sic semper tyrannis!"

"Please," I said, in a tone that made it clear I was objecting to her words, not begging for my life. "If I'm a tyrant, you're a fluffy little duckie. Which might be more welcome than whatever the hell this is right now. Where's Nessa? Who *are* you? I'd say you only have a few more seconds before the royal archers are in position, so I'd talk fast if you're trying to deliver some sort of message."

"The only message I need is written *in your blood*," she said, voice dropping toward a register that managed to be deeper and shriller at the same time, a neat trick, made less exciting by the fact that I could feel the hand on my throat changing shapes, the fingers getting longer, the nails getting sharper, the skin getting cooler and faintly clammy, like I was being clutched by some terrible thing that had slithered out of the closed cave where it was meant to linger.

"Okay, that's enough of that," I said, and stomped down, hard, on her foot. No matter how much her body shifted, she still had feet, and feet are filled with lots of convenient little bones that go "crunch" when you subject them to sufficient pressure. There was a satisfying cracking sound, and she cried out in pain, still in that higher-lower impossible voice.

I yanked myself away from her, drawing my own knife, all too aware that I was only feet from the High Table and was probably committing some degree of mild treason by daring to fight, even for the sake of protecting myself, but unwilling to stand back and just get stabbed.

Although when I spun to face her, she didn't have a knife anymore, and I realized maybe that was because she had already used it to stab something. Dammit. I glanced down, and there was the knife, a simple copper thing with a basic cross hilt, sticking out of my side where a knife definitely wasn't supposed to be.

Shock is a hell of a drug. If there was going to be pain—and there's always going to be pain—it would come later, probably when I tried to pull the damn thing *out*.

"This is a new dress," I snapped, my attention going back to not-Nessa.

She was getting taller. Taller, and thinner, almost insectile, losing all roundness from her face, arms, and torso, losing all the softness. Her skin was taking on a new shade, becoming a mottled mix of gray and green, patches that seemed to shift in the light, making it harder to focus on the shape of her. Her clothing tore as she grew, exceeding what Nessa's own body had needed in an outfit, and the ragged pieces began to drop away, even as her teeth sharpened into fangs.

"Doppelganger," I said, and started to circle. I only had the one knife, and the urge to pull hers out of my side and add it to my petty arsenal was strong. It was also a bad idea until I could be sure the edge wasn't serrated. I'll recover from a little stab wound faster than anyone else alive. Disembowelment takes longer, and I didn't have the time for that.

She hissed at me—actually hissed, like some kind of giant lizard—and leapt into the air, a single pump of her legs propelling her high enough to reach the ceiling, where she grabbed onto an amethyst spire and kept on hissing, looking down at the room.

"Shit," I said, taking a step backward. "Tybalt? Luidaeg? Anybody got any ideas?"

"Archers," said Raj. He sounded almost bored.

"I was right about that?" Bowstrings twanged around the edges of the room as the royal archers I had only been guessing about released their arrows, firing at the Doppelganger, who sensibly wasn't there anymore as soon as she saw the arrows flying in her direction. Unfortunately, the arrows were still there, and they were doing what arrows do when they encounter gravity: flying in a high arc toward the center of the room, where they should have embedded themselves in their target, which they missed by a considerable margin, and then beginning to descend.

"Shit shit *shit*," I chanted, dancing backward, out of the area where the arrows were likely to hit. "Chelsea! Nolan! I need portals!"

"What in the world—" Nolan began.

"Follow my lead," said Chelsea. The smell of smoke and calla lilies swirled as she concentrated, and a portal easily ten feet across opened in the air above our heads. Nolan made a small sound of understanding, and a similar, if somewhat smaller, portal appeared above the guards who were still trying to move High Queen Maida out of the way.

There were other Tuatha in the room, and their mingled magics filled the air as they emulated Chelsea and Nolan. The air above us became a virtual firework show of glittering portals, each showing a little slice of somewhere else. A few of the portals opened onto what I assumed were other spaces inside the knowe. Some showed open forest or meadows, and one showed the parking lot behind a Tim Hortons.

And the arrows, falling, fell into them, and didn't come out on our side of things. Instead, they embedded themselves in whatever the portal showed, and no one was hurt. The Tuatha began closing their portals, and I started looking around for the Doppelganger, no longer afraid of being impaled by falling arrows.

The room was big enough that she was almost impossible to spot, her shifting skin allowing her to blend into whatever part of the ceiling or wall she was now sticking to. "I hate Doppelgangers," I muttered, and used my knife to open the ball of my left thumb, spilling hot blood into the air. It seemed a little wasteful to go cutting myself when there was already a knife sticking out of my side, but again, disembowelment is hugely inconvenient.

It was a small cut, already half-healed by the time I got my hand to my mouth. The taste of the blood coated my tongue in an instant, brighter than the lights, sharper than the blade of my knife, eager to do my bidding. Sometimes I think my magic is like an abused dog learning to trust its new owner. It doesn't fight me the way it used to, but its eagerness to be put to use can be somewhat overwhelming when I'm not properly braced.

Blood filling my mouth, I closed my eyes and breathed sharply

in, looking for the scent of Doppelganger. It was a good thing
Nessa, wherever she really was, apparently favored form-fitting
clothing; if it had been wearing something more adaptable when it
transformed, it would have been able to assume a new face without
worrying about the sudden appearance of a naked person in our
midst.

Doppelgangers can only weave illusions when they have access
to the blood of the person they're emulating, and every attempt
uses up a little more of that blood up. Either Nessa's beauty becoming blunted had been an illusion, or the result of an actual
physical transformation. It was hard to say without more information. If the Doppelganger was smart, it would have been a transformation, to preserve the blood it had access to.

I breathed in again, looking for the slick swamp-slime smell of
the Doppelganger itself. With the blood amping my magic up well
beyond casual limits, it didn't take me long to find. I opened my
eyes, pointing to a seemingly unoccupied space about ten feet
from the still-open door. "There!" I yelled. "Right there!"

Still holding onto the scent, I started running. The knife in my
side made that more difficult, the shock wearing off to be replaced
by waves of stunning pain. Fuck worrying about disembowelment;
I yanked the knife free and flung it away from myself as I ran,
hoping I wouldn't hit anyone. The King's Court was in a panic,
with people running in all directions to get away from the onslaught of arrows, blood, and strange changeling women throwing
knives around like it was no big deal. Only the group I'd brought
with me was still reasonably calm.

Emphasis on *reasonably*. Someone pulled up alongside me as I
ran, and I looked to my left to see Tybalt keeping pace with my
steps. Some of his normal mien had melted away, leaving him with
rather more feline features than he usually chose to display around
the Divided Courts. "Scarce here an hour and you're getting
stabbed?" he hissed.

"Could have been worse," I said. "Could have kept my mouth
shut and let someone who heals more slowly than I do get stabbed."
The knife, which had not been serrated, had left a clean wound
that felt like it was already healing.

Tybalt scoffed.

I smiled as winsomely as I could while sucking blood off my

molars and running across a formal dining room to intercept an invisible hired killer. I wasn't ready to credit the Doppelganger with being an assassin yet, as it hadn't tried to stab anyone who was actually politically important. Calling me a tyrant didn't indicate a high level of intelligence on the creature's part, and yes, it had probably come prepared to say that as it killed a king, but it could have switched gears if it realized it was stabbing someone much lower on the pecking order. ·

Creatures aren't known for their mental flexibility, and that's exactly what it was: a creature. Doppelgangers are monsters, born through some strange alchemy of blood and magic and momentary need by one of the Three. They claim no progenitor because they're no one's descendant race. They crave chaos, and most of who they are is stolen, at any given moment, from the people they emulate. Without a face to wear and a voice to speak with, the Doppelganger was little more than a dangerous, cornered animal.

Animals have claws and teeth and can do a hell of a lot of damage when they feel like they have to. We kept running, until we reached the open patch of air that held the swamp-slime scent of the Doppelganger's bloodline, and I leapt, knife poised to descend, only to feel a clawed foot slam into my middle and knock me backward, away from the fray.

And it *was* a fray. Seeing me fly back from a hit of nothing had told Tybalt exactly where the Doppelganger was standing, and the thing suddenly found itself dealing with an entire pissed-off King of Cats who really needed a target for his aggression. Tybalt snarled, claws slashing at the air, and between one hit and the next, the Doppelganger reappeared, bleeding from multiple wounds in its arms and torso and snarling.

I pushed myself back to my feet, already recovered from both my stab wound and the blow to my middle, and rushed to grab one of the creature's arms, wrenching it around behind its back. "Hi," I said amiably. "Care to tell us who hired you?"

It snarled at me, head snapping forward in an attempt to bite. I punched it in the face. It reeled but couldn't break my grip on its arm without doing something more drastic than failing to bite me. It raised its free hand to slash, then stopped as Tybalt grabbed it, grasp tight enough that I could hear bones cracking.

"Wrong answer," I said.

The king's guard was moving into position around us, but hesitantly, as if they weren't sure who they were supposed to be arresting. If this was the best the Westlands had to offer, maybe we were in more trouble than I thought.

"The Doppelganger, you jerks," I snapped, gesturing toward the monster in question with my chin. It was still struggling against us, frantic to escape, and as we held on, it began to shift in our hands. Its arms grew no thinner, but they did grow rounder, softer with the natural fattiness of a mammal's body. The creature itself shortened and straightened, long blue hair cascading down its back.

"Please," pled the Doppelganger, in Nessa's voice. "Please, they're hurting me. Please."

"You can look directly at her from only a few feet away, and your eyeballs aren't melting," I said, voice low, to the nearest of the guards. "You know that isn't right." She was beautiful in this shape, yes, but it wasn't the sort of beauty that left a trail of corpses in its wake. It wasn't the beauty she'd been wearing when she came to greet us. This was beauty within the normal ridiculous standards of Faerie, which could be painful, but not fatal.

"Nessa has served here faithfully for fifty years," said the guard, wresting his eyes away from her with what looked like palpable effort. "She deserves to be treated gently."

"And if you've known her for fifty years, then you know this isn't Nessa," I said. "We'll find her if she's still alive. You have my word on that. And if she's stopped her dancing, we'll find what the night-haunts left for us, and we'll make sure her family knows to mourn."

The Doppelganger-turned-Nessa seemed to realize its ploy wasn't working, maybe because it's harder to play the innocent ingénue in front of people who've just watched you change shapes and stab a visiting dignitary. She turned and hissed at me, displaying a set of teeth an anglerfish would envy.

"Got it," I said genially, and shoved her at the guard. Two of them grabbed her arms before she could react to her momentary freedom. I pushed my hair out of my eyes, suddenly aware of the mess I'd made of all Stacy's hard work. "Oh, Stacy's gonna *kill* me," I groaned.

"Not just Stacy," said Tybalt. I turned. "I don't fault you for having suspicions," he said, "but did you consider, even for an instant, the possibility of voicing them to someone in a position of authority? Not simply as an aside to me in the hall, but precisely and privately?"

"Given how quick she was to pull that knife, I think I did the right thing," I said. "She was planning to kill someone." *Sic semper tyrannis*—thus always to tyrants—that's the sort of thing someone who's come to kill a king is primed with.

"You couldn't have known that," said Tybalt.

"True," I agreed. "If she hadn't pulled a knife, she would have either blown her cover trying to argue with me, or I would have sniped at her until she did, and she would have been arrested without anyone getting hurt. But we needed her not to be wandering around the knowe as an unmarked danger, and we really needed her not to replace one of *us*."

Tybalt looked uneasy at that. "Not an option I would have preferred," he admitted.

"So let's not fight, please." The guards were still standing there, restraining the Doppelganger, which now looked entirely like a naked Gwragedd Annwn woman—only not quite. She was wearing no illusions, and still her beauty failed to assault the eye. Yes, she was a gorgeous, naked woman, but she didn't hurt to look at. Doppelgangers can emulate form, face, voice, and even certain mannerisms, picking them up from the people they copy. They don't need blood to do it, either. Transformation is water magic, and wherever they come from, they've always been assumed to have more of Maeve in them than anyone else.

But because they don't *have* to use blood to fuel their transformations, they can't naturally use other forms of magic. If they have access to their target's blood in the beginning, they can use it to replicate that person's magic, but doing that will use up the blood, like taking shots of some illicit energy drink. When the blood runs out, what they'll have left is what comes naturally to them—shapeshifting, mimicry. This wasn't Nessa, but it had been near her at some point, long enough to bleed her for its initial transformation. Without more of her blood, it couldn't achieve that level of accuracy again.

"I suppose I'd be a fool to try to change you now, when I've already admitted my affection for the woman you are naturally," grumbled Tybalt, and moved into position beside me, putting one hand on my waist. On the side where I hadn't been stabbed. He had a tendency to avoid the location of recent wounds, no matter how often I reassured him that once I was externally healed, I was internally healed as well, and he couldn't do any further damage.

"You would," I agreed, with a small smile, before focusing on the guards. "Why are you still standing here?" I asked. "You need to get her somewhere secure, with a door that locks and a guard who doesn't navigate purely by sight."

"You don't have the authority to order an arrest in my knowe," said High King Aethlin, voice uncomfortably close. I looked behind me, and there was the ruler of the Westlands, a sword in his hand and an expression on his face that managed to mingle exasperation, concern, and amusement. He didn't look angry, and there weren't any arrows sticking out of him, and that was about as far as the positives went.

He turned his attention to the guards. "Take the Doppelganger to the dungeons," he said, firmly, managing to make it sound like this was all his idea, and not the inevitable conclusion of the evening's events. "Do not harm the creature more than it already has been, but do not allow it to escape."

The Doppelganger hissed and struggled as it was dragged out of the room. It didn't budge from its Nessa disguise. Apparently, the new plan was to let anyone the guards passed in the knowe see that they were dragging a naked, defenseless, unarmed woman away.

Charming. With the danger of the Doppelganger removed, I was free to focus my attention on the potentially greater, if less immediate, danger of the High King. I turned to face him, dipping into a low curtsy—which coincidentally put my hands on a level with my sheath and allowed me to put my knife away before Aethlin took offense at my waving it at him.

"Your Highness," I said gravely. "You have my abject apologies for the disruption to your dinner."

"I think if anyone's supposed to be apologizing here, it would be me, who allowed a Doppelganger to infiltrate my knowe without detection." He frowned then, looking pensive. "It seems odd, that such could be successfully done before one of the Firstborn."

"Is the nature of the sea witch well known here, against the shore of the Atlantic?" If she had been in contact with the Roane of Beacon's Home as recently as the 1700s, she might still be a familiar danger to these people, but Faerie, for all that it's full of people who make octogenarians look like infants, doesn't have as much in the way of institutional memory as you might expect. Purebloods forget things, quickly, when they can't see them anymore. It's like true object permanence is one of the costs of immortality.

"Well enough."

"Then you understand that unless you make a bargain with her and meet whatever price she chooses to set for you, she can no more offer you protection while she walks your halls than a mountain can offer protection to the creatures who scurry on its sides." I saw Oberon's failure to act as a slightly bigger problem, but since the false Nessa hadn't even forced him to give a fake name, I had no way of mentioning that without outing him, and I wasn't willing to do that. Not even to the High King.

"I remember the stories spoke of bargains, but I don't understand why the absence of one would cause her not to act."

"The bindings that control her are tight ones, woven by someone even greater than she is." And, apparently, even Oberon couldn't remove them since she was still bound. "Unless you bargain with her—something I do *not* recommend—she can't help you."

He blinked. "The stories I've heard about you include several bargains with the sea witch."

I struggled not to glance at the table where Quentin sat, living proof of another bargain. "Yes, and that's why I'm one of the people most qualified to tell you not to do it. She can't refuse you if you ask her, and it . . . it isn't kind to impose on your guests in such a way. You can, of course, if you really want to—it's not like I can stop you—but it's not kind." I shrugged helplessly. "That's all."

"How did you know Nessa had been replaced?" asked the High King, apparently abandoning the idea of asking the Luidaeg for her protection. I was grateful for that. She told me once that she could only do things for free when she could somehow spin them around to being selfish, and I didn't see a way that protecting a monarch she didn't answer to could be selfish.

"My loyalty is pledged to Duke Sylvester Torquill of Shadowed Hills," I said gingerly. The fact that I was here without my liege, and that he had, so far as I knew, not been involved at any stage of getting me permission to come here, could reflect badly on my honor, as well as his, if I wasn't careful. "I was trained in my knightly duties by his seneschal, Sir Etienne. And even in a backwater Duchy run by a politically unambitious man, the seneschal knew enough not to bring strangers before his liege without verifying their names and natures. The Doppelganger pretending to be Nessa offered us the hospitality of the house immediately, without asking our names."

"She mistook the Luidaeg, who looks human when she so wishes it, for my lady," added Tybalt. "October's changeling nature is well-known, and effort has never been made to conceal it. She is proud of where she comes from."

"But there's still a difference between 'human' and 'part-human,'" I said, with a nod. "She should have verified my name, and if she couldn't do that for some reason, she should have avoided assumptions that might cause offense."

"Wouldn't want to offend the king-breaker, after all," drawled Raj.

I turned. He was sitting at on the edge of one of the nearby tables, which had been summarily upended and abandoned when the fight broke out. Apparently, much as this place was set up to invoke the idea of a Viking longhouse, they weren't big on Valhalla-esque nightly brawls.

Pity. He had snatched a pretzel roll from one of the breadbaskets and was gnawing on it idly. My stomach grumbled. It had been a long time since lunch, and what with everything that had happened, we were unlikely to get dinner.

To my surprise, High King Aethlin laughed. "Ah, the little Prince of Cats," he said. "I was unsure you would be able to attend, or that you would be willing to, without your shadow by your side." He raised an eyebrow, clearly waiting for someone to answer the question he was leaving unasked.

Raj toasted him with his pretzel roll. "My regent gave me time off for good behavior. The Court of Cats of San Francisco is well-kept in my absence, and in the absence of my uncle, which is a fine thing, since he will be unable to resume his throne when you're done with him. Are we getting dinner or not?"

Raj being rude to the High King is sort of a recurring theme when we put the two of them in the same room, and yet we keep doing it, thus maintaining the relationship that's existed between

Cait Sidhe and the Divided Courts for centuries. The relationship that might well be universal, if not for me and Tybalt fucking
it up.

Of course, I didn't trust Aethlin not to push the issue of Quentin's location if I let them keep talking, and so I broke in
hurriedly.

"Before dinner, we should find Nessa," I said. "Do you have any
good trackers among your court?"

"We have a family of Cu Sidhe who work with the grounds-
keeping crew," said Aethlin. "I can call for them."

"I am not a bloodhound," said Tybalt, clearly anticipating my
next question. "But I can track by scent well enough, when the
need arises."

"And I can track by blood. We'll need to start with seeing her
quarters," I said. "Can someone lead us there?"

"Yes," said Aethlin. "I'll escort you myself."

"Raj, tell the others where we're going, and then catch up with
us," I said. "You're going to need to be one of the trackers."

What I didn't mention was that if Nessa had been taken blood-
lessly, my own tracking abilities would be effectively useless. I
didn't know the scent of her magic, although I might be able to
pick it up from her rooms, so it wasn't like I could trace it through
the knowe, and if she'd been knocked unconscious, she wouldn't
have been casting anyway.

But she was Gwragedd Annwn. She needed an illusion to move
safely through the world. If the Doppelganger had knocked her
out, that illusion would have dissipated, lacking the attention necessary to maintain it. If it had killed her, it would still have needed
to dispose of her body. Either way, it needed some of her blood to
mimic her beauty the way it had initially, and whatever its plans, it
wouldn't have been able to look at her for long.

"I am?" asked Raj, eyebrow raised. But he shivered, the scent of
pepper and burnt paper rising around him, and his pretzel roll fell
to the floor, rolling to a stop next to Aethlin's foot, as he was replaced with a russet Abyssinian cat. Raj meowed loudly, stretched,
and leapt down from the chair, racing back to the others in half the
time it would have taken him on two legs. I smiled. It's rare for one
of the Cait Sidhe to take orders from a member of the Divided
Courts, but the only reason Raj isn't officially my squire is because
of our respective Courts. If I'd been Cait Sidhe, or he'd been

anything else, I would have accepted him at the same time I accepted Quentin. So he didn't mind as much when I did it.

Let anyone else try, though, and things could get messy.

Aethlin started toward the exit. Tybalt and I followed. When a King in his own knowe walks, those who don't wear the crown are bound to accompany. He made a small gesture with his hand as we went, and four guards peeled off from those remaining on the wall, falling into step around us like the corners of a compass.

Outside in the hall, there were small knots of former diners gathered together and talking in the low, anxious voices of people whose pleasant state dinner had just been interrupted by an unexpected knife fight and a rain of arrows. Some of them stopped talking to point at us and stare as we passed with their king, and I smiled weakly in response, unable to figure out the etiquette of this admittedly unusual situation.

"You've come at an interesting time, Sir Daye, and I find myself grateful that you left the item you have in keeping for me at home." He cast a sharp sideways glance in my direction. My stomach tightened. So he was concerned for Quentin's safety, and he was afraid someone in his own Court knew that Quentin was fostered with me. Interesting.

It made sense, though. Quentin had told me that Eira, in her guise as Evening Winterrose, respectable Daoine Sidhe Countess, had traveled to Toronto to discuss fosterage for Quentin and his younger sister, Penthea, or, as he sometimes said mockingly, "the heir and the spare." She had somehow managed to convince Aethlin and Maida that the safest place to send their son and Crown Prince was a backwater Duchy whose Duke was rumored to have gone mad, and Quentin had been thrown to Shadowed Hills like a steak to the hyenas, there to sink or swim on what preparation he brought with him from his time in his parents' shadow.

He'd gotten surprisingly lucky when he was sent to deliver a message to me and somehow became my private page when I was dealing with my liege. From there, it had been a small series of misadventures and disastrous almost-quests that led, inevitably in hindsight but unbelievably at the time, to him becoming my squire. Eira's plans for him had fallen apart when one of her allies turned against her and forced her to fake her own death.

Couldn't have happened to a nicer lady, really. Couldn't have gotten me a better kid.

If the High King was *grateful* that I hadn't brought Quentin with me, something was really wrong. "How long ago do you think Nessa was replaced, Your Highness?"

"I don't know," he admitted. "I speak to her daily, but rarely alone, and usually about matters of scheduling and protocol. My wife's chatelaine would have a better idea—we find it works better with the household staff if they each know who they answer to and divide the duties accordingly."

It made sense, since he and Maida were ostensibly equal rulers, rather than her serving as Queen Consort. It still made me bristle somewhat although I couldn't put my finger on precisely why. I'd probably figure it out if I thought about it long enough.

"And where is her chatelaine?" I asked politely.

"Honey? I haven't . . ." Aethlin paused, looking briefly stricken. "I haven't seen her all day. You don't think . . ."

"I don't think we can dismiss the possibility," I said grimly. One Doppelganger could be an isolated incident. Two would definitely be proof that something bigger was going on.

"But she's a Centaur. Can a Doppelganger even impersonate one of those?"

"I don't think so. Any Doppelganger impersonating her would need to be able to double their mass, coordinate extra limbs, lots of other fun exercises." I wasn't even sure that was possible for a Doppelganger. They can definitely change their size, but they have limits. They can't impersonate pixies or Bridge Trolls. Even the largest exemplar of their type would be too small to safely twist themselves into a Centaur's shape. "And they'd have to do it while mimicking the woman who knows the High Queen better than anyone else, save for Aethlin himself. Nope. Can't replace the chatelaine. Can get her out of the way, though, as long as you keep the High Queen too distracted to go looking for her before you're ready for her to. She's probably shoved into a closet some-where, waiting for us to find her."

There was a soft pop next to us, and the nearest guard jumped, grabbing for his sword before Aethlin shook his head and ordered, "Stand down."

Raj, who had just stepped out of the shadow of High King Aethlin's body, gave the guard a curious look. "Was he going to try to stab me?" he asked. "Is he better at stabbing than the last batch was at shooting arrows? Because I barely know which end of the bow is supposed to point away from me, and I still understand the physics of the thing enough to understand that if you fire something *up*, it's going to come *down*." He managed to sound faintly bored while insulting the prowess of the entire royal guard.

Oh, he was going to make an amazing King of Cats.

"My guards have no training at fighting adversaries on the ceiling," said Aethlin, matching Raj's boredom with amusement. *See, kitten?* his tone seemed to say. *You can't get to me.*

"Maybe they should," I said.

We had left the main hall and were heading down a smaller, narrower one that was just as opulent as the others, maintaining the maple-and-amethyst theme but also somehow making the aesthetic look somewhat shabby and lived-in, like we were walking through a deeply strange-themed hotel. Why anyone would theme a hotel on "smell faintly like pancakes at all times" as the Canadian dream, I didn't know, but hey, who am I to judge? My house is furnished in early thrift store, with a side order of don't these people know that recycling is a thing, and you don't have to keep every single scrap of paper forever.

"The servants' quarters are this way," said Aethlin, leading us on as the guards pressed in closer around us, both due to the span of the hall and out of apparently increasing concern. I gave them a narrow-eyed look. We were going to have a little talk later, I and them, when we were no longer in close proximity to the king.

When you want to know what's really going on in a knowe, ask the servants. When you want to know who's been trying to kill the king, ask the guards.

The hall ended in a sort of a flat hammer shape, with doors at either end of the "head." Aethlin indicated one door. "Maida's chatelaine, Honey, keeps her room there. I believe it's a nickname, although I'm not sure for what. She came highly recommended and has served without fault for fifteen years." He indicated the other door. "Nessa's chambers. Aron, if you would please?"

"Yes, sire," said one of the guards, and stepped forward.

I realized a moment too late that if the Doppelganger had been here for any length of time, this probably wasn't a good idea. "Wait—" I said, raising my hand to motion him to stop.

I wasn't fast enough. He grasped the doorknob, only to yank his hand away, shaking it vigorously as he squinted at his fingertip. "Blasted thing *bit* me," he said, turning to face the High King.

So we had a perfect view of the moment when his eyes rolled back in his head and he collapsed, dead before he struck the floor.

SEVEN

THE OTHER THREE GUARDS rushed to their fallen compatriot, clustering around him but thankfully not touching him before one of them looked up with an expression of wild-eyed terror and almost shouted, "Aron's not breathing, sire!"

"Let me through." I pushed my way between two guards, a stocky Satyr and a surprisingly well-groomed Redcap, to drop to my knees beside the fallen guard. The third guard who *wasn't* flat on the floor was a Daoine Sidhe, who looked at me warily.

Him being the one to move to help his companion made sense. Daoine Sidhe don't go into the healing arts very often—something about Eira ordering them to amass as much power as they possibly could puts a damper on most altruistic urges—but their blood magic is strong enough to make some things come easily to them. Realizing that one of their compatriots has stopped their dancing is on the list.

"Let me," I repeated, more softly this time, specifically to the guard. He hesitated, looking past me to King Aethlin, who must have nodded or otherwise signaled his approval, because the guard sat back on his haunches, allowing me access to the unfortunate Aron.

He was a Gwragen, with the gray-white skin his kind are heir to, which would have made him look like a walking corpse to the unfamiliar eye even before whatever had just happened to him. Now, though, there was a waxen pallor to his complexion that told me as clear as anything that he had suffered a sudden, dramatic injury.

I still leaned close enough to press my fingers to his throat and my ear to his chest, checking for pulse and heartbeat. It only took a few seconds to verify what wasn't there. I sat up, turning to face the High King, and shook my head.

That was all it took. The Daoine Sidhe guard wailed disbelievingly, an unprofessional sound for someone wearing the formal livery of a noble house, but hopefully forgivable under the circumstances. I pushed myself to my feet, turning to Raj. "The nighthaunts will be here soon, and we should be gone when they arrive," I said. "I'll need your lockpicks."

"Why, Sir Daye, I am offended and affronted that you would suspect me, a Prince of Cats, of carrying thieves' tools on my person! How could you *presume—*".

"Raj. I know you have them because I gave them to you for your birthday. Stacy took mine while she was dressing me, or I'd use my own. Lockpicks, please. This isn't the time." I paused, taking a breath. Some things are rarely said bluntly among the fae. But blunt force trauma is my specialty. "A man is dead."

Raj stopped talking immediately and reached inside his tunic, pulling out a small, leather-wrapped bundle. I held out my hand, and he dropped the bundle into my palm.

"Sorry, Toby," he said, sounding chagrined.

"I know, kiddo." Raj can never formally be my squire, but he's learned when it's time to stop screwing around and listen to me.

The other guards helped the Daoine Sidhe guard back to his feet and fell back, all three of them moving into position around King Aethlin, like they thought whatever had killed Aron was going to leap away from the door and kill them, too.

It wasn't a completely unreasonable fear. I bit the inside of my cheek until I tasted blood and squinted at the door, looking for the tangle and weave of a spell lain across it. There was nothing on the door itself, the frame or the knob, although the spells worked into the knowe gleamed from the walls, so bright I could barely keep my eyes open. It wouldn't matter if I closed them; I'd see the weave anyway, burning bright against the dark absence of magic that was the world between the strands.

Hastily, I swallowed the last of the blood clinging to my tongue and released the spell, blinking away the afterimages. Being able to see and manipulate other people's spells is still something I'm getting used to—as much as I ever have time to "get used to" anything, rather than lurching from crisis to crisis like some sort of wind-up disaster mannequin—but the Luidaeg assures me it's part of the same function that allows practitioners of blood magic to borrow the abilities of other fae. Magic is in the blood, and the blood is in the magic, and because of what I am, both will yield to me when I need them to.

No pressure.

"It wasn't a spell," I said, satisfied, and waved away the faint cut grass and copper scent of my own magic as I approached the door, moving slowly, scanning my surroundings the whole way.

Aron had moved too fast. That had been his first, and probably fatal, mistake. He was a pureblood, and the sickening feeling of cold iron that radiated from the doorknob should have hit him much sooner than it did me. Only he hadn't had the time to realize the feeling was there, because he'd been going too fast, and his hand had been on the doorknob before the nausea could register.

I moved closer, swallowing my discomfort. Iron isn't fun to be exposed to. It can be deadly if someone with strong fae blood spends too much time around it. Some types of fae are more resistant than others—we're still figuring out where the Dóchas Sidhe fall on that ladder, but given that I've had iron poisoning bad enough to almost kill me twice, and I already felt like I was about to lose the dinner I hadn't had down the front of my dress, I was willing to bet that "pretty susceptible" was going to be the final answer.

Ironic, for a woman who used to carry an iron knife everywhere I went—who still had that iron knife sealed into a rowan box in the back of my closet, just in case, and who held onto my last ounces of humanity in part because I might need to shift my own blood back toward humanity in order to use that knife again.

Tybalt stopped asking why I was so determined to stay mortal right around the time we figured out that I was virtually indestructible. He didn't like the "virtually" part, but I didn't like the fact that he *wasn't*, so we both got to be a little bit unhappy, and I got to be a little bit human, just in case it was ever necessary to kill another Firstborn. You know. The usual plans a girl makes for her future.

Even if the doorknob had been made of cold iron, which it

distinctly wasn't, having the same coppery sheen as all the others
we'd passed, just touching it wouldn't have been enough to kill a
man. I knelt, unwrapping the bundle I'd taken from Raj and laying
it on the floor in front of me. Avoiding iron for the boys meant
their kits had taken one of two forms—antique or ultra-modern—
and ironically, both options left them ill-prepared for high security
locks. The titanium in Quentin's kit was too thick, while the bronze
and carved wood in Raj's kit was too soft.

They'd graduate to hardened faerie silver eventually, when I
thought they were ready for more difficult locks, and in the meantime, Raj's tools would be good enough for the level of security I'd
seen thus far inside the knowe. Most knowes don't invest in very
good internal locks. Why would they? You need to have made it
past the wards and past the initial inspection, whatever form that
took, to reach any door worth opening. It would have been a foolish investment of resources. I pulled the tweezers and jeweler's
loupe from Raj's kit, leaning closer still, trying to find any part of
the doorknob that didn't match up with the rest.

It was so subtle I could easily have missed it, even taking my
time and looking closely. On the left side of the knob, concealed
against the shaft, someone had affixed a small mechanism that
didn't quite match the metal around it. It wasn't a total mismatch,
just a rectangle of slightly duller metal, like someone had failed to
fully polish it. Carefully, I leaned forward and pressed against it
with the tip of the tweezers.

It was a simple spring mechanism, but it was still deeply unnerving when the edge of the plate snapped forward and a needle
stabbed out, hitting nothing but empty air. I held up my free hand,
signaling the others to stay back.

"I'm going to need a minute to disassemble this safely," I said.
"If someone could get me a rowan jar, that would be fantastic."

Yes, wooden jars exist. They're not common, glass being so
much cheaper and having the advantage of transparency, but they
exist, and they're not difficult for even a semi-competent wood-
turner to make. Rowan wood has a dampening effect on iron; it
would make it safer to keep the little mechanism, even if there
wasn't much we'd be able to learn from it.

"Go," snapped Aethlin, looking to the Redcap guard, who nodded curtly, spun on his heel, and ran away down the hall. He was
probably relieved to have an excuse to get away from the corpse

and the taint of iron hanging in the air. "Sir Daye, what did you find?"

"Someone set a trap on this doorknob," I said. "Poisoned needle under a pressure plate. I mean, I'm guessing on the poison, since we haven't given this thing to Walther to analyze yet—"

"Walther?" asked Aethlin, sounding faintly baffled.

"Oh, he's one of our wedding guests. He's also Arden's court alchemist, and the one who developed the cure for elf-shot. You met him at the convocation." I continued prodding the mechanism, trying to verify that it was as straightforward as it seemed. It didn't seem to have any backup attacks concealed behind its thin metallic frame, but did I want to risk my life on that? No.

We were pretty sure I was unkillable, and to be fair, I *had* recovered from half a dozen different ways to die. But I could still be elf-shot, and the poison still stayed in my system long enough to require administration of the cure before I woke up. Magic could still hurt me. If this was a magical poison—and who uses a purely mundane poison inside a knowe? That would be silly—there was a chance it could do the impossible and kill me.

As if sensing the direction of my thoughts, Tybalt cleared his throat and said mildly, "I would prefer not to be a widower before I've enjoyed my wedding night. Please be careful."

"I am," I said. "Anyway, whatever's on this, Walther will be able to work it out in no time."

"I have my own alchemists," said Aethlin. "I know them, and I trust them."

I did twist and look around at that, taking in the small formation behind me; Raj and Tybalt, the two guards, and the High King. Not a predictable combination from where the night had started— but an understandable one. "I am willing to wager a good deal on the fact that you have not spent as much time, even cumulatively, with your court alchemists as I have with Walther," I said. "He has saved my life on multiple occasions, and I trust him completely. If your own seneschal could be replaced for some unknown period of time without anyone noticing, how can I trust that your alchemists, with whom you do not have remotely as much contact, would not have suffered the same fate? Hmm? Give me a good reason, and I'll stand down. Or don't, and we'll use my alchemist."

"You can't speak to him like that," snarled the Daoine Sidhe guard, whose shock and grief was apparently beginning the transition into anger. Well, that was probably easier to carry, at least for a little while.

Grief is a weight that you can't put down, only transmute into other things, and once it lands on your shoulders, you have to wait for time's erosion to lift it off. We're all Atlas, in a way. We carry all the sins of our past, and all the things we think we've lost, and we might as well do it forever for as long as it can seem to last.

"I can, I did, and I will, and I wouldn't talk if I were you, since I haven't seen the royal guard exactly covering themselves in glory so far," I said, with what must have seemed like almost obscene cheerfulness. "I'm not sure how big 'the realm' is, whether it's kingdom by kingdom or what, but Queen Arden Windermere in the Mists declared me a hero of the realm, and we've got a dead man and a poisoned doorknob and a missing seneschal and a Doppelganger on our hands here, so I'd say this is pretty solidly hero territory, and that means it's absolutely *my* territory, and telling people what they need to do if they want this to work out for the best is a big part of my job."

"Is that so?" Aethlin's voice was mild, but when I shifted my attention back to him, there was something in his eyes that I would have called amusement if a member of his guard hadn't been sprawled dead on the ground between us. "For your information, 'the realm' is usually accounted kingdom by kingdom, although as being a hero really only gives you the authority to call yourself by that title and to be asked to involve yourself in rather ridiculous amounts of trouble, I have no qualms about assigning the role to you here as well as at home."

"Great, then it is literally my job to tell the High King that we'll be using my alchemist, who I'm sure will be thrilled to find out he's going to be working during my wedding. Then again, so am I."

"I am shocked, *shocked* that you have managed to involve yourself so quickly in an apparently ongoing crisis of the monarchy," said Tybalt dryly.

The air next to him ripped open, and a slender figure clad in the royal livery slipped through, like an acrobat through a hoop. Two globes of yellow-white light followed them through, rising promptly to spin in air at roughly eye level. The figure bowed deeply and formally to the king, then offered him a small jar of rowan wood.

"Give it to her, Caitir," said Aethlin, pointing at me. "This is our visiting hero, Sir October Daye in the Mists. She's the one who requested the jar."

"Yes, Your Highness," said the Candela, bobbing a quick curtsy before turning on her heel and walking toward me. I held out my hand, waiting for the jar. She dropped it into my palm.

"You may all want to move back," I said. The guards didn't like that. They moved to put themselves more firmly between me and the High King, stranding Caitir in the middle. That wasn't as big of a problem as it might have been; as she had just so aptly demonstrated, Candela can teleport, shortcutting through the shadows in a much simpler, faster way than the Cait Sidhe.

I wonder if Candela who live in a place where there are no Cait Sidhe find their access to the Shadow Roads disrupted, or if the anchors the Cait Sidhe provide apply only to the Court of Cats.

Her Merry Dancers spun lazily around her head, getting brighter when they faced me, reflecting her curiosity. "You should probably also move back," I said. "I don't know what's going to happen when I remove this."

She frowned, then turned and dove into the shadows that had gathered at the bend of the hall, vanishing. She reappeared a moment later, behind the rest of the group, expression perfectly serene.

Teleporters. They never seem to believe distance exists for the rest of us. I pulled the lid off the wooden jar—it slotted into the container like a bolt, rather than screwing onto the top like a nut—and maneuvered it carefully under the little metal plate, setting it on the floor. "I'm going to take this off now," I said as I picked up the largest of Raj's lockpicks, using it to pry up the edge of the plate while I used the tweezers to press it down, keeping the needle in sight the whole time.

It was well-concealed but not particularly well affixed. After only a few seconds of prying, it came off with a scraping sound and fell, tumbling toward the waiting jar.

It did not bounce off. It did not swerve in midair and stab me in the arm. For once, the thing did exactly as it was meant to do, behaved exactly as it was meant to behave, and I was able to put the lid on the jar and stand, offering it to whoever wanted to take it. "This goes to Walther Davies," I said firmly. "Blond man, Tylwyth Teg, traveling with my group. You really can't miss him." For one thing, he was our only blond. For another, he was our only Tylwyth

Teg. We were rich in Daoine Sidhe, but Tylwyth Teg tend to be a little thinner on the ground.

One of the guards cautiously took the jar. "Are you sure that was the only trap?" asked Aethlin briskly.

"On the doorknob, yes; that's what stabbed Aron in the hand, and killed him before he could hit the ground," I said. "There could be more traps inside."

"Understood," he said. "Caitir?"

"Yes, Your Highness," said the Candela, and stepped backward into shadow, vanishing. I stared, first at the space where she had been, and then at the High King.

"We don't know what's in there, and you sent her in alone," I said slowly and with great deliberation. Raj stepped away from the High King and slightly behind Tybalt, trying to look nonchalant about it, like he wasn't getting out of the potential blast radius. "You sent a single Candela, *alone*, into a room that could contain a corpse—and that's sort of our best-case option right now since the whole place could be trapped to Annwn and back."

"It was that or continue to wait for you to open the door," said Aethlin implacably. "This seemed the more efficient option."

I stared at him for a moment. "We have two Cait Sidhe with us," I said finally. "If sending someone in, alone, without a way to scout ahead, were the most efficient option, don't you think I would have already sent one of them?"

For the first time, the High King's confidence appeared to waver. I couldn't tell whether it was because he was listening to me, or because his Candela had yet to return. Caitir was hopefully alone in there, and not setting off any more traps, but we had no real way of knowing. I turned back to the door, putting the King behind me.

I didn't have to wait long for the reaction to that. "A commoner does not turn her back on the High King," snapped one of the guards.

"Not a commoner," I replied, studying the door, especially the seams between it and the wall. The hinges were external—again, bad, if sadly predictable, security—and I could see that they hadn't been tampered with, at least not on this side. That was a small break. "Knighted for services to the crown of the Mists, named hero of the realm by the Queen in the Mists, acknowledged as such by the High King, just now, in your hearing. If I need to turn my back on him to do my job, he can understand the necessity and forgive me for it."

There was no more iron anywhere on the door. That didn't mean I wanted to touch it with my bare hands. One of the first real killers I ever met was Oleander de Merelands, and she specialized in poisons. Contact poison was one of her favorite tricks. I stooped to wrap the hem of my dress around my hand, then stepped forward and grasped the doorknob.

People who put deadly traps on doorknobs often forget the obvious, which is that it's a good idea to lock doors. The knob turned easily, and I jumped back as the door swung inward, revealing the short entry hall of what looked like a plushly furnished chamber. It wasn't as large as the one where I'd been expecting to stay with Tybalt—we were probably going to have to move now, or at least have the place thoroughly swept for traps, several times—but it was equally well-appointed, at least from the slice I could see.

Of course, that slice included a motionless Candela lying sprawled on the floor, which was a little less pleasant to look upon.

"Caitir!" shouted one of the guards, and the Satyr rushed past me, diving into the room without glancing back. If he had accomplished nothing else, Aethlin had done a good job of convincing his people to be loyal to each other.

As the Satyr ran, there was a small snapping sound from floor level. I jumped away, putting still more distance between me and the open door. It was a good idea. The wire he'd broken was apparently connected to a small silver dipper hidden along the line of the wall near ceiling level. It snapped down, showering him in glittering green dust. He kept running for several more steps before he started to wheeze, clutching at his throat in terrified confusion, and collapsed to the floor next to Caitir.

I spun around, focusing on the sole remaining guard. "Get the High King out of here now," I snapped, then switched my attention to Aethlin. "Sire, I need to secure this location, sweep for further traps, and get your people out of there, assuming they're not both dead."

Aethlin had gone pale and was staring in horrified fascination at the two unmoving bodies visible through the open door. "Y . . . yes," he said. "Yes, of course. You have my permission to do whatever you feel necessary to resolve this and bring Nessa home, if possible."

"Yes, Sire," I said, dismissing him as I turned to Raj. "Go back to the others. Tell May I need her to get the biggest canister of canned frosting Kerry has, and that she, Jazz, and Cillian should come join us as quickly as possible." "Cillian" was our code name for Quentin. Hidden in plain sight or no, he was still my squire, and I wanted his help.

"On it," said Raj, and dove into shadow, vanishing. The Daoine Sidhe guard was already hurrying Aethlin away down the hall, leaving me alone with Tybalt and the corpses.

So a pretty normal date night for us, really.

"Canned frosting?" he asked, raising an eyebrow.

"Kerry's addicted to the stuff," I said. "She puts it on her Oreos, and I've seen her use it to make cheap-ass eclairs by shooting it into donuts from the grocery store bakery case. I can't imagine she came to Toronto to make a formal wedding cake without bringing an entire case of it."

"And what are you planning to do with, ah, canned frosting?"

"Spray it all over that damn hallway," I said. "The problem with relying on tripwires is that not everyone has the same gait. A Silene will step higher than a Bridge Troll. So there are probably multiple wires set, with multiple associated traps. I hate to leave them in there when there's any chance they're still alive, but . . ."

"But if you decide you're willing to die rather than marry me, I will be deeply disappointed," said Tybalt, voice dropping lower and taking on an undertone of resignation that I didn't like one little bit.

I took the three steps necessary to close the distance between us and touched his cheek, trying not to dwell on how often I ran off alone when danger loomed, and how not seeing that look on the faces of the people who cared about me was at least half of why. It's a lot harder to be casually self-destructive when people keep looking distressed about it.

"Hey," I said. "I'm not charging in there without a plan. I'm not being stupid about this. I'm *going* to marry you, and I'm going to do it this week, in Toronto, before Kerry's cake has time to get stale." Which was a sort of ridiculous thing to say, since Kerry had probably layered that thing in so many preservation spells that it would still be good on my hundredth birthday.

It was also apparently the right thing to say, because some of the tension left Tybalt's shoulders. Not all of it—we were still standing in front of a room potentially full of traps and at least one corpse.

Delaying the night-haunts' dinner is a hobby of mine, I guess.

The smell of pepper and burnt paper came from behind me a split second before Raj was tapping on my shoulder. Because his magic had already given his location away, I neither jumped nor stabbed him, only turned and held out my hand.

"May and the others are on their way," he said, dropping a canister of spray frosting, the shitty kind they sell in grocery stores, into my hand. "Cillian knows how to get here, and he seemed relieved to have something to do."

"I thought I told you to have May get the frosting." Kerry guarded her sweets jealously, and always had. She didn't know Raj well enough to have handed the can over voluntarily.

"I told her it was an emergency, and that you'd buy her fancy Canadian canned frosting as an apology." Raj shrugged. "It seemed more efficient."

It was, and I was putting off dealing with the room. That wasn't kind to the people inside, who might not be past saving, or to the High King, who had to live with the knowledge that he'd sent one of his courtiers in there without thinking through the possible consequences. All these deaths were on the person who'd set the traps, but some of them also belonged, a little bit, to him.

I walked back to the doorway, shook the frosting canister as hard as I could, and started spraying bright pink frosting into the room. Silly String would have worked better, since it wouldn't have broken when it hit the wires, but the frosting was vividly colored, and it stuck to the wires as it hit them, making them increasingly visible as it built and caked along their length.

In addition to the wire our Satyr friend had tripped, there were two more at floor level, and one at slightly more than average head height. Someone had *really* wanted to make sure no one made it into this room.

"You can follow me if it makes you feel better, but no magic, and don't touch *anything*," I said to Tybalt and Raj. "I'd prefer if one of you could stay here to tell the others what's going on."

"Raj will remain," said Tybalt, in a voice that left no room for argument.

I couldn't blame him for that. I've run off into certain danger often enough without giving him the chance to come along, and if he wanted to stay with me now, that was reasonable. Ridiculous, but reasonable. "Make sure you don't hit any of the wires, and try to avoid bumping the walls," I said, starting for the door, canister of frosting still in my hand. "The tripwires activated powder, so we're looking at something inhaled, but it could be something that acts as a contact poison."

"Poison existed before I knew you," Tybalt said, sounding half-amused, half-exhausted. "I assure you, I understand how it works."

"Then let's go."

EIGHT

STEPPING OVER THE FROSTING-COVERED wires was easy enough, although I had to hike my dress almost to my knees to keep it from dragging in the mess on the floor. It would have been easier to cut it off at mid-thigh, but—and this was key—Stacy was already going to kill me over one little easily mended stab. I didn't want to antagonize her further until it was me or the dress.

The frosting was slippery, but not quite slippery enough to knock either one of us down. Once, it would have been. Once, I would have gone ass over teakettle before I made it to the first body.

And sadly, it *was* a body. Any regret I'd had about showing sense and not immediately charging after the Satyr went away when we reached him. He had fallen face-up, and his eyes were red, like every blood vessel he had had had burst at once, flooding his field of vision. A narrow trickle of blood had run from his nose to his upper lip, and when I inhaled, I could smell it, rich and loamy and cold. Satyrs are almost as connected to the land as Dryads are, and it was reflected in his magic.

I could also smell the poison. Not in the magic, but in the blood, which resented its intrusion and warned me away at the same time. To try to ride this man's memories would be to invite the same death upon myself, and while I couldn't be sure it was a death I wouldn't recover from, it felt like it could be.

Maybe "will this kill me" isn't the best game to play by gut feeling alone, but when my choices are that or risking exposure, I'll go with my gut, thanks.

Tybalt was only a step or so behind me, navigating the hall with a Cait Sidhe's grace. I paused when I reached the Candela. She was lying on her side, face toward the wall. Unlike the Satyr, her eyes were closed, and there was no blood. There was also no broken glass. The carpet around her was plush and clean. I looked up.

There, clustered together in a corner like frightened puppies, were her Merry Dancers.

Which meant that Caitir, whatever else she was, wasn't dead.

"Tybalt," I said softly, and elbowed him in the side, pointing. He followed my finger, eyes widening as he saw what I was pointing at.

"Oh," he said, voice hushed. "I see."

"Yeah." Dammit. I should have asked that last guard to stay behind rather than escorting the High King to safety. We needed someone who knew the knowe well enough to tell us how to get to their infirmary. "I know this is asking a lot of you—I understand that—but will you go and ask Maida where we can get a doctor in this place? I don't want to touch Caitir until she's been looked at by someone with actual training, but I don't know how long she has without intervention."

The look Tybalt gave me was anguished. "Your request is reasonable, little fish, and I hate you for making it," he said. Then he grabbed my shoulders and turned me to face him, staring at me for a long moment before he pulled me close and kissed me.

It was the kind of kiss that usually gets described as "last." He kissed me like the world was ending and he was never going to have the chance to kiss me again, like he knew that the moment he left, I was going to do something genuinely foolish.

"I will be *right* back," he said, and stepped into shadow, and was gone, leaving me alone with the unconscious and the dead.

I sighed, closing my eyes and tilting my chin upward, toward the ceiling. I stood there, perfectly still in this room that smelled of blood and poison and unfamiliar magic, and said quietly, "It's all right now. I'm alone, but that's not going to last."

The whisper of wings almost too soft to hear rustled around me, and a voice I knew all too well and didn't know at all spoke from the air immediately in front of me. "You don't belong here."

"Hello, Gordan." I opened my eyes and tilted my chin down, looking at the Barbie doll-sized figure that hovered in front of my face, tattered autumn-leaf wings beating frantically to keep it aloft. "You don't either. You died in California. Why so far from home?"

"The dead go where they please, and I had no interest in joining a flock that would intersect so often with the one that held your loved ones." She had a face deeply seamed with lines, like crevasses in rock or wrinkles on the face of a human, and a short, spiky shock of bone-white hair. I hadn't seen her since the day she died.

Technically, I wasn't seeing her right now. The night-haunts wear the faces and carry the memories of our dead, but they *aren't* our dead. They are a questionable immortality, one that lasts only as long as the lives they carry. As Gordan, this night-haunt might get fifty years before she needed to feed again.

Other members of her flock weren't so lucky. Some of them had forms as solid and realistic as hers. Others were charcoal sketches, bleached-out ghosts held aloft by the vibration of ephemeral wings. Faerie's dead. Not as common as they'd been when we still went to war at the drop of a hat, but still . . . too common for comfort.

At least this flock was far enough from home that there was only one face I recognized, even if it was the face of a woman who had tried to kill both me and Quentin, who *had* killed several people I was now sublimely fond of.

She glanced at my feet, then back up. "No protective circle," she said. "Nothing to keep you safe from us. You *dare* . . . ?"

"You're not allowed to consume the living," I replied. "And I didn't summon you. The dead did. They've been poisoned." Maybe that was an unnecessary explanation, but better too much than not enough when it came to something like this. "I can't ride their blood. I can't ask them anything. I was hoping you could."

I'm not the Luidaeg. I can lie. These bodies held no secrets for me; I'd seen them both die, done in swiftly and painfully by poison. Learning the exact nature of that pain wouldn't help me. But I could see the flock now, and the solid members were few enough that I could pick them out easily, lacking a crowd to hide themselves behind.

And not a one of them had a face beautiful enough to stop a heart, or long blue hair, or perfect breasts.

Nessa wasn't here.

Gordan's haunt looked at me suspiciously. "So you risked our wrath just to ask a few questions?" she asked. "I know what you've done. I know you brought back everyone I killed. It should have been impossible, but you did it, Liar's daughter. Why let us come at all?"

"I was able to raise the dead that time because it was a unique situation," I said. "It involved a lot of blood. These people were poisoned, and if I drank enough of their blood to even attempt to bring them back, it would poison me, too. I don't know if I could recover from that."

"So your own life is more important than theirs? Typical." She laughed, shrill and bitter, and several of the more faded members of the flock took that as their cue. They dove for the bodies, and I tilted my face away, so I wouldn't see what came next.

A corpse was too much for a single night-haunt to consume. The meal would be shared out amongst the hungriest of them. I didn't know how they chose which one would wear the face of the dead, and I didn't want to know. That felt like a secret too far for the living to carry. Instead, I focused on the night-haunt with Gordan's face.

"Everything that lives wants to survive," I said. "I never claimed to be any different."

"No, but your actions claimed it for you, *hero*." She spat the word like it was the worst slur imaginable, like she had never said anything so disgusting. "Changeling filth, pretending at the place of your betters—but not as changeling as you were, are you? You've been shedding your humanity while you dally with kings and queens, climbing the social ladder in ways that were never available to the rest of us. Well, all are equal among the dead. We had the answer all along. All Faerie ever had to do to change itself for the better was end."

I looked at her, this tiny being who wore the face of a woman who had tried her best to murder me when such was still entirely possible, and all I felt was pity. She'd died thinking her mortal blood made her less than everyone around her; they'd told her it was so, sometimes openly, sometimes in quiet, cruel little ways, and she'd believed them. Now she carried that belief on autumn wings among the dead, and for all that she said the dead were equal, they couldn't be, not when those thoughts still weighed her down.

"I am sorry not to die for the sake of someone I don't know, and your ideals," I said. "I am also not sorry in the slightest, because I *am* making Faerie better. I save lives. I fix things. I shore up the walls when the tide is coming in, and I bring the lost ones home. I do the things a hero is meant to do, and if those things can't always include the impossible, I can live with that. Besides, saving all the dead would mean starving the flocks, and regardless of the faces you wear and the prejudices you carry, you're alive, too."

The night-haunts might spend their lives effectively in exile from the rest of Faerie, unable to join in our kingdoms or community, bound by Oberon himself to be scavengers when otherwise they would devour us in their endless hunger, but they're alive. They exist because they live and they live because they exist, and that's the kind of contradiction Faerie thrives on.

The haunt with Gordan's face scowled at me and kept scowling as more solid-looking haunts came to hover in the space around her. All of them looked like they had mass and heft, which was more than I could say for the members of the flock still hovering around the edges, their bodies translucent and foggy, like they might be tricks of light and shadow, only here until someone opened a window or turned on a light. Two of them had new faces.

One was Satyr. One was Daoine Sidhe. None of them were Candela, but I still glanced up to the corner where the Merry Dancers bobbed, staying well away from the flock around me.

"You'll come to us soon enough," said the Gordan-haunt. "You'll come to us, and we'll suck the marrow from your bones like sugar candy." She smiled, baring suddenly sharp teeth, before she zipped upward with a single mighty flap of her wings, which should have been too frail to propel her at that kind of speed. The rest of the flock followed, even the ones verging on insubstantiality, and I was alone again.

Well. That could have gone worse. I ran my hands down my sides as if to check that I was still undevoured, and upon confirming that my too, too solid flesh had not begun to melt away, turned my attention back to the motionless Candela sprawled on the floor. I didn't dare touch her, not without knowing the nature of the poison that had knocked her down, and without the benefit of blood, I couldn't even start to figure out what was wrong.

It was sort of nice to be reminded that I had limits, even if the timing couldn't have been worse.

The smell of musk and pennyroyal rose behind me, and I turned to see Tybalt standing there, clutching the arm of a slight, brown-haired Ellyllon whose wings were beating so rapidly they had become a blur, casting translucent cascades of glittering, colorless dust into the air around the pair of them. That was fine. It would dissipate as soon as it touched literally anything, unless the Ellyllon was trying to make it stick. My crime scene, such as it was, wouldn't be disrupted.

"I found your healer," said Tybalt, pupils narrowing to slits as he took note of the absence of the Satyr's body. I hadn't turned to look yet; the night-haunts wouldn't have bothered to craft a manikin to replace the corpse, not here, not inside the High King's knowe where there was no need to pretend the dead man had been anything other than immortal. They would have left something behind to mark the fact that he had fallen if I hadn't been here to see him taken and know that he was dead, but I knew the body was gone.

"She hasn't moved or woken up," I informed the Ellyllon, who was looking around the room with the short, sharp motions of someone truly terrified. "Her Merry Dancers haven't dipped or even started to fall, so I'm assuming she's stable, but there's a very good chance she was dropped by some sort of poison, possibly contact."

"I'm about ready to shed this skin anyway," he assured me, and moved to kneel on the floor next to Caitir.

When his knee hit the carpet there was a small snapping sound, and a tiny arrow, no bigger than a matchstick, was released from somewhere against the wall. It zipped past, missing him completely due to his small stature and place on the floor, and embedded itself in the baseboard of the opposing wall. "Ah," he said, utterly calm. "Elf-shot. Well, that explains a great deal."

He rolled her onto her back, revealing the matchstick arrow protruding from her upper arm. She had landed on it when she fell, shattering the shaft. He gingerly touched the remains. "Fletched with hummingbird feathers, if I judge correctly," he said. "You're looking for someone with very small hands. Cornish Pixie, perhaps, or Piskie."

Cornish Pixies are the size of humans, but they're one of the only types of larger fae who can communicate easily with regular pixies, and frequently recruit their smaller cousins to help them with delicate matters. Knowing Poppy and the Aes Sidhe, I sometimes wondered if Cornish Pixies weren't the result of Aes Sidhe crossbreeding with something else. Tylwyth Teg, perhaps, or Ellyllon. It was an interesting thought, if not strictly relevant to the task at hand.

Piskies, on the other hand, are definitely the result of the Aes Sidhe breeding with true pixies, as confirmed by the Luidaeg herself, making them one of the few fae races with no Firstborn. They're size-changers. They can move through the world of the large fae and the world of the small fae with equal ease, and it would have been easy for a Piskie to make an arrow as small as the one in Caitir's arm.

"Why, though?" I asked. "We have a treatment for elf-shot now. It's not a good way to take someone out of commission on a long-term basis."

"No, but it is a good way, if you've been discovered, to cause exactly the scene we saw unfold," said Tybalt slowly. "Someone who can enter the room without disturbing the traps at the door goes in, and they fail to come back out, causing their companions to rush the door. The traps are triggered, your cover is blown, but you can still potentially question the first intruder, to learn how much they knew before they led their friends to slaughter."

He sounded incredibly calm, given that if I had taken a step in the wrong direction, I could easily have been elf-shot. "Any idea what triggered the trap?" I asked the Ellyllon. "Did you feel something break or hear a click or anything like that?"

"No, sadly," he said. "If it was a tripwire, it was a very thin one, and I didn't notice breaking it. I can check for more, if you like?"

"I would appreciate that," I said. Being able to treat elf-shot doesn't make it a fun way to pass a morning, and if I got elf-shot before my wedding, May would never let me hear the end of it. People already thought I didn't really want to be here.

"You may want to cover your noses," said the Ellyllon apologetically, and ducked his head, arching his back in a feline way that would have looked much more natural on Tybalt. Then he began to beat his wings, frantically.

Ellyllon are somewhat unusual among the winged races of Faerie in that they can't actually fly under their own power once they reach adulthood. Their magic focuses on other things. They can glide, but that's about the extent of the time they spend in the air. That doesn't mean their wings are useless. Much of Ellyllon magic manifests through the dust they shed, commonly referred to as "pixie-sweat"; they're rare in that their magic has no scent to it, only the glitter in the air. I put my hands over my nose and mouth as the Ellyllon filled the air with his magic, but some of it still got in my mouth.

It tasted sweet, like the powder that comes off a stick of wax-wrapped convenience store bubble gum, and I wondered whether Jin's magic would taste the same, whether this was the element of Ellyllon magic that I had always been missing.

I swallowed, and watched as more and more dust filled the room, drifting lazily downward to collect on every level surface. Including, I saw, a web of thin strands, barely as thick as cobwebs, that crisscrossed the floor only an inch or so above the carpet, too fine to be seen by the naked eye, but present all the same.

Whoever had booby-trapped this room had wanted to be absolutely sure they took out anyone who entered. Looking down, I could see that our seemingly miraculous avoidance of the elf-shot was more a consequence of coming straight down the middle of the hall—what should have been an impassable danger—and hence stepping into the footprints of the person who'd lain the tripwires in the first place. The scale was such that while they might have had a Piskie involved in crafting the elf-shot, someone bigger had been involved in setting the actual traps.

"Charming," said the Ellyllon, sitting up straight as his wings stilled. "I would recommend not moving if you don't have to."

"Wasn't planning to," I said. We were in a minefield all of a sudden, and I was glad I hadn't tried the frosting trick here. These wires were thin enough that I would probably have broken a few with the weight of cheap canned frosting, and if there's a more embarrassing way to get elf-shot, I certainly can't think of it.

"October!"

I turned. May and Jazz were rushing down the hall, Quentin and Raj close behind them. Quentin, for one, looked like he was on the verge of panic. I guess the possible consequences of gambling his face on me surviving long enough to get married were finally hitting home.

"Stay there," I said, pulling my hands away from my face and gesturing empathetically for them to keep their distance. "Do *not* come past the door."

"Why?" May pulled up short, putting out her arms to stop the

others before their momentum could carry them past the thresh-
old. "What's going on in there?"

"Massive boobytrap," I said. "It's not safe to move in here."

"But you're moving in there," said Quentin.

"Believe me, I've noticed, and I'm not thrilled about it at the
moment, so just give us a second to figure out what to do, okay?"

The Ellyllon had broken several strands when he knelt next to
the fallen Candela. I offered him my hand. "Come on, get up," I
said. "Tybalt?"

"As always, I am your faithful servant," he said, and when I
pulled the Ellyllon to his feet, Tybalt was right there to sweep the
startled healer into his arms. "You may want to hold your breath,"
he said, politely enough, and hurled himself into the nearest patch
of shadow, dragging the healer with him.

If his passing broke any further trip wires, their arrows didn't
hit anyone—namely, me. I held perfectly still, looking at the gleaming lines all around my feet, exquisitely aware of how precarious
my position was. At any moment, I could set off a trap and be
sleeping for a long, long time. And this was only the first room!

Even if the High King's own seneschal didn't warrant more than
a glorified hotel room, I had to assume there were at least two
more rooms here—the bedroom and the bathroom. And there
would probably also be closets, and any one of them could be
trapped from here to Mag Mell, and she could be in any of them,
assuming she was here at all. Nothing said she'd been taken inside
the knowe. Maybe she'd been abducted out in the mortal world,
where she would have been less protected even in public. Thanks
to the night-haunts and the Doppelganger's use of her magic, I was
reasonably sure she was still alive, but that wasn't necessarily a
good thing.

Tybalt and the Ellyllon reappeared in the hallway outside, Tybalt shoving the Ellyllon at May before diving back into the shadows. That was my cue. Careful of the remaining strands, I stooped
and lifted the fallen Candela into my arms, positioning us both to
keep her from breaking any more pieces of what I could only reasonably call a web as I straightened. She dangled limp and loose
against me, and her Merry Dancers slowly began to descend from
ceiling level, drifting closer.

"My fiancé is going to come get us," I said. "He's going to take
us into the shadows, and we'll be right back. If you come down

here, you can come with us, or you can go into the hall, and we'll come to you."

The Merry Dancers dropped faster, coming to circle around my head. I smiled at them. That was what I'd been expecting. No one I know of has ever intentionally separated a Candela from their Merry Dancers; no one knows what it would do.

As expected, Tybalt stepped out of the shadows behind me. "Ready?" he asked briskly.

"I am." I turned, taking a deep breath as I offered him my hand. He took it, looking wryly at the woman in my arms, and shook his head.

"Always on a quest for heroics to be done," he said fondly as he pulled me toward him.

He shouldn't have done that.

As he opened the doorway to the Shadow Roads, my ankle hit one of the unbroken strands and it snapped, flinging another tiny arrow across the room. He heard the sound as surely as I did because he froze, hand tightening on mine.

Then the arrow struck his calf and he toppled forward, into the open gateway to the Shadow Roads, pulling me, the Candela, and her Merry Dancers all with him into freezing, airless nothing.

NINE

I'D ALWAYS BELIEVED THERE could be no light in the Shadow Roads, but two things registered at the same time: I was falling, and I could still see, thanks to lambent glow coming from Caitir's Merry Dancers. I'd dropped her when I lost my balance, and she was lying sprawled on whatever served the Shadow Roads as ground, the Merry Dancers circling wildly in the air above her. They looked distressed. I didn't know how I could know that, but I did.

I could see, but I was freezing, and I couldn't breathe. I looked down at Tybalt, his hand still clasped firmly in mine—even drugged into an enchanted sleep, he hadn't let me go—and saw that he was breathing normally, protected by the natural magic of the Cait Sidhe.

I couldn't just borrow his power and use it to navigate us out of here. There was too much chance, given the weakness my line was heir to, that I would immediately transform into a cat and be unable to change myself back, or to drag two human-sized bodies out of the darkness with my teeth. Plus, I had to admit, the idea of seeing the memories of the man I was about to marry when he had, once again, every reason to be disappointed in me, was . . . unsettling, at best. I know Tybalt loves me. I know I frustrate him more often than I should. I didn't need to have it confirmed.

That left Caitir. Candela have access to the same space as the Cait Sidhe, they just travel through it faster and for shorter distances. I crawled toward her, pulling my knife with one increasingly stiff and unresponsive hand. She had elf-shot in her blood, and I would have to be careful of that, but as long as I stayed awake long enough to open a door, it would be all right. It would be *fine*.

My first cut was shallow and drew no blood. My second was deeper, and I was rewarded with a sluggish trickle of blood that smelled, although probably only to me, incongruously of lemons. I bent and pressed my mouth over the cut, sucking as hard as I could without actually allowing myself to take a breath. My lungs were already beginning to ache.

Caitir's memories rose up, threatening to overwhelm me. She/I had been honored to be given a directive by her King, to be asked to do something as important as checking on the well-being of his seneschal, Nessa, who was a beloved figure among the courtiers, always fair, always balanced in her judgment. She/I had only been with the High Court herself/myself for a few years, not long enough to build a reputation, but long enough to know she/I wanted to continue to serve—

I forced the memories away, becoming singular once more, and focused on the lemon-bright sweetness of her magic. It was lemon and raspberry, an oddly flavorful combination. I swallowed again. No, not lemon; lemon verbena, which made a little more sense. And as I identified her magic, I understood it, and what it was created to do.

Raising my hand, I traced a circle in the air, and was delighted to see the hallway appear, May and Raj holding Quentin back as he tried to throw himself through the open door to Nessa's quarters, Jazz standing a few feet behind them, watching helplessly. Out of all of them, she was the one who might have been able to enter safely, as long as she did it in her raven form. And was very, very careful.

And I didn't have time to focus on that right now, since I still couldn't breathe, despite the magic I had borrowed from Caitir. The Candela didn't linger in shadows long enough to need to breathe there, apparently. I scrambled back over to Tybalt, slinging his arm over my shoulders and hoisting him along as I rose into a half-crouch, suddenly grateful that I'd never been overly attracted to tall men. Step by step, I dragged him toward the portal I had opened, unsure whether my growing sluggishness was cold, hypoxic shock, or the elf-shot in Caitir's blood beginning to do its work.

The fact that I hadn't fallen asleep instantly meant it was unlikely to be elf-shot, which usually works in an instant, but maybe the stuff is different when ingested orally and on purpose. Faerie is confusing sometimes, and alchemy is finicky enough to make conditional potions.

I reached the portal and shoved Tybalt through, leaving him to fall in a heap on the hallway floor. The sound made everyone turn. Quentin made a strangled sound at the sight of me standing framed by a circle of borrowed magic against a background of absolute darkness.

I stuck my head out into the hall, where the warmth of normal air was like a slap to the face, and took a deep breath, filling my aching lungs with much-needed air. "We have an elf-shot Candela in here," I said, quickly. "She's alive, and I'm using her magic to maintain this portal. Give me a second and I'll get us both out." I took another breath, already regretting what I was about to do, and pulled back through the portal, turning toward the Candela.

I felt, rather than heard, the moment when the magic I'd borrowed from her blood ran out and the portal slammed shut again. I grimaced, shuffling toward her, the cold making it increasingly difficult to move. It would be so nice to lie down, just for a few minutes, and let my legs recover . . .

And I would freeze to death, and so would she, and even if my magic resurrected me to suffocate again, hers wouldn't. She'd die, and she'd take her magic with her, and we'd never get out of here.

Someone grabbed me from behind. I didn't scream; screaming takes air. I didn't stab the person either, having sheathed my knife when I was done cutting Caitir. If I dropped it in here, I'd have to gnaw through her shoulder or something to get more blood. Instead, I drove my elbow up and back at the same time, catching my assailant in the solar plexus. They staggered away, and I whirled.

Raj gave me a pained look, face a sketchy outline in the dim glow from the Merry Dancers. ". . . ow," he said, able to speak in the Shadow Roads the same way his uncle could, by breathing the air that wasn't there for the rest of us. "Could you not?"

I blinked at him.

"I followed the light," he said. "I knew roughly where you were, and I just followed the light. Can't leave my knight to freeze, can

I?" His expression shifted from pained to pleading. "Now will you let me get you out of here?"

I nodded and pointed to Caitir. He walked past me, scooping her into his arms and slinging her over his shoulder, and I had never in my life been so glad to see him, or so grateful for the fact that both my boys have gotten taller and stronger as they've aged. I hadn't paid quite as much attention with Raj, since I'd never been allowed to claim him officially as my squire, but he was almost as tall as Tybalt now, with the rangy, defined musculature necessary for a Prince of Cats who was preparing to challenge for his throne. He'd been working out more since Ginevra came to stand regent for him and made the prospect of becoming King devastatingly real.

The Merry Dancers followed their Candela, swirling around Raj's head as he straightened and walked back over to me, offering his hand. "Hold me fast, and don't let me go," he said, a note of caution in his voice.

Raj wasn't as accustomed to taking passengers through the shadows as Tybalt was, and I didn't know if he'd ever done two people at once before. I nodded, grabbing onto his hand, and he smiled at me before crouching slightly down, tensing, and leaping into the deeper dark.

I jumped with him, and together, we crashed out of the darkness and into the warm light of the hall. Raj dropped us both when he landed, catching himself on the hallway wall with both hands while he gasped and wheezed. I rolled to a stop against the same wall, my hip pressed to the baseboard, my eyes fixed on the ceiling. The ghosts of Caitir's memory still rattled their chains at the corners of my mind. They would fade soon enough, as long as I didn't focus on them strongly enough to make them memories of my own.

"What," said May, pausing portentously before she continued, "the *fuck*?"

"Are you hurt?" The first face to appear in my field of vision belonged to the Ellyllon healer, his wings working frantically and spilling glittering dust into the air. "You have blood on your lips. Did you injure yourself?"

"It's not mine," I said. My limbs were starting to thaw. Awkwardly, I pushed my way into a seated position, rubbing my aching forehead with one hand. "Check on Caitir. I had to cut her to borrow her magic, and it was dark, so I'm not sure how deep the knife went."

The healer blinked at me. He wasn't used to this sort of thing, not having been around long enough to become acclimated to the level of casual chaos that the rest of us live with on a daily basis. There are days when I think Dóchas Sidhe aren't designed so much to manipulate the workings of the blood as we are to cause problems everywhere we go. It would make a lot of things make a lot more sense if that were the case.

"Um," he said.

"It's all right. She's always like this," said May, moving to the Ellyllon's side. "Let my sister think about what she's done."

"Um," he said again, but allowed himself to be led away. Jazz stepped up to take his place.

"Two people got elf-shot, and neither of them was you," she said.

"Nope."

"But you *did* drink an elf-shot victim's blood," she said, almost hopefully. "Does that mean you're going to fall asleep soon?"

"I know we've always worried about that, but no, I don't think so." I rubbed my forehead again. "I think I got little enough of it that I'm going to be okay. Walther should probably still give me something prophylactic."

"Nice use of 'prophylactic,'" chirped May. "And it doesn't matter either way, because even if she falls asleep, she didn't get elf-shot, so you don't take the betting pool."

"Aw, nuts," said Jazz.

"You are all weirdoes," I said, and that was when Quentin slammed into me, wrapping his arms around my shoulders and yanking me close. It was like being hugged by a particularly enthusiastic tsunami, and after a moment of confusion, I relaxed and hugged him back.

"I see how it is," said Raj. "I grab you and you assault me. Cillian grabs you, and he gets a hug. I know which kid you actually give a damn about, *Mom*, and it's not me."

"Go to your room," I said, looking past the tangled scrim of Quentin's hair that covered my eyes to where Raj stood, smirking. I patted Quentin on the back with one hand, trying to give him the time to collect himself, then blinked. "Hang on—betting pool?"

"On whether you make it to the wedding," said May. "So far, you're doing pretty well."

"Two people are dead, the groom has been elf-shot, the seneschal is *missing*, and I have to explain to Kerry why I used up almost an entire container of her canned frosting for no apparent reason," I said flatly. "I'm not sure how you class that as 'pretty well.'"

"You've really skewed my sense of normalcy," said May.

Quentin finally let go of me, glaring. "I thought you were *dead*," he said. "We all saw Tybalt fall, and we know you can't navigate the Shadow Roads by yourself."

"Luckily, I had a Candela with me to borrow from." I looked past him to where the Ellyllon was kneeling next to Caitir. "She's going to be okay, right? It's just elf-shot?"

"The fact that I now live in a world where the word 'just' can precede 'elf-shot' is a genuine miracle, for which we should be thanking Oberon on a daily basis," he said, looking up from his patient. "That being said, yes, it appears that she has been elf-shot, and should wake in a hundred years, or upon administration of the counter-tincture, whichever comes first."

I raised an eyebrow. "Do I get a vote? Because I was just in her memories, and I'm reasonably sure she'd prefer the counter-tincture to missing the season finale of *Canada's Got Talent*."

"She does like her modern media," agreed the Ellyllon, rising and moving to kneel again, this time beside Tybalt. He leaned forward as he pried one of Tybalt's eyes open, peering into it. "Yes, again, elf-shot. Both should be fine."

A knot I hadn't been allowing myself to admit I felt untied itself somewhere behind my sternum, in the birdcage enclosure of my ribs. "I'm grateful to hear that," I said, forcing my voice to stay steady. "Walther will be able to treat and wake them both—he's our—"

"Walther *Davies*?" asked the Ellyllon, wings buzzing again, this time with excitement. "The alchemist who first developed the treatment for elf-shot? The man who woke the sleepers? I know who he is, I just never expected him to be willing to travel here with you. No offense intended, ma'am, I know your marriage is an event of some significance, but an alchemist of his stature—surely it must be difficult for the Mists to spare him."

I turned my face away to hide my smile. "Indeed," I said. There was no point in telling the man that Walther had yet to allow Arden to name him her court alchemist, even though there was no one else available to take up the position. Until he had tenure, he said, his first fealty had to be to the University of California's

Berkeley campus, where he spent his days teaching mostly mortal students what he called "new and better ways to poison themselves."

He was on a tenure track, so he'd probably let her convince him sometime in the next few years, but until then, he was staying stubbornly exactly where he was, freelance alchemist and chemistry professor, officially unaffiliated with any Court except for the one Tybalt and May occasionally jokingly accused me of putting together in my living room.

As if. I would be the *worst* liege. Everyone's duties would be based around whose turn it was to pick up the pizza this week.

"I would be honored to share the treatment of these patients with Master Davies," said the Ellyllon, as I finally picked myself up off the floor and shook my skirt out, amazed at how little blood was on the fabric. Stacy was going to be so proud of me.

Once she got done yelling about the stab wound in my side, that was.

Slowly, I turned and looked at the open door to Nessa's quarters, showing the frosting-smeared hall and the place where the Satyr's body had been. In its place, the night-haunts had left a bundle of twigs and straw twined around with dried wildflowers. It was pretty, in a terrible way, and I had to wonder whether that was what lay beneath all of their manikins. If so, January O'Leary was going to have a nasty surprise the first time she got too close to a match . . .

"Does High King Aethlin have any Bridge Trolls in his service?" I asked abruptly.

The Ellyllon blinked but nodded. "Three in the guard, two more on the landscaping team," he said.

"Good." I turned to fully face him. "We're gonna need them. Also, do you have a name? Thinking of you as 'the Ellyllon' is getting old, and maybe a little bit insulting."

"Galen," he said, smiling. "As for the Bridge Trolls, I can relay your message to His Majesty, unless you wanted to send the Cait Sidhe boy who came for me . . . ?"

"Raj is a Prince of Cats, not an errand boy," I said. "We'll need to move both Caitir and Tybalt to the infirmary and notify Walther that we need the tincture readied."

"I can do that," said May.

"Great," I said. "I'll stay here and wait for the Bridge Trolls."

Galen blinked. "Oh, you meant—well, I suppose now is as good a time as any to—yes, of course." He bent and scooped Caitir into his arms, wings working overtime to let him stay upright with her weight pressing against him. Raj wasn't quite as able to lift Tybalt, but with May's help, they were able to get his arms slung around their shoulders and hoist him to his feet.

It was wholly undignified, and I found myself half-wishing I'd given in the last time April had tried to talk me into letting her upgrade my phone to something that didn't fit in my pocket but *would* take pictures. These would have been great to bring up the next time he laughed at me, however delicately, for tripping over my own feet trying to get into Muir Woods.

Oh, well. Some moments are meant to be savored, not preserved.

Jazz and Quentin didn't move, waiting for me to tell them what we were going to do next. I turned to them, running my hand through my hair, which had managed to escape the last of Stacy's styling in all the chaos and was increasingly coming to lay loose and flat around my face.

"Okay," I said. "The room is *heavily* booby-trapped. Cillian," we all knew better than to use Quentin's real name inside the knowe, where the walls were quite literally listening, "what have you managed to pick up about this Nessa woman? Is there any chance she went willingly with whoever sent the Doppelganger?"

"No," he said staunchly. "If she's gone, it's because she's been replaced. She's completely loyal to my—to the royal family."

I gave him a look, trying to communicate that he needed to be more careful. A slip like that in front of the wrong person and I could be up on charges of treason. He shrugged, expression sheepish. He knew he'd messed up, but that didn't mean he could stop himself from making mistakes. I sighed, allowing my face to soften. I would always forgive him, and he knew it. When he'd called me family, he'd been acknowledging a bond that each of us knew went both ways. Maybe my daughter still didn't want me in her life, but I could be there for my son.

Sons, if Raj was to be taken seriously, which he probably wasn't. It can be hard to tell with him. Cait Sidhe seem to come into the world already speaking fluent sarcasm.

"And you're sure she's that loyal?" I asked.

He nodded vigorously. "She's had opportunities to leave, and she's always refused them. All the core staff—the ones who have access to the private family quarters, who can get near the heirs when they're home—agree to submit annually to interview by the Court Seer, Fiac, and he's an Adhene."

Adhene can taste lies. They become enraged when people deceive them—sort of like I do, only with more violence and murder. No one with any sense would intentionally lie to an Adhene. Fortunately, they can tell the difference between intentional deceit and repeating someone else's falsehood, and while they don't like innocent deception any more than they like the on-purpose kind, they're pretty good about directing their rage at the right people.

They don't usually hang around noble courts voluntarily. Either Aethlin had something on this Fiac, or he was a better king than I had ever guessed he might be.

"Nessa proved her loyalty to this house over and over again," continued Quentin, looking down at his feet. "She would *never* have let a monster in voluntarily or agreed to laying traps in her rooms, and now she's missing, and I don't know . . . I don't know . . ." He trailed off, sounding miserable.

"Hey." I put a hand under his chin, pushing gently until he lifted his head enough to meet my eyes. "Hey. I saw the night-haunts."

"You—what, *again*?" He was almost sputtering. That was a good thing. If he was upset about my behaving recklessly, he wasn't focusing on a missing woman who might have been important to him, before his family had been convinced to send him away.

Will Eira ever be held accountable for all the damage she's done, not only to me, but to all of Faerie? I don't know, but sweet Oberon, I hope so.

And I hope I'm part of the accounting.

"I saw the night-haunts," I repeated, keeping my eyes locked on his. They were all wrong—they were supposed to be a deep, almost startling blue, like the Atlantic off the Canadian coast, but they were a pale dustbowl brown, the color of the sky over the ghost towns of Kansas—but they were still his eyes, still Quentin's eyes, and he was all I saw looking back at me. "They came to claim the dead, as is their due, and Nessa was not among them. She wasn't part of their number. She's the reason I stayed and was silent, so they would come while I was there. They told me she was still alive for us to find, and they did it without saying a single word. I swear to you, by the root and the thorn, the ash and the oak and the rowan and the rose, that she is not yet among the night-haunts, and if she lives, we'll find her. We'll find her."

"Thank you," he whispered, and threw himself into my arms.

He had never been this affectionate before—or at least not this demonstrative. I didn't know whether that was because Banshees were genuinely more emotional, or if it was because, for the first time in his life, he didn't feel the weight of the crown to come pushing down on him and preventing him from standing unburdened. I wasn't sure it mattered in the moment. I just put my arms around that boy, who would be a man soon enough, who would be so far beyond me that looking for him would be like scanning the sky for a single star, and I held him.

I held him like I was never going to be asked to let him go.

After a moment, he began to relax against me, accepting the hug as the sincere offer it was and not something I was required to give. I let my chin rest atop his head, breathing in the scents of the hall. The gorse and vetiver scent of his magic was the closest and strongest, of course, since I was literally holding him against me; under it was the raspberry and lemon verbena of Caitir, still strong because I had been using her magic so recently.

The scents under that were more faded. I could smell the traces of Tybalt's magic, and Raj's, and May's, all familiar and comforting—the scents of home. I could smell the sunbaked feathers and cool fog of Jazz's magic, which was subtle and hard to pin down, but part of the atmosphere I lived in on a daily basis, and thus welcome.

The scents layered under the mingled scent of family were harder to identify because they were more blurred, but I kept breathing as I pinned them down one by one for further examination. White mountain heather and celandine poppies was High King Aethlin, and chestnut rose and moss was our poor doomed Daoine Sidhe. Pitch and burnt hay was probably the Satyr, given how strong it was, and that it only smelled like it had traveled in one direction, here, not here and back like the High King or the other two guards, both of whom had left their own scent trails behind.

It was a complicated, layered web of perfumes, and picking them apart was like trying to separate the layers in a croissant without tearing them, but I've had a lot of practice with this sort of weird magic trick in the last few years, and so I lifted them away from each other and filed them, one by one, matching them to their owners until all that remained was a scent of indefinable decay which I immediately identified as the Doppelganger, and two unfamiliar magical signatures.

One, which smelled of bitter almond and carnation, came and went over and over again, and had been this way no more than a few days before our own arrival. The other was limestone and creeping thistle, and it was complicated, thick enough in the air even after all this time that I could tell its owner had been here frequently enough to wear a groove into the world, but absent now for several days. It still clung, but it was fading. It would be gone soon enough.

"I've got her," I said dreamily, letting my arms fall to my sides. Quentin kept hugging me for another second or so before he let go in confusion.

"Got who?" he asked.

"Nessa," I said. "I think I've found her magic."

"How could you find her magic? You've never met her."

His confusion was understandable. All blood-workers can smell magic to some degree, and I've always been good at it, but it was only recently that I'd started to understand it well enough to make it something more useful than a party trick. I'm more fae right now than I've ever been before in my life, the consequence of entering a transformational trance when I had nothing but myself to transform, and that's heightened everything, including my sense of the magic around me.

For Quentin, magical signatures were simple things. They could be smelled, they could be tracked, but they could also be confused. He would smell the heather in his father's magic as identical to his own, while for me the two couldn't have been more different without one of them becoming something other than floral. Magic is unique. Give me a hundred people who smell of roses, and I'll still be able to tell which one of them wove which spell.

"The Gwragedd Annwn were born in Wales," I said. "There's a lot of limestone in Wales, and creeping thistles grow there. That wouldn't be enough, if this weren't a short hallway with two apartments at the end of it. A Welsh-based magical signature this strong outside of Nessa's rooms? That's got to be hers. The other signature's owner was here much more recently, probably recently enough that they were here last night at the very latest. Hers has been missing for about—" I inhaled again, even though I already knew the answer. Sometimes you want that moment of explaining to a room full of captive nobles how the murder was committed. Sometimes you want to be theatrical. "—I'd say three days since she was here last. That's got to be her."

Three days would match up with the amount of time needed to prepare rooms for visitors and get all the security arrangements in place, but more importantly, it would also come *after* the hard work of convincing the kitchen staff to allow Kerry to touch their equipment had been performed. Doppelgangers can perform an exquisitely accurate impersonation of the person they're pretending to be, as long as it doesn't require them to pull up anything beyond surface memories. There was no possible way a Doppelganger would have been able to perform that negotiation, and yet Kerry was baking, so someone had done it.

I opened my eyes. Quentin was staring at me with something like hope and something like resignation in his eyes. Or maybe that was exactly the blend he was trying to contain.

"You're sure?" he asked.

"I'm sure." I turned to Jazz.

She held up her hand before I could open my mouth. "I know, I know," she said. "Stay here. And where, pray tell, are you going?"

"I'm going to follow this trail to wherever it leads me, and Cillian's going to come with me, and if Nessa isn't there, we'll come back," I said. "When Galen comes back with the Bridge Trolls I asked for, ask them to go into Nessa's quarters and trigger or deactivate any traps they find. They should avoid the tripwires in the hall, because those are apparently connected to 'I've already been caught, may as well kill everyone' poison pouches, but the threads in the main room just set off elf-shot."

"And Bridge Trolls can't be elf-shot, because their skins are too thick," said Quentin, stating the obvious.

Well, he had more emotional connection to the situation than I did. For me, this was an abduction and possible planned assassination that had had the bad taste to get in the way of my dinner appointment. For him, it was a missing woman who had been a part of his life since infancy, who he had apparently missed while he was in California.

I'd never put too much thought into the fact that Quentin would have had friends, acquaintances, even enemies before the start of his fosterage, but he'd had the time; he'd spent his entire childhood and the beginning of his teenage years in these halls. I'd met Stacy, Kerry, and Julie all before I turned thirteen, and we'd stayed friends well into adulthood. No matter what else changed, I'd been able to hold onto my gang of four. There was a time when I would have called them the most important people in my life and meant it. So why hadn't I dug too deeply into the idea that Quentin might have had friends he wanted to see again, or even that shining spec-ter, the first love, waiting somewhere in Canada?

He'd given up so much more than just his face for the opportu-nity to attend my wedding. He'd given up his homecoming, and the reunion that could have followed it, in a kinder, less dangerous world. He'd given it up for me.

Well, that being the case, I could find one missing woman for him.

"Got it," said Jazz. "And *after* they've defused all the traps?"

"If any of them likes to watch mortal crime dramas, they can search for clues, and I'll be very grateful to them when I get back," I said. "If not, just ask them to come back out into the hall and not touch anything. I'll be back as soon as I can. Cillian, you're with me."

Quentin fell into step beside me as I started down the hall, chin tilted slightly up so I could keep sniffing the air for traces of Nes-sa's magic. I felt like some sort of weird bloodhound, and for the first time I really appreciated how annoying Tybalt must have found my tendency to assume that because he was a cat, he could track people by smell alone. I mean, he *could*, but it looked silly, and it wasn't as easy as it sounded.

"I'm glad you're letting me help," said Quentin.

Oh, I did *not* need another distraction while I was trying to do something silly and kind of difficult. "Of course, kiddo," I said. "You're my . . . you're mine. I'll always let you help . . . when it doesn't mean getting us both killed. Where's Dean?"

I was hoping the question would distract him enough to let me focus. Instead, he huffed a sigh.

"Since his dads won't be here until tomorrow, the Luidaeg said he didn't have parental permission to do anything stupid and dan-gerous until they showed up." He sighed heavily, looking put-upon and briefly betraying his age. "I think she just doesn't want to deal with Dianda if something goes wrong."

"She's a smart one, that sea witch," I said. "I don't want to deal with Dianda either, honestly. Or with Patrick looking disappointed in me." I didn't mention Dean's other father, who isn't related to me at all, but is legally my father, too. Our laws are complicated and sort of stupid sometimes, which is all the more impressive considering they supposedly don't exist.

We have one law, Oberon's Law, which forbids us to kill each other unless it's during a time of formally declared war. Or unless the person being killed is a changeling since the Law doesn't protect us. It doesn't protect humans, either, which is one of the many reasons the fae don't make good neighbors. Now that I have actual access to Oberon—when the Luidaeg lets anyone get near him, which isn't often—I'll have to ask him why he set things up that way. Excluding changelings from the Law basically guaranteed that we'd never be anything more than second-class citizens in a world where we were already disadvantaged by our own mortality.

Everything else is custom and agreed-upon practice, but it's not actually *law*, and if you try to say it is, people get pissed. Suggesting that maybe Faerie needs a few more laws to keep us from making each other miserable all the time, and you might as well have suggested the nobility be forbidden to wear clothing when conducting formal courts.

That might not be the worst thing. Court would almost certainly be shorter.

Anyway, the small-L laws of Faerie are more like . . . traditions everyone has decided to treat as absolutely inviolate. Since the big-L Law says changelings don't count as people for purposes of whether or not you're allowed to kill them, they have no standing under those traditions, and when my mother went out and got herself knocked up by a human man, it was treated as an immaculate conception. My father, quite literally, didn't matter to the situation. And since she was still married to Simon Torquill at the time, I was considered his daughter when I was born. We have no blood in common save for Oberon's; he's a distant descendant, while I'm a direct granddaughter. But if Faerie had an organ donor registry, he'd be the first person my doctor called.

Simon and I have a complicated history, to understate things so dramatically that they barely make sense. He's my liege lord's brother, and the man who turned me into a fish for fourteen years for the crime of getting too close after he literally kidnapped his brother's wife and young daughter. I didn't find out until years later that he'd done it because the person who was giving him his orders had wanted him to kill me to remove me from the playing field. I was more human then. He could have done it.

Instead, he had transformed me, an old pureblood technique for getting an enemy out of the way for a while, and left me to swim away a decade and a half of my life. I'd lost everything because of Simon.

I was still trying to figure out how I felt about the fact that I'd been the one to help him get everything back.

Oh, it was a new everything—he had divorced my mother and immediately remarried, this time to both the Duchess of Saltmist and her Ducal consort, a move most people seemed to be regarding as purely tactical, putting him as far outside my mother's reach as possible while he recovered from his years of abuse, neglect, and worse in the service of Eira Rosynhwyr. Sadly for my sanity, I knew there had been nothing tactical about it, at least not for Simon and Patrick—they truly loved each other, with the deep, immutable love that sometimes rises out of the deepest friendships. It might have been partially tactical on Dianda's part. I've never met a woman who was as primed to fight the world as Dianda Lorden, and the chance to poke a Firstborn she'd hated for decades in the eye may have been too much to resist.

I don't think so, though. I think she loves Patrick enough that when he asked to bring the man he loves home, she agreed, and I think she's learning to love him, too.

So yeah. I try not to think about the situation with Dean's parents and my legal father more than I absolutely have to, and I dare anyone in the world to blame me.

We had continued walking while I didn't think about Dean's parents, following the thin, attenuated trail of Nessa's magic. The hall ended, merging with another, wider hall, and we continued onward, until the trail led to a seemingly featureless wall. We stopped there, me still occasionally sniffing the air to keep myself from losing the trail, Quentin balling his hands helplessly.

"If we were in Shadowed Hills or Goldengreen, I'd know what signs to look for in order to open this door," he said. "I'd know how the servants hid their comings and goings from the nobility, and I'd be able to get us in."

"But we're not," I said. "We're just in a place that has good reason to love the person we're looking for, and probably good reason to love you, too."

I stroked the wall with one hand, leaning forward until my lips nearly brushed the wood. I stopped short, mostly because smearing dried blood and whatever remained of my lipstick on something clean and polished seemed unnecessarily rude. "Hi," I said, voice pitched low. "I don't think we've been introduced."

"Oh, Maeve! Do you have to?" groaned Quentin. "It's so embarrassing when you do this."

I ignored him. No one was coming and even if they did, Faerie doesn't actually have any taboos against sweet-talking buildings. Most people don't believe knowes are alive, much less that they can have opinions about things, but they are, and they can. I've proven it, over and over again.

"My name's October," I informed the wall. "October Daye. I'm standing as knight to Quentin Sollys, who you probably remember used to live here. He's going to live here again someday, and when he does, he'll remember who was nice to me, and he'll reward them."

"Oak and ash," muttered Quentin, putting his hand over his face. "Just hurry up and make out with the architecture before somebody sees you."

"Sure, kid," I said with amusement. To the wall, I added, "You can ignore him. He's at that age where everything adults do is embarrassing. I'm looking for your seneschal. I know she came this way, and I know she didn't go back to her room, and I've been in enough knowes to know there's a door here. If you could just open it for me, I'd be able to find her, and make sure that she's all right. I think someone may have done something bad to her, and I'm concerned . . ."

This was one of the rare situations where being elf-shot was the best option we could hope for. If Nessa had been elf-shot, she wouldn't need to eat, drink, or use the bathroom. She'd just sleep for as long as it took us to find her. Up to a hundred years, if it took that long.

It wasn't going to take that long. Elf-shot was Eira's creation, and it used to be the best way the purebloods had to both wage war without killing each other and reassert their natural superiority. They could put each other to sleep for a hundred years and consider it a mere inconvenience! They could come back to the world after a century had passed and slide right back into their lives as if they had never been gone at all! Even if elf-shot hadn't been designed to be fatal to changelings, we didn't have that option. A hundred years of slumber would leave us stranded in a world that we couldn't recognize, bereft of the entire mortal side of our family, with no way of ever going home.

Eira thought elf-shot would prevent Faerie from ever being anything like equal. How could it be, when one of your best weapons killed part of the population and gave the other half a refreshing nap? And maybe she would have been right, if not for my ridiculous sensitivity to the scent of magic. I'd been able to accurately identify the type of rose she'd used in brewing and enchanting the original elf-shot, and Walther was a talented enough alchemist that he'd been able to use that information to blend a countercharm that could cancel out the effects of elf-shot, no matter when it was administered. Five minutes or fifty years, it didn't matter. If Nessa had been elf-shot, she was going to wake up.

If she hadn't, I just hoped she hadn't been left somewhere that would do her damage.

I stroked the wall again, whispering, "*Please*," and there was a soft clicking sound, like a trigger pulling back or a latch letting go. I took a step back, not wanting to be in the line of fire for the former and not wanting to impede the latter. A previously unseen door swung open, revealing a narrow hall paneled in the same maple as the rest of the knowe.

"Do you not have any other trees in Canada?" I asked.

"Arden uses redwoods in all of her decorating," said Quentin, and pushed the door wider, stepping into the hall beyond. I scowled as I followed him. He knew better than to take point.

Only apparently not, because here he was, leading the way deeper into the servants' passage. I closed the door behind me, whispering a quick, "I appreciate it more than I can say," to the knowe. The wood seemed to warm beneath my fingers, and I smiled, hurrying after Quentin.

TEN

THE AIR WAS STILLER here. Apparently, there wasn't much service to this part of the knowe; that, or High King Aethlin's servants didn't feel the need to move around the knowe in secret all that often. The smell of limestone and creeping thistle was accordingly stronger. I pushed my way past Quentin, who made a wordless sound of protest.

I held up a hand to stop him. "No," I said. "I understand that you feel like this is a place where you can be the one to take on the danger, because you've worked in halls like this and I haven't, but her magic is so close at this point, and I don't want to lose it because I get distracted by yours." It wouldn't have been a problem if his body had been his own, radiating his quiet, familiar magical signature. I could tune that out easily. The signature of this new body was less familiar. It still attracted my attention.

Frowning, Quentin stepped back and yielded the lead to me.

I put my hand on the wall to keep myself on an even keel and closed my eyes as I started walking again, following nothing but the scent. There had been nothing consistent accompanying it; the Doppelganger had dragged her here, somehow transporting her through the knowe without being seen. That implied a level of surveillance and study of the normal patterns of the staff that was frankly unnerving and meant they might have a much bigger problem than one infiltrator and one abduction.

We kept walking for what felt like forever but was probably no more than fifty feet when the scent of Nessa's magic grew suddenly, substantially stronger. I stopped. Quentin slammed into me from behind, and I opened my eyes.

"Ow," he said.

"Stay *right here*," I said, and took three long steps forward before scenting the air again.

No limestone. Nessa's magic didn't extend this far. I returned to Quentin, sniffing first one wall and then the other before tapping on the left wall. "Here," I said. "Should there be a door here?"

"I don't know," he protested. "I've never been in here before! Maybe there's supposed to be a door, maybe not!"

"It feels like there should be a door," I said, and I tapped again. The sound that came back was hollow. I pressed my palms against the wall. "I don't suppose you can help me out again?" I asked. The wood grew cool under my hands, as if the knowe itself was saying no. I nodded, taking my hands away. "That's what I was afraid of."

"What do you mean?"

"I mean the doors in the main hall are hidden because the courtiers and nobles don't want to think about the servants they don't see. The people who clean the rooms and deliver the drinks have to be able to move privately and discreetly around the knowe. In here, on this side, there's no reason to put that amount of work into smoothing out the seams. The architects wouldn't take the time, and neither would the knowe. If there's supposed to be a door here, someone is hiding it."

"Meaning what?"

"Meaning you need to be quiet and let me work."

Gwragedd Annwn are fabulous illusionists, second only to the Gwragen. That's never really made sense to me, since we like to simplify the types of magic to illusions being Titania's purview, but the Merrow are her descendants, and they thrive entirely in the water, and so are the Daoine Sidhe, whose strength is in the blood. Maybe being descended from the appropriate member of the Three makes things easier, rather than making them likely. I don't know. What I do know is that the Gwragedd Annwn can weave illusions so perfect they seem realer than reality, and if Nessa's magic was stronger here, it was probably because she had been awake and cajoled into producing her own prison.

I drew the knife from my belt, my own magic gathering around me as I stared fixedly at the wall. This time, I was going to be using my own blood to fuel the working, and I drew the blade across my palm, tensing my hand enough to split the skin and muscle beneath in a single smooth line. Quentin winced.

"I know you heal faster than is fair, but I really wish you'd stop cutting your *hands*," he said. "What happens when you turn yourself mostly human again by mistake and you don't heal like it's your job, huh? What happens when you cut a tendon and it doesn't just snap back into place?"

I shot him a quick look as I raised my cupped hand to my mouth. "But you can make a bowl with your hand, so the blood doesn't just run down your arm," I said. Ease of delivery is why most of the blood-workers I've known have focused on the hands, even though most of them don't make cuts as large or deep as I do. They're not racing against their own bodies to get to the blood before their skin seals up again and locks it safely inside.

For as much as people yell at me for bleeding too much, it's surprisingly difficult to get as much blood as I need.

Fortunately, this cut had been deep enough to bleed considerably before the skin healed over. I lowered my head and drank as deeply as I could, tasting the cut-grass flavor of my magic in the coppery richness of my own veins. I used to hate the taste of blood. I'm still not the biggest fan, given the memories and complications it brings with it when it comes from someone else, but at least these days I can appreciate how much blood is informed by magic.

I raised my head again, resisting the urge to wipe my bloody palm against my still mostly-clean dress as I closed my eyes and focused on the idea of the wall, relaxing as a twisting web of tangled purple and pale gray lines sprang into existence. It was nestled atop a deeper purple and polished maple macramé that looked . . . more stable, somehow, like it had been here long enough to root and settle itself. The two magics were entirely separate and distinct, which was a relief. I wasn't going to unweave the knowe by pulling on the illusion I knew had to be keeping me from the door.

Of all the gifts of my bloodline, the ability to unweave other people's magic seems like it would be the most useful, but it's actually the least helpful in a crisis because it takes time and concentration; it isn't something I can do swiftly, not like picking out a scent or borrowing the magic in someone else's blood. Maybe I'll get faster with practice. Maybe I won't. Everyone needs limits.

I reached out with one hand, grasping the first glittering gray strand where it lingered in the air and giving it a short, sharp yank. It unraveled, releasing several purple strands to wave languidly in the air. I pulled on them, and then on another gray, and another, continuing to pull and twist and separate until the whole structure began to look frayed around the edges. This time I reached out with both hands, grasping what remained and yanking sharply.

The spell collapsed with a sudden rush of limestone and creeping thistle, perfuming the air so heavily that Quentin gasped, finally catching the familiar scent of his childhood—what? Babysitter? Guardian? What would a seneschal have been to the Crown Prince of a High Kingdom?

I opened my eyes. The smooth stretch of wall was gone, broken by the outline of a humble door, the kind of door that led to nothing special, closets or storerooms and the like.

"Cover your eyes," I said. He gave me a startled look. "If she has no illusions and the sight of her kills me, I'll get better." Probably. "You won't. So cover your eyes, or my nerves won't be able to handle opening this door."

He put his hands over his eyes. I reached for the doorknob, pausing at the last moment to check it for pressure plates like the one that had been on her quarters. There were none. "This is either a solution or massive stupidity," I said, and tried the knob.

It was locked. Of course, it was locked. If you're trying to get someone out of the way—or to hide a corpse—you don't shove them into an unlocked room if you have any choice in the matter. That's not hiding someone; that's putting them on a shelf until someone needs a roll of toilet paper and opens the wrong door.

I sighed heavily. The problem I'd had earlier was looming again. I didn't have my lockpicks with me, and I'd given Raj back his. I glanced at Quentin. "I don't suppose you have your lockpicking kit with you, do you?"

"My knight would send me to my room without dessert for a week if I didn't carry them with me everywhere I go," he said, and produced the kit from inside his tunic, offering it to me with a cheeky grin that was no less recognizable for being on the wrong face. I took the kit and wrinkled my nose at him, then bent and began working on the lock.

It was a fairly old-fashioned piece of hardware, good enough for locking someone in a room and not letting them out, but not remotely good enough to stop me. In under a minute, I was bundling the tools up again and passing them to Quentin, who tucked them back into his tunic. "Sounds like your knight is pretty good at her job," I said lightly.

He kept smiling. "She has her moments," he said.

I rolled my eyes and grasped the doorknob again. This time when I twisted, it turned easily, and the door swung inward to reveal what it had been hiding.

On the other side was a storeroom filled with racks of towels and pristine, sparkling dishes, like something out of the Bed Bath & Beyond attached to Medieval Times. Half the room was also filled with a wall of water.

It split the room almost flawlessly, reaching from the floor to the ceiling, glimmering and clear. On the other side of the water, towels and napkins floated on a gentle current, moving around the figure of the woman who hung suspended in the center of the flood.

I blinked. "That's new," I said. The water was acting as a sort of refraction device. I could tell the woman—whose eyes were closed, and who appeared to be sleeping—wasn't wearing any illusions, but the sight of her didn't hurt with the water in the way. She was a modern-day Medusa, wrapped in the loving embrace of her own rippling mirror. "Keep your eyes closed."

"What's going on? Did you find Nessa?"

"Pretty sure, yeah, and not sure," I said, reaching out with my bloody hand to touch the surface of the water. That was either the best thing or the worst thing I could possibly have done, and I had no idea which it was going to be.

Eventually, I was going to have to learn to figure that out first, but since I'd been doing pretty well with my "be basically indestructible and refuse to stop moving forward" agenda so far, this didn't seem like the biggest risk.

As soon as I touched the wall of water, it popped like a soap bubble, cascading down on us and driving me back until I hit the opposite wall. Quentin, who had been standing to the side of the doorway, was merely soaked to the skin. He made a protesting noise, but he didn't uncover his eyes, and I appreciated his obedience more than I could say.

I coughed and spat, trying to get the water out of my nose and mouth even as I wiped my eyes. Nessa was sprawled facedown in

the middle of the storeroom, not having been washed remotely as
far as she should have been. I picked myself up and took a step
forward, my dress impeding my motion as it hadn't before now that
it was soaked through and clinging to my legs.

"Excuse me, Nessa?" I said. "Are you awake?"

She didn't move. That didn't necessarily mean anything. My
voice was unfamiliar, and she'd been abducted; if she was awake,
she had no reason to make this easy on me. If anything, she had
good reason to make it as hard as possible.

"If you're awake, please veil yourself," I said. "My name is Sir
October Daye, Knight of Lost Words. I have been invited from the
Kingdom in the Mists to hold my wedding here, and you're supposed to be the one overseeing the organization. Your quarters are
full of boobytraps, including a bunch of pixie-sized elf-shot—that's
pretty awesome, considering that my groom is currently unconscious, and supposed to stay that way for a century—and a Doppelganger has been pretending to be you." I didn't tell her about
either of the dead men. She could handle the knowledge and the
guilt, if it came with any, once she was herself again.

She tensed but still didn't lift her face from the floor. I realized,
perhaps belatedly, what she was waiting to hear.

"The High King was not harmed; the crown remains where it
was placed," I said. "The High Queen sits her throne, sick with
worry for her absent seneschal. I have yet to see the chatelaine, but
her magic was fresh in the hall outside your rooms, and I believe
her to be unharmed."

Slowly, Nessa moved, sliding her hands under herself and using
them to push her torso away from the floor, slowly moving into a
seated position. She kept her head bowed, hair hanging to conceal
her face.

"The *thing* was in my quarters when I returned from my duties
in the kitchen," she said, voice low and dull. "I had to convince the
staff to allow your friend to bake a cake in their ovens, to cast stasis spells in the presence of their supplies. It was no easy task, but
it needed to be done before the rest could be put in order. And
when I went to wash the flour from my hands and wipe the grease
from my brow, there was a monster in the place where I should
have been safest." She was beginning to shake. "I lowered my illusions and showed the thing my face with nothing to protect it, and
it only laughed. It looked on me and *laughed*."

I suppose if your best weapon had always been your face, having someone shrug it off without noticing would be disconcerting. I certainly don't like it when people shrug off being stabbed, even though I do it all the time. "Doppelgangers don't see the world the way the rest of us do," I said. "They look at people as pieces to be stolen, and it wanted to steal you."

"I know that," she snapped. "It held iron to my throat and bade me make myself disappear, and then it dragged me through the halls to this room, where it sealed me inside."

That didn't answer how she'd been compelled to cast a nigh-unbreakable illusion over the door. Thankfully, Quentin was as curious as I was.

"How did it make you hide the door?" he asked.

Nessa was still for a long moment before she said, anguished, "It told me it had only come to kill the High King, and if I concealed the door, it would spare the High Queen. I'm sure it was treason to do as I was bid. I know my life is forfeit, but the children have been gone so long, and I miss my babies so much, and I was not willing to let a monster make orphans of them if I had the chance to stop it. *Ní dhéanfainn dílleachtaí de mo mhuintir.*"

She sounded utterly miserable. I shook my head, wet hair slapping against my cheeks. Any curl Stacy had managed to tease into it was gone, done in by the combination of horrible things I'd done to it instead of having dinner.

"No one's going to be tried for treason," I said. "You had iron at your throat, you're allowed to make some bad decisions."

"Have you been in here this whole time?" asked Quentin.

Nessa made a small sound of distress, but there was no hint of recognition in her tone as she continued, for which I was honestly grateful. The last thing we needed right now was for her to figure out who he was somehow and rat us out to the High King. "Once the door was sealed and hidden, I had nothing to eat and no way to escape. If I wrapped myself in water, I would need nothing else. The illusion I spun at the monster's command—it was *ró-láidir.* I had nothing else to give. I still . . ." She made a sound, a small hic-cupping sound that was neither a laugh nor a sob, but something trapped in the middle. "I still have nothing more to give."

Meaning she couldn't cast an illusion strong enough to protect everyone else from her. Oh, this wasn't great. "What do you need? What will make you feel better?"

"I need water from the lake where I was born," she said. "I keep a supply in my quarters." She raised her head a little, enough for one eye to peek through the curtain of her hair, which was already dryer than my own, as if her body was drinking in the water. "If you could . . . ?"

I wasn't sure anything that had been in her quarters over the last three days could be trusted, given the circumstances, but I wasn't going to tell her that. "Hey, Cillian," I said, voice as light as I could make it. "Can you go and find my aunt for me, please?"

We were only traveling with one person who could arguably be called my aunt, even if I wasn't stupid enough to call her that to her face. Quentin's eyes widened. "You think she can help?"

"Based on what she told us earlier, if anyone can help, it's going to be her," I said, glancing back at Nessa. "It's worth a try."

"All right." He retreated to the door, where he paused. "Are you sure it's a good idea for me to leave you alone?"

"Kid, Tybalt's not going to kill either one of us any more than he already is."

"Got it," said Quentin, and nodded decisively before he ducked out the door, leaving me alone with Nessa.

It was almost a relief to be left with someone who didn't know me or expect anything from me. I sagged where I was, and must have sighed a little, because she looked up through her hair again, a furrow marring her perfect brow.

"You do not like the boy?"

"I love the boy," I said. "He's my son by all but blood, and I love the boy so much it scares me, because I'm going to have to give him back to his parents eventually. They didn't agree to lose him forever when they handed him off to me, and there's no way for me to keep him. He's not mine."

Even when she didn't know we were talking about Quentin— even when she didn't really know me at all—it hurt to admit that I was going to lose him. No, not lose; loss implied that he was going to be taken, when anyone who knew me knew I was going to let him go.

And when he came back here, when he stopped being Squire Quentin of no particular name or bloodline and became Sir Quentin Sollys of the Westlands, named and anointed next ruler of our High Kingdom, I wouldn't even be able to say I missed him. He'd have a place and a family and a world that didn't have any room left in it for me, and Oberon damn it all, this wasn't a problem I'd seen coming back when I could have gotten out of this. Back when he'd asked me to be his squire and I'd offered my pathetic list of reasons I was a bad choice for any sort of real responsibility, I had never thought to include "if you're my squire, I'll love you too much, and you'll take a piece of me with you when you inevitably have to leave."

I'd been so broken when I came back from my exile in the pond, so convinced that no one was ever going to really love me and I was never going to really love anyone, ever again. I'd been a fool.

Nessa's frown deepened before she ducked her head again. "I've never had children," she said. "Men of the Gwragedd Annwn are rare, and no one else can lie with us past the dawn without fear of being struck dead when the sun comes up and our illusions come down. It seems like a great challenge, to allow your heart to rove freely outside your body, and not spend all your time kept rigid by fear. If you are the woman whose marriage I was to facilitate, I know you have a child of your body, as well as this boy who is the child of your heart, yes?"

"So you do know who I am, then."

Nessa scoffed. "As if anyone could *not* know who you are? King-breaker and chaos-chosen, who's been overthrowing regimes up and down the Pacific coast as if it were some sort of wild game. The High King speaks of you with both admiration and horror. I think you know where my boy is." Her tone changed on her last sentence, becoming sterner, almost demanding. She didn't raise her head, however. She wasn't threatening me.

"I don't know what you mean," I said carefully.

"The Crown Prince was sent to the Mists for his fosterage," she said. "I'm not meant to know that, but I knew the woman who came to make your kingdom's case to the High King and Queen. I had seen her before, when good King Windermere died, and it was necessary to name a successor to his place."

I blinked. I hadn't heard about Evening actually traveling to Maples when Gilad died, and I knew the High King hadn't come to us. He would never have placed her puppet on the throne if he had. Anyone who looked at the false Queen could tell in an instant that she wasn't Gilad's daughter, as she had claimed to be; she was of a completely different bloodline, for one thing, and she looked nothing like him. Also she was terrible, but if Faerie had a rule about not handing terrible people thrones, we'd have a lot fewer Kings and Queens.

"She traveled here in the aftermath of the earthquake, carrying King Windermere's bequeathments and begging his daughter be allowed to take the throne despite the challenges against her. He had never married, you see, and her mother was of mixed blood, which carried almost as much stigma in those days as human blood. Since the hope chests have been lost, one after another, it has become more and more difficult to correct a course once it has been etched in blood and bone."

That made sense. I nodded before realizing that she couldn't see me with her head bowed. "Yeah, okay," I said. "That was Evening. She's sort of . . ." I paused. I couldn't call her the worst anymore, not after dealing with my own mother over the past year or so, but I couldn't call her anything much better. ". . . awful," I finished.

Nessa laughed. "Yes, awful. She came, and she spoke to the King and Queen, and when she left, they were different than they were. The King had always been far too aware of how his own parents died, at an assassin's hands, and he restructured his guard in the wake of her time here, dismissing the soldiers who remembered what it was to fight and replacing them with the untried children of the nobility. He seemed to care less for his own legacy. And then she came again, although I advised against allowing her, and they sent my boy into fosterage, even though they had always promised him they would never do such a thing. They took him away and left us with barely the time to say farewell. I was hoping he might accompany you to your marriage."

"Why would you think that?"

"Sollys heirs are drawn to heroism. He would have gravitated toward you as a moth flies toward a flame, looking for his own immolation."

I wasn't sure how I felt about that description. Luckily, I didn't have long to dwell on it, as voices drifted in from the hall.

"—this way, come on!"

"Slow down, kid, I don't rush." The Luidaeg sounded more amused than anything else. Good. This was going to be easier if she wasn't already in a rotten mood. "I'm too old to rush. I did my last rushing in the 1500s. Didn't want to hang out too close to a bunch of humans who'd gone and contracted the Black Death.

Humans were *filthy* during the 1500s. I don't know how we got any changelings out of that century. Yuck."

"I left Toby alone and armed with someone she doesn't already know."

"Yes, so you've said, multiple times. I still don't rush. It's not in my nature."

Quentin appeared in the doorway, a worried expression on his face. I had no idea how large the knowe was, but even assuming it was only the size of Goldengreen, he must have taken at least part of the trip at a dead run to be back so soon. I made a mental note to be properly impressed once I knew the actual distances involved.

"They're in here," he called, over his shoulder.

"Anyone bleeding?" The Luidaeg managed to make the question sound almost academic, like she didn't particularly care about the answer one way or another. She appeared behind him, once again wearing her human teenager disguise: overalls, no shirt, no bra, electrical tape in her hair. She paused to take in the sight of me sitting on the floor in my drenched gown, next to a virtually dry Nessa. I raised one hand, wiggling my fingers in a small wave.

"Hey," I said.

"Hey," she replied, and stepped around Quentin, into the room. "So why exactly am I here?"

"Nessa spent the last three days in some sort of big, weird water bubble," I said. "At least, three days is the best guess I have so far for how long she spent there. Could have been longer if this has been brewing for more time than we currently think. Before she bubbled herself up, her captor forced her to cast an unbreakable illusion and hide the door."

"Looks broken to me," said the Luidaeg.

"I am a breaker of the unbreakable," I said, aiming for the level of pompous portent that Tybalt could put into asking for a toaster waffle.

The Luidaeg snorted. "Sure, kiddo, keep telling yourself that. So if the illusion's been broken, the problem is . . . ?"

"She spun a really strong illusion and then spent three days in a bubble with nothing to eat and I'm guessing no real sleep to speak of," I said. "She can't spin the illusions that would make her safe to be around without water from the lake where she was born, and that's in her quarters, which are heavily boobytrapped, and which the Doppelganger has had unfettered access to for at least three days."

"Oh, is *that* all?" The Luidaeg came fully into the room, walking toward Nessa, who kept her head bowed and her face hidden behind her hair. The Luidaeg bent, touching the top of Nessa's head with surprising gentleness before grasping her upper arms and pulling her, carefully but inexorably, to her feet.

"I'll hurt you," cautioned Nessa.

"You won't," said the Luidaeg, and released her arms, reaching out to move Nessa's hair delicately aside. She had angled the Gwragedd Annwn so Quentin and I still couldn't see her face, but we could see the Luidaeg's as she looked into Nessa's eyes. Her expression softened, her own eyes bleeding from the muddy blue-brown she favored toward their true—or trueish, it's hard to tell when you're talking about the Luidaeg—clear glass green.

"*There* you are," she said, with absolute and unmistakable fondness in her tone. "Now I have to ask, Nessa, daughter of Donal, son of Tosia, daughter of Ismene, called Black Annis by those who speak of her in this modern world, will you consent to my concealing your splendor from those it might harm? Even knowing you will have to trust me to remove my own working?"

Nessa stiffened, not pulling away, but clearly startled. She started to raise her hand, then appeared to think better of it and stopped with it somewhere around the level of her heart. "You . . . you're . . ."

"I am," the Luidaeg affirmed.

"Then is . . . Ismene?"

"No," said the Luidaeg, with deep and genuine sorrow. "Your First died as she was rumored to have died, when Conláed hunted her through marsh and fen with fire in his hands and murder in his unthawed heart. His own death followed on his heels, but not fast enough to save my sister."

Nessa sighed, deep and slow. "And they . . . they know?" she asked, with a little gesture of her head toward me and Quentin. In that moment, I believed she could find the strength to drown us both if she felt like it would keep the Luidaeg's secret and was glad beyond measure that she wasn't going to have to.

The Luidaeg followed Nessa's gesture, her eyes lighting on me. Then she smiled, a bright, earnest expression that would have seemed entirely alien on her face not all that long before. When I'd met her, she had been an angry, bitter woman living in self-imposed isolation on the edge of the sea, where she could watch the descendants of the people who'd slaughtered her children without ever being a part of their lives, where she could hold her breath and let the world pass her by.

Now, she was still angry, and she was still bitter, and she had good reason to be both of those things. But she was also thawing out, one tiny bit at a time, mellowing into the warm, generous woman she must have been before Titania and her descendants had committed truly monstruous acts in their efforts to make her Faerie's greatest monster. Protective and kind, within the limits of her geasa.

All she'd ever wanted was a family.

"They know exactly who I am," she said, attention going back to Nessa. "Better than anyone has in centuries, and the best part is, they don't care. The kid beat me at chess last week."

I glanced at Quentin. He hadn't told me that.

The Luidaeg continued, "Me, the sea witch, terror of the tides, he beat *me*, and he didn't even have the common sense to look ashamed of himself. Called me an old woman and said I should learn some gambits invented in the last century because he knows who I am, and he knows what I am—and he's *not afraid of me*. Now, normally, I'd have to charge you for an illusion, but in this case, both of the people behind you owe me debts for favors done, and I need them alive so I can collect. That means hiding your pretty face from the world is an act of selfishness, and I'm still allowed to be selfish, thank Mom. So, will you allow it?"

"It would be an honor," said Nessa, sounding faintly awestruck.

The Luidaeg laughed. Her magic began to gather, the smell of the sea, brackish and sweet at the same time, a living contradiction. The corners of the room darkened and swelled with unspeakable power, and what felt like a wave of pressure crashed down on all of us, weighing and compressing the room as the spell was finished and the magic broke. The Luidaeg took her hands away from Nessa's face.

"There you go," she said. "Perfectly safe, until I release you. I *will* have to charge you if you want your lake water purified and rendered safe for use, but the price will be small—a lock of hair, or a rude word said in the High King's presence. I swear to you, the price will be small."

Nessa nodded to the Luidaeg and turned to face the rest of us. She looked like the illusion of herself the Doppelganger had worn, the woman robbed of her supernatural power to hurt us with a glance. She sagged slightly, wobbling, and I realized how tired she had to be. This was a woman who had been ambushed in her home, taken captive, and held herself in magical stasis for three days while believing she was responsible for the death of her liege.

"Please," she said, and there was a world of pleading in that single word.

I shook my head. "He's alive," I said. "No one blames you for what happened. We all know you didn't do this willingly. But I'm afraid I can't let you rest yet."

She blinked. Whatever response she'd been expecting, it wasn't that. "He's truly alive?"

"He's alive," I echoed. People who aren't used to being knocked out by Doppelgangers and stuffed into closets sometimes need a little more reassurance when that kind of thing happens to them. For me and most of the people who spend any amount of time with me, this was sort of a best-case kidnapping. Nessa hadn't been seriously hurt and neither had the High King. She'd just taken a stressful three-day nap.

Of course, two members of the guard were dead, and that was going to be heartbreaking for everyone who knew them, but I hadn't. I could keep moving forward like this was any case, and I've found that when I do that, I tend to drag the investigation along behind me.

Nessa blinked again. "I thought . . . when that creature took me, I thought . . ."

"Near as I can guess, it was waiting for us to show up so that it could assassinate the High King with a known king-breaker in the knowe," I said grimly. "No one with any sense would look at that situation and *not* believe we'd either smuggled the Doppelganger in with us or hired them in the first place—if people even believed there had been a Doppelganger. I'm pretty sure that if I hadn't forced the issue, the plan was to replace one of us during the day, and then have the Doppelganger perform the assassination while they looked like me, or May, or Stacy."

Depending on how much the Doppelganger knew—which hadn't been all that much, as such things went—it could have decided to target the Luidaeg, or even Oberon. I couldn't quite decide whether that would have ended with Oberon locked in a supply closet, still unwilling to be anything more than a silent tag-along, or whether it would have ended with the King of Faerie returned and the Doppelganger in pieces all across the Eastern seaboard. Either way, it would have been a disaster, and I was incalculably relieved by my own inability to let anything go.

"Ah," said Nessa. "I see. It may also have been waiting to see if you brought the Crown Prince with you."

I raised an eyebrow.

"I apologize if you didn't know," she said. "As I said before, the rumor in the knowe is that he was sent to the Mists, to place him as far from Toronto as possible while Their Majesties addressed the pressures that had demanded a fosterage to begin with. Further, the rumor states that he has been squired to begin his proper knightly training, and that he serves a king-breaker."

"Huh," I said. "Don't know of any other king-breakers active in the Mists right now. We're not the only Kingdom on the Pacific Coast, you know. He could be in Silences, or Angels, or shoveling cow shit on the Golden Shore. I brought my squire with me." I gestured for Quentin to step forward, in all his faded Banshee glory.

Nessa looked at him without recognition, studying his face for a moment before she sighed and turned away. "Then the rumors were wrong," she said. "But believing them may still have motivated the timing of this attack. Kill the Crown Prince and the High King at once—and change the course of a continent."

"Um, isn't the High Queen considered an equal ruler?" I asked. "And then there's the little sister—she could inherit."

"But not for years yet," said Nessa. "If Quentin were to be killed, Penthea would require a regent to hold the throne, and war would surely follow, for those who seek power are not going to sit idly back while a little girl plays at being High Queen. And there are . . . aspects of the High Queen's past that would preclude her taking the throne in the eyes of many of the same individuals."

Meaning Nessa knew that Maida had been born a changeling, and even though she hadn't been mortal in decades, maybe centuries, the prejudices in Faerie can run deep enough and be arbitrary enough to prevent a peaceful transfer of power. Kill the sitting King and his eldest heir, make sure the truth about the High Queen gets out, destabilize the Westlands.

I was going to have to give Quentin an extra slice of wedding cake to thank him for realizing he needed a new face if he was going to attend the wedding.

"But it's all right, it didn't happen, and October here is a hero and a busybody, meaning she's going to do everything in her inconsiderable power to annoy whoever arranged your abduction into giving themselves up," said the Luidaeg, soothingly. Nessa turned to look at her. "Now, where can we take you that you'll feel safe? Your quarters are out of the question, I'm afraid. It's going to take a while to clean and search them and verify that they're safe."

"Can I stay with you?" asked Nessa. "Please, I won't be any trouble, I won't ask for anything else if you allow it, but please . . ." She was looking at the Luidaeg the way the Roane did, eyes bright and wide and filled with depthless pleading, like this was the only thing she had ever really wanted in her entire life. Like the Luidaeg could make her dreams come true by saying yes.

The Luidaeg sighed. "I'm not your First," she said. "I love you, but not the way she would. I don't have that in me anymore for anyone who isn't already mine. I'm sorry. I know how lost you have to feel, not knowing your beginnings, but I can't be your harbor. You can stay with our group, for now, unless the High King calls you, but I can't promise I'll be there the whole time."

Nessa nodded. "That will be . . . more than I have any right to have asked you for." She bent until her forehead nearly brushed her knees. "Thank you," she said, in a very small voice.

The Luidaeg grimaced. "And with that settled, Toby, we should get back to your room, both so you can help with searching it for traps, and so your kitty cat can see some actual proof that you're not dead *before* he starts a diplomatic incident."

I felt my eyes widen. That was something I hadn't considered. If Tybalt lost his temper inside the seat of the Westlands . . . "Let's go," I said, standing hurriedly.

The Luidaeg smirked. "Yes," she agreed, "let's."

ELEVEN

QUENTIN GETTING BACK SO quickly with the Luidaeg made more sense once we were in the hall and I started to understand the geography slightly better. From the storeroom where we'd found Nessa to the hallway where the guest quarters were linked was less than a ten-minute walk, and he hadn't been walking. He'd been running as fast as his legs would carry him, anxious to resolve a bad situation that managed to touch on both sides of his life at the same time.

Poor kid. I'd always known my getting married in Toronto would be hard on him, but I hadn't expected quite this level of difficulty.

Nessa held tight to the Luidaeg's hand as we walked, ignoring the startled looks we got from passing locals. Anyone who knew her also knew what had happened, and clearly didn't understand how she could be walking so calmly with a group of strangers. But as long as she was with the Luidaeg, she was calm, and we could use that.

The door to my temporary quarters was open, and voices, raised in argument, drifted out into the hall.

"—one good reason why I shouldn't go and find her?" Tybalt sounded incredibly collected, almost calm, which didn't match up with his volume, which had a strained quality that told me it had been creeping steadily upward for some time.

"Because you've just been elf-shot and you're going to be wobbly for a while," said Walther, reasonably. "If I didn't carry the elf-shot counter whenever I was going anywhere with Toby, you'd still be unconscious while I finished brewing, so I think you can afford to take a little time to recover."

"Because she's *fine*," said Raj, sounding bored. "She's Toby. She's always fine."

Oh, I teach the worst lessons to my squires. Whether I mean to or not, I'm forever in the process of breaking them.

"Because the sea witch is with her, and that means we need to be more worried about everyone else in this knowe, and possibly everyone along this seaboard, than we are about the indestructible king-breaker," said Nolan.

"Because the air says she's right outside in the hall," said Cassandra.

There was a pause. We walked a little faster.

Not fast enough: Tybalt appeared in the doorway, gripping the frame with one white-knuckled hand, clearly recovered from the elf-shot, although he was still paler than I liked. The strained look around his eyes was probably more attributable to me than being woken from a century-long sleep before the alarm went off, and I had a split second to feel bad about that before he was sighing my name like it was an undiscovered sonnet by Shakespeare and flinging himself the last few feet between us.

I braced for the collision, opening my arms, and when he slammed into me, it was a very mutual embrace, his arms locking around my torso and mine around his shoulders. He buried his face in the damp but drying tangle of my hair, taking a deep, shuddering breath.

"Come on, kid," I heard the Luidaeg say to Nessa. "Let's take you to meet the rest of this sideshow of ridiculous horrors. They're going to be a few minutes."

"I'll see you inside," said Quentin.

As soon as we were alone in the hall, Tybalt pulled back, sliding his hands up to press against the sides of my jaw as he studied my face. "You weren't there," he said. "The last thing I remembered was opening the shadows, and then sleep claimed me, and I had been pulling you with me to the other side, and I woke up, and you *weren't there*."

"You fell into shadow," I said, voice soft. "Carrying me and Caitir. Candela can access the Shadow Roads on their own, and I can borrow magic from blood. I didn't dare try yours, not with elf-shot in your system and your memories likely to make me lose control of your magic, and so I had to use hers to open us a gate out of the Shadow Roads. I'm not hurt. Out of the three of us, I'm the only one who wasn't hurt."

"I'm supposed to *protect* you," he said, hiccupping with the effort of not sobbing. He leaned forward, resting his forehead against mine. "I'm supposed to protect you, and I let myself drop you in the dark, alone, with no way out."

As afraid as I had always been of being stranded on the Shadow Roads, how much more afraid must he have been, knowing them the way he did, understanding them as intimately as only a King of Cats could. I reached up and gripped his wrists, holding his hands where they were.

"I got out," I said, voice low. "You don't always have to protect me, as long as you want to keep trying. The trying is what matters, and when we fell into the dark, I had two ways out. You, and her. I used her because it was safer for me, because I'm going to make it to our wedding."

He laughed, a little unsteadily. "Am I?"

"Of course you are. You're the King of Cats, and you're my fiancé, and I think there's a very good chance at this point that you're my one true love." I smiled at him, as earnestly as I could. "We're going to be the sort of story people write ballads about, only we're not going to end with either one of us lying in a shallow grave somewhere, because I flat-out refuse to let that be the last verse for us. You're going to be at the wedding. You get to make me deal with whatever pureblood bullshit you've dredged out of your ancient books of etiquette, and see me in my wedding dress, which I know is going to be gorgeous, because you have much better taste in clothing than I do, and is also going to be covered in blood before the end of the ceremony—"

"I have already taken that into account," he said, sounding much more composed.

"I knew you would. Now, are we good? This time, I didn't run off and endanger myself without you."

"No, I endangered you quite enough for the both of us." His expression darkened a bit, but didn't return to its earlier misery, and that was more than good enough for me.

"Excellent. So let's go see how chaotic things are in our room— you didn't think we'd have actual privacy before the wedding, did you?" I let go of his wrists. "You're too smart to have made a mistake that massive."

Tybalt scoffed and let me go, taking a step away before capturing my hand in his and pulling me along with him into the room where our friends—and Nessa—were waiting.

And boy howdy, were they waiting. They seemed to cover every available surface, making me feel abstractly as if I'd just walked into a drama club meeting from one of the terrible teen movies that Chelsea liked to co-opt my living room in order to watch. Her mother didn't care for cinema of any kind, and Etienne apparently had a tendency to become completely enraptured by moving media, making him the binge-watcher to end all bingers. I thought that was hilarious, but apparently straining my friend's marriage because I thought it was funny wasn't appropriate, so the works of John Hughes and Kenny Ortega got to dominate my television instead of theirs.

Weirdly, Tybalt didn't seem to mind the teen movie festival intermittently spinning up in our living room. When I'd asked him about it, he'd just laughed and said it was payback for the number of Shakespeare productions he made the kids sit through.

So walking into a scene from one of those movies was startling, but not as jarring as it could have been. The teenagers had claimed one of the short couches, the four of them piled on it like so many puppies, personal space forgotten in their rush to make sure no one sat on the floor. Raj hadn't bothered switching to cat form before sprawling across Quentin and Dean's laps, while Chelsea was perched on the back of the couch with one leg over each sitting boy's shoulders, twisting a lock of Quentin's hair between her fingers.

Walther and Nolan, on the other hand, were both on the floor, Walther slouched and Nolan as ramrod straight as if he were settled in a proper throne. Cassandra, interestingly enough, wasn't sitting with her boyfriend; instead, she and her mother were sitting on another of the short couches. Kerry was bustling around the room, offering cookies to anyone who didn't already have one. Which was everyone, meaning either the cookies had just come out or they were really, really good.

May and Jazz were standing, leaning against each other, both blessedly awake. Nessa and the Luidaeg were already seated on the last of the short couches, Nessa leaning into the sea witch like she knew no other comfort in this world. Oberon was leaning against the wall between the two couches, still in his nondescript "I don't matter, don't pay attention to me" guise. They all looked around when Tybalt and I stepped inside, and I offered them a wan smile.

"Um," I said. "Hey."

"October Christine Daye," said Stacy, voice getting louder with each passing syllable. She stood, Cassandra leaning to the side to clear her way, and strode toward me, jabbing a finger at my chest. "What. Did you do. To that *dress*?!"

"Um." It didn't feel like a question with any good answers. Plus there were so many of them. "I got it wet? And cold? And I think maybe I bled on it a little . . ."

Quentin made a stifled choking noise. I glanced at him. "A *little*?" he asked. "Toby, you had a whole knife sticking out of your side! A knife, just jammed into the side of you like it had any business being there in the first place! You bled on that thing a *lot*."

"Yeah, but only on the black part." I looked back at Stacy, who seemed like the much more immediate danger. "I got stabbed, if that's what you're asking, and it feels sort of like you already knew that before you said anything, so I guess I don't understand why this has to be some sort of a production when we have other things we need to be worried about right now—"

"I am never going to live in a world where you getting *stabbed* isn't something to worry about!" snapped Stacy.

I turned pleadingly to Tybalt. "A little help here?"

"Oh, I think she's doing quite well without my assistance," he said. "But if you insist, I have never been one to leave a lady fair in distress."

"See? Even Tybalt thinks you need to worry more about getting *actually stabbed*." Stacy jabbed her finger at my chest again. "If you won't worry about yourself, you shouldn't be surprised when we do the worrying for you!"

"I'm not surprised," I sighed. "More just frustrated that you want to focus on this *now*."

"She has a point," said Walther. "Two people are dead."

"Speaking of dead people, where's Caitir?" I asked, looking around like our temporarily resident Candela might be crouching in the corner with her Merry Dancers. "Did you wake her up?"

"He did, and she immediately ran off to tell the High King what was going on," said Raj, sounding incredibly bored with the whole situation, which was apparently not rising to meet his standards for a stirring afternoon. "If you didn't want him to know that you were causing trouble, you should have asked us to sit on her."

"I don't think sitting on a Candela will stop them from opening a doorway into the shadows," objected Chelsea.

Raj waved a hand, brushing her objections away. "We would have tried, which is more than we did in the absence of instruction."

"The High King was there when we discovered the Doppelganger, and when we found the traps on Nessa's room," I said, more amused than aggravated by his ongoing attempts to be as frustrating as possible. "Pretty sure he already knows I'm causing trouble. Or, well, not causing trouble, but trouble-adjacent once again."

"That should go on your business cards," said Quentin.

"We are getting away from the point," said Stacy, jabbing her finger at me a third time. "You were supposed to be sitting down to a nice, calm, diplomatic dinner with the High King, not causing an inter-Kingdom incident and getting yourself *stabbed*!"

"It's a pretty small hole," I said. "You can stitch it up later, right?"

Stacy made a disgusted noise, throwing her hands up, and turned to stalk back to the room she'd claimed as her prep space. "It's fine, let her go," said May when I started to turn and follow. "You know how she is."

"I do," I agreed, slumping as I turned back toward the group. "I mean, I thought she knew how I was, too, but I do know how she is." Stacy had been like this since we were children, upset when thwarted, slow to recover from a seeming offense, then all smiles and sunshine once the moment passed, like a thing only mattered while it was actually happening, and could be dismissed as past and resolved the second it was done. Me being stabbed had apparently offended the princess wedding fantasy she'd constructed around the occasion.

To be fair, we'd spent the normal amount of time daydreaming about our weddings when we were children, and she had always wanted the big ceremony and the impossible ideal. And she was the one who'd gotten a local community center and a family friend ordained by the Universal Life Church. I was about to live her dream, and I wasn't taking it nearly seriously enough to deserve it.

"Here, you look like you could use these," said Kerry, pushing two cookies into my hand and offering an encouraging smile. "I'm just going to go talk her down." She handed the tray to Tybalt, and followed Stacy's path to the changing room, letting herself inside with a little wave for the rest of us.

Walther pushed himself off the floor and moved to join Cassandra, pausing along the way to collect the tray of cookies. "What?" he asked when Tybalt lifted an eyebrow. "They're good cookies!"

"They are at that," I agreed, looking at the two in my hand. Chocolate chunk and maple ginger, from the look and smell of them. "But we still have the whole Doppelganger and boobytraps issue to deal with."

"Spoilsport," said Raj.

"This was an attack on the Mists as much as it was an attack on the High Kingdom of the Westlands," said Nolan, with unusual gravity. "Had the Doppelganger impersonating the Lady Nessa been successful in the attempt to harm the High King after Sir Daye's arrival, the attack would no doubt have been attributed to her reputation as a king-breaker. Even if we could prove she had been in no way involved, the rumor would have spread and undermined any faith in the High King's heir."

"Princess Penthea is still too young to inherit without a regent, and very few would stand for High Queen Maida ruling alone," said Nessa. "I cannot speak to the reasons why, but they are well known among the highest ranking of the nobles, the ones who circle like wolves, seeking to sink their teeth into the first available throne."

"So you call forth the Crown Prince from wherever he's hiding," said Walther, not looking at Quentin himself, who was sitting stiff-backed in his spot on the couch. Walther nonchalantly bit a cookie. "He hasn't reached his majority yet, but he should still be able to weigh down the throne long enough to convince the wolves to go after an easier target."

"There was a rumor that he had been concealed in the Mists," said Nessa carefully. "Sunk deep in the concealing gray, where no one would be able to find him. If so, the rumor ran, he would accompany Sir October's party to the knowe for the wedding. The timing of this matter is no coincidence."

"What do you think now?" asked Raj.

"I had more of the raising of that boy than his own mother when he was very small, and I would know him," said Nessa. "He is not here."

Quentin flinched. Chelsea squeezed his shoulder. Neither of them said anything, and we let the moment pass without comment. His disguise, which had seemed so ridiculously extreme when he bartered it from the Luidaeg, was seeming more and more like it was going to be his salvation. It's funny how things work out sometimes. The things you think will save you don't, or can't, or won't. The things you thought were little, or unnecessary, change everything.

"So the assassin replaced Nessa because it recognized Nessa as a way to get to Toby," said Cassandra slowly. "That doesn't explain why it didn't know which one of us she was. Wouldn't it have made more sense for whoever hired them to give them a picture to refer to?"

We all looked to Walther as the one who'd survived a coup against the crown in recent memory. Maybe not *this* crown, but the principle was the same. He frowned, taking a bite of his latest cookie, and swallowed without chewing. "During the siege of Silences, the older purebloods seemed to go into this—this fugue, almost. Like they thought it was somehow still the fifteenth century. I'm not sure anyone who was plotting sedition against the crown would be *able* to send a picture. It wouldn't even occur to them."

"Also, I'm pretty sure anyone who's plotting sedition against the high throne isn't going to be able to get April to jailbreak their phone," said Chelsea.

"I did not understand a word you just said apart from 'sedition' and 'April,'" I said. "But I'm going to assume you're probably right: the people who would be plotting governmental insurrection on the East Coast are unlikely to have modern access to the Internet. Which may be useful."

"How so?" asked Jazz warily.

I grinned. "They don't know exactly what to expect when they look at October Daye. They probably know she has mostly brown hair, pale eyes, and a bone structure that could pass for Daoine Sidhe, even if it's not quite right. Oh, and a little bit of mortal blood. That's going to be key."

"Meaning . . . ?" said May.

"Meaning if we can get Stacy to come out of the room, we have four potential brides," I said. "You, Stacy, and Cassandra are still mostly brunettes who can almost but not quite pass as Daoine Sidhe. And you're a pureblood, but because of when you were made, you still ping changeling to people who want to go looking for the indicators."

May nodded, not moving as she looked to Tybalt. "Well, you heard her, big guy. Sounds like we're getting hitched."

"Indeed," he said dryly. "I have long been awaiting this happy day."

"Too bad I don't like dudes," said May.

"Too bad I don't share," said Jazz.

May laughed. I turned to Nessa. "Since you got stuffed in a storeroom while your quarters were turned into a murder maze, I'm pretty sure we can trust you not to be working with the people behind all this. Can we trust you not to say anything about setting decoys to keep the focus off of me?"

Nessa nodded slowly. "I heard rumors you were very hard to harm," she said, voice careful.

"You mean 'virtually indestructible, heals like it's my job'?" I asked. "Yeah, that's true. May doesn't heal as fast as I do, but she's even harder to cause serious harm to."

"I, on the other hand, bleed like a normal person, and if you hit me, I will be hurt, and not recover from being hurt until I'm given the normal quantity of time to heal," said Cassandra. "I've seen the kind of damage you can take, Aunt Birdie. I don't want *anyone* to mistake me for you, or vice versa."

"But if I stayed with you, I'm better with a sword than anyone expects a chemistry professor from Berkeley to be," said Walther. "I was trained by the same master as trained my cousin, and he was Crown Prince. Our parents needed to be able to trust that either one of us could defend ourselves if we were caught without a guard. So just stick with me and you'll be safe."

"I feel certain the next words out of my lady's mouth will be words I have no interest in hearing," said Tybalt, tone dry.

I twisted to look at him, a strained smile on my face. "And on that count, I'm going to need you to stay with Stacy."

"No," said Tybalt. "Absolutely not. I have already been elf-shot and dropped you into eternal darkness since arriving in this frigid kingdom. I will not free you from my company, loose to find whatever troubles you desire."

"This isn't about finding trouble," I objected. "This is about saving the High Kingdom."

"Really? Because it sounds to me as if it's about finding yet another excuse not to marry me!"

"I feel like I maybe shouldn't be here," said Nessa nervously.

Oberon, who had been silent through the whole conversation, nodded in commiseration. Great. We were even making the King of Faerie unhappy by fighting in front of him.

"I wish people would stop acting like me not swooning over the idea of a big diplomatic wedding means I don't want to be married to you," I said. "I agreed to your proposal because I wanted to be your wife. I *still* want to be your wife. I never thought I'd have the chance to marry the man I loved or live in a world where you were willing to love me. So excuse me if I'm currently focused on trying to keep the High Kingdom from falling before you can stick a ring on my finger, or whatever weird-ass tradition the Divided Courts use instead!"

"Yes," said a voice from the doorway. We all turned, me first, to behold the High King standing there, unruffled and perfect as ever, flanked by a whole new contingent of guards. The ones who had survived the earlier encounter at Nessa's quarters were there, but standing back, letting the fresh guards take the lead. "I, too, would prefer that we guarantee the safety of my crown and Kingdom before such time as we move on to your wedding." He smiled, but his eyes were sharp.

"So can we focus?"

TWELVE

"**H**EY," SAID THE LUIDAEG. "Be respectful. You're talking to guests."

"This is my knowe and my Kingdom and my continent," said the High King. "Unless you can produce a title that proves your rank above my own, even being Firstborn of Maeve does not place you over me in my own halls." He bowed then, exaggeratedly. "My lady."

For the first time, I could really see where Quentin got it. I'd always assumed I was the reason he thought smarting off to the sea witch was a good idea, but he'd grown accustomed to the idea with faintly horrifying speed, all things considered. I fully turned to face the High King, taking a half-step backward so I could lean against Tybalt's chest. He responded by sliding his arms around my waist. Even mad at me, he knew how to present a united front.

"Highness," said Nessa, rising and stumbling across the room to stop a few feet from the King, dipping herself into a deep and formal curtsy. "I have failed you. I am so very, profoundly sorry, and as soon as I'm informed that I may safely enter the rooms I have occupied during my service here, I will pack any things you deem mine to take with my unworthy self."

"Well, yes," said the High King, sounding baffled. "You'll need to move your things to new quarters while yours are cleaned and sterilized for you to move back into them."

She glanced at him through her hair, clearly startled. "But—but I have *failed* you."

"Yes, Nessa, I heard you the first time." High King Aethlin shook his head, looking pleadingly at Nolan. "Does your sister have to deal with this every time one of her vassals is overpowered?"

"My sister's vassals include Sir Daye," said Nolan blandly. "She rarely contends with failure, so much as she contends with unrealistic changes to the status quo that will of necessity have ramifications for the entire kingdom."

"Hey," I said, without heat.

"Even so," sighed Aethlin. He returned his focus to Nessa. "Did you ask the Doppelganger knowingly into our halls? Did you surrender yourself to danger with no fear for your life or attempt to defend mine? Did you create a situation where someone could be harmed intentionally and with malicious purpose?"

"I—n-no, sire, I would *never*! I fought as hard as I could without losing my own life in the process!" Nessa sounded genuinely horrified at the very thought that she could have played an intentional role in a plot against her regent.

"Then be at peace and cease this silly talk of leaving us," said Aethlin. "You are my seneschal, for as long as you remain loyal and wish to be. I know, in my heart, that you will still be standing by my side when my children return home and offer you their warm regards."

Nessa ducked her head, clearly overcome. The Luidaeg rose and moved to stand behind her, eyes on the High King.

"That was kindly done," she said. "Too many in your position would have let it turn them hard and treated her as disposable."

"Too many in my position have forgotten what it means to serve," he replied, and turned to me. "Sir Daye, I beg your indulgence, but a matter has arisen that requires your attendance."

"Look, I know we're a feudal system and everything, but we're living in a modern world," I said, exasperated. "My underwear has elastic. I have a phone. We can talk like normal people. No one's going to take points off the final score if we stop sounding like we gargle with bad BBC dramas."

"Yes, but where's the fun in talking like normal people?" asked Aethlin. "Half the time I'm a King of Faerie. The other half, I'm standing in line at Tim Hortons and some asshole in a hockey uniform has just taken the last sour cream glazed. We have to wallow in the aesthetic when we get the chance."

"I will overthrow your kingdom *myself*," I threatened genially. Not genially enough: several of his guard reached for their swords.

High King Aethlin sighed and raised a hand for them to stop. "Your reputation precedes you, Sir Daye. Could you please not make jokes about sedition?"

"Yeah, sorry," I said.

"Appreciated," he said. "As I was trying to say, I need you to come with me. The Doppelganger we captured before is awake and willing to talk, but only to you."

"Me? Why?" It probably shouldn't have been such a surprise. Half the homicidal jerks I deal with are out to get me in specific, and the other half think if they just bat their eyes and word their pitches for world domination correctly, they'll be able to sell me on their new form of governance, which will somehow be so much better than the one we have already.

That and a timeshare in Annwn and I'll be set for life.

"That part is less than clear," he said. "My Court Seer will be in attendance. I don't know if you've ever encountered one of the Adhene before."

"Can detect lies and have a nasty tendency to kill people who try to lie to them," I said curtly. "Will he try to kill someone for lying in his presence if they're not lying to *him*?"

"No, he'll just become agitated. Will you come?" A flicker of amusement crept into his voice. It wasn't mirrored in his eyes. "I could order you, but I prefer not to command my guests to do things without their willing consent."

"This is one of those things where you ask me for my consent, and it's cool and all, but if I say no, you order me, and I have to do it anyway, isn't it?" I asked.

Aethlin nodded. "It's good to see that you understand the way things work," he said.

"Right. I guess I'm going with you. Tybalt, Cassie, you're with me."

Walther, May, and Quentin all immediately protested, their voices overlapping and rendering their words unintelligible. I put my hands up.

"Quiet," I snapped. To my shock, they all obliged. "Fiancé with good reason to be anxious about my safety and niece who can occasionally see the future, coming with me to a controlled interview with a Doppelganger who has been securely restrained and isn't going to be stabbing anyone else today, much less me. Right, sire?"

"Right," said Aethlin, amused again. Glad to know I could serve as someone's traveling comedy show. If this whole heroism thing didn't work out, maybe I could get a new job as a court jester.

"Tell Stacy where we've gone, and catch her up on the decoy plan," I said to the Luidaeg, as we moved toward the door.

"If you can call that a plan," she said mildly though she didn't argue otherwise.

Oberon didn't say anything or move away from his place against the wall, where he lurked as unnoticed as ever. What was even the point of having the King of All Faerie back among us if he was just going to stand around like some sort of creeper, not helping, not contributing what had to be a considerable store of knowledge and experience to the cause of keeping the people I cared about from getting hurt?

But maybe that was the reason he'd left. I knew he'd gone voluntarily from the stories, if not from the man himself: with his queens gone, he'd been a danger to the balance of Faerie, something that made a lot of sense when I considered that he was supposed to have an amount of power that was, "as much greater than his children as His children were to their own." With Maeve and Titania gone and most of the Firstborn either dead or missing, he could have been a god without raising his voice. Considering he'd been kind enough to leave us rather than hurt us once before, I didn't think he wanted to be a god.

But that didn't make it any easier to feel like we had a literal deus ex machina following us around, not doing anything, demonstrating his power only in how good he was at blending into the background. Someone as strong as he was should have been lighting up the air like a beacon, making it difficult to breathe. Instead, he was as much a part of the scenery as a courtier at a royal banquet, basically furniture that occasionally moved and refilled your water glass. I'd done that job a few times in my youth, before Sylvester had figured out that I was constitutionally unsuited for any position that required me to make nice with people who considered themselves more important than I was.

Which did nothing to explain why I was now following the High King of the Westlands through his own knowe, trailed by a King of Cats and a changeling of blended descent, whose appearance seemed to have been cobbled together from recessive traits stolen out of all three lines. It was the only thing I could think of that explained the tufts of fur that tipped her ears, like a lynx, or the blonde-to-brown gradient of her hair.

Magical genetics means never having to say, "Dd your Mommy have an inappropriate relationship with the milkman?" I guess. Titania only knows what my own kids were going to look like, blending Dóchas Sidhe and Cait Sidhe genetics. The thought was, as always, a pleasant one; the idea of a little girl with Tybalt's eyes, or a little boy with pale blond hair and a serious expression, could get me through a lot. I couldn't wait to meet them.

The High King's guard fell back as we walked, expanding their formation to surround the three of us as well as the High King himself. It was such a smooth, practiced change that I had to assume it was something they'd rehearsed as part of their training. There was a level of studied formality to their motion that made me feel like certain things were taken a lot more seriously here than they were in Shadowed Hills. As seriously as they eventually would be in Muir Woods, where Lowri was already in the process of whipping Arden's guard into shape.

It was another pleasant thought. The idea that the Mists would be stable enough to waste time on things like teaching your guards how to expand a formation. Your relatively untried guards if the scene at Nessa's room was anything to go by. All the training in the world isn't a substitution for actual experience. They knew where to stand and when to draw their swords. They didn't know how to handle actual danger.

They were going to have to learn sooner or later.

People passing in the halls either moved aside to let us go by or stopped to stare, depending on how close they were to being in the way. High King Aethlin nodded to them as we passed, but didn't stop, didn't acknowledge them beyond that initial bob of his head. It was like they were ghosts passing through the scene, or maybe we were, a long chain of haunting being whisked through an endless hall.

And then it ended, giving way to a flight of stairs spiraling downward into the brightly-lit depths of the knowe. No darkness here; the amethyst spires that lined the walls made it impossible, lighting up from within with a strangely white light, ignoring the purple they should logically have been projecting. The smell of maple syrup grew even deeper as we descended, until I couldn't decide whether I wanted a plate of pancakes or to never eat sugar again. It was disconcerting, and my stomach grumbled, reminding me of my missed dinner and the cookies I had eaten too fast to fully appreciate them.

"Kerry said to tell you she can get us plates from the kitchen, as soon as you remembered that it's past dinnertime and you decided it was better to get stabbed then it was to eat," said Cassie, voice low. One of the guards still shot her a sour look for opening her mouth in the presence of the High King.

"Good," I said. "I could really use a sandwich."

"She remembers that blood must be replaced with actual food and cannot be generated out of the fabric of the cosmos itself," said Tybalt, rolling his eyes toward the ceiling in exaggerated delight. "A miracle is upon us this day."

"Don't be sarcastic," I said, elbowing him lightly in the side. "I know it's your primary means of communication, but that doesn't make it appropriate right now."

The stairs ended at a short hall, the way forward blocked after only about eight feet by a rowan door. Rowan is standard for royal and noble dungeons: it makes it safer to keep certain tools in the knowe without hurting anyone who hasn't already been imprisoned. It was still jarring, after all that maple, to see something made from any other wood. It was carved with a pattern of maple leaves and common loons in flight, maintaining the "yay for Canada, Canada's cool" theme of the rest of the knowe. That helped a little.

Not enough. The feeling of not enough grew stronger as one of the guards produced a key from his pocket. It was rowan wood, like the door, but the lock wasn't: the lock was made of pure iron, radiating quiet malice as we grew closer.

High King Aethlin looked over his shoulder at me, apparently anticipating my discomfort. "The prisoners are not bound with iron, or sealed in iron cells," he said. "We keep only as much around as we need to dampen the magics that might allow them to escape."

That didn't help the way he clearly meant for it to. "Um, cool," I said.

The guard unlocked the door. The air that rushed out was cold and stale, smelling the way all dungeons did: like wet stone and rotting wood and the slow, inexorable decay of iron. The nicest dungeon in the world will still have that smell because iron degrades magic. Knowes are living magic, so if they must contain iron in order to maintain a stable dungeon, well . . . It's a little pocket of infection in the body of the knowe. I can't imagine it feels very good for the knowe, which has to keep doing everything else that's expected of it, all with this horrible sucking wound deep in its body.

When we got home, I needed to talk to Arden about her own dungeon situation. As far as I knew, there was no iron in Muir Woods, but that didn't mean the situation hadn't changed. Situations change all the time.

"This way," said the High King, gesturing for us to follow him through the door.

One of the guards stepped in front of him. The High King stopped, blinking. The rest of us did the same. "Sire, I must object," said the guard. "The dungeon is no place for a seated monarch. The iron here could do you harm, and if someone were to take advantage of the moment—" He glanced at me as he spoke, and I managed not to snarl at him. Instead, I bared my teeth in something that could only be interpreted as a smile under the most charitable of umbrellas, shifting position slightly to lean against Tybalt. He put a hand on my shoulder, and he *did* snarl at the guard, who quailed but held his ground.

"If someone were to take advantage of the moment with both the Crown Prince and Princess absent, it could be dire for the future of the High Kingdom," continued the guard, refusing to be intimidated.

"I understand the risks," said Aethlin. "We need to speak to the Doppelganger. You won't be disciplined for standing up for what you feel is right, but you need to stand aside now."

The guard grimaced but stepped out of the way, and we continued forward, into the dimmer light on the other side of the door.

Maybe it was because the knowe was lit entirely by its own power, glowing crystals and radiance from the walls, instead of torches or witch-lights or the less-fashionable than it used to be and extremely inhumane shoving of pixies into jars and letting them starve while they light up the room around them, but the light here was definitely less intense than it had been outside. The iron was impacting the knowe's ability to remain stable.

It hung heavy in the air, and I flinched as the door closed behind us. Maybe it's because I used to be human enough to handle the stuff with relative impunity, and maybe it's because I've had severe iron poisoning twice, but I can't stand to be near it in any real concentration, even if the purebloods around me are fine.

Tybalt looked almost as shaken, shifting his stride so that he was walking closed beside me, slipping one arm around my waist. Cassandra on the other hand was looking around, completely unperturbed.

The High King was equally unshaken, as were his guards. They must have been down here often enough to be comfortable with the danger, but not often enough to have side effects to deal with. That was nice for them.

The hall widened, becoming more of a long room than a hallway, and doors appeared along the walls, spaced like the rooms in a luxury hotel. They would have seemed almost pleasant, if not for the fact that every one of them was made of rowan and covered in a thin lattice of iron bars, bent and twined into something elegant that couldn't fully conceal the poisonous reality behind it.

The High King paused at the first of the doors, waving to the guard. "Let us in," he said.

"Sire," began the guard.

"No," said Aethlin. "I'm tired of people arguing about whether or not I'm allowed to do my job." He cast a commiserating look at Tybalt. "Do your subjects argue with you like this?"

"If they try, I slam them into the nearest wall," said Tybalt stiffly. "The Court of Cats is managed in a much more direct manner than the majority of the Divided Courts."

"I see," said Aethlin. "The door, please."

The guard moved to unlock the door, casting unhappy glances back at both the High King and the rest of us. He didn't want to be doing this.

Well, that was cool. Neither did I.

The guard unlocked the door and pushed it open, revealing a dimly-lit room. Two guards were already there, standing to either side of a man about the size of an eight-year-old human child. He was clearly an adult, with the face to match, and a short brown beard a few shades darker than the hair atop his head. His eyes were the smooth yellow of a lizard's, no white or distinct iris, and his ears were pointed.

Like almost everyone else we'd seen since arriving in Canada, he was dressed in the royal livery, tailored for his smaller than average frame. Unlike almost everyone else, he was also handcuffed. The cuffs were silver, not iron, delicate things that held his wrists about a foot apart. I blinked.

"Um, hello," I said.

"Fiac," said the High King, with obvious relief. "I appreciate you taking the time from your duties to assist us with this interrogation."

"I prefer not to disrupt my schedule when I don't have to, but for you, my liege, anything," said the Adhene, with prim, studious precision. He reminded me oddly of Etienne. I suppressed the urge to smile.

In addition to having a near-pathological addiction to the truth above all else, Adhene are very fond of their own dignity. Embarrassing them can have fatal consequences. His nature explained the cuffs; if someone bumped him in the hall and lied casually about what they'd been doing or where they'd been going, he could have done serious harm.

Most Adhene choose to live as far away from the rest of Faerie as possible, due to not wanting to break the Law over someone saying they look nice in an ugly blouse or something equally pointless. I offered Fiac a deep nod, trying to wordlessly project how much I respected the fact that he was here at all. He responded by raising an eyebrow and snorting.

"You're that October girl, aren't you?" he asked. "Amandine's daughter? You know what the Firstborn call your mama? Amandine the Liar. You a liar, girl?"

"Not on purpose," I said. "And while she's still biologically my mother, I'm not her daughter anymore."

"Ah," said Fiac. "That husband of hers finally got the sense to ask for a divorce? And you chose his line, even though he's not really yours. I've known some who would take you carrying the name 'Torquill' as a falsehood, but I'll take it for the slap in your mother's face it truly is and applaud you for finding a way to split yourself from her."

"Okay," I said. No one who knows Mom seems to be her biggest fan. I used to think Simon was, but he gave up that title when he left her. And good for him. He deserved a chance at something better.

Not sure I'd personally call a three-way relationship with a no-
toriously violent mermaid "better," but hey. Everyone has their
own idea of what makes a happy ending.

"Gentlemen." Aethlin nodded to the guards before starting
deeper into the room. The rest of us followed him.

It was a reasonably spacious room. The luxury hotel comparison
I'd come up with in the hall wasn't entirely inaccurate; the main
space was the largest, but from there, it opened up into a bathroom—
indoor plumbing had caught on even in a knowe this old—and a
small kitchenette. The lighting was dim throughout. The Doppelganger was in the kitchenette area, not tied to a chair like it should
have been. I shot the High King a quick glare, which he ignored.
The Doppelganger was in its natural form, all leprous gray skin
mottled with unnatural green, long limbs and sharp teeth. It turned
at the sound of our footsteps, perfectly round eyes widening before
it shimmered, shrank down, and resolved itself into a perfect mirror image of me, even down to the dress I was wearing.

"Much better," it said, voice as stolen as the rest of it. Hearing
myself from the outside had stopped being strange within the first
six months of May living with me, but that didn't make this any
more pleasant. Tybalt set his hand back on my shoulder, squeezing
just tightly enough to make it clear he was going to keep track of
the real me even if he had to do it by holding on the entire time we
were here. Cassandra hung back, being unobtrusive, as the Doppelganger continued: "To what do I owe the honor of this visit?"

"You stabbed me," I said.

"You interrupted me," it replied, with a casual shrug, as if stabbing me had been no more important than anything else that had
happened today.

I scowled and kept scowling as Cassandra moved to stand next
to me, eyes very wide. "Whoa," she said. "It looks *just* like you,
Aunt Birdie. How is it doing that?"

"Doppelgangers can mimic anything in Faerie, even if it means
changing size, within a certain limit," I said. "It probably couldn't
emulate Danny, but it can copy any one of us."

"What happens if we get confused about which one is which?"

"We will *not*," snarled Tybalt.

"In the event that Tybalt lets go of me for long enough for the
Doppelganger to replace me, just stab us both," I said, eyes on my
double. "The one that recovers immediately is me. Hey, Fiac, how

is it you're not scratching this lady's eyes out? Her whole body is a lie right now."

"If we reacted to silent lies, we would have to assault everyone who wears mascara," said Fiac, sounding amused. "As long as she keeps a civil tongue in her head, she remains safe from me."

"Got it, cool." I frowned, turning my attention back to the Doppelganger. "There a reason you're impersonating me? Did you just want to see how badly you can piss my fiancé off before you go too far and he causes a diplomatic incident?"

"Your form is the most useful one currently in this room," said the Doppelganger. "I'd prefer the one I wore earlier. She was a pleasure to be."

"Okay, cool," I said. "Nice to know you have aesthetic preferences, and I can't deny that she's objectively hotter than me." Tybalt made an annoyed noise. I shrugged. "What? It's true. She's Gwragedd Annwn. Being hot is literally her superpower. Mine is more useful." I smiled at the Doppelganger, making a point of showing every single one of my teeth. Sensibly, the thing flinched away, stopping when its hip hit the counter.

It wasn't restrained in any way, no rope or cuffs, which was a little disconcerting, given the cuffs on Fiac, and made it more concerning that the High King was with us. Did these people have no concept of basic security protocols? I took a step forward, still smiling.

"Do you know what my superpower is?" I asked.

"Being terrible and serving the oppressive, illegitimate government of the Westlands?" asked the Doppelganger.

Tybalt glanced to Aethlin. "I knew your rule could be considered oppressive. Every effective rule can be, by the people it constrains from running rampant. But how, pray tell, have you rendered yourself illegitimate?"

"I have no idea." Aethlin shook his head. "I inherited from my parents, and I was their only born child. If someone's staged a coup, no one's bothered to tell me."

Cassandra made a smothered sound of amusement.

I fought to keep my attention on the Doppelganger. It was hard, with the lot of them at my back, but if I asked them to stop, it would break whatever air of menace I had managed to construct.

"No," I said. "Healing. No matter what's done to me, I'll recover before they pull the blade out of my body. Can you say the same?"

The Doppelganger wavered, and then it wasn't me anymore. It

was the High King instead, an uncharacteristic look of fear on his handsome face. I backed off, before the guards could decide that even menacing a representation of their liege was grounds for a stabbing.

"Why is this thing not restrained?" I asked, gesturing to the Doppelganger. "I don't think free-range prisoners are the best plan."

"We tried," said one of the guards. "It simply . . . stopped having hands."

The Doppelganger looked smug.

"I guess that took cuffs out of the equation, but did you consider tying it up?" I asked. "Most living creatures need a torso, if only so they'll have someplace to keep their lungs, and iron chains would probably make it harder for the thing to shapeshift."

The Doppelganger's smugness melted into displeasure.

"*Iron* chains?" it asked. "It's true, then, what they say of the Mists. You spent too many years under the hand of a monster, and you've all become monsters yourselves, unable to tell the difference between right and wrong . . ."

The High King touched my arm. I turned to look at him. He shook his head. "We do not use iron for disciplinary purposes, Sir Daye," he said. "It concerns me that you would."

I blinked, several times. "I'm sorry, sire," I said, and bowed my head. "I was trained and spent most of my life under the false queen's rule, and she was less discerning with her subjects. I intended no offense."

"Truth," said Fiac, sounding almost bored. "Can we get back to the interrogation?"

I guess when you're a living lie detector with a legendarily vicious temper, you don't have to show deference. I flashed Fiac a quick smile, then returned my attention to the Doppelganger.

"We won't use iron on you, but you have to see that you can't escape," I said. "This room is secured and sealed, everyone here is prepared to commit violence to protect the High King, and you have nowhere left to go. Tell us why you're here."

"To kill a tyrant," said the Doppelganger. It opened a cupboard and took out a plastic tumbler, which it proceeded to fill from the tap. "I don't see why that's so difficult for you to understand. The word on the street is you've taken out a few of those yourself."

"We knew they were tyrants when we went up against them," I said. "We know no such thing about High King Sollys."

"Oh, no? Why not try asking the Crown Prince, greatest living threat to his father's rule? I'm sure he would have a few things to say about tyranny."

Fiac still wasn't reacting. That's the trouble with lie detectors, whether magical or mundane: they can't help you if the person you're trying to catch genuinely believes what they're saying is the truth. Still, maybe I was missing something. Carefully, I asked, "Crown Prince Quentin Sollys?"

"What, was there ever another one?" The Doppelganger sipped its water, seemingly unperturbed. "He was sent away on 'blind fosterage,' and disappeared, just as he was getting old enough to learn the truth about his parents. If you could find him—if he's even still alive—he could tell you a great many things."

Only the presence of the guards, who probably didn't know where Quentin was being fostered, kept me from busting out laughing. If I'd looked at Cassandra or Tybalt, I would have lost my composure instantly. Instead, I schooled my face to careful neutrality and said, "That's an interesting way to look at things, since blind fosterage has been a tradition for centuries. Can you tell me about the High King's tyranny?"

"The usual. Theft of land, theft of crown, theft of the lives of the hundreds of common folk who serve and suffer under him, who should be free to pursue their own passions in life, not serve at the pleasure of an unforgiving king." The Doppelganger sipped its water again. It seemed to be enjoying this. "All kings are monsters."

"It sounds like you want to overthrow the entire monarchal system." That was a lot more ambitious than I had ever been. Sure I'd replaced a couple of monarchs who weren't treating their people fairly, but I had never aspired to taking down the system, mostly because I didn't feel like I was in any way qualified to decide what was going to come next. Democracy didn't seem to work all that much better; it just came with fewer beheadings.

"No," said the Doppelganger. "The people I'm working for aren't interested in throwing a perfectly good system away. They just want to make sure it's replaced by something closer to what it was always intended to be, and that begins with putting the rightful King on the High Throne."

I raised an eyebrow. This was all sounding very calm and logical, and when added to the speech the Doppelganger had given us upon our arrival, it pointed to one clear conspirator. But surely no one who was going to make a run at the High King would be that stupid?

"So tell me," I said pleasantly, "how long have you been working for the Shallcross family?"

The Doppelganger sipped its water one last time before putting the tumbler calmly down, transforming again, this time into an exact duplicate of Tybalt. "They were always meant to hold the High Throne, you know," it said, in an eerie replica of his voice. "No one knew about the iron in the harbor, but the convocation that was called somehow locked king to kingdom, rather than looking at what was best for the continent. It should have been High King Shallcross of Maples, not High King Sollys. The theft was committed in the dead of night, quick and clean and all but unremarked. You serve an imposter."

"And it was a long time ago, and if your employers were going to try and do something about it, that should have happened almost as long ago," I said. "You've condemned yourself for nothing more than sour grapes. I hope they paid you enough to justify losing everything."

"We'll see who loses everything," said the Doppelganger, and leapt, heading straight for the High King, hands up, fingers hooked, and claws exposed.

The guards had taken the creature's weapons away and given it no replacements. But Tybalt was a King of Cats. He didn't have weapons that could be taken away, and no matter how much he shifted his form toward the Daoine Sidhe "ideal," he would always have his claws. The Doppelganger's recreation of those claws were easily an inch long and wickedly sharp, primed to strike and cut.

"Look out!" I shouted. I know better than to get in the way of Tybalt's claws, whether or not they were really his. Tybalt slashed my throat open with them once, when he was under the control of the false Queen of the Mists, who had used the talents inherited from the Siren side of her heritage to seize his will and turn him into her puppet. I'd been more mortal then, but it had still hurt like hell, and poor Tybalt had been shy of touching me for what had felt like weeks afterward, convinced that any moment I was going to come to my senses and blame him for what he'd done.

I couldn't say for sure whether he'd react the same way to me getting flensed by a Doppelganger wearing his face, but I could say that I didn't want to find out right before my wedding night. There

are some sacrifices too great to be made even for the sake of a
High King. Still, I wasn't going to go back to Quentin and tell him
I'd stood idly by while his father died. I drew my knife, angling my
body in front of the High King, ready to defend him. Cassandra,
wisely, had already taken a step back, early enough that I guessed
she'd seen this moment coming—although not with enough time
to give us a warning. Stupid prophetic gifts.

Two things happened at the same time. One of the guards drew
his sword with the distinct shimmering twang of metal scraping
against hide, and Tybalt leapt, matching the Doppelganger's approach with his own. He roared as he moved, and the two of them
became, briefly, a rolling, roiling ball of limbs and flailing claws. I
backed up, knife at the ready, prepared to defend myself if necessary. It didn't seem likely to be necessary.

One of the Tybalts caught the other by the hair and slammed his
forehead into the wall. There was a cracking sound, and the Tybalt
who'd been injured groaned, swiping feebly around behind himself. I wanted to intervene. It wasn't like I was exactly concerned
about my own safety. But when I tried to press forward, Tybalt
waved me off, and I had to trust that my centuries-old fiancé could
handle himself against a shapeshifter bad enough at infiltration to
have made such obvious mistakes.

Tybalt slammed the other Tybalt's head against the wall again,
and the second Tybalt blurred, features melting into a mixture of
Tybalt's and Nessa's, wavering like it couldn't decide which face
was more likely to see it to safety. A trickle of greenish blood ran
down its cheek from a cut just under the eye.

"Ack," it said.

"Good job, hon," I said brightly. "Excellent violence. A plus."

There was a noise from behind me, and I turned just in time to
watch the second guard pull a dagger that was shaped remarkably
like my own out of the High King's back. Aethlin fell silently, eyes
very wide.

"Sic semper tyrannis," said the guard, raising the dagger, and
slit his own throat.

Fiac, still bound, watched him fall with a dismayed expression
on his face. Then he looked at me, suddenly gone pale as whey.

"No lies here," he said—and fainted.

THIRTEEN

"SIRE!" I DROPPED MY knife and rushed to kneel at the High King's side, falling to my knees and reaching for his head, like that was going to help when he'd just been stabbed in the back. The remaining guard was standing next to Fiac, sword in hand, looking baffled. His position was probably why the second Doppelganger hadn't killed them both.

"Is he alive?" asked Fiac, who had risen from the floor after a relatively short period of shocked unconsciousness.

"Yes, for now," I said, already regretting the speed with which I'd dropped my knife. Approaching the fallen High King with a weapon in my hand hadn't seemed like a good idea, in the half-second I'd been given to decide what was or wasn't a good idea. And now here I was, with no reasonable means of making myself bleed.

"He doesn't have long," said Cassandra. "Aunt Birdie—"

"I know. I *know*."

Aethlin was breathing, little hitches of his chest that sounded increasingly labored. The knife had been slotted between his ribs, probably piercing a kidney, and he could be bleeding out internally.

The knife. The Doppelganger's knife was less than a foot from the High King's body, as yet untouched by the spreading pool of ichor that was all that remained of the actual Doppelganger. They melt when killed, creating a horrible, caustic slime that *never* comes out of carpet.

Go on. Ask me how I know.

Suddenly realizing what I had to do, I lunged for the Doppelganger's knife, only for the remaining guard to slam his sword into the carpet bare inches from my fingers.

"No, king-breaker," he snarled. "You will not harm him farther."

"She's on his side!" cried Cassandra.

I did my best not to get distracted, focusing on the guard. "I'm not trying to *harm* him, he's Daoine Sidhe, that makes him a blood-worker, I'm Dóchas Sidhe, I heal like it's a contest, if I can make myself bleed, I can help him." I was talking fast, all too aware that the High King's time was limited. He was going to lose consciousness soon, if he hadn't already, and then he wouldn't be able to use the magic he got from my blood, no matter how useful it could have been. We were on a countdown, and I didn't know how much time was left before we ran out of options.

The guard looked to Fiac hopelessly, clearly awaiting the Adhene's answer before he made his final decision. Fiac looked briefly pained, looking between the two of us, then sighed and settled on a mild:

"She speaks truth. Let the girl try."

The guard pulled back his sword, a mistrustful expression on his face, and I grabbed the knife, covered as it was with the High King's blood.

In a mortal setting, at a mortal crime scene, interfering with the weapon would have been the worst thing we could do. But here—the Doppelganger wouldn't have left any useful fingerprints behind. If it left any, they belonged to the missing guard, not to the dead monster. And we already knew the High King had been stabbed, so contaminating his blood wasn't a concern.

"Tybalt?" I called, voice higher and less steady than I liked.

"Yes?"

"Is it dead?"

"Very." He didn't sound satisfied or smug about that. He just sounded tired.

"Good," I said, and slashed the knife down the length of my arm, cutting deep before dropping the blade to the floor, in easy reach in case I needed to cut myself again. Hopefully not. I needed this wound to last for at least a few seconds. The blood was hot and immediate, cascading free, and I moved my arm, pressing it to the High King's mouth.

"Come on, come on," I said. "Drink and get better."

Did his lips move? Did he swallow? I couldn't tell. I kept my arm in place until it had healed completely, then sat back on my heels, watching the High King's motionless form sink just that little bit deeper into the carpet. I couldn't tell whether he was alive or dead, and I didn't want to be the one to find out one way or another.

"Is he alive?" demanded the guard. I gave him a hopeless look, sighed, and began to bend forward, to press my ear to the High King's chest.

I was still in motion when Acthlin gasped, opened his eyes, and sat up, all at the same time. Unfortunately, the speed of the gesture meant his forehead cracked against mine, sending me reeling. He stayed where he was, looking wildly around.

"Sire?" asked the remaining guard.

Aethlin turned slowly to look at him. "Artyom?" he said, sounding puzzled, like he hadn't been expecting to see his own guard.

"Yes, sire," said the guard, with naked relief in his voice.

Tybalt, meanwhile, was moving to help me up, hooking his hands under my arms and tugging me back to my feet. I let him, doing my best to get my feet under myself and help the process along.

Lips close to my ear, he murmured, "Are you well?"

"Yeah," I said. "He didn't even hit me hard enough to crack the bone. I'll be fine as soon as I've had a chance to catch my breath." My stomach grumbled. "And eat a sandwich or something."

"Yes, or something," he agreed.

"Maybe *two* sandwiches," suggested Cassandra.

There was a marshy patch on the carpet behind Tybalt, green sludge spreading out across the kitchen floor. He looked shaken, like he was on the verge of tears, and there was nothing romantic about the way he ran his hands along me. He was checking for injuries that had somehow failed to heal, not trying to get inappropriately frisky in front of the High King.

"Hey," I said. "I'm *fine*. I'm more worried about you and the High King."

Fiac had moved, despite his hands still being tied, to give Aethlin something to lean against as he levered himself off the floor.

The back of the High King's tunic was completely soaked through with blood, as was the carpet where he had fallen. This had been an unreasonably nice cell, as prisons went; they were going to be rewarded for that with a remarkable amount of cleaning. Well, at least their Bannicks would be happy.

The last guard—Artyom—moved to put himself between Aethlin and Fiac and the two of us. "What did you do to the High King?" he demanded.

"Healed him," I said. "Saved his life. You're welcome." Aethlin still looked dazed. I sighed and relented, explaining, "He's a blood-worker and he's just swallowed a considerable amount of my blood. He'll lose access to my magic soon enough, but my memories may linger a little longer."

Aethlin swung his head around, staring at me with wide, puzzled eyes.

"You're you," he said.

"Yes," I agreed.

"You're October Daye."

"Yes."

"But *I'm* October Daye."

"No," I said, and remained exactly where I was as his eyes rolled back in his head and he collapsed to the floor in a dead faint. Artyom stepped between us again, sword at the ready. I sighed heavily. "I think we're going to need to get some backup in here. Tybalt . . . ?"

"I came with you on a simple questioning, and you found two Doppelgangers and the High King got stabbed," he said. "Why you would think me willing to leave you is entirely beyond me."

"Because you love me and don't want Artyom here to arrest me for crimes against the High King?" I said, as endearingly as I could. "I will stay right here, and I will not stab anyone, including myself, unless it's in self-defense. But we need someone else who understands blood magic and is unquestionably loyal to the crown, which means we need the High Queen." Technically, we had two members of our little crew who could potentially help someone who was struggling with blood memories, Dean and—no. No, Quentin couldn't help.

Quentin had traded his natural magic for a Banshee's compelling, repelling wail. He couldn't help. And Dean's natural magic had always been somewhat suppressed by the unique blend of his heritage, which seemed to focus most of its energy on keeping him locked in an air-breathing shape, rather than sliding into a form that couldn't breathe on land *or* in water. He'd never shown any inclination toward transformation, but the magic didn't lie.

"I'll make sure she behaves herself," said Cassie. "Cross my heart. And you should go. The air says you'll be able to convince the High Queen to come."

Tybalt blinked, but as Fiac didn't contradict her, he couldn't really argue. Instead, he made a frustrated sound and turned to rest his forehead against mine, sighing deeply.

"You are running out of reasons to bid me to leave you behind, little fish," he said. "Be careful you do not exhaust your supply. It will not, I fear, regenerate as quickly as you do." Then he kissed the bridge of my nose and wrenched himself away, walking in long strides toward the wall.

Fiac was looking oddly at Cassandra. "I don't know you," he said. "I know all the seers of the Westlands, but I don't know you. How does the air speak to you, girl I don't know?"

"The High King has been poisoned," said Artyom sharply. "I think we have bigger concerns than a girl you don't know."

Fiac sighed, turning briefly to me. "This is the trouble with putting most of your magic into seeing the truth," he said. "We can't be around people unless they're so careful with us that it's not sustainable, and so our numbers dwindle, since we can't even stand each other most of the time, and people still lie to us, or twist the truth to suit what they want it to be, and it doesn't rouse our tempers because they don't know they're lying. If I had just come into this room, I would believe him when he said the High King had been poisoned, and all my wrath would be for you."

"And now?" I asked carefully.

"Now I know what I saw, and I know what a blood-worker overwhelmed by stronger magic looks like." Fiac shook his head. "I might be able to blame you if you had bled to prove your good intentions, or to share a memory, but given you bled to save my liege's life, it's not fair to hold you responsible if he's blood-drunk on what he got from you. He'll recover."

"But—" protested Artyom.

"No," said Fiac. "No buts. She didn't poison the man, and right now, I have no more important concerns than how she can be traveling with a seer I don't know. We're few and far between in this world. Eira Rosynhwyr saw to that."

I blinked. I knew Eira had been responsible for the original slaughter of the Roane, as part of an elaborate attempt to make a monster of her sister—to make the Luidaeg seem like the one who had wiped out her own descendant line, one of the few crimes unique to the Firstborn, and one of the few that Faerie could never forgive. This was the first I'd heard of her targeting all prophets.

I'd wondered, of course, whether that could have been a part of her motivation, whether she'd worried the Roane would foresee and reveal some other plan of hers and twist it somehow out of true. It was impossible not to wonder. But I'd never wondered whether she could have been going after other seers, too. Maybe that explained why they were so rare. Having one of the most ruthless of the Firstborn targeting them without concern for the consequences would certainly have done a lot to reduce their numbers.

"I'm an aeromancer," said Cassie, voice a little unsteady. It wasn't an admission she made often. "I can see the way the air moves, and it tells me things, whether it means to or not. I don't know where I got it. Neither of my parents is a seer."

"But your sister is," I said. She turned to look at me. "Karen's an oneiromancer. We don't know where that came from either."

"That's different," she said.

"How?"

"Karen doesn't read dreams so much as she moves through them," said Cassie.

"She's called me before because she had a dream that told her something that was about to happen. She sees the future in dreams."

Fiac blinked again, before looking at Cassie like he was seeing her for the first time. "I see," he said. "Well, that explains almost as much as it asks."

"What do you—" I began, then stopped as the door slammed open so hard it bounced off the wall. I'd have to grab a knife from the floor to arm myself, and so I settled for shifting into a defensive stance, fists raised, ready to brawl. I'm not the best brawler, but my ability to take a hit that should knock me down and keep on kicking means that I can definitely be a challenge.

Cassie moved to put herself behind me, while Artyom moved, sword in hand, to put himself in front of Fiac. Whoever was coming was going to find themselves with at least a little bit of a challenge before they took the High King.

Then Maida rushed down the short entry hall, two more guards in her wake, and we all relaxed, Artyom already apologizing as he lowered his sword with the speed of a man who expected to be executed for threatening his Queen.

Maida ignored him, hurrying to drop to the floor next to her unmoving husband and gather his head into her lap. She glanced at the ruined carpet, and I could tell from the way her shoulders tensed that she knew exactly what that volume of blood meant, possibly down to the drop. She knew she should be grieving, not trying to comfort her unwounded husband.

Tybalt came in behind the rest of them, strolling more calmly, projecting casual unconcern as only a cat can. He didn't have his hands in his pockets, but everything else about him screamed "whoever's problem this is, it's not mine." None of this blunted the relief in his face when he glanced across the room and saw that I had kept my word and was still standing where he'd left me, not wearing any more blood than I had been before.

The concerns of our relationship aren't unique, but they probably ought to be. They're hard on the nerves.

"What *happened*?" demanded Maida, voice just a little shrill, just a little too loud for the space we were in.

"Well, Highness—" began Artyom.

"No," Maida's voice was flat, leaving no room for argument. "I don't want to hear it from you. I want to hear it from *her*." She turned to look at me, an almost feral expression in her eyes. I was the interloper here, after all, and I'd brought chaos in my wake. I'd come without her son, at least as far as she knew, and my arrival had been marked with infiltration and assault, and now with the injury of the High King. She had good reason to be upset with me. If I'd been in her position, *I* would have been upset with me. Maybe even more upset than she was. I don't react well when people hurt Tybalt.

"The High King came to the room where my party is currently housed," I said. "I know those rooms were prepared for us by the imposter, not the real Nessa, so we may have to move if there's something wrong with them, but for right now, that's where we are. He requested I come with him to interview the Doppelganger who had been masquerading as your seneschal—that's the Doppelganger all over the kitchenette floor, by the way, I'm sorry we weren't able to keep it alive for further questioning—"

"I'm not," interjected Tybalt, walking daintily around Maida and the guards, and around the bloodstain on the floor, to stand behind me. I resisted the urge to take a step back so our shoulders could touch. I was in the presence of the High Queen. I needed to at least pretend to be following the rules of court behavior.

"Well, no, it was trying to kill you at the time," I said. "Anyway, the Doppelganger got everyone to focus on it, and the second Doppelganger, which had replaced a member of the King's guard—"

"Enzo," supplied Artyom. I supposed that would matter if the man was still alive somewhere in the knowe, as Nessa had been. Since the Doppelganger had appeared Tuatha de Dannan while impersonating him, I didn't have a good feeling about that. Keeping a teleporter confined is difficult at the best of times, and if the Doppelganger had had access to the original Enzo's blood, it would have been able to teleport away.

"All right," I said. "A second Doppelganger had replaced Enzo. You need to check all your staff for indication that they've been replaced. This is clearly bigger than we thought it was at first. The second Doppelganger stabbed the High King in the lower back, I believe piercing a kidney, from the location of the wound and the volume of blood involved. I don't believe the blade was poisoned, since I went on to use it to cut myself and have suffered no ill effects. They just wanted to stab him. Like the first Doppelganger, this one said 'sic semper tyrannis' after the deed was done, but unlike the first Doppelganger, it slit its own throat so it couldn't be taken captive. The High King had fallen by that point, and I know he's Daoine Sidhe, meaning he can borrow magic if he has access to blood. So I bled myself into his mouth before he could die from his injuries, and he was able to heal."

Through all this, Fiac stood silent and stoic, waiting until I stopped before he looked at the High Queen and said solemnly, "She speaks the truth."

Maida made a sound that was caught somewhere between sob and sigh, stroking her husband's hair with one hand. "So he'll live?" she asked. "He's uninjured?"

"I didn't roll him over to check, but he's still breathing, and he wouldn't be if he hadn't been able to use my blood for *something*, so probably, yeah," I said. "You can check if you want. He was stabbed . . . here, roughly." I put my hand on my own back, indicating the place where I'd seen the knife come out.

Maida nodded and sniffled, pulling on the High King's shoulder until she had rolled him onto his side. The rent in his tunic was easy to see from this angle. She slid her hand inside, feeling around for several seconds. Finally, her eyes widened. "There's no injury," she said, allowing him to roll back into his original position. "You saved my husband's life. Our kingdom owes you a debt of gratitude."

Still Fiac said nothing. I had never considered how intensely disconcerting it would be to have a living lie detector who could fly into a killing rage at the slightest falsehood in the room with me. Then again, it wasn't a situation that came up all that often.

I hoped he wasn't going to be a witness at our wedding.

"He needed me," I said. "I couldn't stand by and let the High King die if there was something I could do to save him." Quentin would never have been able to forgive me.

"So why is Artyom saying he was poisoned?"

"The High King is Daoine Sidhe," I said carefully. "I'm not, but I know blood memory can be very overwhelming, especially if you swallow too much—and I had to give him a lot of blood to be sure he'd have access to my magic and be able to put himself back together without lingering injury. He's just a little confused about who he is right now, that's all."

"Treason," spat Artyom.

"I think for it to be treason, I would have to have been trying to permanently replace the High King's mind with a copy of my own, which was not the goal here," I said. "The world doesn't need more of me."

"One is more than sufficient to most needs," muttered Tybalt.

I glanced at him sharply. He put on his best expression of innocence though he didn't try to deny saying anything.

Right. I turned back to Maida. "I think your guard may have mistaken the passive effects of blood magic for an intentional attack," I said, as delicately as I could manage. "The High King should recover soon. Has he been trained in the use of blood magic?"

"It's never been his strongest suit," said Maida, stroking Aethlin's forehead with one hand, "but he manages the basics well enough to be considered competent, and I find him quite impressive on occasion."

"Then he'll be fine," I said. Riding the blood is one of the first and simplest lessons young Daoine Sidhe receive, and I know that to be true in part because I'd believed I *was* a young Daoine Sidhe when Sylvester Torquill had sat down with me to teach me how to coax a memory out of a drop of blood. He'd started with dilute mixtures, a single drop in an entire glass of water, and for years I'd felt a little hurt by how frustrated he'd looked as he mixed me stronger and stronger samples, adding more blood to less water until I could hear the faint echoes of someone else's memory.

That hadn't been a fun summer. For either of us. At the time, I hadn't been able to understand why he'd even bother, since it was blazingly obvious I would never have strong enough magic for it to matter. Now, I wondered how he'd been able to convince Mom to let him give me even that much training—although it could also have been her idea. I'd been a stubborn child. I know, big shock. But she'd been dedicated to the idea that if I thought I was powerless, I would be, and she'd never wanted me to understand my own potential, or the ways in which it deviated from the Daoine Sidhe norm.

If the High King had received even the most basic training, he'd be able to fight his way through my memories and back into himself in due time. And until he did, he probably shouldn't be trusted with knives since the regenerative capabilities of my magic wouldn't last as long as the memories did. He could easily stab himself, thinking it was something he'd be able to shrug off, only to find that most people don't do well with knives jutting out of their bodies.

Sure, the fact that he currently thought he was me could be taken as raising some uncomfortable questions about identity in Faerie, but no more uncomfortable than the questions raised by the existence of Fetches and night-haunts. We had better things to worry about.

"We need to interview your entire staff," I said. "And by 'we' I mean 'you,' and by 'you' I mean 'someone you trust implicitly, probably with Fiac present to verify people's responses, because if you were to find another Doppelganger, you'd probably get stabbed, too, and that's not a fun family activity.'"

"Can I . . ." The High Queen faltered, swallowed, and then began again, asking, "Can I beg a vial of your blood to carry with me, until such time as this is resolved? I would rather not be stabbed, but if it becomes inescapable, I would like a way to not succumb to my wounds."

It was an interesting question, and one that gave me momentary pause. I glanced to the side, where Tybalt and Cassandra were observing the scene. Tybalt gave a very small nod, indicating that he wouldn't disapprove. Cassie was watching the air between me and the High Queen, giving no indication that she had heard a single thing we were saying.

Seers. What can you do? I looked back to Maida. "If you promise me you're not going to give it to anyone else or save it to use against me later. Blood is a dangerous thing. We can't just leave it lying around for anyone to find."

"I promise," she said swiftly. "If we get through this without issue, and I still have the blood, I will return it to you if there is any possible way to do so. By the root and the branch, the rose and the thorn, the ash, the rowan, the oak, and the yew, I swear."

Fiac nodded when she stopped, approving her words as true. But let's be honest. I was always going to agree to her request. She was the mother of my squire, and the same laws of sympathetic magic that would allow someone to use my blood against me would have allowed me to use her son against her. Yes, she'd only sent him away because Eira made it sound like a great idea and it's almost impossible for Daoine Sidhe to go against her wishes, but if Maida could trust me with her entire son, I could trust her with a little bit of my blood if it would help her feel safe in her own knowe.

"The first Doppelganger, before it attacked us, was explaining how it believed King Shallcross should have been granted the title of High King even if Ash and Oak wasn't chosen for the Kingdom seat," I said. "It said High King Sollys was an imposter who sits upon a stolen throne."

"The convocation was to decide both where the High Kingdom would be seated and who would wear the crown," said Maida. "Everyone involved agreed the high crown would travel with the seat, to make matters as simple as possible. It wasn't until his kingdom was passed over that Shallcross began making claims of illegitimacy and theft. He'd been so sure no one could choose *Muddy* York over *New* York that he never bothered to raise a complaint until the matter was settled and done."

I nodded slowly. "I know you weren't there," I said. Maida had been born toward the end of the last High King's rule, so she couldn't possibly have been in attendance. "I also know the Luidaeg was because she told us as much, and she can't lie. Is there anyone else in this knowe who attended the convocation in the flesh? I'd like to speak to them, if so. I need to understand what's going on here."

Doppelgangers in their natural forms don't have blood as such; they're an undifferentiated flesh, more fungal than anything else, and while the slime they leave behind when they die might contain traces of their magic, you're not going to catch me putting that stuff in my mouth. I looked at the slime eating its way into the carpet and nearly gagged at the thought alone. No: blood magic wasn't going to be the answer here, save in the sense that it was going to let me give High Queen Maida the peace of mind she needed to go back to her life.

In the meantime . . . "How long has King Shallcross been calling the legitimacy of the throne into question?" We hadn't heard anything about it in the Mists, but without reliable phones or Internet, news travels more slowly in Faerie than it does in the mortal world.

Not that that had been enough to stop the rumors of my king-breaking from spreading with enormous speed. I guess "October Daye will stab you until you die if you're naughty" was a much more interesting rumor than "maybe the High King, who hasn't really been an asshole or demanded anything unreasonable from his vassal kingdoms in over a century, was not supposed to inherit the throne after all." People are people no matter what.

"Since the convocation," said Fiac. "He didn't like the answer when he asked, 'May I have the crown?', and so he began objecting. He insisted Ash and Oak should have been chosen despite the testimony of the Roane—called them liars and slaves to a First-born's fickle fancies—even after the first signs of iron poisoning began to make themselves clear in the subjects of his own demesne. The man could have seen his courtiers melt and still claimed it was safe to remain in the kingdom."

I looked to Fiac. "Were you there?"

"My predecessor was. My mother served the first High King as I serve his son, and she told me what had happened in precise and unyielding terms. I would have known had she lied to me."

"Yes." Intentionally, anyway. Recollection is imprecise. If he'd been there, I could have asked for a sample of his blood and lived the memory for myself, studying it from every angle. Blood magic allows me to be an eyewitness to events I couldn't possibly have seen for myself, and that's valuable.

The Luidaeg had been there, of course, but asking for her blood wasn't an option. I've tasted it before, and it's overwhelmed me every time, knocking me down and damaging my ability to manage my own life. The blood of the Firstborn is too powerful to be consumed so casually, as Simon Torquill learned to his dismay.

"I'm so sorry, Sir Daye," said Maida. "I'm afraid this will interfere with your marriage."

"No." Tybalt's voice was a wall, slamming down over the High Queen's words and forbidding any further passage. "We *will* be wed before the end of this visit. I refuse to consider any other outcome."

"Is it really responsible for us to divert resources to a celebration when there's a possible coup in progress?" asked Maida.

"Had we not agreed to come to your domain for our wedding, had we remained in the Mists and allowed Queen Windermere to perform the ceremony, as she volunteered to do, your coup would be proceeding without my lady's intervention or assistance," said Tybalt flatly. "We came here for diplomacy's sake, not because we needed you. If you declare yourselves unable to host, we will of course be disappointed, and we will remove ourselves from your halls immediately. I have delayed my marriage to this woman frequently enough to allow her a great many injuries, at least one act of impossible, inadvisable magic, and more poor decisions than we have time to list right now. No. I will not delay any further."

"He speaks truth, Lady," said Fiac.

I said nothing. I didn't feel the need to be married now, right now, this second as strongly as Tybalt did, but I probably would have, if he had shared my talent for getting himself stabbed every time I let him out of my sight. Much as it rankled when Tybalt got overprotective, I had to admit he'd earned the reaction, every scrap of it, and all he was doing was asking me to lie down in the bed I'd made for myself.

"I'll go with him if he says we have to move the wedding," I said abruptly, earning myself a wounded look from Maida and a thankful one from Tybalt. I couldn't comment on either of them. "It's important for us to finally get married, and we wouldn't have been here to get involved if not for that. So while you can absolutely say you're not comfortable hosting right now, if you do that, we'll have to leave, and you'll have to handle your coup on your own."

"We could order you to stay," said Maida. "Hero of the realm or not, you are a knight of the Divided Courts, and you answer to our authority."

"Do you really want an angry, resentful, known king-breaker being held captive in your knowe when you're already dealing with an outside enemy?" Artyom tensed, raising his sword. I looked at him flatly. "That was not a threat. That was a question. Believe me when I tell you that you'll know if I start making threats. They're pretty damn hard to miss, coming from me."

The High King groaned before Artyom could respond, shifting in Maida's lap, lifting one hand to rub his forehead before he opened his eyes and blinked unsteadily at the ceiling. Maida leaned forward slightly, making sure he could see her face as she smiled.

"Hello, sweetheart," she said. "Welcome back."

High King Aethlin gasped and sat upright, causing all three of the guards present to tense. They were primed for a fight. Pity they were also massively outmatched. Aethlin looked frantically around, eyes finally settling on me.

"You!" he bellowed. "Take me to my son!"

Well, crap.

FOURTEEN

"HOW COULD YOU *DO* this? Don't you understand the danger this places the entire Kingdom in? I trusted you to behave responsibly when I allowed you to stay in the Mists! Not to do—" High King Aethlin gestured frantically with both hands, trying to encompass all of Quentin in one gesture. It wasn't working.

Arms crossed, Quentin looked at him flatly.

"—whatever *this* is," Aethlin concluded. He dropped his hands, glaring. "What do you have to say for yourself?"

"I wasn't planning to say anything. You weren't supposed to know."

"Obviously, *that* didn't work the way you planned it. This is disrespectful to me, to your mother, and to your Kingdom. That woman has been a terrible influence on you, and I should never have allowed you to stay in her custody. I should—"

"Fuck you," said Quentin, voice bright and almost chipper. Aethlin stiffened.

"What did you just say to me?"

"I'm sorry, was that disrespectful? I meant fuck you, *Your Majesty.*"

On the other side of the room, Dean put a hand over his mouth to cover his smile. Chelsea had acquired a movie theater-style bucket of popcorn somewhere and was sharing it with Raj. Most of the rest of our company had decamped for the kitchen while Tybalt, Cassie, and I were off with the Doppelganger, leaving only

Walther and the assorted teens. Walther looked as amused as
they did.

High King Aethlin didn't look amused at all. He looked like he
was about to give himself a heart attack through sheer rage.

"You do *not* speak to your father in such a disrespectful manner,
young man! You were raised better!"

"Yes, I was, but not by you." Quentin balled his hands into fists
and glared at his father. I suppose the difference in his transformed
height didn't make any real difference, since it wasn't like they'd
spent much time together since he was a child. "Not even when I
was here, not even when people knew me by name and smiled at
the sight of me. No, you left the raising to Nessa and the rest of the
staff, except when it was convenient to trot out the proof that you
were virile enough to have produced an heir *and* a spare. So impressive! You think I didn't hear the way your courtiers talked
about us when we were supposed to be in bed?"

"You were supposed to be in bed," said Aethlin.

"I was a *kid*! Kids sneak out of bed to see what their parents are
doing while they're not around! Kids get into mud and mischief
and messes, and they're not pretty little accessories that you can
just pack up and mail to California when you don't want them
anymore!"

Aethlin froze. "Is that . . . is that what you think happened?"

"I think you sent me away, and you sent Penny away, and you
couldn't even bother to send us away together," snapped Quentin.
This had been brewing for a while, clearly, and I wasn't going to
interrupt it. Beside me, Maida was stiff as an iron bar, her eyes
locked on the stranger who was her son, her hands buried in the
folds of her skirt and her nails, I was sure, digging into her palms.
I could smell blood.

"She was my only friend and the only person who knew me,
really *knew* me, who I was when I wasn't 'the Crown Prince,' and
you sent her away like I wouldn't care. You left her alone in the
world and you shipped me off to a bunch of strangers." Quentin
shook his head. "Did you ever even bother to check and make sure
I was okay in Shadowed Hills? Did anyone bother to tell you the
Duke was mad, or that his wife and daughter had been kidnapped,
leaving him tearing at the walls as if it would somehow bring them
back?"

"I didn't—Countess Winterrose made the case for your fosterage, and she was . . . she was *very* compelling," said Aethlin helplessly. "Before she came, we had never even considered the virtues of sending you and your sister away."

"I think this is one where you have to back down a little, kiddo," I said. "You've been in a room with her, you know what it's like to have her full attention focused on you. Daoine Sidhe literally can't say no to their First, and when she stops talking, everything she said sounds so reasonable that you'll justify anything to yourself to keep from contradicting her. I don't know how long the effect lasts."

"Not long enough if it's something you really care about," said Maida. "I started regretting what we'd done before the end of the first year. I started asking your father to call you home before the end of the second." The look she gave Aethlin's back was nothing like the adoring glances she'd been directing his way back in the Doppelganger's cell. This was the face of a mother who'd been denied access to her children by the man who was supposed to help her protect them, and I was glad, for Aethlin's sake, that he couldn't see it. He might have started to worry about his marriage.

Fortunately for everyone involved with this little family disagreement, Aethlin's guards had agreed to wait out in the hall while he spoke with Quentin, and hopefully they could be trusted to keep their mouths shut, since they definitely knew Quentin was in the knowe. The High King's disorientation upon waking up hadn't lasted long, and he'd realized that if Quentin was safely hidden, he should probably be allowed to stay that way. Even if Aethlin still wanted to yell at him for possibly muddling the lines of succession.

It seemed to me that there was a long tradition of using magic to conceal princes and princesses until the time was right to reveal them, and with both Fiac and the Luidaeg on hand, no one reasonable would dare to contradict them if they were to say Quentin was the Crown Prince—not that they were going to. The fact that he was currently a Banshee would be secondary to the woman who can't lie identifying him in front of the man who reacted to falsehoods with aggression. But no, the High King needed to yell, I guess.

And he was doing an admirable job of it.

Had I not been distracted by the fact that he was dying at the time, I would have thought more about the fact that Quentin's father would get enough of my memories with the blood that healed him to realize the Banshee boy who'd accompanied me from the Mists was actually his son in a very good, nigh-unbreakable disguise. I would still have given him the blood—you don't sit by and watch the High King bleed to death, causing a potential crisis of succession, when you have a choice in the matter—but I would have tried harder not to think about Quentin while I did it.

Then again, the best way to make someone think about elephants is to tell them not to think about elephants. I supposed I was lucky he'd only twigged to the location of his son, and not to the fact that the nondescript, somewhat boring man following the Luidaeg around like a really tall antlered puppy was actually Oberon, King of all Faerie. That would have been a lot harder to explain.

Of course, this was distracting from both the matter of the coup at hand and the need to finish getting ready for my oft-delayed wedding, but it was still better than outing Oberon before he wanted to be.

"I know what *that woman* can do," said Quentin. "She's done it to me. I also know that if you're loyal enough to something other than her, the effect is blunted. Dean shrugged it off entirely."

"To be fair, I'm only half Daoine Sidhe," said Dean, looking faintly alarmed at being dragged into this. "I have two Firstborn to answer to. Resisting one of them wasn't as hard as it could have been."

"Remind me to tell you a funny story about your other Firstborn," I said. Maida blinked at me. I shrugged. "Long story."

"We went to the Duchy of Ships to do a favor for the Luidaeg, and we met the Merrow Firstborn while we were there," said Quentin. "Her name's Amphitrite, but she mostly goes by 'Pete,' and she's kinda awesome but kinda annoying, too. Which describes most of the Firstborn I've met, I guess."

"Okay, I guess it wasn't that long of a story," I said. "But it illustrates why you should stop being pissed at your parents, Quentin. If they hadn't sent you away, you would never have met Pete, or the Luidaeg—or Dean."

"Or Toby," contributed Raj, who had clearly been silent for too long and was starting to feel left out. "Or me."

"So many wonderful people to enrich and endanger your life," said Tybalt dryly. "Are we quite done with the family dramatics? I would like to resume the process of preventing a coup before it interferes with my wedding date."

"I want that also, honey," I said. "But this feels like a fight that's been a long time coming, and it needs to happen."

"Do you have any idea how many years I spent feeling like no one in the world wanted me?" asked Quentin, attention back on his father. "Like I must have done something *wrong*, or you wouldn't have separated me from Penny? There was no one in Shadowed Hills who was equipped to be the kind of adult I needed to have in my life. A couple of the Hobs tried, but I was enough of a pampered prince not to recognize kindness as sincere when it came from the staff. I was drowning when October came along. I didn't know who I was or where I stood or how I was going to survive long enough to prove to you that I was worthy of coming home, and then there was this woman—this ridiculous, careless, *rude* woman, who didn't want me any more than anyone else did, but at least she was honest about it. At least she didn't lie to me."

"Quentin . . ." I stopped. I didn't know what else to say, honestly.

"Oh, don't pretend you wanted me around in the beginning. We both know you didn't." Quentin smiled a little, shrugging. "It's okay. You were still sad, and I was sort of a spoiled brat. We weren't good for each other yet. We learned how to be good for each other, and we did it together, which made it even better."

"I've always liked you," said Raj. "Of course, the circumstances of our meeting were traumatic enough without adding abandonment issues to the mix."

"Yeah." Quentin focused back on his father. "If I wanted someone to love me, I had to force them to see me for who I was under all the fear and resentment and propriety, and I did this to myself so I could be here to see Toby get married without endangering your precious throne in the process. So I'm not going to apologize to you because I'm *not* sorry."

They glared at each other, and although they currently looked nothing alike, there was no mistaking the fact that they were family. Only family can look that angry, in that specific, focused way. Family means never having to say, "I forgive you."

Aethlin was the first to look away. "I'm sorry," he said. "Last time I saw you, you were . . . you seemed well, and you told us you loved us, and I thought things were all right between us. I didn't really have a choice about sending you away, not given who was making the suggestion, but I could have kept you and Penny together, or I could have found a way for you to contact your sister without invalidating the protections of a blind fosterage in the process. I'm the High King. I could have found a way, and I'm sorry I didn't."

"That's all I wanted to hear," said Quentin. He released some of the tension in his shoulders, not sagging, precisely, but becoming less of a sculpture in the shape of a Banshee boy. "I'm sorry I didn't find a way to tell you who I was. How *did* you realize who I am?"

"I don't . . . I don't actually know." Aethlin looked back to Quentin, frowning again, but this time with confusion. "I remember pain, and then blackness, and then redness filled with moving figures and places I had never been, people I had never seen. I think . . . I think I saw Annwn." His voice took on a lilting note of awe, like the idea of catching even a glimpse of deeper Faerie was something to be treasured and dwelt upon.

I might have felt that way once before it had actually happened. There was nothing like *seeing* deeper Faerie to make me never want to do that again.

"Toby, did you bleed on my father?"

"Had to," I said. "He'd been stabbed in the kidney and he was bleeding out. I needed him to be able to heal before his injuries killed him." And possibly even immediately after those injuries killed him—if his magic had still been capable of working fast enough.

That's something I have no interest in advertising. I made that mistake at Tamed Lightning, allowing Li Qin and the rest of the staff to realize I could occasionally, under the right circumstances, raise the dead, and my repayment had been an invitation to bleed myself virtually dry to bring back their loved ones. It's not the sort of thing I can, or should, be doing on a regular basis. Death is a part of the order of things, even in Faerie, or we wouldn't have the night-haunts.

If I raised all of Faerie's dead, what would the night-haunts eat? I would be condemning an unknown number of them to a slow withering away, and all for the sake of denying the way things were meant to go. And I would still do my best to save the people I cared about . . . if I had the opportunity.

I guess I'm as much of a hypocrite as everyone else. I'm just a hypocrite who admits it.

Quentin rolled his eyes. "I was all prepared to yell at you for telling on me, but you didn't, did you? You just didn't think."

"In my defense, if I'd stopped to think, he would have bled out on the floor," I said. "That would have been worse, I think."

"Maybe," muttered Quentin. He shot his father a sharp look. "Maybe not." Then he thawed and sighed, and admitted, "Yeah. It would have been worse."

Aethlin took a half-step backward, visibly stung, but didn't object. Instead, he turned back toward me and Maida, hands by his sides and still covered in flecks of dried blood—whether his or mine, I couldn't possibly have said.

"Now what, Sir Daye?" he asked plaintively. "My kingdom is under threat, my son rejects me, my staff is infiltrated and cannot be trusted . . . what more can I lose for your sake?"

"Hey," I objected. "Don't you blame *any* of this on me, unless you're blaming a general shortage of eggs in your kitchens after Kerry finishes baking the wedding cake, or blood in the carpets after I've been allowed into a room. I didn't send your children away, I didn't foment a coup, and I certainly didn't replace your staff. If we can help you—any of us except for the Luidaeg, since her services are not mine to promise, and must be paid for whether you're a king or not—you need only to ask. If we can't, we'll stay out of the way. I have a wedding to prepare for."

Any unease I might have felt at talking back to the High King—which admittedly, wasn't much—was washed away by the surprised, grateful look Tybalt shot my way, his whole face softening, like he couldn't quite believe I was still focused on our wedding. I smiled at him. He deserved this. Everything else aside, he deserved this.

"That's my cue," said Walther, and levered himself out of the short couch where he'd been reclining. "As I have no official wedding-related duties to perform, and some experience with the intrigues of royal courts, I volunteer myself to assist in interviewing your staff."

"Really?" asked Maida.

"Really," Walther confirmed. "If you have access to a stocked alchemy lab whose owner won't object overly much to my presence, I can even brew up a decent draught of truth to give to anyone whose motives seem in the least questionable."

"You were able to brew the elf-shot countercharm in this room," said Aethlin, dubiously.

"That formula is my own creation, and probably the single thing I've been called upon to brew most frequently since I was in training with my alchemy instructor," said Walther. "I carry the base ingredients whenever I travel with Sir Daye. I could mix it in my sleep at this point although you probably shouldn't swallow anything mixed by a sleeping alchemist, no matter how much you trust us. Doing it out of a suitcase with people breathing down my neck was no big deal. Draught of truth involves ground castor seeds and pressed iris blossoms, as well as several other moderately toxic compounds. If I don't have the proper equipment, I'll kill half your staff. And it won't be murder, it will be negligence. I doubt that will make it any more forgivable for their families."

Aethlin stared at him for a long moment. Walther looked implacably back, going so far as to reach up and adjust his glasses.

"Cassandra can assist me," he said. "She's been spending a lot of time in my lab, and she knows her way around a mortar and pestle."

"Mom will probably be happier if I'm off doing alchemy with Walther, and not wandering around playing decoy with you and May," said Cassandra apologetically. "Sorry, Toby."

"No worries. You do what works best for you," I said.

"All right," said Aethlin. "A lab can be found, and basic supplies. We would welcome the assistance." He looked back at me. "I'll send someone we've verified as trustworthy if we need you."

"All right, sire," I said, and offered him a cursory bow.

"Hmm," he said, and started for the door. Maida grabbed my arm instead of following.

"The blood?" she said, anxiously.

"Right, almost forgot," I said, and pulled my knife. Maida let me go, having enough common sense not to hang on to an armed knight. I offered her an encouraging smile and walked over to Walther. "Jar, please."

"Really? What am I, a Container Store?" He still bent to open his valise, pulling out a small glass jar about large enough to hold a cup and a half of liquid. "I assume you're about to bleed into this, and I don't want to ask you to fill something large enough that your lurking King of Cats glares at you."

"He's not the only one who'd be glaring," said Quentin.

"Appreciated," I said, and took the jar in my free hand. Unscrewing the lid without stabbing myself was difficult, and Walther didn't offer to help, the jerk, just watched with the dry amusement of someone who knew he wasn't about to be bleeding, no matter what.

Once I had the jar open, I pressed the edge of my knife against my wrist, where experience had shown me the blood would come fast and easy. Then I looked at Maida, to be sure she was watching me. If I was bleeding for her, I wanted her to see it.

She met my eyes and nodded, very slightly. She understood that no matter what else I was doing, I was hurting myself for her sake, and she acknowledged it. That was all I ever wanted from her, or from anyone, really. For them to see that I was hurting myself on their behalf, and not let them pretend they had no part in it.

The knife bit into my arm as sharply as it always did, the pain not dulled in the slightest by the number of times I'd cut myself in that exact spot. I healed fast enough not to scar, and that meant I also healed too fast for nerve damage to take hold. That was definitely good in the grand scheme of things, but sometimes I wished it would hurt just a little less. I hissed between my teeth, the sound small. Not small enough to keep Tybalt from catching it. He tensed, moving, not toward me, but toward the High Queen.

"Do you see what she does on your behalf, on the behalf of all these cursed, divisive, Divided Courts?" he asked, in a low, unforgiving voice. She glanced at him, startled, before her eyes were pulled back to my bleeding arm, as if she couldn't look away for long.

The wound was already starting to heal, and the jar was less than half full. I pressed down again, trying to stay focused on my task.

"I would take her into the Court of Cats if it were allowed," said Tybalt. "I would ask her to forsake her title among your kind and come to live with me. But alas, the shadows would never welcome her, and so I must set aside my crown for her sake, and come into your rotten, ruined world to live by her side. But never mistake the fact that she is the best of you. She is the fairest flower of Oberon's garden, and she bleeds for your sake, who would call yourself her better, who has never earned that name."

"Why are you angry with me?" asked Maida, finally turning her eyes away from my efforts. "Because I allowed my Firstborn to convince me to send my children away? I've been angry with my-self for doing that since I did it, and I dare you to sit in front of your own First and do any differently. Because I sit upon a throne? You know how much I gave up to hold that place and call it my own. You know what it cost me better than almost anyone, save maybe for your lady herself, who has forgiven me for more than you ever could. Or is it because my husband was direly injured and she took it upon herself to save him—a favor I did not ask her to bestow, although I would have, had I been there to intercede. Is it because you know that were our positions reversed, she would have been unable to save you, King of Cats, whose magic bends down other paths?"

"*Maman*," said Quentin. "Leave him alone."

"He came first to me," said Maida, and looked at her son with painful longing. Painful because even though I knew he loved her, the look his face reflected back at her didn't match the degree of affection I could see so clearly on her own, and I had been stand-ing where she was now not all that long ago, watching my child choose another woman over me.

But unlike Maida and Aethlin, I had never voluntarily sent Gil-lian away. I put the lid back on the jar and wiped my knife against my hip, further bloodying my already hopelessly-bloodied dress. "Here," I said, walking across the room to offer it to her. "A mouthful should be enough for anything but a truly mortal wound."

"And if the wound is truly mortal?" she asked, gingerly taking the jar.

"Drink until you choke," I advised. I honestly had no idea how much of my blood she'd need to heal herself, but more was proba-bly a good idea. "And make sure you warn your guard once you've vetted them. It's my blood, so it's going to be full of my memories, and you might get confused the same way the High King did."

"Confused?" asked Chelsea.

"He thought he was October when he first woke up," said Maida.

Quentin laughed out loud. "I wish I could have seen that," he said. "It would almost have made up for the rest of this." He turned his back on his father and walked—stalked, really—over to the couch where the rest of the teenagers were sitting, compacting himself onto the arm of the couch with his feet resting on Dean's lap. Dean didn't object, just hooked an arm around Quentin's knees and gave the High King a challenging look, like he was daring the literal regent of the entire continent to say anything about this seating arrangement.

Dear Oberon, was I training an entire army of disrespectful teenagers who didn't care who they offered insult to? I hoped not.

"Chelsea, do you know when you're supposed to go pick up the next wave of guests?" I asked, more sharply than I intended to.

"Um . . ." Chelsea pulled out her phone, checking the screen. "Now looks about good. Boys, you wanna come with me?"

In short order, the teens were trooping toward the door, taking Chelsea's popcorn bucket with them, leaving me alone with Tybalt, Walther, Cassie, and the two Sollys monarchs. Quentin didn't say goodbye to either of his parents. His mother looked stung though she didn't say anything.

"You can't tell anyone else he's here," I said. "Even with Fiac in the room, you shouldn't have cause to mention whether or not you know where the Crown Prince is, and if you let us get through the wedding and leave, there won't be any questions about the validity of the line of succession."

"I know," said Aethlin. He sounded utterly miserable. "Does my son *actually* hate me? Have I failed so completely as a father?"

"I don't think he hates you; I think he's just a teenager and under a lot of stress and lashing out at someone it's safe to be mad at. I also don't think I'm the person you should be asking," I said. "Take Cassie and Walther with you and start interviewing your staff. We need to know who we can trust, and I need to change my clothes before I go find the others and talk to Nessa."

"Nessa?" Maida didn't bother to conceal her surprise. "Why do you need to talk to Nessa?"

I glanced at Tybalt and smiled warmly. With everyone else taking care of their respective errands and nothing, for the moment, that demanded our immediate attention, it was time to do a little more toward keeping my word.

"She still hasn't shown us the venue, and I need to make sure it doesn't smell like maple syrup."

Tybalt's look of surprised delight was worth all the possible charges of insurrection in the world.

FIFTEEN

THE ROYAL KITCHENS WERE, unsurprisingly, enormous and much more industrial than I'd expected them to be. Obviously, they couldn't use steel in a knowe, but every surface was either polished marble or equally polished maple; it *gleamed,* with the warm, organic slickness that only ever comes to well-oiled and treated wood. It was like walking into the medieval equivalent of one of those Food Network cooking shows May sometimes puts on after midnight when she wants to unwind.

One entire wall was ovens and stoves and open holes leading to oceans of flame that probably had some reasonable name like "pizza ovens" or "big fucking baking place," but looked to me a lot more like gateways into the human concept of Hell. You could burn in one of those open ovens for a long, long time. The opposite wall was all shelves of dry goods, joints of meat hanging on wooden hooks, and closed doors leading into an assortment of pantries. It was dizzyingly expansive, and not made less so by the veritable army of Hobs, Brownies, and Hobgoblins bustling around the sinks and stoves, all of them working at preparing the next meal for the high table.

I wondered whether there was any chance we'd get to eat this one, or whether our time in Toronto was going to be one long chain of missed opportunities to sit down and stuff our faces like civilized people. Maybe the knowe understood that we really weren't civilized people and was just trying to save us the embarrassment of me forgetting which fork was supposed to go in my salad versus which fork was supposed to go in the person I was trying to kill.

One of the Hobs looked up from her work and smiled brilliantly at the sight of us—an emotion I was sure had to be at least somewhat dishonest, since even the Hobs of Shadowed Hills, who genuinely loved me, never looked that happy to have their territory invaded.

Then, still smiling, she said, "Your friends are at the tables in the back," and I saw the frozen edge of terror behind her smile. The Luidaeg must have introduced herself, then. That made things make a lot more sense. People with more of a concept of their own mortality than I and my friends tend to possess get a little weirded-out when Firstborn walk in and announce themselves just for the sake of a sandwich.

And to be fair, we're only that mellow about certain Firstborn. Three, to be precise, out of the six I've met so far, but Eira is unpleasant enough to make up for ten of her kinder siblings.

"Cool," I said. "Do we need an escort?"

"No, no," she said, shaking her head. Then, in case there had been any question about her nerves, she added, "Please. Be our guest."

I realized all the other kitchen staffers were watching us warily, like mice all too aware that a snake had just slithered into the room. I reached back to take Tybalt's hand, answering her smile with one of my own. If mine had a few too many edges, well, hers was about as sincere as Evening complimenting a changeling's hairstyle.

"Appreciated," I said. "Do you know where Kerry is?"

Her smile turned even more strained, crumbling around the edges like a riverbank during a rainstorm. "She has commandeered one of the cold pantries, and demanded—quite imperiously, might I add—that we not allow you anywhere near it, or tell you precisely which one she's in, as you are not allowed to see the cake before the wedding."

"Really?" I asked, amused, and glanced toward Tybalt. "Is this a weird pureblood thing? Because with humans, it's the dress that the groom isn't supposed to see ahead of time, not the cake and the bride. And since my groom designed my dress, I think we've already opted out of most of the traditions, and you told me I'd get to approve the cake."

"Far be it from me to override a Hob where hearthcraft is concerned," he said, with no sign of remorse. If anything, he looked amused.

"I don't know if it's a tradition where you come from, ma'am, but when a stranger commandeers part of my kitchen, I do whatever seems likely to keep them calm and not damaging things and might convince them to leave slightly sooner than they would be otherwise inclined to do." The Hob shook her head. "The High Queen herself requested we allow the use of our space, and so we allow it, but permission is not the same as approval. Please. Your friends are waiting."

I knew a dismissal when I heard one, no matter how politely it was couched. "Gotcha," I said, with a small mock salute. I grabbed Tybalt's hand, pulling him along with me as I followed the Hob's gesture toward the back of the banquet hall-sized room.

"Have *you* seen the cake?" I asked, once I judged we were safely out of hearing range. "She's not, like, sculpting an animated model of Godzilla out of fondant or something, right?"

"Not as such," he said, sounding a little shaken. "We discussed flavors and design once, and I showed her the early sketches of your gown, and then she said she would take care of everything and I shouldn't worry my pretty little head about it and went away. Should I have pressed the matter further? I wasn't concerned until this moment."

"No, I'm sure it's fine." It felt frivolous, to be concerned about my wedding cake in the middle of a possible coup, but for the first time, it wasn't my responsibility to stabilize a kingdom alone. There were other people with the skills and authority to handle the current phase of the problem, and while they would probably call on me once we reached the "people getting stabbed and doing lots of bleeding" part of the proceedings, the fact of the matter is that I'm a blunt instrument. Sometimes a situation needs a scalpel.

We kept walking toward the indicated back of the room, continuing for what seemed like an utterly unreasonable amount of time for us to still be in a kitchen. Almost every workstation was occupied, even down to a row of dishwashers scrubbing serving platters and rinsing out goblets. They all watched us suspiciously as we passed, but none of them asked where we were going or challenged our right to be there.

I remembered the way Oleander de Merelands had been able to

infiltrate Shadowed Hills, under the guise of a serving girl, and the Barrow Wight girl who had stood as servant of the former King and Queen of Highmountain. In both cases, they had been able to cause a remarkable amount of trouble by being beneath the notice of the people they were trying to hurt. I made a note to myself to remind Aethlin that interrogating the staff had to include *all* the staff, not just the ones he thought were important enough to matter.

Everyone matters. If there's one thing I've learned from how hard Evening and her ilk have tried to convince me I *don't* matter, it's that everyone matters. The alternative is a world where no one matters, and since I know that isn't true, "everyone" is the only option we have left.

Finally, after far more walking than was reasonable, we reached a corner and turned it to see a series of rough-hewn essentially picnic tables, probably set up for the use of the kitchen staff themselves when they took breaks from their work, or as a staging area for banquets in the process of being delivered. The tables were far from full, being extensive enough to easily seat at least fifty people, but as they held the rest of our party, plus Nessa, and a remarkable number of serving trays of cold cuts, cheese, and sliced fruit, I didn't care.

"Toby!" called Stacy, catching sight of us. Then she got a better look at me, and sighed. "Where in the world is your dress? You shouldn't have taken that off without help."

"I *do* know how to work a zipper," said Tybalt, in a primly offended tone.

I laughed, patting him on the arm. "I had help, and my jeans seemed like a better choice if people were going to be stabbing me." Which meant they were always a better choice for me, given how much time I spent bleeding.

As a child, the idea of wearing comfortable, mundane clothing inside a royal knowe would have been unthinkable, not least because the false Queen had been so fond of transforming whatever I was wearing into something she liked better. Even when I showed up in gowns originally commissioned by my mother, intricate assemblies of rare fabric and layered enchantment, there had been a decent chance the false Queen would change them around me, asserting her control of the situation through the cut and color of my underpants. It was amazing how long I'd gone thinking that was normal, that monarchs were always careless and capricious with the lives of their subjects.

And then I'd met Arden, who hadn't been a queen for long, but who had learned the art at the feet of her father, who was widely regarded as the best king the Mists has ever had. Arden, who didn't abuse her people for fun, and who wore jeans and sweatshirts when she wasn't officially on-duty. Not that a queen was ever distinct from her throne, but sometimes she was speaking officially as the crown and sometimes she was just Arden, amused and exasperated by her attempts to teach her staff about toaster pastries.

If Arden could wear jeans, so could I.

"I left it in the dressing room," I said, before Stacy could get even more upset over its absence. "It's beautiful, and I'm sure the staff Bannicks will be able to get the blood out. If they can't, we just take it home with us, and Elliot will be delighted to take care of it." I brought Elliot's fiancée—now wife—back from the dead. He'd be happy to do my laundry for the rest of my life if I asked him to. Then I paused, blinking. "And *what* is that on your *head*?"

She was wearing a headband of sorts, one festooned with red plastic roses, sequins, and tiny plastic pearls, with a short veil glued down in the middle. It was tacky. It was ridiculous. May beamed across the table at me.

She didn't have a headband, but she did have a gaudy button that said, in large, cheerful letters, "Here comes the bride!" "Do you like it?" she asked. "We got one of the Tuatha to open a gate to the local party supply store for us and got bachelorette party swag for all the decoys."

I sighed, not having the heart to tell her that after an assassination attempt on the High King, we probably weren't going to need any decoy brides. When May gets the opportunity to decorate something, she tends to go all in.

Stacy huffed, sitting back on the bench where she'd settled herself and folding her arms. Narrowing her eyes slightly, she asked, "Where's my daughter?"

"Cassie is with the High King and Queen, assisting in the interrogation of their private guard," I said. She narrowed her eyes further, and I sighed. "She's a Seer, Stace. I know you don't want her to be, I know you don't want her to be anything that attracts the attention of the nobility, but she's my niece, she's brilliant, and she's a Seer. All the wanting in the world won't change that."

"I don't like this," said Stacy. "Mitch is coming with the rest of the children. You're not going to let *them* go off with the High King, are you?"

"She can't stop Karen if she wants to go, since that girl is under my protection, and I outrank you both last time I looked," said the Luidaeg, gesturing with a pickle spear. Not to be left out of the bad style choices, she had several strands of Mardi Gras beads around her neck, and a stack of cheap bangles on one arm. That party supply store had enjoyed its time with May's credit card.

"And the rest aren't Seers, so it shouldn't be a problem," I said. Stacy looked away, not meeting my eyes. I blinked, hard, and decided that cornering her on the issue in front of everyone else wasn't going to do us any good. But we were *going* to have a conversation about this as soon as I could get her alone.

Poppy snorted and waved at me from the other side of the table, chirping, "Get a plate and make a sandwich. You've not eaten since before I ate last, and I've had three!"

"She hasn't eaten, *and* she's been bleeding again," said Tybalt, nudging me toward the trays. I looked between the two of them and sighed, moving to pick up two slices of bread.

"I don't need the entire world telling me I need to eat more," I objected. "I'm a grown woman and I can feed myself just fine."

Tybalt made a scoffing noise. "Perhaps it's for the best the court Adhene has gone off with his liege lord for the interrogations," he said. "Since a lie that blatant would surely have roused him to attempted murder."

"I'm pretty hard to kill," I said, stuffing roast beef and sliced melon between the bread.

"Hence the 'attempted.'"

"You know, my sister will be thrilled when I get home and report the day's events to her," said Nolan easily. "Oh, don't look at me like that. You all know I'm here as an observer for Queen Windermere. She only has one hero of the realm right now, and one presumptive heir. She wouldn't allow us both to go off at the same time if she didn't have good reason, and being sure Sir Daye is neither plotting insurrection against her nor overthrowing anyone else absolutely qualifies. She's going to be so happy to hear that you don't vex her on purpose, you're just like this. All the time. No matter how important the people you might be insulting are. Sir Cat," he switched his attention to Tybalt, not missing a single beat of his sentence, "are you quite sure you wish to marry the Lady October? She does seem rather akin to the month she was named for, and will no doubt cause you no end of troubles. It seems like a marriage to her is a poor way to guarantee a peaceful future."

Tybalt blinked at him, expression more amused than offended, but before he could say anything, a new sound introduced itself. It was low and rich and slightly gravely, with a strange kinship to hoofbeats racing across the open moor. Faerie is remarkably good at presenting itself in complicated metaphors, but this metaphor was incredibly simple, for all that it was also inescapable. It was a sound no one had heard in centuries, except for maybe the Luidaeg, maybe Poppy, locked up as they were in their apartment by the bay.

It was the sound of Oberon laughing.

"A peaceful future is never guaranteed," he said, dark eyes bright below the crown of his antlers. Everyone was silent, listening raptly, as if he were saying the most important thing ever spoken in these halls. And as he was the father of us all, who was to say he wasn't? He represented our past and our future, all tangled up in a single confusing, often nondescript man.

"The right wife doesn't somehow magically buy you peace and plenty," he said. "I found the right wife twice over, or thought I did, and found no peace there, only endless conflict. My beautiful ladies are stories now—to most of you, anyway," and there he glanced to the Luidaeg, infinite warmth in his expression, "but to me, they were the most wonderful women in the world. The *only* women in the world, when first we met, but I would have chosen them out of millions. I would choose them for the first time today if that choice were set before me. And they never brought me peace or plenty, not one day in our long, long days together, and I would have all those days over again if the world allowed it to me. Do not try to direct your heart's desires based on presumption of peace. It will never once bring you joy, and it will never lead you home."

"Daddy," sighed the Luidaeg, sounding every inch the teenager she appeared to be, like she belonged with the teens who swarmed my living room almost every night of the week, laughing and teasing each other and throwing food even when they knew they'd be expected to clean up after themselves.

Nessa startled, looking at the Luidaeg with new understanding in her terribly widened eyes. "Did you call him . . ." she began, only to taper off into silence as those same eyes, still wide, seemed to glaze over. There was a long, silent pause before she slumped forward, her head hitting the table only inches from her sandwich-laden plate.

The Luidaeg sighed and moved one of Nessa's arms so that it was cradling her head, giving her something to rest upon. "Sorry," she said. "That was my fault."

"Wait," I said. "I thought no one noticed him because he didn't *want* to be noticed. Are you putting the whammy on people who figure out that he's your dad?"

Oberon picked up his sandwich, seemingly unconcerned by the scene unfolding around him. The Luidaeg sighed.

"He's not entirely himself yet," she said. "He doesn't want people demanding things from him before he's finished the process of pulling himself back together."

"I don't know if you've noticed, but we're in some serious shit here!" I gestured wildly with my sandwich. Tybalt caught my wrist and gently guided it back down in front of me.

"Eat," he said. "Don't attempt to conduct an orchestra."

I shot him a quick look, then returned my attention to the Luidaeg. "So you've been wiping the minds of anyone you don't feel deserves to know that he's here?" That answered a lot of questions. It raised almost as many more, like how could she do that? Titania had bound her powers long before she disappeared, making everything something to be paid for.

"I'm allowed to act when it's for selfish purposes, and wanting my father to be left with the time he needs to heal is about as selfish as it gets," she said. "You have to understand, October, I'm so much older than anyone else you know. Only Eira comes close, and I had a century without her, when it was just me and my sisters—my *true* sisters, the ones who knew me and loved me exactly as I was, who worked no conspiracies against me, who laid no plans to make themselves sole heirs to our parents' love—and the moors, and nothing to come between us and the heart of Faerie. So no, you *don't* understand my loneliness, or my selfishness. You've helped the former in the last few years, you and Quentin and your Fetch and Poppy."

"That's me," chirped Poppy.

"But you can't *understand* it, not the way my father can—my father, who left me, and came back to me, and he *will* have the time he needs to heal before Faerie starts beating down his door again, demanding he settle every petty problem they've created for themselves. He will have all the time he wants." She glared at me, eyes as black as pitch and somehow bright with sorrow at the same time, a sorrow I knew better than I wanted to, because she had been showing it to me since the day we met. The Luidaeg couldn't lie, but she didn't have to say everything she felt unless she wanted to—unless she was compelled to. She could keep her secrets, and so she did, when it suited her. When they were things she didn't want to share.

"Hey," I said uncomfortably. "It's cool. I didn't say it was wrong for you to be stunning people, just that I was surprised. I'd been wondering how it was no one seemed to notice him. The High King swallowed some of my blood, and he saw Quentin in my memories, but he didn't see Oberon. And that doesn't make a lot of sense unless something's hiding the actual, you know, One King of all Faerie."

"Why was the High King drinking your blood?" asked the Luidaeg. Everyone else leaned a little closer, clearly anxious for my answer.

I added some cheese and a few slices of tomato to my sandwich. This was more like normal, solid ground, and I was going to enjoy standing on it, for however long it lasted. "Oh, because he'd been stabbed in the kidney," I answered, voice light.

The Luidaeg narrowed her eyes. "*What.*"

"Turns out there's more than just the one Doppelganger—that's why Walther and Cassie are helping with the interrogations, by the way, the Sollyses have to interview all the members of their guard and anyone else who might have access to the royal family, which pretty much means all the staff in the knowe—and the second one managed to stab High King Aethlin before committing suicide to avoid interrogation. The High King was going to bleed out, but he was still breathing, which meant he could still borrow magic."

"So what, you just gambled with bleeding?" asked Stacy. "That seems a little bit extreme."

"It was that or gamble on a healer showing up fast enough to do something to save him, and that pretty clearly wasn't going to happen." I shrugged. "It worked, he healed himself, I didn't get accused of regicide. Now I have a sandwich, and as soon as Nessa wakes up, she's going to show us where in the knowe I'm supposed to be getting married."

Stacy blinked. The Luidaeg blinked. A whole lot of blinking happened from the rest of the group, all at pretty much the same time, which made noting them all individually both pointless and more work than I felt like doing right now. I took a bite of my sandwich. It wasn't my best work, but the ingredients were fresh, and it had been so long since the last time I'd eaten that I had to resist the urge to shove the entire thing into my mouth and gulp it down like a snake. I'm pretty sure I made an inchoate noise of delight before taking my second bite, barely pausing long enough to swallow the first one.

Nolan was the first to recover. "The High King was assaulted in your presence, and your concern is for the venue of your marriage?" he asked.

"Yes." I looked up from my sandwich to focus on him. "I owe the High King exactly as much loyalty as anyone else on the continent does. I don't want him to die, and did I mention I *saved his life*. But I owe Tybalt a great deal more, and I promised him we'd actually be getting married this week, which means I need to stay halfway focused."

Nolan blinked. "I think my mother would have liked you," he said, in a dazed tone. "Whether that is compliment or dire criticism, I leave to the judgment of those who knew her before she stopped her dancing."

The Luidaeg actually laughed. "All right, so you're finally marrying the kitty-cat, and the High King's not dead, and I'm guessing you're missing the Ames girl because she's gone to get the rest of your guests, as you continue your campaign to put everyone in one place for the first time. A single dragon of sufficient size and my sister could take care of everybody you care about at the same time."

"She's asleep," I said stiffly.

"She is," the Luidaeg affirmed. "If she wakes, I'll know. Unless she wakes due to magic so far outside my experience or so much greater than mine that I can't perceive it, I'll know, and you know you're the first call I'll make. But she could still have agents, and I can't find them unless they do something to make themselves apparent."

"We have enough trouble already without trying to borrow

more." I leaned across the table to gently prod Nessa in the arm. "When's she going to wake up?"

"When you finish that sandwich, make another one, and drink something," said the Luidaeg. "You can lose a lot of blood without suffering the consequences that would come for a person who lacks your specific gifts, but you still need to hydrate. Eat, drink, and she'll wake up."

I rolled my eyes. As Sleeping Beauty clauses went, "you just need to eat something, not kiss anybody" was reasonably mild and probably nicer than it had to be, but it was still annoying. I settled myself to consuming the rest of my sandwich in bites as large as I could manage without choking, and Tybalt began assembling a sandwich of his own. He was old enough not to overly judge my fondness for combining fruit and meat, thankfully, something which had been much more popular in his youth than it was in modern America. It was one of the few habits I'd picked up from my mother that I didn't mind holding onto. Amandine was bad at raising children and bad at being a decent person, but she was great at building a sandwich.

Maybe that's a mundane virtue for a daughter of Oberon, but when you have as few of them as she does, I guess you need to do what you can with what you've got.

Tybalt settled beside me with his own plate, smiling warmly. I smiled back. Everything else aside, we were getting married. He was finally going to stop worrying that I somehow didn't want him, and I was going to stop getting ambushed with bridal magazines every time I entered my own kitchen. What were matters of dynastic succession compared to that?

Quite a lot, actually. My second sandwich was sliced chicken, spicy mustard, and nectarine, giving me the salty-savory-sweet combination I preferred, and I ate it almost too fast to taste, before filling a glass to the brim with what I assumed was orange juice. I took a large gulp and managed to swallow rather than aerosolizing it. Melon juice. Of course it was. Faerie doesn't do anything normal when we can find a way to make it weird.

"Good enough?" I asked the Luidaeg.

"What's your hurry?"

"Sedition, still don't know who on the staff is trustworthy, a bunch more of our friends are about to arrive here, and they won't know what's been going on."

"Hell, *I* barely know what's going on," said Stacy. "You haven't been exactly forthcoming, October."

"You know as much as I do," I said. "High King got stabbed. Doppelgangers in the knowe. Apparently, there's a question of legitimacy of the throne, thanks to King Shallcross being an asshole."

"There's only a question in his own mind," said the Luidaeg, before leaning over and tapping Nessa twice on the forehead. The Gwragedd Annwn gasped and sat up, eyes suddenly very wide.

"Did I fall asleep?" she asked, pushing her hair out of her still-illusioned face and looking around the table. "I'm *so* sorry, that was *so* unprofessional of me. You're guests in this knowe, and it's my duty to remain attentive to your needs—"

I took another swig of melon juice to pacify the Luidaeg before putting the glass down. "Well, right now, what we need is to be shown to the place where we're getting married tomorrow. I want to know that the Doppelganger didn't make a mess of everything."

Since I had no idea what the decorations were supposed to look like, or even what "everything" entailed in this situation, the request was somewhat more pressing than it might have been under normal circumstances. Nessa rose. So did Nolan. I blinked at him.

"I will be accompanying you," he said solemnly. "Not to fault the choices of your swain or this sweet maiden fair," he somehow managed to make that sound endearing, rather than sexist and a little creepy, "but I doubt the King of Cats has attended many pureblood weddings among the Divided Courts, and I do not know the Lady Nessa's qualifications."

Nessa giggled, hiding her mouth behind her hand. "I would be delighted to have you accompany us," she said.

"I admit, I have an ulterior motive of sorts." Nolan offered his hand, helping her to her feet. "Tuatha de Dannan are limited by our ability to visualize the place we want our portals to open. Our journey here was possible primarily due to the fine mortal art of photography and the assurance of the courts who helped us on our way that the pictures were clear, accurate, and recent. By visiting the wedding hall myself, I will be able to return there in an instant, should trouble arise."

"You kids have fun with your little coup," said the Luidaeg, waving a baguette vaguely in our direction. "I'm going to stay here and hold down the table."

"I'm going to go make sure you haven't managed to bleed on the rest of your wardrobe, and also be seen being a possible decoy," said Stacy. She rose, brushing her hands against her hips to knock the crumbs off. "That way I'm there when the rest of my family arrives."

"Sounds like a plan." I glanced over at Poppy, Oberon, May, and Jazz, but all of them seemed content to remain exactly where they were, munching their way through an actual meal. It wasn't sophisticated, but sometimes that matters a lot less than being made of food. I offered them a little wave and took Tybalt's arm, pulling him to his feet along with me.

"Well, we're off," I said. "Be safe, all of you, and if someone approaches without being verifiably themselves, throw things."

"No one's sneaking up on us today," said May. "Come find me when you need a decoy. Otherwise, I'm going to stay here and use bride privilege to demand more snacks."

"Yes, ma'am," I said, and followed Nessa, on Nolan's arm, back the way we had come.

The kitchen seemed smaller now that we knew where we were going, or maybe that was just me feeling less leaden and weighed-down after putting something in my stomach. Nessa paused to exchange a few words with the Hob who had directed us to the others in the first place, smiling at the other woman's reply, and then led us onward, out of the kitchen.

Once we were safely outside, the door closed behind us and the maple-and-amethyst walls of the hall enveloping us, Nessa looked at me. "When you said the High King and Queen would be verifying the identities of their staff, you meant . . . ?"

"The entire staff," I said, and watched as some of the tension left her shoulders, replaced by an ease that seemed far more natural to her. She was someone who liked rules and order enough to have risen to the position of seneschal of a royal knowe. This must all be very upsetting for her.

"Thank Maeve," she sighed. "It's all too common for the higher nobility—no offense, to any of you—"

"None taken," said Nolan.

"But it's all too common for the higher nobility to overlook anyone below the rank of Baron, and sometimes they don't even remember the baronial titles when it comes time to account for their underlings."

"Are all the guards titled, then?"

"Oh, yes." Nessa led us along the hall, an earnest expression on her face. "The domains close enough to us to have easy access to our staffing needs send their second sons and daughters here to serve. The majority of the guard are knights and dames at the absolute least; most are barons or more. It keeps them occupied, and not planning insurrection."

"I see. Is that commonly known?"

"It would have to be, wouldn't it, since everyone is released come the end of their term of service," said Nessa. "They go back to their home domains and resume whatever duties they have in their families, and we honor and remember them for their time with us."

"We knew when we were children that had our father been able to openly claim us, I would one day be expected to travel to Toronto to serve my time," said Nolan. "Because he couldn't, I couldn't, and had Arden been called to the throne in the normal way of things, that would have put her at a disadvantage against our peers, who would already have known me, as we would have been brothers in arms. And sisters, I suppose. There should be a way to express that thought without getting hung up on the difference between the two . . ." He trailed off, expression turning pensive.

"While Nolan invents modern gender theory, how long has this been going on?" I asked.

"Since the High Kingdom was founded." Nessa frowned. "You truly didn't know?"

"How would I?" I shrugged. "I'm a knight, but I earned my title, I didn't inherit it. My mother has no title." Amandine's Firstborn, but that doesn't come with a crown. Thankfully. If she were a literal fairy princess, she would be even more insufferable than she already is, and that's really saying something. "My father, depending on which of them you're referring to, was either absent or human during my childhood. Even if he'd somehow known I was going to be titled one day, he couldn't have warned me about this particular practice."

If King Shallcross, whoever he was, was actually trying to destabilize the Westlands, arranging for the mass slaughter of the second-born nobility might be a decent way to get started. And at least three members of the guard were dead after just this one day's work.

Although many of them being hereditary nobles made their poor performance in the banquet hall make a little more sense. Etienne had spent more than a few afternoons during my training ranting about hereditary knights and how they were never properly trained or tested, all because they were born of noble stock and assumed to know how to sheath a sword without stabbing themselves, whether they had even the slightest clue of which end to hold and which end to swing.

I blinked, the thought that maybe this was why he'd been in no hurry to get Chelsea squired suddenly occurring to me. She'd never be able to live up to his impossibly high standards, and any knight who was willing to take her on would be doing it partially to please him, making it likely that her training would be brutal. The only knight I could think of who wouldn't treat her differently because of who her father was . . .

Was . . .

I groaned, letting my head drop forward. Tybalt gave me a side-long look. "Are you well?"

"Just realized something about my future, which means it's your future, too, which means I'll tell you later." I smiled as winningly as I could. "Don't worry, it's not going to interfere with the wedding."

"Why does that glib reassurance only make me worry more?" He shook his head, attention swinging back to Nessa. "The Court of Cats manages succession through different means, and we lack most of your lesser titles. There are no counts or barons among our number, no knights or marquesses or baronets. We have Kings and Queens, Princes and Princesses, and it is rare beyond remarking for a single Kingdom to have multiple possible heirs. We would never risk them by sending them away."

"You make us sound careless with our children," said Nessa, sounding stung. "I assure you; the opposite is entirely the case. Service and fosterage are not the same. We do foster the children of noble houses who wish to send them here to learn the ways of our Court and will usually have some of them who choose to stay on at the end of their term of fosterage, dedicating themselves to service in turn. But never more than a few, and never against their will."

It was a system that would lend itself easily enough to abuse. Even if I assumed it hadn't been abused in this specific situation, there would still be generations of nobles with intimate firsthand knowledge of the royal knowe. I was suddenly more glad than I could say that Quentin had been sent away from here when he had. For all that I'd gotten him shot, stabbed, tortured, and transformed, it felt like he was safer when he was with me.

Maybe I was flattering myself. Maybe not. "Do you have a title, Nessa?" I asked abruptly.

"Oh, I'm a dame," she said. "Dame Nessa of Maples, that's me. My mother was a Baroness of a small demesne in Beacon's Home, which she chose to cede when she came to serve here, though she retained the title without the land. Because so much of the staff is titled one way or another, they tend to be recalcitrant when working with commoners, and as she intended to stay here with her sisters, she thought it best if she, and eventually I, had a title to brandish before them."

"And your father?"

"I never knew the man, nor cared to. He was a minor noble, I'm sure, and as he never married my mother, I owe no debt to his lines."

Gwragedd Annwn are an interesting case among the sometimes surreal breeding patterns of the fae. Unlike the occasional all-female or all-male descendant line, they have both male and female children. But their blood doesn't blend. A Gwragedd Annwn woman will always carry a Gwragedd Annwn child, period, no matter what the father contributed. The few changelings that have been sired by Gwragedd Annwn men have been uncommon enough that, while I've heard rumor, I don't know of anyone who says for sure that they've met one.

Mom seems to be the same way. Her children are always Dóchas Sidhe. I suppose only time, and someone else stupid enough to sleep with her, will tell us whether she can carry boys, or whether we're destined to be nothing but a bunch of tiny duplicates of my grandmother, Janet Carter, whose blood has been removed almost entirely from our line, but still carries through in coloring and composition. We take "family resemblance" to an extreme new level.

I nodded. "All right."

"I am sorry I had no opportunity to serve here and know you better," said Nolan.

"And I am sorry to have been surprised by the news that King

Windermere had been a father," said Nessa. "He was a kind man, considerate and devoted to the care of his kingdom. You could have done far worse for a family line."

So Nessa had known Gilad? It made a certain amount of sense, since I knew she'd been serving here for a long, long time. It still seemed like a stretch. Faerie makes coincidence inevitable, given enough time to spread itself across.

"I could," said Nolan. "He loved me and my sister both, and it's not his fault he had to go."

"It rarely is," Nessa agreed. She paused as we approached a set of double doors, finally freeing her hand from the bend of Nolan's arm. He let her go reluctantly, looking disappointed that their mild flirtation seemed to be at an end.

"I apologize if my duplicate has in some way interfered with the plan I was given for the room and will do my utmost to see whatever is wrong will be made right before the ceremony," she said as she pushed the doors open, revealing an open-air courtyard that couldn't possibly exist within the confines of the knowe. It didn't make any sense, which meant it was part of the structure as it existed in the Summerlands.

Nessa stepped through. Silent in the face of what I was seeing, I followed her.

We were standing in what seemed to be a natural bowl eroded into the peak of a mountain. Even the air felt different, thinner and cleaner and so crisp it hurt the back of my throat, like it was coming from much higher up. The hillside around us was covered in trees, bushy-branched evergreens reaching for the lilac sky, where four suns, each smaller than the one at home, rotated through a long, slow dance.

I've never been sure how the sky functions in the Summerlands. The number of moons and suns seems to be almost random, shifting from moment to moment regardless of whether there were that many the last time someone looked. The sky over Mom's tower usually has at least three moons, but I've seen the number go as low as two and as high as seventeen. The constellations are equally changeable, varying night upon night—and the cycle of nights and days doesn't really care about the passage of time, preferring to set itself to the internal clock of the local regent. For there to be that many suns overhead, High King Aethlin had to be pretty upset.

The trees were veiled in sparkling silver and diamond white, like the perfect fairytale snowfall had dusted them lightly before moving on, not accumulating on the ground, which was all dark loam and mossy green, forming a perfect, remarkably curated pathway deeper into the bowl. Nessa kept walking, and we followed, gaping like schoolchildren on their first trip to the museum.

The path's natural end was obvious, coming as it did to a small dais made of polished maple—of course—and flanked by two long staves that looked for all the world like maypoles, garlanded in ropes of roses and peonies. There was less pink than I'd been worried about after seeing May's ideas about appropriate wedding flowers. That was nice. So was the outdoor setting, which felt about as close as it was possible for me to get to being married in Muir Woods.

Multiple rows of chairs had been set up around the dais, filling the base of the depression with space for our friends and families. The boundaries of the path, the space in front of the dais where I assumed we were meant to stand, and even the rows themselves, were marked with tiny toadstools that glowed a deep shade of lavender when Nessa approached them, reacting to her presence like the motion-detector lights in a supermarket.

I glanced at Tybalt. He was beaming, eyes flicking from one aspect of the natural amphitheater to the next, looking more settled with every passing moment.

"Normally, we would have trapped and released pixies to provide lighting, since the suns will likely be down come time for the marriage proper," said Nessa. "However, your fiancé was very firm that you would not appreciate what he referred to as 'the exploitation of our smallest kin,' and that if we wanted them, we would have to invite them as guests. Some of the kitchen staff will be going to the locations frequented by the local flocks in the morning, to buy them donuts and offer them an opportunity to attend. So I'm afraid I can't guarantee how well-lit the space will be."

It took me a moment to realize she was speaking to me. I blinked. "Oh, um, yeah, he's right, I definitely prefer the option that doesn't make all the local pixies hate us. I have a pretty good relationship with the pixies in the Mists, and I don't know how often they migrate."

Nessa nodded. "Even so, we'll have witch-lights on reserve in case they prove necessary. Does this meet with your expectations?"

"It's *perfect*," said Tybalt. "When I requested an outdoor area or courtyard, I didn't expect you to have access to a proper cirque."

"Maples has been shaped by glacial progress both in the Summerlands and in the mortal world," said Nessa. "The knowe was built to incorporate and accommodate the local mountains. If you kept walking west, you would come to the croquet fields and the children's wing."

Sometimes trying to figure out how knowes reconcile the two aspects of their existence gives me a genuine headache. Maybe that's why we get along so well. They're changelings, too, in their own way.

"What time is it?" I asked abruptly. "We left the Mists at like, ten o'clock at night, and I know it's three hours later here. But what time is it *now*?"

"The sun just rose in the mortal world," said Nessa. "Today is your wedding day, Sir Daye, and I am honored to be the first to say such to you."

Ah. Swell.

Tybalt looked at me and smiled, and I managed, barely, to dredge up the same expression in response.

Well, damn.

SIXTEEN

STACY AND KERRY WATCHED without sympathy as I paced back and forth in the enclosed space of the changing room. I was gesturing wildly as I paced, whacking my hands against racks of dresses I'd never seen before and was absolutely sure I didn't own. Where Stacy had gotten the budget for this many changes of clothing, I didn't want to know. Someone's college fund had probably been raided to pay for components.

She was still wearing her little bridal veil headband, and if it wouldn't have made Tybalt kill me, I might have suggested we trade places. Just until my heart stopped beating so damn hard.

"—even *came* from," I said. "One second I was going 'yay, finally going to have this crossed off the list,' and the next second, it was like the whole world was pressing down on top of me."

"You want to take this one, or shall I?" asked Kerry.

"You go find the group Chelsea just brought in and see if it included Julie," said Stacy. "We're going to need to get the band back together for this."

"What?" I demanded, snapping out of the conversation I'd been admittedly mostly having with myself. Stacy and Kerry had been sitting, nodding, and interjecting the occasional understanding noise since I'd arrived. "Julie's not coming to my wedding. Julie hates me."

They exchanged a look. "Well, I hope someone told Julie that, because last time I checked with May, Tybalt had put her on the guest list, and she had RSVP'd 'yes,'" said Kerry carefully. "Maybe she hates you a little less than you think she does."

"That's ridiculous; he wouldn't have done that."

"Or maybe he just assumed that if you couldn't find a reason to bleed on your wedding dress, you'd invent one, and wanted to give you a decent starting point." Stacy rose, crossing to smooth the wrinkles out of my collar and tuck my hair back behind my ears. "That man really loves you, October."

"I know."

"Do you? Because this looks like a pretty severe case of cold feet, and while that's normal and okay and even expected, you need to chill out before he comes looking and realizes something's wrong." Stacy settled her hands on my shoulders, looking at me gravely as Kerry slipped out of the room. "Your abandonment issues are not new to me. You've been my best friend since I was a kid, and I know how your head works. When something seems like it's too good for you, you run away from it as fast as you can. You ran away from Shadowed Hills when Sylvester wanted to take care of you—"

"Which we now know he only did because I'm his niece and he felt obligated," I muttered.

Stacy sighed. "—and as soon as you started feeling like you could be really happy at Home, you went and found yourself a human to fall in love with, because you had enough self-hatred from dealing with your mother to feel like anything involving a human couldn't possibly end happily ever after. Don't you argue with me. I can see you getting ready to start, and you're not going to win."

I shut my mouth.

"You're getting nervous because you're getting close to actually marrying the man, and once he puts a ring on your finger or a tiara on your head or whatever weird bullshit it is they do at pureblood weddings—and believe me, I'm so excited to watch you get subjected to it that I could just *spit*—you're going to have to admit what the rest of us have known for years." She finally took her hands off me and stepped back, giving me space to move. "Which is that the boy is stupid in love with you. He makes you better. He makes you care enough about yourself to actually take *care* of yourself once in a while. Do you know how long it's been since I've seen you voluntarily sit down and eat a sandwich? I wasn't even surprised when we found out that your secret superpower is recovering from whatever sort of abuse you want to put your body through, but I was a little disappointed. Maybe if some of the bruises you got would last more than five minutes, you'd at least pretend not to think everyone who loves you is a fool!"

"I never said that," I protested, blinking and resisting the urge to gape at her.

Stacy glared at me. "Yes, you did. Every time you forgot to eat for three days, you did. Every time you stopped sleeping because you had to do something that might finally make your mother proud of you, you did. Every time you decided you could challenge someone five times your size to a fistfight in an alley. Every bad decision that reminded us how much you think you're expendable was another reminder that you think we're all liars or losers for daring to love you. Honestly, I'm not sure which is more insulting."

"Stacy, I . . ." I rubbed my face with one hand. "I'm sorry," I said finally. "I'm trying to do better. I *am* doing better. You're right, because Tybalt makes me feel like I have to do better to be as good as the person he sees when he looks at me. But not just him. Quentin. He's my squire. He depends on me to take care of him, and that means taking care of myself once in a while. And May."

"You built yourself a family." Stacy offered me a wan smile. "I just wish the people who've been there since the beginning had been enough to provide you with the foundation you needed."

My mouth moved silently, not finding the words I needed to tell her how much of my foundation she was; how essential she was to me, even when she wasn't in the room. She was a constant. Sometimes the only constant, it felt like, the one brick in the wall that, if removed, would bring the whole thing crashing down. The words, if they even existed, refused to come, and so I stepped forward, wrapped my arms around her, and pulled her tight against me, hoping she'd understand.

Stacy sighed heavily and wrapped her arms around me in turn, and that was that. I almost didn't hear the door open behind us.

"You figure out how to tell Toby she's being an asshole without getting stabbed, or is she in the middle of a murder right now?" asked Kerry genially.

Stacy pulled away, smiling as she wiped her eyes. "No stabbing," she said.

"No stabbing," I confirmed, turning.

Kerry was already fully in the room, as relaxed as ever. The only time I'd ever seen that woman look like she wasn't sure she belonged somewhere, we'd been in the process of crashing a local high school prom, having used way too many illusions and way too much eyeliner to blend in with the human kids around us. It had seemed like a great idea when we'd been safely in Shadowed Hills—go out for a night, get in touch with the mortal side of our shared heritage—but in practice, the lights had been too bright, the music had been too loud, and everyone had talked way too fast for our comfort. We'd ended up sneaking back out again, spending the rest of our rare night of freedom at the local Denny's, charming the staff into bringing us bottomless pancakes and coffee.

The woman in the doorway behind her looked a lot less sure of herself. She was dressed much as I was, in a T-shirt and jeans, her tiger-striped arms bare to the world. The stripes continued up the sides of her neck and onto her face, where they cupped her cheeks like fingers. Her hair was a mass of brown-and-gold streaks, surprisingly similar to my own, just more densely pigmented, and she couldn't have seemed more nervous if she'd been facing a man with a chainsaw.

Given where she spent most of her time, she probably would have looked *less* nervous if faced with a chainsaw.

"Hi," she said. "I know you probably didn't invite me, and I wasn't sure I should come, but I promise I'm not going to try to kill you on your wedding night, so I guess that's probably better than nothing—"

"Julie, get in here," I said, beckoning her forward.

The door slammed behind her as she hesitantly approached.

"You're right. I didn't invite you. I didn't invite *anyone*, technically, since May and Stacy handled all that. Maybe I invited the two of them—"

"Nope," said Stacy cheerfully.

"—but I don't think so," I continued. "Tybalt wanted you here because he cares about you, and if I'd been consulted at any point, I would have said I wanted you here, too, as long as you didn't try to kill me. And you've already said you're not going to do that, so we're doing pretty well so far."

Julie blinked, looking baffled. "But I *tried* to kill you."

"Several times, and I'm not going to lie—I was pretty pissed about that for a long time. And then I stopped and asked myself what I'd do if someone killed Tybalt, and I didn't feel like it was my fault." Technically, he's died a couple of times since we met. But he's a King of Cats, and sometimes they bounce back. I felt my expression sour. "I'd do a lot worse to anyone who did that than you tried to do to me."

"I tried to *kill* you," Julie repeated.

"I'd tell you to join the club, but most of the members are assholes, and I don't think you'd care for their company." I smiled warmly. "You're fine, honestly. I've missed you."

"And you're getting *married*," said Julie, in much the same tone that she'd been using to remind me of her attempted murder. "To my *uncle*. Who you *hate*."

Stacy laughed. "You've missed a lot, sugar. I don't think they ever really hated each other the way they tried to let on. They had a lot of mistrust and pent-up stupid to work through, but it was never real hatred."

"And now they're so sweet on each other it's kind of sickening, and I'm the baker," said Kerry. "He gets all flowery and romance novel from the Austen era when she's around."

"Actually, I think that's a little modern for him," I said.

"Toby actually tries to get punched less when Tybalt can see," continued Kerry blithely.

Julie gasped. "No!"

"I hate you all," I said. My three best friends since childhood broke into unified laughter, and the sound was so familiar, so comfortable, that I joined in, unable to resist the urge.

The door banged open again. Quentin fell into the room, Dean close behind him, both of them breathing heavily.

"You need to come with us," said Quentin, not waiting for us to stop laughing or acknowledge their arrival. "You need to come with us *right now*."

"What? Why?"

"Caitir's waiting for you. Come on." Quentin bolted back into the main room, leaving Dean behind.

Dean looked at us gravely, and said, "The High King has been poisoned. Please come."

I went.

Caitir—the Candela from before, now fully recovered, Merry Dancers bobbing around her head—was waiting for us. "Alchemist said you'd ridden my blood," she said. "Means you know I'm me."

"Yes," I agreed. I would have known even without riding her blood. Much like Nessa's impossible beauty, the Doppelgangers couldn't mimic a Candela's magic without access to their blood, and even access to their blood wouldn't duplicate their Merry Dancers, which are technically separate entities born at the same time as their Candela partner. They die at the same time, too. Caitir would be the last person in this knowe to be replaced.

"Good. So we're leaving." She waved her hand. A hole appeared in the air, and she looked at me expectantly, waiting for me to go through.

I glanced around the room. It was even more crowded now than it had been earlier, packed with what was starting to feel like every person I'd ever met in my life . . . except for Tybalt.

"He's already gone to talk to the guard," said Dean, catching the direction of my search. Quentin was standing next to Caitir, bouncing on his toes in the anxious need to get moving. "He knows where you'll be. You're not running off without telling him."

"I appreciate that," I said, and leapt through the portal Caitir had opened, barely taking the time to catch my breath first.

Quentin was close behind me, and Caitir close behind him. Our feet never hit the ground. Unlike the long run through the Shadow Roads that always awaited me when Tybalt was in control, this was a swift and terrible passage through the darkness and cold, lit by the flickering glow of the Merry Dancers, which had the time to swirl around us once before we were tumbling into the bright light of what looked like a gentleman's study.

Like what seemed to be everything else in this knowe, the walls were furnished in polished maple, with brass fittings and witch-lights burning in verdigrised silver sconces. Books filled the shelves, and while they all looked rarified and old, I recognized a couple of the titles. The High King was apparently fond of high-end leather-bound reproductions of classic science fiction novels. There were worse things he could have been doing with his time.

Like, at the moment, dying. He was collapsed in the highbacked leather chair behind the desk, clutching his chest with one hand, breath coming in shuddering, uneven gasps. His color had shifted, going from his normal healthy peach to a waxen pallor that was frankly a little unnerving.

Maida was on one side of him, clutching his hand in her own, watching Walther with the rapt attention of a cobra trapped in a room with a mongoose. Walther had set up his alchemy kit on the desk, sweeping everything that had been placed there onto the floor in the process, and was mixing chemicals and herbs as fast as he could, hands a blur. Cassie stood nearby, one of the witch-lights in her own hands, eyes fixed on the air above it.

"Cassowary plum," she said, tone gone dreamy and distant. "Milkweed, eucalyptus, and ground beetle wing. Hercules beetles, species nonspecific."

"I brought them, Majesty," said Caitir. Maida's gaze snapped to me, like it was following a preset grid. She took a deep, shuddering breath, shoulders slumping.

"He's *dying*," she said. "Fix him."

"I can't."

"As your High Queen, I *order* you to fix him."

"And again, I can't." I shook my head helplessly. "I can put a body back together. I can't remove poison. I'd have to exsanguinate him, strip the poison out of his blood, and put it all back when I was done, and by that point, he'd be dead, and I'm not actually sure there's anything I could do about that."

Someone coughed in the corner of the room. "Technically true, but close enough to falsehood that it makes my head ache."

I glanced sharply to where Fiac lurked. "I've managed to raise the dead before, under tightly controlled conditions that might or might not be replicable, and not when I was trying to bring back the High King. The pressure alone might be enough to make things go wrong. *Can* I raise the dead? Sometimes. Occasionally. *Should* I raise the dead? Not according to the night-haunts. It's not something I should be doing casually or something we can count on working every time I decide to give it a go, and it's *certainly* not a decent reason to call off a perfectly good alchemist just because hey presto, Toby the magic cure-all walked into the room!"

I was yelling by the time I finished. On a moment's reflection, I realized I didn't care. Sometimes, yelling is the right thing to do.

Quentin stepped around me, grimacing as he glanced over at Fiac, and hurried to kneel beside his mother, who wrapped him in a tight embrace. So tight that for a moment he went a little cross-eyed, looking like he couldn't quite remember how to breathe.

"My chest hurts," he said, pulling away and pressing two fingers to the base of his sternum. "Why does my chest hurt?"

"That's the wail trying to break loose," said Walther. "Don't let it. Swallow it down. Kick a wall or punch yourself in the dick or whatever you have to do to keep it from getting away."

"I'll probably wail if I punch myself in the dick," said Quentin dubiously.

"Yes, but it won't be the same wail," said Walther. "When a Banshee wails because they feel it, not because they're hurting, people die. If you wail, there won't be anything else I can do. It'll curdle the alchemy and break Cassandra's prophecy into shards."

Quentin looked deeply alarmed, as did Maida. Fiac stayed in his corner, looking distraught but disinterested, like he couldn't understand exactly why a Banshee wailing would be a bad thing.

Interesting. "So if he wails, the High King's doomed to die?"

"Yes," said Walther. "So whatever you do, swallow that urge. Don't let your magic out. Don't let it take form. Not right now. Not with everything that's at stake."

"Someone else could be dying right now," said Fiac. "If the boy screams, who's to say the death will fall on the High King?"

"This is an interesting debate, but it doesn't seem like the most important thing we have to deal with at the moment," I said, a little louder and a little more stridently than I needed to. "What the hell *happened* here?"

"We were interviewing the staff," said Maida, still clutching Aethlin's hand like she thought she could be the reason he stayed in this world. It was impressive, given how hard she was clinging to Quentin at the same time. She wasn't letting go of her family if she could possibly help it. "This is Aethlin's private office. He conducts much of the household business here. We had a full complement of guards; we took all precautions . . ." She sounded less like she was trying to convince me, and more like she was trying to convince herself.

"Did something happen?" I asked, and immediately felt foolish. Clearly, something had happened. Clearly, the High King had been poisoned.

Thankfully, Maida didn't seem to notice my gaff. She shook her head. "No," she said plaintively. "Everything was normal. Aethlin was speaking with Hiram, one of the palace historians. He's been with our household since the Kingdom was founded. If someone was attempting to infiltrate the scribes, he would be the place to start. They've been friends a long time. Aethlin relaxed when he entered the room. He sat down, and leaned back in his chair, and his hands were resting on the desk, and . . ."

She started to sob, great, racking gasps that shook her entire body. I turned to Walther.

"Contact poison?" I asked wearily.

"Contact poison," confirmed Walther. "The desk blotter. You shouldn't touch anything in this room without asking me first. I've found three different poisoned surfaces. They've been expecting to be found out long enough to have been making preparations."

"Makes sense, since their fake Nessa went down pretty publicly." I moved still closer, staying slow, so as not to alarm Maida. She looked like she was as close to snapping as Aethlin was to dying, which was closer than I liked. Turning toward Fiac, I said, in a loud, clear voice, "I am October Christine Daye, Knight of Lost Words, here by invitation, and am not working for any hostile power or attempting to undermine the High King in any way. Although I may tell him he's being an asshole when he's being unreasonable, which he seems to be fairly frequently. For example, it would be really unreasonable of him to die right now, thanks."

The High King's mouth seemed to twitch for a moment, although it was difficult to tell, under the circumstances, whether he was trying to smile or grimacing in pain. Fuck. Since Fiac wasn't attacking me, I moved closer to the High King, holding up my hands to make sure Maida saw I was unarmed. There were no guards in the room.

"Where's the guard?" I asked.

"I asked them to leave," said Walther. "I'm doing delicate work, and I didn't need a bunch of jocks freaking out because their liege was trying to die. They were upsetting Cassandra. They were upsetting *me*. We're safe enough in here, between her watching the air for changes and Fiac standing guard. More bodies in the room only complicates things."

"He was fine. He was *fine*, and then he wasn't fine. It all happened so *fast*." Maida sniffled, and I realized how close she really was to breaking into tears. "I didn't want to send the guards away, but Fiac and your alchemist both said it was safer for us to be in a closed room where we knew everyone was safe and who they said they were, and their first responsibility is to the High King, not the High Queen. And I think the guards felt bad for not somehow detecting the poison before he could be exposed."

"No one will attack him again while I still breathe," said Fiac. "I should have been faster the first time. I will be faster if it happens again." His lips set into a thin line. "I will be *much* faster."

I wouldn't have wanted to be the next person to attempt to kill the High King. Fiac looked like he was about ready to break anyone who tried. "As soon as Aethlin fell, I gave him the blood you'd given me," said Maida. "I thought it would make him better, but it didn't make him better."

"It did, however, stop him from getting any worse," said Walther, eyes on his braziers and beakers as he added a pinch of this and a dash of that to one or the other. His valise was open, revealing a dizzying array of tiny bottles and jars, none bigger than a few ounces, most visibly at least partly full. "So kudos for that. You did no harm, and you may have saved yourself from a sedition charge. If this is where you want to suddenly remember the High King's evil grand vizier who you just forgot to tell us about until now, that would be *great*."

"Why do we always jump to 'vizier' as the title for the evil member of the court?" asked Cassandra. She and Walther exchanged a look, said in unison, "Racism," and went back to work.

"No . . . no one in my husband's council would want to harm him. Most of them served here when they were younger, learning how governance is done, and then returned to serve again when they failed to inherit. He doesn't elevate unfairly or put people into positions they aren't suited for simply because of their titles."

"Sounds more functional than the human government," I said. "But clearly, someone holds a grudge, against both of you. We're finding Doppelgangers all over your knowe, and this attack was an obvious attempt to incriminate you."

Maida looked confused. "What do you mean?"

"I mean when a Doppelganger attacked in full view of the court, they did it with a knife, while they were standing next to someone who's pretty well known for preferring knives to just about any other kind of weapon," I said.

"Because any other kind of weapon would keep the violence at a sensible distance, and we can't be having *that*," said Quentin.

I ignored him. "And when a Doppelganger attacked in a small room with a limited number of people, it used another knife, and went for a quick kill that could easily have been over-looked and would have left no time for even the fastest healer to work. And now, when the High King has been attacked in his private rooms, they used poison."

"Traditionally a feminine means of murder," said Walther, holding up a glass beaker and swirling its contents, a thoughtful look on his face. "Maybe that's sexist—probably that's sexist—but if a King dies alone in a room, and he dies by poison, everyone will assume the Queen did it. No matter how much proof you provide that she didn't."

Maida looked horrified. "I would *never . . .*"

"We know that, and we know you didn't, but if you hadn't had my blood ready to go and the poison had killed him, would the court have agreed?" And given the timing, would it have mattered? The Luidaeg was here for our wedding: even if Oberon stayed silent and hidden in plain sight, all she had to do was declare the High Queen's innocence and any debate would be immediately ended.

Only I knew the world didn't really work that way. Everyone would listen to her, sure, because failure to listen to one of the Firstborn is a good way to wind up very, very dead, and then we would leave, and no one would actually believe Maida hadn't killed her husband to claim the throne. Her reign would be destabilized, and by its very nature, brief.

Maida slumped, still on the floor, still clutching her transformed son and holding her dying husband's hand. For a moment, I felt almost like I could see what it was like to collide with the daily chaos to which we had all become accustomed, where this sort of thing happened before lunch five times a week and we just had to figure out how we were going to deal with it before we could finish ordering our pizza. This was all new and shockingly terrible for her.

And she had thrown her only son into it. Poor woman. "Fiac, will the court believe you when you say the attack was carried out using contact poison on the High King's desk?"

"They will," he said gravely. "Adhene can lie, but they know that we find it abhorrent, and this court has no cause to doubt me. And if the High King lives, there will be no question at all of the Queen's innocence, or of recalling the children from their distant fosterage." He had to work not to look at Quentin, who was still hugging his mother.

Good man. "I'm sure Penthea would prefer to remain where she is until it's safe for her to come home," I said. Fiac had to know by now who the Banshee boy clinging to the queen was, but if I could talk around it, I would. "I know Quentin is happy with his current arrangement."

"That's all I had ever hoped for them," said Fiac.

"Who benefits from throwing the High Kingdom into chaos?" I turned to Walther. "And how long before you know whether you can fix this?"

"I'm not a magician trying to pull a rabbit out of a hat, I'm an alchemist trying to come up with a counteragent for a novel poison that seems to be more iron-based than it has any business being," said Walther. "You'll forgive me if it's not the fastest process ever."

Cassie gasped, eyes still fixed on what looked to me like absolutely nothing.

"Ash and Oak," she said. "The Kingdom fell, and no one came for the people who lived there. Look for their signatories, look for mistletoe and Virginia creeper and holly. They brew their poisons on what remains of a blighted land."

"Of course, they do," said Walther, grabbing several more small jars and adding their contents to his mixture. For all that he spoke like there was no urgency to his task at all, he moved like it was the most urgent thing in the world, like he could never have done anything less.

The contents of his beaker changed colors, going from pale gold to a rancid slime green that glittered from within with tiny specks of captive gilded light. Walther sniffed the mixture and wrinkled his nose. Given some of the things he'd given me to drink in the past, that didn't speak well for it.

"Toby, I need some of your blood," he said.

"I thought we just established that my blood doesn't counteract poison," I said. "See, the High King's right there, and he's still all poisoned, despite being doped up with my blood before he could die."

"Yes, but your blood will let him heal himself, and the poison has done—and is still doing—a considerable amount of damage to his body," said Walther, producing a scalpel from inside his kit. He offered it to me. "If you don't want the High King to need dialysis for the rest of his life, bleed for me."

"Every time I think my life couldn't get more like a horror movie, something like this has to go and happen," I grumbled, taking the scalpel and using it to lay open the side of my hand. Walther moved his beaker into position, holding it there until he'd gathered what he judged to be a sufficient quantity of my blood. Which was reassuringly not all that much since I was pretty tired of bleeding.

I tossed the scalpel onto the desk and wiped my bloody palm on my jeans. Quentin wrinkled his nose.

"You know Tybalt's going to notice that," he said. "If you wanted to bleed without getting caught, you'd keep it off your clothes."

"If I wanted to bleed without getting caught, I'd wash my hands and put on some perfume," I said. "Don't teach your grandma how to conceal forensic evidence, kid. You know it never ends well for you."

"Both my grandmothers are dead," he said, somewhat sourly, and glanced back at his father.

Walther had finished reheating and stirring his mixture. He held it carefully in front of him as he approached the High King, eyes on Maida. "This should counteract the poison in your husband's system," he said. "I believe I identified and isolated all of the compounds doing him harm. Fortunately, to be stable enough to linger on surfaces and be absorbed through the skin, the potion couldn't be overtly magical, and had to rely on its contents to do the most damage possible. Unfortunately, that reliance involved a great deal of cold iron. I can't promise this will be enough to save him, but I can promise you there's not an alchemist in this Kingdom who could have done a better job."

Fiac neither moved nor spoke, clearly accepting Walther's words as truth. That was reassuring. That reduced the odds of his being arrested if this didn't work.

"May I give this to the High King?" Walther paused respectfully, waiting for Maida's answer.

When it came, it was in the form of a laugh that bordered on hysterical. "Can you save my husband?" she asked. "The man who gave me everything I have, the man without whom I don't know what to do or how to do it or even where I'd go, where I'd live, where to find my children, can you *save my husband*?" Her laughter died, replaced by a look of bleak despair that chilled me to the bone. "Please. Try."

Maida had been a changeling when she met Aethlin. I knew her father, her fae parent, had died in one of the wars. Her mortal family would be long since dead, the farm where her parents had lived sold to other hands. She knew the knowe and the throne and nothing else. Did she have friends? Did she have people like Stacy and Kerry, or even Julie, who could take care of her if the High King was gone?

Sweet Titania, was she a prisoner here even though she was supposedly in charge?

No, bad Toby. Fix the feudal system later, after you've prevented its current round of victims from dying. Walther pressed the edge of the beaker to the High King's lips. Aethlin stirred, making a noise that was neither loud nor strong enough to be classified as a moan, but not shrill enough to be a squeak, either. "I know, it smells terrible," said Walther, in a soothing tone. "You still have to swallow it, because if you don't, I'm going to pour it in your hair."

Aethlin didn't react.

"I'm pretty sure the smell won't ever come out. You're going to have to shave your head." Walther's tone never varied, and his hand didn't shake. "The choice is yours. Swallow this or wear it."

"Can he hear you?" asked Maida.

"If he can't, we're past the point where I can help him, and the kid's not howling yet," said Walther matter-of-factly. "He can hear me."

Aethlin made the sound again, stronger this time, and I saw his throat move as he swallowed whatever of the mixture had managed to trickle into his mouth. "Good man," said Walther, and tipped the beaker a little further forward. He still wasn't pouring very fast—the liquid would be entering the High King's mouth at barely above a drip—but now that he knew Aethlin wasn't going to choke, he could focus on getting it into him as quickly as possible.

"Human hospitals use IVs," said Quentin.

"So do I, when the issue is dehydration, or when I'm working with a changeling kid who needs human-developed medication delivered over a long period of time. When it's hormone replacement or a painkiller, I usually use a syringe." Walther kept his attention on the High King as he spoke, eyes scanning Aethlin's face in quick, sharp motions that looked far more urgent than anything else he was doing. "When you're dealing with an alchemical tincture, direct injection is almost never the answer."

"Why not?"

Walther glanced at Quentin, a wry, frustrated smile twisting at his mouth. "Because most of the things in this beaker are technically poisonous whether ingested or injected, but the magic that goes into the brewing process renders them inert when administered in the correct way. There may be an alchemist somewhere who's been working on applying more mortal means of draught completion, but I am not he, and I still use traditional methods. Which say swallow."

"So you're giving my—my king," Quentin caught himself clumsily, barely managing not to glance at Fiac, who surely had to know his identity by now. He'd been in the room when Aethlin demanded to see his son, after all, and Maida was clinging to Quentin like a lifeline. "Poison to get rid of poison? How does that make sense?"

"Most medicine is poison," said Walther. "It's just poison that kills you more slowly than whatever's been making you sick."

High King Aethlin groaned again. An actual groan this time, strong enough to be worth the name. Maida sat up straighter, pulling Quentin along with her as she clutched at her husband's hand.

"Aethlin?" she asked—pled, really, voice dripping with the desperate need for him to reply. "Sweetheart, can you hear me? Are you awake?"

He groaned again, louder this time, and raised his free hand to bat weakly at the beaker Walther was still holding to his lips.

Walther, though, was resolute. This was a man who gave pro bono medical care to any changeling kid who stumbled across him—something that happened with increasing frequency as word spread—who brewed elf-shot cures for the nobility of the West Coast, and who, maybe most importantly, was often charged with putting me and my allies back together. A little feeble struggling from a High King was nothing to him.

"Nope," he said, almost cheerfully. "Sorry, Your Majesty, but I'm going to need you to finish drinking the whole thing before I can let you stop. It's like reciting a proclamation. If someone interrupts you in the middle, technically whatever you were trying to decree isn't finished."

Something about that sounded important. He was right, though. Interrupting ranking nobles with a coup when they were in the middle of declaring something—usually land rights, titles, or the naming of a formal heir—was a time-honored way of disrupting the political structure.

"Hey, Fiac, you know a lot about the founding of this Kingdom, don't you?"

"The Librarian would know more, or Hiram," Fiac looked around the room as if the absent historian might still be lurking there. "But I know a great deal," he continued. "I know if the High King dies while the lines of succession have been somehow muddled, we shall have to break the seal on the Princess' fosterage, and even that might not be enough to save the kingdom."

"Cool, cool," I said. "Do you know the wording of the founding decree?"

Fiac blinked at me. "Not precisely," he said. "I know where they're stored, if you feel they matter for some reason."

"They might," I said. "Walther?"

"Almost there." He tipped the beaker a bit further and smiled encouragingly at Aethlin. "You'll be finished soon, Your Majesty, and then you can yell at me for making you drink something so nasty."

"Will he *live*?" demanded Maida.

"Oh, sorry, didn't I say? If he was going to die, this would have killed him already." Walther stepped back, taking the now-empty beaker with him. "He's going to be fine. Exhausted for a while, because his body's not built to heal itself the way October's is, and twice in one day is probably pushing things, but the poison has been counteracted, and the damage is being repaired even as we speak."

High King Aethlin gasped, opening his eyes and sitting up in the chair—or trying to, anyway. He seemed to get caught partway into the motion and sagged back into his slump. The color in his face was improving at an unnatural rate, the waxen pallor removing itself like a film running in reverse.

"Is it that weird to watch me put myself back together?" I asked Walther, in a low voice.

"Weirder, since you're usually doing it without help, and with half your blood on the outside of your body," he said. "We've had time to get used to it."

"I haven't," said Cassandra, staring raptly at the High King.

Aethlin coughed and tried again to sit up, succeeding this time, although the effort appeared to exhaust him. He clutched at Maida's hand, seeming to realize she was there for the first time as he slumped against that side of the armchair. "Maida . . ."

"I'm here, love, I'm here." She laughed, tears rolling down her cheeks. "I'm here with you, you foolish man."

"Told me not . . ." He stopped, running out of breath, and just leaned.

"Yes, I told you not to hold the interrogations in the room where you spent so much of your time. I didn't anticipate poison—I was hoping to keep the space from being tainted by association—but I was right all the same." Maida didn't let him go, not even as Quentin pulled away from her to keep himself from being crushed. He glanced to me as he did, something pleading in his eyes. I couldn't tell whether he was begging me for rescue, or to understand why he didn't want to be saved.

Eventually, he was going to have to decide where he wanted to be on his own, and I wasn't going to begrudge him that decision. I also wasn't here to come between him and his family.

"You stay here," I said, focusing on Quentin. Then I glanced back to Fiac. "Are you free to come with me? I need someone to show me the way to the library."

Fiac blinked. "The library?"

"You said the Librarian would know the exact terms of the kingdom's founding paperwork. I need to get a look at that."

Fiac frowned slowly, tilting his head. "You think you know something," he said, sounding confused.

"I suspect I may have found the start of why this is happening," I corrected. "I don't *know* anything, except that when I get that feeling that tells me something is important, it usually is. And I feel like the wording is important in this case."

"We already know who's doing this," said Quentin sourly. "Shallcross."

"Absalom Shallcross hasn't been seen in years," said Maida. "Not since the 1950s at least."

Almost seventy years of silence from a human would have meant they were no longer a concern, and we could start looking for someone else. Seventy years of silence from a Daoine Sidhe King who'd lost his throne was the equivalent of a long nap followed by a sulk in the corner of the playroom. They think in a different time scale than the rest of us do. Sometimes it's possible for me to forget that, to pretend they have the same number of years to plot and plan and get things right and get things wrong as I do, and I guess they do, since I could have forever if I would just go ahead and get rid of the last traces of my mortality. But in the here and now, the chances that the original King Shallcross was still out there were pretty decent.

"And I'm pretty sure no one knew where the Luidaeg was when she left the East Coast, until she resurfaced in San Francisco," I said. "Doesn't mean she didn't exist while she was out of sight, or that she wasn't doing Luidaeg things."

"Luidaeg things?" asked Aethlin, managing to sound weak and amused at the same time.

"You know, the things she does when no one's keeping tabs on her. Brew horrifying potions. Harass the Selkies. Eat really weird ice cream with too many ingredients listed on the carton. Cookies and cream makes sense, sure, but cookies and cream and gummi bears and chocolate peanuts and Twizzlers and strawberries and marshmallow and M&M's and graham crackers? There are limits to how far you can push things while still having them taste even halfway decent."

Acthlin and Maida were both staring at me by the time I finished. Maida turned to Quentin, asking delicately, "Is she *always* like this?"

"Pretty much," said Quentin. "Sometimes she gets a little weird." He shrugged broadly. Given that he had turned himself into a Banshee to be able to attend my wedding in his parents' house without getting caught, and they seemed to decorate entirely in the kind of giant uncut crystals that belonged in a New Age catalog for really wealthy Wiccans, I wasn't sure any of the three of them got to judge how weird I was or wasn't.

But none of that was relevant. "So yeah, we know who's behind all this, and we know it's Shallcross," I said. "What we don't know is whether it's the original model throwing a fit because he lost his throne and thinks he deserves a consolation kingdom, or a descendant."

"Absalom and Vesper Shallcross never had children that I'm aware of," said Fiac. "And while Absalom was seen after the fall of Ash and Oak, Vesper was not. Most have assumed her body lies in the harbor along with so many others." He bowed his head, expression going solemn.

I wondered if the fae of Maples thought New York had fallen along with Ash and Oak. "If she died there, either she's joined the night-haunts, or her body was buried by the humans who still live in Manhattan," I said delicately. "And since there wasn't a huge blow-up about aliens or fairies or whatever moving among the humans of New York, I'm going to say the night-haunts were able to come as normal."

Quentin looked unfazed. Maida and Aethlin both looked nervous. Which made sense; they weren't used to casual dismissal of the death of hundreds. Quentin, on the other hand, is basically immune to terror at this point.

"Fiac, my point stands," I said. "I need to talk to your Librarian. Please."

"The alchemist will remain here," he said. It wasn't a question.

I nodded. "The alchemist and the seer will both remain here."

"The boy?"

I glanced at Quentin. "Will go where he chooses," I said. Maida scowled, but didn't argue. She knew she couldn't, not without confirming aloud what Fiac already knew.

"Can you ask my guards to return if you see them?" asked Aethlin wearily. "Caitir is an excellent guardian, but she can't do it alone."

Caitir smiled wanly but didn't say anything. That wasn't unusual; neither was the fact that she'd been silent since we arrived. Candela are terse at best, and that's usually in times of low stress. Seeing her liege assaulted had to be stressful for her.

"We will, Your Highness," said Fiac, and offered a shallow bow.

"If Tybalt shows up looking for me, tell him we've gone to the Library," I said.

Walther nodded, as Quentin pulled away from his mother, pausing to kiss her temple before he moved to stand by me. She looked after him, sorrow in her eyes, but didn't say anything.

Poor woman was going to need a hug and an extra slice of wedding cake when this was all over, I swear. I offered her a sympathetic smile, then turned to Fiac. "Lead the way," I said.

"As my lady says," said Fiac, and opened the door into the hall.

We followed him out and away.

SEVENTEEN

THE HALL OUTSIDE THE High King's study was long and gently curving, as pleasant and well-appointed as the rest of the knowe. I scowled as we followed Fiac along it.

"I'm starting to feel like we're lost in a mall," I muttered.

Quentin hid his smile behind his hand. "Now you understand why I was so disoriented when I moved to Shadowed Hills," he said. "It was so *tiny*, I didn't understand how people could stand being on top of each other all the time. No one had any space."

"And yet you moved into my makeshift motel for some ridiculous reason," I said mildly.

Fiac didn't look back, but he did say, in a calm tone, "You do realize I can hear you both. I would take care with what I say. A lie, even from an ally, is likely to ignite my blood."

"We aren't lying to you."

"I know. If you were, there would already be blood on the floor."

I walked a little faster, pulling up even with him. "I've never actually met an Adhene before."

He glanced at me. "Then how can you be sure you know what I am?"

"I'm not actually sure how to describe this honestly, so please try to forgive me if I get this in some way wrong, but my mother was Amandine the Liar, and she drilled me after my Changeling's Choice, to be sure I could identify all the known children of Faerie by appearance and common attributes," I said. "My parents have since divorced and I repudiated her, so I don't know if she's my mother anymore, but she was when I was younger, and she told me what to watch for in the Adhene."

"Why did she do that, I wonder?" Fiac kept his eyes fixed straight ahead as we continued. "Only princes and princesses need that level of tuition to avoid giving accidental offense, and when last I checked, the Last among the First was not considered a princess of any line, not even her father's."

"I don't know why she did that either. I always just sort of assumed it was normal for pureblood parents. That they made sure their kids wouldn't embarrass them, or themselves, by getting things wrong in the wider world. By the time I was old enough to start meeting people who weren't her or the folks at Shadowed Hills, embarrassing her was one of my major goals."

"Ah. A rebellious child."

I smiled a little. "I guess you could say that. I didn't want her to be proud of me. 'Ashamed to admit she was connected to me in any way' was more of the idea."

"Then we may never know her motivation." Fiac turned down a wider hall. It was substantially more opulent, the ceiling growing high and cathedral-arched, lined with more of those vast panels of amethyst crystal, gleaming in the light they cast on one another. If they ever had an earthquake in this knowe, absolutely everyone was going to get impaled.

At the end of the hall was a single set of broad double doors, and a small, plain door set off to the left-hand side. Fiac ignored the larger doors, heading for the single. Quentin and I followed.

Fiac touched the door, murmuring something I couldn't hear. It swung open, and he stepped through. Quentin and I followed him into a room that consisted entirely of towering bookshelves reaching toward the misty depths of an unseen ceiling. There were no walls. Rolling ladders moved along the shelves seemingly at random, with no one in sight to operate them. Pixies clung to the higher shelves, occasionally chiming, their wings waving lazily as they fanned themselves.

There didn't seem to be anyone there. I looked both ways down the endless row of books before turning to look at Fiac. "Is this a capital-L Library?" I asked. "From the way you were saying it before, I assumed it was, and this looks like one, but if it's just a small-l library, I don't want to break any rules."

"This is the Library of Stones," said Fiac solemnly. "The first

High King Sollys granted them space and connection to the knowe's magic in exchange for Library cards for himself and his Queen, and for the highest-ranking members of his household."

"So you have one, and the chatelaine, who I still haven't seen, has one, and who else?"

"In the normal course of things, the Crown Prince, once he returns home and agrees to take up his royal duties," said Fiac, resolutely not looking at Quentin. I hoped the kid was proud of the fact that he'd managed to make an Adhene skirt the truth. "We're all allowed guests, when using the entrance through the knowe. The entrance on the mortal side moves around the province, although I understand it mostly stays in Toronto. The Librarian is uncommonly fond of mortal coffee."

Maybe that was an attribute shared by all Librarians. The Librarian we knew in San Francisco, Mags, was also fond of coffee. I smiled a little. "None of this makes sense to poor, provincial little me, you know. Where I come from, Libraries are considered independent of all noble ties, and don't answer to Kings or Queens."

"Oh, that's true here as well." Fiac touched one of the rolling ladders as it passed. It paused, vibrating, then reversed and rolled off in the other direction. "The High King has no authority within the Library. When he walks these walls, he is merely a man, and the Librarian treats him as such."

I blinked. "Then why . . . ?"

"When this knowe was opened, the political situation along the Eastern coast was much more dangerous than I think you can understand," said Fiac. "Death was common, war was constant, and chaos reigned in both the human and fae worlds. The American Revolution rendered the streets hazardous, and shops which seemed safe and stable today could be ashes and memory tomorrow. He offered the Librarian a stable doorway into the Summerlands, with no need to fear insurrection or collapse leading the Library to become unmoored. They can be lost easily, if their connections are severed, and the Library of Stones contained a great deal of information that was deemed too valuable to risk. The first High King kept his word, and never attempted to use the Library for political ends, and so when his son took the throne, the Librarian willingly renegotiated the treaty to maintain the same terms. It is assumed she will do the same, if she retains power, when young Quentin comes into his ascension."

"Has it been the same Librarian the whole time?"

"No, there have been several Librarians in the time the Library has been anchored here. They change every fifty years or so, either due to retirement or because they've transferred to another Library. The Libraries prefer to keep their staff well-informed, which means moving them between locations from time to time."

All knowes are alive and self-aware. The Library knowes are weird enough that it made sense they might be able to tell their Librarians what they wanted and see to it that their will was carried out.

"Huh," I said.

The ladder came rolling back along the line of shelves, now carrying a dainty woman in a floor-length pink velour bathrobe with white bunnies embroidered all the way around the hem. Her sleek black hair was gathered into a messy braid that fell down her back in snarls and puffs of tangled strands, capped at the bottom with a sparkly rhinestone butterfly clip. She looked more like a teenager who'd been raiding May's closet than a Librarian, and I blinked.

"Sorry, sorry," she said, hopping off the ladder, which rolled on into the dark without her. "I was in the children's section, and you know how those picture books can get."

She was even wearing pink bunny slippers. The corner of my mouth twitched with an involuntary smile.

Fiac bowed. "Librarian Yenay," he said solemnly. "These guests would like to speak to you on matters of history and the records you have custody of."

"Seneschal Fiac," said the Librarian, voice much lighter. "Do any of them have Library cards?"

"Nope, although I've been a patron of the Library of Stars in the Mists," I said. "Hi. My name is—"

"Sir October Daye, Knight of Lost Words, most recently known of the Dóchas Sidhe, proof that Amandine the Liar can fail to do her duty more than once without attracting the vengeance of Oberon himself, oh, yes, I know who *you* are," said the Librarian. "I'm Yenay Ng, and this is my Library."

"It's very . . . misty," I said. "The walls don't look like they've quite committed to the idea that they need to keep existing when no one's looking at them."

"That's one of my favorite things about the place," said Yenay, and looped her arm through mine. Her skin was a remarkably clear medium brown, so smooth it was like she had no pores, and her eyes were black from one side to the other, lacking the aura of vague menace that the Luidaeg took on when her eyes were in the same state. "I mean, that, and somehow I can always find fresh donuts in the breakroom, when I can find the breakroom at all. Sometimes it doesn't exist because *someone* wants me to eat more salads." She tipped her head back to yell her final words at the ceiling. Then she shrugged. "But breaking in a new Librarian has got to be frustrating, so I guess it's okay if this one wants me to last for a little while. Come on."

She started leading me between the shelves. Quentin, who didn't want to be left alone with Fiac, followed.

"So what is it our humble Library can do for a daughter of Amandine the Liar?" she asked brightly. "I've seen the biography you helped Magdaleana Brooks write of her. Lots of pieces missing. Plenty of room for an update if you wanted to make one."

The Libraries trade in information, and for a Librarian, knowing something no one else knows is sort of like getting a gift card to Willy Wonka's factory, along with permission to buy as much candy as they can carry. It's a big deal. "I can't give you any secrets about my mother," I said. "Those are promised to the Library of Stars."

She turned to me so I could see her pout. "Well, then, what do you have to bargain with? I assume there must be something, or you wouldn't be here looking for information."

"I can tell you where the other Dóchas Sidhe is."

Yenay blinked, pout fading into a look of profound confusion. "But August Torquill was lost in 1906, when she went looking for Oberon himself, at the behest of the sea witch," she said. "She was bade not to return until her quest was complete."

"That's true."

Her eyes widened. "You mean . . . you mean she found Oberon?"

The Libraries are independent of the Kingdom structure, immune to the word of Kings and Queens, but they're still part of Faerie, and that means they have to answer to someone. That someone is and has always been Oberon himself. If he had returned, their days of independence were over.

For some reason, that hadn't been a big enough concern to occur to me before now, at least in part because I still didn't have permission to tell anyone he was back.

"No," I said carefully. "She did not find Oberon. But I found her, at the request of Amandine the Liar, and I was able to work with her father and the Luidaeg to bring her safely home. She's living with her father in the Undersea demesne of Saltmist, having chosen him in the divorce."

"Hmmm," said Yenay. "Human interest angle is strong—I wish we had a better way of saying that, but since we decided to go all-in on stealing language from the mortals, I don't really have an easy-to-follow way to construct the phrase 'fae interest angle.' That's just word salad. But anyway, people will be interested in hearing how she came back, given how long she was missing, and how little we know about her. Don't suppose you're down for narrating another biography?"

Giving Mags the information she'd asked for about my mother had been a relatively painless process, although I probably needed to talk to Janet and then talk to Mags again—it was time for a second edition now that we knew who my grandmother was. But Mom had given up her right to privacy when she spent my entire childhood keeping secrets from me. As far as I was concerned, she no longer had any reason to expect me to stay quiet about private matters.

August, though . . . August was a different case. We weren't what I'd call friends, but we were sisters, and we'd chosen the same side during the divorce. We were both daughters of Simon Torquill in the eyes of Faerie. I had no doubt that meant something, in the tangled and self-contradictory web of rules and traditions that increasingly governed my life. I didn't want to cross any lines I didn't know existed.

"Sorry," I said, honestly. "August's life story is only on the table if she puts it there. But I can tell you the parts that involved me. Maybe that's enough to buy the information I need. Maybe it's not. I don't really know. I don't think I'm asking for anything that valuable."

"True, we should figure out what you want me to pull before I get down to barter." Yenay cast a sour look over her shoulder at Fiac. "Blame these people. They act like we're the Kingdom's private Library because of where we're anchored, and half the time they're sending their people here looking for the latest bestseller or really *weird* erotica. I don't care what gets people hot and bothered, I don't judge, but if Cait Sidhe are your thing, why not just date one, instead of reading about someone else doing it?"

"I'm marrying one later today," I said, fighting the urge to smile.

"Oh, right, the King of—fuck, what's he King of these days? Man's had so many crowns I lost track somewhere on the other side of the Atlantic. Doesn't that mean he'll have to give up his throne? I bet he's relieved. Everything I know says he never wanted to be King of anything in the first place. But yeah, I knew that. Anyway." Yenay let go of my arm and stepped away, waving her hands across her chest at the same time. Her bathrobe melted away, replaced by an equally pink-and-white dress that seemed to be made almost entirely from intricately interwoven strips of ribbon. Her braid adjusted itself at the same time, wisps and flyaways replaced by smooth perfection. The butterfly clip remained.

"I am Yenay Ng, chosen Librarian of the Library of Stones," she said, with sudden solemn gravity. "What is your request?"

"I need to see the original proclamation declaring the Kingdom of Maples as the seat of the High Kingdom of the Westlands and dissolving the original crown," I said. "I need to know exactly what was said in the process of making the first High King Sollys into, well, the first High King Sollys."

Yenay blinked. "Why didn't you just say so? The Kingdom's founding documents are basically public domain, or they would be, if we had any concept of the public domain. Wait here." She turned and dashed off into the stacks before I could reply.

"She didn't really leave you room *to* say so," said Quentin, stepping up next to me.

I glanced at him. "I get the feeling she gets talked over a lot. Tends to make people talk faster to make it hard to interrupt them."

"Huh."

"Shyi Shuai aren't that common in the Westlands. Finding one not working as a Court Seer is a little weird."

Quentin snorted.

I glared. "What?"

"Toronto has one of the largest Chinese populations outside of China," he said. "And unlike the Mists, we didn't try to burn their Chinatown down with all of them still locked inside. Our Shyi Shuai never left."

"Huh." A whole community of luck-bending fae. Maybe there was a reason the Kingdom of Maples—and by extension, the High Kingdom of the Westlands—had enjoyed more than two centuries of relative peace and prosperity.

Fiac loomed up beside me. "I understood you had a Shyi Shuai standing as a temporary Duchess in your home Kingdom."

I jumped. "Man, we are gonna *bell* you. Don't sneak up on people!" I pressed a hand to my chest, trying to calm myself. "Li Qin, yeah. She took up temporary regency of Dreamer's Glass when Duchess Riordan vanished." I knew exactly where Treasa Riordan was, and I hoped she liked it in Annwn, because as far as I was concerned, she could rot there. I certainly wasn't going to lead the expedition to get her back.

"So you know they still exist."

Unlike the Roane, the Shyi Shuai had never been rumored extinct, just rare. "I do."

"We are very fond of Yenay. If she chose to leave the Library, we would find her a place in the archives, or working with the scribes. Whatever she desired. But she seems to enjoy the relative obscurity of serving the Library's whims, and she treasures her time with the books." Fiac continued looking straight ahead. "Please do not confuse autonomy with a lack of loyalty."

"I generally try not to." Yenay came rushing back through the stacks, clutching a leather-bound ledger to her chest. She didn't look distressed; on the contrary, she looked very nearly jubilant, as if she hadn't expected her evening to be so interesting.

"I found what you were asking for," she said brightly, thrusting the ledger at me before pausing, blinking, and pulling it back again. "But they weren't big on consistent spelling in the eighteenth century, so you probably can't read it. Would you like me to tell you what it says?"

"That might be for the best," I agreed.

She beamed and turned the ledger around, opening it and reading aloud, "'I, High King Clement Pemberton of Europa, do certify and attest that the High Kingdom of the Westlands has successfully petitioned for their independence as a noble demesne, to be ruled by their own power and to set their own laws and demands upon their citizenry. They shall no longer be subject to our law, nor heir to our kindnesses, but shall endure alone, and upon their own power. We guarantee to them as a condition of this decree that Europa will not make war upon them or seek to encroach upon their domain for a term of one hundred years as measured in the mortal world, unless there has been some disruption to the royal line as declared and agreed upon here.'" She looked up. "That's fancy pureblood jerk talk for 'we swear to leave you alone unless you depose the King we decided was a good idea. If you do that, we can do whatever we want.'"

"I picked up on that part," I said dryly. "Is the whole thing like that?"

"Pretty much. You think the nobility is into being overly flowery today, you should go digging in the historical records." She cleared her throat, then resumed, "As has been agreed upon by the Convocation of Crowns, the former regional Kingdom of Maples is henceforth to be dissolved and replaced with the High Seat of the Westlands, to be initially held by High King Oakley Sollys, with the throne to be passed along his descendant line according to the custom of our kind until such time as his line is sundered by either war or a failure to provide issue. In the event that High King Oakley is unable to perform his duties, and no male heir is available, the crown and throne will be passed to King Absalom Shallcross of Ash and Oak, who would have been named High King on this day had his land not been deemed unsuitable by the gathered Seers of the newly-formed Westlands, whose word was to be heeded . . ."

"Okay," I said. "So if the High King died right now, it wouldn't matter that Quentin isn't here. He's too young to inherit the crown, which means the line is broken, and the crown of the Westlands passes to Absalom Shallcross."

"King Shallcross was the second candidate for the role," said Fiac stiffly.

Something rustled in the stacks behind us, telling me my timing had been about as I'd hoped.

"Yes, but it's bad wording." I flashed Quentin a wry look. "It doesn't cede the crown to his line; it cedes it to him in specific. Probably because Europa figured things would either go well or fall apart completely in pretty short order, and all the players they knew would still be on the board when the first High King Sollys got assassinated or caught syphilis or died from a staph infection or whatever they were into dying from in the Revolutionary days. So they bet on a horse they already knew and tried to prevent a crisis of succession in the process."

"I fail to see the relevance," said Fiac.

"Of course you do," I said. "As long as you succeeded in assassinating the High King, you'd get to take over the Kingdom on the authority of the High King of Europa, and without an available heir, that would be the next best thing to Oberon himself stepping in and saying you were supposed to be in charge."

Fiac blinked, staring at me for a moment like he couldn't understand what I was saying. Then he sputtered, saying, "You don't know what you're *talking* about."

"Don't I?" I shrugged. "I know the King's seneschal was replaced, and I haven't seen the Queen's chatelaine at all, even though she should be glued to her side during a crisis like this one. She's one of the only people who doesn't look suspicious if she starts following the royal couple around, which means her absence indicates some difficulty in replacing her. Yenay, do you know what the Queen's chatelaine is?"

"Honey?" she asked, voice blank with confusion. "She's a Centaur."

"That's what the High King said, too. A Doppelganger couldn't replace her if they wanted to. But they must have tried for *someone* other than Nessa in a high position. So who do you replace? Not the High Queen herself, she'd be caught in an instant. The Court Seer who everyone knows can't be in the presence of falsehood without losing his shit, though? That's a great cover."

Fiac glared at me. I smiled sweetly.

"And you're sort of stuck right now, because if you *were* Fiac, you'd be attacking me if anything I said was untrue, which means either you're Fiac and I'm right, you're also King Shallcross of Ash and Oak, or you're not Fiac and it doesn't matter if I'm lying, because you don't have his magic, either in the positive or the negative sense. You've been faking it pretty well, but that's not the same. So which is it?"

Quentin moved closer to me, eyeing Fiac sidelong, uncomfortable. He knew me well enough at this point to know that once I start breaking down the reason someone should be on the wrong side of my suspect list, I'm probably about to get stabbed.

Fiac scowled. "What leads you to this conclusion?" he asked.

"No competent seer would allow the King they served into a room with a known assassin present while searching for an imposter. There's bad advice and then there's ridiculously misguided advice that could lead to someone getting seriously hurt—as this did. You already knew the Doppelgangers were willing to use both physical weapons and poisons, and you still allowed the High King to leave himself underdefended in the face of the unknown. I'm told you've served both loyally and long, so tell me, how did that decision make sense?"

Yenay moved closer to me. "What are you doing?" she asked.

"Gloating, a bit," I said. "Antagonizing him, mostly. If I can get him angry enough, there's a chance he'll do something stupid, and then the fun begins."

"You're trying to get him to attack you?" Yenay sounded horrified, and more than a little confused.

"I'd like to wrap this up, so yeah, it'd be nice." I smiled at Fiac. "Centuries of planning, time and resources and *breeding*, sweet Oberon, the *breeding*, doing exactly what your Firstborn commanded you to do, marrying a good Daoine Sidhe woman and getting yourself a crown, getting yourself within an assassination and a badly-worded founding document of the highest office in the land, and it gets fucked up by a changeling who wouldn't be able to out-deduct the kids from Scooby-Doo. How does that feel? Bet it feels pretty lousy. Bet it makes you wish you'd chosen a different inciting incident, instead of waiting for the arrival of a convenient king-breaker. With the resources you have, you could have pulled this off, if you hadn't been searching for someone to blame."

Fiac's eyes narrowed. Then he snapped, both verbally and literally.

"I have enough men still in this knowe to take it even with your meddling," he said, reaching for his belt, which seemed bare, but nonetheless provided him with a knife when he pulled his hand away. It was a nice trick that I didn't have time to fully appreciate. "The High King *will* die, and you'll go down in the process of attacking the young Librarian who could have given your horrifying deception away."

"Leave me out of this," said Yenay, taking another step toward me. Apparently, she thought being closer to me was also worth being closer to Fiac. "I'm not a part of your power struggle."

"You wouldn't have been, if she hadn't insisted on involving you," snarled Fiac, gesturing for me with his knife. His face twisted, seeming to warp around the edges as he scowled. "This didn't have to be so difficult, you know. If you'd been properly focused on getting married, like you should have been, I could have killed you all and spread the blame across the kingdom. No collateral damage. No need for anyone to suffer."

"Mmmm, no," I said. "I'm pretty sure I'm suffering if I'm dead. What do you think, sweetheart?"

"I think baiting a treasonous bastard into attacking you is a poor wedding gift," said Tybalt, voice garbled from the effort of speaking around more teeth than his mouth was currently shaped to contain. He reached out and settled a hand on the air about two feet above Fiac's visible shoulder, tightening his fingers around an obvious obstacle.

"Pureblooded Cait Sidhe can see through illusions when they focus," I said cheerfully. "Just in case you forgot that little tidbit."

"I knew you were masked, but assumed it was cosmetic until I heard my lady's line of questioning," said Tybalt, tone reasonable. "I looked more closely once I realized there might be something to see."

Fiac—who wasn't Fiac at all—laughed. Actually laughed. "I heard the news about your mother," he said. "It was carried all the way to the East Coast, faster than news ever travels. A new First-born! What a cause for celebration among those who'd never met her, what a cause for mourning among those who had."

"If you think making fun of my mother is a good way to get under my skin, you're dead wrong," I said. "Making fun of my mother is a good way to make friends." My hand inched toward my knife. I wouldn't say that I was aching to stab something, but it would certainly have been a nice bonus to the situation.

"How shamed she must have been, to carry a mongrel child," he continued, as if I hadn't spoken. "How painful for her to know that her bloodline, the flesh of her flesh, was trapped in a mortal vessel, doomed to die."

"Not dying any time soon," I said. "You made bad choices when you decided to use us as your scapegoats. I am not your excuse for regicide."

"Oh, but you are. You just don't realize it yet." Fiac's outline shimmered, growing taller, slimmer, altogether elongated, until his visible shoulder was settled firmly into Tybalt's grasping palm, until nothing about him so much as resembled the Adhene Seer he had been masquerading as.

He was a beautiful man. Of course he was: all Daoine Sidhe are beautiful. Eira would have tolerated nothing less. His hair was the deep burnt orange shade of the perfect jack-o-lantern in waiting, and his eyes were only a few shades lighter, inhuman and compellingly bright. His clothes transformed with the rest of him, becoming the livery of a kingdom I didn't recognize but assumed must be the lost, inconsistently lamented Ash and Oak.

He was wearing a crown. It was a nice touch, given everything else that had just happened.

"You have no idea what you're toying with, little girl," said the man—King Absalom Shallcross of Ash and Oak, I presumed. Yeah, making guesses doesn't always pan out, but everything I had so far pointed to the man, and I like betting on the sure thing when I can.

"Neither do you," snarled Tybalt, and whipped King Shallcross around so that they were facing each other. Tybalt's illusion of civilization was slipping. His eyes had gone fully feline, pupils narrowed to hairline slits, and his mouth bristled with teeth. The stripes traveling along his cheeks and down the sides of his throat betrayed his tabby nature with perfect clarity. He looked like he was on the verge of losing control.

I wasn't the only one who saw it. Yenay stepped forward, the precious ledger clutched to her chest like a teddy bear. "Please don't get blood on the books," she said, in a gasp. "They don't deserve that."

"Ask him where the Seer is," I said.

Tybalt tightened his hand further on King Shallcross's shoulder, claws breaking the other man's skin. The smell of blood snaked its way through the room, savory-sweet and far more appealing than it had any right to be. I refused to turn my face away. This was part of my job more than it was part of Tybalt's. This was my squire's family and the throne I was ultimately sworn to.

"Your people have been replacing the loyal members of this household," said Tybalt, and as he spoke his voice leveled out, teeth shrinking back toward their normal size. I guess now that I wasn't in immediate danger of taunting my way into getting stabbed again, he didn't feel the need to be quite as threatening. That was almost flattering. "Have they been killing them?"

"Not for the most part, and never directly," said King Shallcross.

"The Doppelganger who replaced Nessa had set some pretty deadly traps in her quarters," I said.

"Bah," said King Shallcross. "Traps are not the same as murder, under the Law."

I stared at him. "People *died*."

"Yes, but they pulled the trigger themselves." He turned toward me, expression unnervingly triumphant. That smug smile made me want to punch him right in the middle of his pretty, pretty face. "No one can be said to be responsible."

Faerie doesn't so much have a definition of "negligent homicide," and I didn't so much have a reason *not* to be punching him. Sure, he was a King, but he had no Kingdom, and I had an assortment of people with crowns who'd willingly pardon me for assaulting the man.

The feeling of his nose crunching under my fist was surprisingly satisfying. Tybalt actually let him go as he reeled backward, knocked off balance by the blow. Blood cascading down his face, King Shallcross lifted his head and stared at me.

I smiled at him, making deliberate eye contact as I raised my hand and licked the blood off my knuckles. It tasted of spruce and hazelnut, echoing the magic that eddied around the man when his illusions were released, and when I closed my eyes, I could see myself through his eyes, plain, unassuming knight of a backwater kingdom, named hero for political reasons, with a reputation all out of proportion to anything I could possibly have achieved. All those stories of me deposing corrupt monarchs and consorting with Firstborn were just that—stories, and the people who took them seriously deserved to be exploited and overthrown.

"What's wrong with her?" demanded Absalom. "A changeling should *never* lay hands upon their betters!"

"I didn't, and stay quiet, because if I lose this blood memory, I'll have to hit you again," I said calmly. "I may do that anyway, for the fun of it."

He stopped talking.

"He heard we were coming because it wasn't a secret, and he's been waiting for a while for an opportunity," I said, not opening my eyes. "Please understand that by 'for a while,' I mean 'since the fall of Ash and Oak.' Man's been hiding in the royal kitchens for *decades*. They need to vet their people better."

Especially considering that he couldn't have done it without illusions and enchantments to make himself look like something other than one of the Daoine Sidhe. Even assuming no one in the knowe would have recognized the former king, which was a pretty big assumption, no one would ever believe a pureblooded Daoine Sidhe's greatest aspiration was to serve under a Hob in someone else's kitchen. It went against everything Eira had decreed for her descendants. He'd been hiding for well over a century.

The thought brought another rush of memories, feeling thwarted, overlooked, relegated to a place well below what he deserved by both the fall of his kingdom—brought about by its human occupants, and not his fault, no, not his fault in the slightest—and the knowe policy of hiring courtiers and guards from among the ranks of the nobility. He couldn't even serve as a page without a household to support him, and so he'd been forced to clear tables and serve people whose station was below his own.

His rage and resentment, which had been building for years, had been given plenty of time to swell, curdle, and sicken him, destroying any vestige of the man who had once been noble enough to be considered for the high throne. Even his lady wife, the lovely Vesper, had left him alone in the wake of his kingdom's fall, slipping away in the night without a—

I gasped, breaking free of the memory and opening my eyes. Tybalt was staring at me, visibly concerned. He had hold of Absalom again, one hand clasping each of the man's shoulders. Absalom's nose had stopped bleeding.

That was too bad. I needed more blood.

"Are you all right?" Tybalt asked, eyes never leaving my face.

"I'm fine, but I need more blood," I said. "I lost the memory, and what I saw—I need to see more."

"Very well."

"No, not 'very well,'" snapped Absalom. "I am a pureblooded descendant of Eira Rosynhwyr! I demand to be treated as my position demands!"

"You are a king who ignored the warning signs when iron poisoning began to seep into your people, who allowed far too many to die when they could have been saved," I said. "You are a small man rendered corrupt by power, only to see that power stripped away when you failed to protect it as you should have done. It's not enough to convince people to put their faith in you. You have to keep earning it every day. You have to be good enough tomorrow for the people who chose you yesterday to know they were right and make the same choice again. You lost everything when Ash and Oak fell, and I can't say yet whether I'm sorry or not. But people have died here, in this knowe, because of actions you took and choices you made, and I'd be a poor hero if I didn't press on and verify the scope of the harm you've done. You *will* bleed for me. The only question is how voluntarily—and how much."

Tybalt shifted his hand from one shoulder to wrap around Absalom's throat, claws pricking against the skin. Absalom swallowed hard and thrust one arm out toward me, wrist turned toward the ceiling.

"Do as you must, filth," he spat.

"Not sure I'd call me that with Tybalt holding onto you like that, but sure, you do you." I drew my knife as I stepped forward, reaching out to take his hand. Carefully—more carefully than he deserved—I pressed the edge of the blade against the place where his hand met his arm, slicing shallowly across. Blood welled to the surface, and I pulled my knife away.

This time, I got a mouthful, and the memories washed over me in an immediate, bloody tide. As always, they carried a certain confusion with them—was I October Daye, daughter of Amandine, or Absalom Shallcross, son of Vitus? And did it matter, either way?

She is lovely, my lady, framed against the moon in the window of her bower, and I would die for her. I would kill for her—I have killed for her, a dozen men, to see the crown safely settled on my brow and its twin upon hers. She carries it as a queen should, my Vesper, my lady of the evening hour, with her pearly skin and her hair as black as polished coal, her manners finer than silk, her touch more precious than pearl—

I knew the woman in Absalom's memories, had known her my entire life. Of course I did. There's nothing beautiful in this world that can't be corrupted by the touch of Eira Rosynhwyr. She hadn't even bothered to change the face she wore between Vesper Shallcross and Evening Winterrose. She was still the woman I'd always known. In more ways than one.

The kingdom is fallen. Iron in the water, iron in the ground, and those damn Roane saw it coming, but not the way it could be set aside. There are no more Roane in the harbors of New York, regardless of the kingdom, but that is small consolation for having lost so much. My lady has left me, and all because the Roane could not speak plainly, could not say "give the throne and the land to Shallcross, for he has been deeded tainted land, and deserves better than his lot." This is all their fault . . .

I gasped and took another mouthful, forcing myself below the memories.

My rival goes to the night-haunts, his son to ascend in his place . . . the boy is weak, his reign will crumble, and the throne will pass to me as it should have from the beginning . . . my lady will return when she sees me holding power again, as I should have done from the beginning. My sweet Vesper will whisper my fears away as she has always done. In her company, I can be a better, stronger man. In her presence, I can be as glorious as our First commanded me to be.

That was because Vesper *was* his First, so of course she'd know how to follow the rules she herself had set down for her descendants. His memories of her were surprisingly carnal for the formal nature of the rest of his thoughts, and I could have gone my entire life without seeing Evening like that, even through someone else's eyes.

But the son holds the throne and finds a bride, although no one seems to remember her mother; she springs from nowhere, like Venus from the tide, and she is beloved, because she is the Queen. I hate him all the more for having her by his side, when my own Queen is absent, gone to parts and places unknown until such time as I can be a man for her.

Is there anything Evening can't make worse? More, is there anyone in Faerie who *doesn't* need therapy?

Time is the only coin I have to spend in plenty. Time, and what remains of the treasury of Ash and Oak, which is no longer replenished, but is no longer needed for the care and comfort of my people. So I gather my strength.

I gather my supporters from among the lowest of the fae, the ones who think like men but are thought of as monsters, all because they were made by the Three rather than born from the bodies of their children. The Doppelgangers thrive in the absence of the Courts and are less troubled by the touch of iron than are so many of us. They have taken the lands that once were mine, and while they answer to no lord, they are willing to negotiate.

The plan is a slow one. The tinder is gathered, the bonfires ready

*to burn, and we build for years. I humble myself before the pre-
tender, keep myself below his notice, serve at his table, sup on his
scraps, and dream of the day when he kneels before me, beaten and
broken and brought low, as he should have been since the
beginning.*

I gasped, breaking loose for a moment, not quite shaking the
memory away. "Still don't know if Fiac's alive or not," I said, almost
apologetically, before pressing my mouth to Absalom's wrist again.
"This would go faster if you'd think about him, and not about how
awesome and cool your grand plan is. It's like sitting through the
arthouse film version of some asshole's evil monologue."

Tybalt shot me a concerned look. I offered him a quick, wan
smile, and dove into the memory again.

*The kitchens are abuzz. There is to be a wedding, and the bride
is apparently a monster who has insisted on bringing her private
pastry chef to make the cake. It's easy, in the offense this generates,
to slip away and move my people into place.*

Oh, Kerry was going to be thrilled about that.

*Things improve; the bride is a known king-breaker and self-
styled hero who causes chaos wherever she trespasses. She will provide the perfect scapegoat for the fall of a king. Some say she may
have the missing Crown Prince in her company. If this is true, he'll
die with his father, and the High Kingdom will be settled on me
with no possible complications. No one will question me when I
appear, heroic savior from the past, to stop a changeling king-
breaker from destroying the proper order of things. I need only get
myself into position—*

The Seer's place will do—

I gasped again, breaking free completely. The shards of Absalom's thoughts cluttered the corners of my mind, unctuous and
somehow slimy, like they'd been as tainted as his land by years of
exposure to ambient iron. I retched, trying to get the taste of his
blood out of my mouth, but had the presence of mind—barely—not
to spit on the carpet. Instead, I turned to Yenay.

"Do you have anything with a stronger flavor than water?" I
asked. "Coffee, whiskey, strawberry soda, *anything*?"

"I have a Cherry Coke in the fridge," said Yenay, sounding a
little baffled. "Why do you—"

"Because I don't actually like the taste of blood," I said. "And
this fucker didn't taste very good, what with all the hatred and

bigotry and ambient iron he's carrying around with him." I shot Absalom a glare. "On the plus side, I think I know where to find Fiac, and it looks like this asshole was serious about trying to pull off a coup without any actual violations of the Law. With Oberon missing, if he killed the Sollys family and claimed the throne, he'd be able to pardon himself. Who's going to pursue a High King for his crimes? Who *can*? So he didn't want to muddy the waters with deaths people could say were unnecessary."

It's been a while since assassination was the most common means of succession. I've always wondered how that was supposed to work, since we're not supposed to kill each other except in times of war, but there have been periods where we knew, or at least strongly suspected, that literally everyone with a crown on their brow had committed murder to get it. Maybe all sitting monarchs are considered at war with one another, and it's something they all know so absolutely that they've never felt the need to tell any of the lesser denizens of Faerie about their perpetual, loophole-creating conflict?

"His Doppelgangers were more than happy to kill in his name," snarled Tybalt.

Yenay, who had ducked away into the stacks, came back without the ledger, and with a bottle of Cherry Coke in her hand, which she offered to me without saying a word. I removed the cap and took a long, fizzy drink, washing the taste of blood away, before looking back to Tybalt.

"They were, and he deserves to be punished for that. Which he will be, once we've finished flushing out the people he still has loose in the knowe—I don't know how many, which I have to assume is because he was intentionally thinking about other things, like how much he missed fucking his wife," I said, eyeing Absalom. He looked unaccountably smug. "But Fiac is alive, and we should be able to get to him before that changes. And the High King is alive, and this one will never take the throne. Now that we know the loophole he was planning to exploit, the foundation documents can be appropriately updated."

Absalom glared at me, Tybalt's hands holding him in place. I smiled sweetly back at him. He glared harder. Villains don't like it when you act like their threats aren't threatening.

"We can update the decree if the High King okays it," I said, in the calm, patient tone of someone who was being forced to explain something to a small child who didn't want to listen. "That's why people don't point these things out when they happen. They're keeping them as weapons to be used later."

Well, this weapon had been used, and while it was bloodied, it had failed to strike its actual target.

I shifted my smile to Tybalt, allowing it to melt around the edges and turn sincere.

"Now what?" he asked.

"Let's get married."

Tybalt blinked. Then he smiled back. "I was beginning to be afraid you'd never ask."

EIGHTEEN

THE HIGH KING HAD managed not to get poisoned again after he resumed interviewing his staff, in part because Walther had swept the room for toxins before lighting several candles for Cassandra, who stared at them as the door opened and closed, saying, "Yes . . . no . . . I can't tell, ask the questions," and throwing the new arrivals off their guard while the *actual* guard stood with swords at the ready. Neither her yes nor her no was being taken as absolute proof one way or the other, but it gave them a starting point, and by the time Tybalt, Quentin and I came back, she had a one hundred percent success rate at identifying the Doppelgangers.

Of whom there were several. Absalom had been moving his people into place for a long time and had only accelerated the process when he heard about our arrival. Not all of his loyal subjects were Doppelgangers, either; a few were the descendants of people who'd sworn themselves to him when he still had a kingdom, or courtiers from Ash and Oak proper. Having centuries to live means having centuries to hold a grudge.

One of them, a Gwragen, had been part of the High Queen's household staff for a hundred and forty years, and had been responsible for the illusions that allowed Absalom to infiltrate the kitchen, and later replace Fiac. She had started to weep when she was revealed as a traitor, insisting over and over again that she'd never done anything wrong or broken any laws; she had simply cast a few illusions when her true liege asked her to, allowing him to pass his days in comfort and care. She was awaiting sentencing along with the rest of Absalom's people, all of them stuffed into the less pleasant part of the dungeon.

Less pleasant, and already occupied when the High King's men dragged them down there. All the people who'd been replaced after Nessa had been knocked unconscious and tucked away there like last week's dirty laundry, intended to be forgotten—including the absent chatelaine. They'd been elf-shot first, so we didn't have to worry about dehydration or starvation. That was the good thing. The section of the dungeons that wasn't designed like some sort of abusive time share contained a lot of iron. That was the bad thing.

Oh, it wasn't a lot of iron by the standards of a truly abusive monarch. The iron in the entire structure wouldn't have been enough to replace one room in the false Queen's old dungeon. But it was enough that all the people who'd been stowed there had signs of iron poisoning, some more severe than others, and the Court alchemists were finally going to have something to do, what with the need to treat them all before they could be woken.

Which Walther would *not* be doing since he needed to be at the wedding with the rest of us.

I stood perfectly still on the low platform Stacy had erected in the middle of the fitting room, my arms stretched out to either side of me, forcing myself to take slow, even breaths as my dearest friends attempted to crush the life out of me at Stacy's instruction.

"Tighter," said Stacy. "Toby, if you let your arms drop, I'm giving Tybalt copies of those pictures we took at the arcade when we were sixteen."

"You're a monster," I managed, as May and Julie yanked the strings of my corset tight again, knocking the breath out of me for a moment. Stacy smiled.

"That should do it, ladies," she said. "Go ahead and tie her off. Toby, you can put your arms down now."

"I hate you," I said, dropping my arms back to my sides. "Why do I need a corset, anyway? It's not like the dress isn't going to fit."

Fae dresses tend to come in two major categories: entirely illusionary or extremely expensive and loaded down with enchantments. Either way, they always fit. Gain weight, lose weight, wear a corset, don't wear a corset, they fit. So this was pointless.

Stacy smirked at me. "Can you breathe?"

"I can, yes." A corset that actually fits properly isn't uncomfortable: it's snug, like wearing a too-tight pair of jeans, but other than making bending difficult, it doesn't really change things all that much.

"Good," said Stacy, and punched me in the stomach.

I blinked at her. "Why the hell did you do that?"

"Did you feel it?"

"Not really."

"That's why you have to wear a corset," said May, walking around to join Stacy in front of me. "A corset means if you get stabbed on your wedding day, you won't be the one bleeding."

"Unless they stab you someplace the corset doesn't cover," chirped Julie.

"Yes, that's very helpful," said Stacy. "Keep being snide while we're trying to convince her she approved the corset when she told us she didn't care about her wedding dress."

I sighed. "Okay. I'm sorry."

"Besides, your tits look amazing," said May.

I grinned at her. "Yeah, they do."

"Close your eyes," commanded Stacy, before we could go any further down the route of discussing my breasts. "It's time for us to get you dressed."

"I'm still not allowed to see the dress?"

"No."

"My own wedding dress. That I'm expected to wear for the rest of the night."

"That is correct."

"That will be on my actual body. That dress. Is the dress I'm not allowed to look at."

"Yes," said Stacy, with surpassing patience. "That is the dress you're not allowed to look at but will be wearing to your wedding. Tybalt asked. I agreed."

"I'm just going along with this because it's funny," said Julie.

"I think it's sweet," said May. "Come on. Let us get the dress on so I can fix your hair."

I sighed and closed my eyes. "This whole thing has just been you arranging a massive 'I told you so' to punish me for abdicating my responsibilities regarding this wedding," I accused.

"Yup," said Stacy. May just laughed.

For the next several minutes, I kept my eyes closed as they poked, posed, and pushed me into the positions they wanted,

occasionally instructing me to raise or lower my arms. A cascade
of heavy fabric descended around me, adding another layer of
snugness to the existing weight of the corset. I smelled roses. Stacy
tugged at the fabric covering my back.

"Laces or buttons?" I asked, unable to suppress the note of despair in my voice.

"Both," she said proudly.

I groaned.

With all three of them working, they were able to get me secured inside the dress in what was probably a reasonable amount
of time yet felt much longer as I stood there with my eyes closed
and listened to the rustling. There were no adjustments required;
the dress did all that itself, reacting to Stacy's tugging and twists.
When they finally stepped away, Julie whistled.

"You clean up good, girl," she said. "Be nice if you had any
color in your cheeks, but we can't have everything in this world."

"You only agreed to come to the wedding to keep an eye on me
for your uncle," I accused, without heat.

"Hey. You're going to be family now. I figured if I could help
him get the wedding day he wanted, I could swallow my pride to
see it happen."

My eyes were still closed, and so I didn't have time to react as
she wrapped her arms around my shoulders and yanked me into
our first hug in years. Lips close to my ear, she said, "This is where
I'd tell you not to hurt him, but you already have, and you're going
to do it over and over and over again, and that's okay, I guess.
That's what you both want. You help him heal more than you do
him harm, and that's even better than never hurting him at all."

She let go, pushing me away from her in the process. I staggered
but didn't fall off the platform.

"Here." Stacy took my hand. "Come sit."

"What?"

She guided me off the platform and across the room to a chair,
where she put her hands on my shoulders and pushed me firmly
down. "We're going to finish getting you ready, and you're going to
sit there and put up with it," she said firmly. "And if you have a
problem with that, you can take it to the complaint bureau."

"That consists of your mother, Evening, and Titania, in case you
were hoping you'd get some sympathy from them," said May.

I made a face. "Ugh, no thank you. I know two out of the three, and anyone who'd raise a kid like Evening can't be someone I want to spend any time with."

"Parenthood is hard," said Stacy. "You know that. Maybe we can't blame Titania for everything."

"We can blame her for more than enough," I said firmly. "No complaint bureau."

"Stop talking. I need you to not be moving your face," said Stacy.

What followed was a familiar dance, one we'd been performing as a group since we were seventeen and Stacy figured out that leaving me alone with a tube of mascara would result in mascara in my eye, not *around* my eyes. She applied my makeup with quick, confident strokes, while May twisted and bent and teased my hair into place. The smell of roses grew even stronger, making me suspect she was using something other than pins to secure her work. With the importance purebloods place on roses, there'd been no way I was going to avoid them. I kept my eyes closed and tried to relax.

Absalom had been arrested, and we had managed to flush out what certainly felt like the majority of his people. This should be the safest possible time for us to distract the rest of the guard. With the size and nature of the crowd we had in attendance for the wedding itself, there was no question as to whether we could defeat whatever army had been raised by a king without a kingdom, however much he'd been willing to exhaust his former treasury in the pursuit of a new throne.

And even with all that being true, I was worried about the distraction we were about to provide. After all, Absalom's entire plan had hinged on the necessity of a distraction, and while blood can't lie, blood memories tend to focus on what the one bleeding has experienced or been thinking about most recently, which is why a lot of blood memory begins with "ow hey that hurt." He could still have kept secrets from me, just by shoving them aside when I cut him, focusing on bigger, more important memories—which would explain why there'd been quite so much sex with Evening in what should have been more recent recollections.

Depending on his skill, it was possible the only sincere look I'd had at his plans was when I punched him, and he'd had no time to settle his thoughts.

Stacy brushed something across my lips, then stepped back. "Open your eyes," she said.

I did, blinking at her in the exaggerated way I knew she preferred when she was trying to check my makeup.

She pursed her lips, looking thoughtful. "Close them, I need to fix your eyeliner."

I closed my eyes. "You know, one illusion and all this is handled."

"I don't want to cast any more spells around your dress if I can help it, and while Tybalt doesn't need you wearing makeup to see how beautiful you are—he's a smart man, he knows who he's marrying—I expect you to be awake come dawn, and I'd rather your mascara didn't disappear between one breath and the next. No illusions. Everything that touches you today is real." She leaned closer as she worked eyeliner along the line of my eyelid, voice low and warm. "This is really happening. He really chose you. You really get to choose him back. Just this once, you get to choose being happy over taking care of all the rest of us. We can take care of ourselves for a little while. So open your eyes."

This time my rapid blinking was less about showing Stacy her handiwork and more about keeping myself from crying. She raised an eyebrow.

"If you ruin that mascara, you get to sit through this again," she said.

I blinked harder.

"Good girl." Stacy stepped back, expression smug as it always was when she made me presentable by her standards. Which had never involved making me look like a proper pureblood but had always involved making sure that they wouldn't be able to find anything wrong with me.

I finally looked down at my dress, receiving little more from my view at this angle than the impression of arctic white and deep blood red. The smell of roses permeated the fabric, getting stronger when I stood, and the skirt fell gracefully to swirl around my ankles. Not just roses—if I breathed in, I could catch a dizzying array of perfumes that seemed to encompass the magical signatures of half the people I'd met in my lifetime. I blinked again, this time in confusion, as I looked sharply up at the smugly smiling Stacy. She was standing next to May, watching me examine myself.

"You said you didn't want any *more* spells around my dress," I said carefully. "What did you mean by that?"

"I mean I'd wait a while before you start popping out little half-Cait Sidhe Tobys to run around getting into trouble, because no one's going to give you any cradle gifts, since May and I have been going door to door convincing people to enchant your wedding gown for weeks," said Stacy. "Pretty much everyone we know who knows how to throw a semi-competent stain-repellent spell gave us one. You could go swimming in the La Brea Tar Pits in that thing and come out spotless."

I looked down at the dress again, this time with more appreciation. "That's a lot of magic."

"Probably the most magical thing you own, so please, for the love of Oberon, try not to set it on fire or accidentally feed it into a wood chipper or anything else like that. It's protected against stains, not Toby." Stacy reached out to grasp my shoulders, pressing them in to make me stand up straighter. "Now go get married."

"Aren't you coming with me?"

"You have a ride." She and May exchanged a smirking smile. Neither of them was dressed for the wedding yet, making me suspect their clothes would be more illusionary and less literal than mine. It made sense. You can't really stain an illusionary dress, but you can't keep it and let it take up too much space in your closet, either.

Julie moved to open the fitting room door. "You look beautiful," she said softly as I passed her.

"I appreciate that," I said, swallowing the forbidden "thanks," and touched her arm as I stepped back into the main room.

Quentin was waiting there for me, perfectly relaxed in his formal stance, which should have been a contradiction but somehow wasn't. Maybe that was one of the prince lessons that managed to actually stick, unlike "leave the sea witch alone" and "when it's time to choose a knight, go for the one who won't get you almost killed on a regular basis." His parents would be *so* proud when they realized he could at least stand like a proper gentleman. He was wearing a wine-colored suit over a stark white shirt, a spray of white violets pinned to his lapel, and he managed not to look like a candy cane. Boy was full of surprises today.

His eyes widened at the sight of me, mouth moving in silence for several seconds before he gave up and just gestured emphatically.

"You look—um." He paused. "I feel like there's probably etiquette here that I don't know."

"There's etiquette you don't know?" My skirt was long enough to brush the floor as I walked, but not long enough—at least in the front—for me to trip on. There didn't seem to be much of a train in the back, either. Maybe this was one area where the purebloods were somehow more sensible than the mortals they insisted on cribbing half their customs from.

"I was a kid when I went into fosterage," he objected. "No, I hadn't already sat down with my parents—or Nessa—for a lecture on exactly what would be expected of me when I chose to get married, only that I would *be* expected to get married, and stay married to the same woman long enough for her to provide me with at least one heir, if not an heir and a backup. But what that would actually look like? No. And it's not like I could ask you, and Etienne never even tried to teach me about how marriage works."

"That's because Etienne married his human lover in a county clerk's office for the sake of keeping her paperwork in order, and doesn't necessarily know anything about pureblood marriage customs," I said blandly. "They left you here alone?"

"Indeed, no, fair lady, but I thought it best to give you a moment with this complete stranger who will be standing in your son's place during the ceremony that is to come," said the warm, familiar voice of Crown Prince Nolan Windermere. I turned, and there he was, leaning against the wall outside the fitting room door, a small smile on his face.

"I need to pay more attention to my surroundings," I said with a blink.

He laughed. "This is perhaps the one day of your life where no one, not even my sister, is allowed to fault your inattention. We have no white horse for you to ride, no fine chariot to carry you to your groom, but we have me, and I would be overjoyed to fill their role." He pushed away from the wall, offering me his arm. "Please."

"Are white horses and chariots the standard here?" I asked, moving to put my hand in the crook of his arm as Quentin moved into position behind me, stooping to pick up the back of my dress, which must have been dragging on the ground more than I realized.

Oh, well. Magic intended to repel bloodstains can handle a little dirt.

"White horses were, once," said Nolan, face falling. "Before our time in the Westlands began, white horses carried a maid to marriage or a man to sacrifice. After Maeve's Ride was shattered, we let them fall to the wayside, favoring carriages instead. A wedding carriage can be a glorious thing when constructed from the right materials, but I hope a Prince will suffice."

"Always," I said as I smiled warmly at him.

"Then, if my lady is prepared, let me take her to her king," said Nolan. He waved his hand through the air, transcribing an archway. On the other side was the not-a-room we'd seen before, all trees and shimmering sky, and the smell of the wind. It smelled of snow and roses, but somehow that didn't remind me of Evening at all. She had no place here.

This place was ours.

Nolan led me through the archway, Quentin following behind. Both of them stepped away once we were on the other side, Quentin dropping the train of my dress as he moved up to stand beside me.

"All right, this isn't about to turn into some patriarchal bullshit about giving me away, is it?" I asked. I couldn't see the platform from where we were standing, or the chairs, but from the sounds drifting back to us, they were full. Our guests had arrived.

"No," he said, offering me his arm. There was a faint rush of air as Nolan gated himself away again, presumably to join the rest of the attendees. "I walk you to the fork where you decide which road you're going to take, and then I go sit down."

"Which road?"

"There are three roads to Faerie. I'm pretty sure I know which one you're going to take, but I'm not allowed to influence you. It's always a squire, a child, or a young relative who escorts the bride to the roads, and then she has to go on alone."

I frowned. "This is gonna be a lot of pureblood bullshit, isn't it?"

"It is," he said, with a solemn nod. Then he grinned. "Shouldn't have married a king, I guess. Even the Cait Sidhe know what a state wedding looks like. Or, if you had to marry a king, you should have taken more of an interest in the arrangements."

"Are you punishing me for not caring more about my own wedding?" I asked, disbelieving.

Quentin shrugged. "At least you get to choose who you're going to marry," he said, voice going soft. "No one's going to tell you that you have to marry another Dóchas Sidhe, or that you have to make sure it's a marriage where you not only get children, but you get a clear line of paternity."

My breath caught in my throat. I kept moving mechanically forward, following his lead. He'd told me several times that things weren't that serious between him and Dean—and maybe they were and maybe they weren't, but who was to say what they could have been if he hadn't been destined to be High King one day, taking a throne that had to be held, one way or another, with blood? He had known his future since he was old enough to understand what a crown was for. A crown was for him. With all of its perks and obligations, it was going to rest on his head, and he was going to carry the weight of it in every choice he ever made. It could be centuries. It could be the day after he reached his majority.

I put a hand over his where it rested on my arm, squeezing lightly. "I'm sorry," I said. "That was ungrateful of me. I know you have expectations to live up to, and I appreciate you explaining this to me, since Tybalt's happy to watch me stumble through it without a map."

"He says you do that to him all the time," said Quentin. The path bent beneath us. I was starting to realize Nolan had dropped us off a lot farther from the site of the ceremony than I'd initially thought. "When you choose your road, I'll stay behind, and your next escort will see you to the place where your groom is waiting. If you had the higher title, Tybalt would be the one making this walk to you. Too bad 'my mother was Firstborn, and also awful' doesn't supersede 'actual king.'"

"I mean, that's probably a good thing, all things considered," I said. "Can you imagine Arden's reaction if I was in a position to pull rank on her?"

Quentin laughed. The path bent, and then split, dividing into three distinct routes deeper into the glade.

The first of them was broad and pleasant, extending away across a wide expanse of grass and wildflowers. Lilies grew along the path's edges, and a figure waited there, barely too far away to see, waiting for me.

The second was narrow, choked with thorny briars that dripped with roses redder than my gown, whiter than the violets at Quentin's lapel. There was no way anyone could walk that way without bleeding. Another figure waited there, distant and obscure.

The third path was the same width as the one I already stood on, winding down a mossy, ferny bank into the shadows of the evergreen trees. A third figure waited there, as impossible to see clearly as the other two. I looked at Quentin, raising an eyebrow.

"So what, I just pick one? What happens to the two I don't pick?"

"They head for the wedding and probably give you shit about it later, even though this is sort of the definition of an uninformed choice." Quentin shrugged. "The Luidaeg says that in state weddings like this one it used to be only the right path that led to the wedding, and the other two would lead you up and down for a hundred hours before dropping you back where you started to try again. I know it must be true if she says it, but that seems like a really lousy way to deal with something that's going to keep half the local nobles from doing their jobs until it's over. But whatever, we're not as hung up on being timeless creatures of forest and fen as we used to be."

He stopped at the point where the paths diverged, pulling his arm away and offering me a small smile. "This is where I go."

"What if I don't want you to?"

"Why, Sir Daye, are you proposing?" I must have looked absolutely horrified, because he laughed, shaking his head. "Not an option. I'll be at the end, along with everyone else who loves you."

Then he turned and walked away, leaving me alone with three unmarked paths, any one of which would lead me to my future. "This is fun," I said, and glared at the air. "Some warning would have been nice."

Faerie and the human world have interacted for as long as they've both existed, brushing up against each other and sometimes striking sparks. I recognized the scene in front of me, even if I had never expected to face it quite so literally. It was from the ballad of Thomas the Rhymer, lover of the Faerie Queen— although the ballad doesn't say which one; I've always suspected Maeve, if only because it doesn't shy away from the bloody nature of Faerie—the point when he faced the three roads that would define his destiny.

What a ridiculous, pretentious, *pureblood* thing to build a wedding ceremony around. I shook my head. "Do you see the narrow road, so thick beset with thorns and briars? That is the path to righteousness, though after it but few inquire."

I looked to the next path. "And see you next the broad, broad

road that lays across the lily lawn? That is the path to wickedness, though some call it the path to heaven."

The last path was the simplest, winding down into the ferns and the dark. "And see you not the bonnie road that winds about the ferny bank? That is the road to fair Elfland, that you and I this night must take."

There was a time when I would have run down that broad lily road without a second thought, trying to move faster than my own demons, racing ahead without looking back. There were dangers there, I knew, and for all that it would be the easiest journey, it would also be the least satisfying.

There was also a time when I would have rejected any road that wouldn't punish me for walking it, when I would have thought a little blood—or a lot of blood—was the least I could pay for pushing my way toward a future where I could actually be happy. I was working on that. It wasn't easy, and the urge to self-destruct was probably always going to be with me, as worked into my DNA as everything else about who I was, but I was trying. That makes all the difference.

The third road, the road that symbolized Faerie, was the only one I could legitimately take. I knew that, taking a step toward it even before I finished admitting to myself that my choice had been made before I got here. Then I paused, looking back at the other two. Last chance to change my mind.

I was standing here in a wedding dress and a thrice-damned *corset*, and I wanted to pretend the last chance to change my mind wasn't already years behind me? I'd been given every opportunity in the world to walk away. I'd even taken a few of them. The people who loved me had never been willing to let it stick, and I can only be fetched back so many times before I start to think that maybe I'm not allowed to leave. "Sorry," I called, hoping the two people waiting to escort me down the paths I wasn't taking would hear me, and plunged onward, stepping onto the path that wound down the ferny bank.

"This is the road to fair Elfland, and also to my fucking wedding," I said, as the trees closed in above me and locked away the light. Everything was darkness and silence under the branches, lit only by the dim glow of tiny white mushrooms half-hidden by fern fronds. The smell of peat and loam rose around me, kicked up by my feet. Maybe this was the wrong road after all. Maybe I'd made the wrong choice, and now I was going to be lost in the woods forever.

Tybalt would never have approved a wedding plan, no matter how traditional, that involved losing me. He'd have given in and agreed to my increasingly broad hints about the county clerk before he would have agreed to any plan where he might not end up with a wife. So this had to be as standard as Quentin said it was. That didn't mean I was going to wander around in the dark and lose the path. I stopped where I was instead, planting my hands on my hips, and said, "I know you're there. I was promised an escort no matter which way I went. This is my wedding night. I don't know how you purebloods do things, but in the human world, what the bride says during her wedding goes, and I say get your butt over here."

A familiar voice laughed in the dark, low and warm and essentially kind, not mocking at all, before a globe of witch-light sprung into life above the outstretched palm of a pale-skinned, red-haired man in a suit identical to Quentin's, even down to the sprig of white violets on his lapel. The light glinted sparks off of his honey-gold eyes, and for a moment—not a long one, but a bright and beautiful one—he was the man I knew he couldn't possibly be: my liege, Sylvester.

Then he smiled, and it was Sylvester's face, but it wasn't, had never been, Sylvester's smile. There was a time when I'd been able to confuse them. I couldn't anymore.

"Hi, Simon," I said. "I'm guessing you're here to lead me to the next part of the wedding? How many of these weird-ass side quests do I have to do while I'm wearing a corset? Since I'm assuming you jumped through every hoop in creation when you married my mom." His marriage to Patrick and Dianda Lorden had basically been the equivalent of "do you wanna? Cool, do *you* wanna?" delivered by the Luidaeg, skipping over all the formal protocols in favor of getting things done as quickly as possible.

Dianda was a duchess, but somehow that hadn't been enough to make her taking a second husband into a formal state wedding. Sometimes I question my life choices.

"Once upon a time, six quests, each more difficult than the last, culminating in the identification of your future spouse amongst a room of people enchanted to look exactly like them." I must have looked appalled, because his smile softened, and he added, "Honey and bees were a common part of the wedding ceremony in those days. A sweetened kiss was the easiest way to locate your intended. But the mortal world demands swiftness and simplicity both. I'm assuming your first escort told you that all three paths would lead to your groom?"

"He had to, or I wouldn't have been willing to go along with it."

"There you are." He sounded smug. "This is your only trial, if allowing me to walk you to the ceremony is such a trial."

"And hey, it matches up nicely with a human tradition."

"Mmm?" Simon looked politely interested, raising an eyebrow in question.

"My father escorting me to the altar," I said, and took his arm. Maybe there wasn't an altar—if there was anything religious about this ceremony, it was going to be a total surprise to me—but there was a wedding, and this was a cultural touchpoint I understood.

And it was worth it for the slow understanding and then acceptance on Simon's face. He put his hand over mine, holding me in place, and began to walk along the path, leading me deeper into the tangle of trees.

"I know I'm not," he said. "I would have liked to have been, but my own choices closed that door before it ever could have opened between us and left it to my brother to fill the place that should have been mine as much as he was willing to—which was never enough for me. On the rare occasions when I came close enough to see his interactions with you, it burned me not to be allowed to step in and offer you the support you so clearly yearned for. You have done, in the balance of things, an excellent job of raising yourself. That task should never have fallen upon your shoulders. But I was gone, and your mother . . ."

He paused, catching his breath. "I knew, even in August's infancy, that your mother was no fit mother to anyone. She tried—she was better for August, I think, than she ever bothered to be for you—but she has her limitations, and I worried, when I saw you playing in my brother's halls, that you would be heir to all of them with no one else to leaven her presence. But you have done incredibly well, and I would bear the title you offer me with pride, not only in the legality of things, if I had any right to it."

I hugged his arm impulsively as we walked. "And that's why you can have it for as long as you want it," I said. "We've had our issues," that was putting it incredibly mildly, "but I think we wound up in the best possible place. You're never going to be my dad, but you can be my father for as long as you want to be. I chose your line, after all. Faerie says I'm yours."

Simon pulled his arm away and turned me to face him, kissing my forehead before he dropped his witch-light into my hands. "Then I'm yours as well, and as your father, I tell you that your heart is waiting."

"You don't mean that literally, right?" Things can be periodically and ridiculously literal in Faerie. My way home—a complicated tangle of memories and motivations that binds me to the person I am now, and not any of the other people I might have been able to become—is apparently a city pigeon that sleeps somewhere behind my sternum. He could mean that my actual heart had been replaced with a stone or a lump of bread or an empty jar when I wasn't looking, and now I'd have to fight a dragon or something to get it back.

Simon laughed. "No. it's just one of those things you say to a woman on her wedding day when you want to sound supportive of her life choices—which, believe me, I am. I always assumed that old cat would find a way into the family one way or another, and if he couldn't marry my sister, my daughter is just as good." He paused. "I suppose that sounds strange, given your human roots."

I smiled beatifically up at him. "Actually, it sounds exactly right."

"Then go," he said. "Get married. Be happy. You've earned it."

Somehow, we had reached the end of the path. It felt like it had taken forever. It felt like it had taken no time at all. The sound of voices was louder than ever, screened off by only the last layer of the trees, and the branches that spread to block them from my view—and me from theirs. I took a deep breath.

I stepped through.

NINETEEN

SIMON FOLLOWED ME out of the trees, moving toward an open seat at the front of the shallow amphitheater. It felt like every seat was filled, and most of them with people I recognized. A reasonable number of the guests were wearing the High King's livery, which told me he'd held back a certain number of spaces for his own courtiers; that was fine, as long as they'd been vetted. It wasn't like we'd been forced to snub anybody due to a lack of space.

The others I didn't recognize occupied about a quarter of the seats, all clustered together. They were dressed the closest to human, in tattered and patchworked finery, leather jackets and denim vests alongside corsets and opera jackets, their faces striped and spotted, their hair much the same. The Cait Sidhe of Toronto were in attendance to see one of their own married to a knight of the Divided Courts, and that made me a little nervous, even as I was relieved to know Tybalt wasn't doing this without the support of his own kind.

There were only a few faces I would have liked to see who weren't present, and all of those absences were at least somewhat expected. Arden wasn't there, being unable to leave her Kingdom; neither was Queen Siwan of Silences, or their current Crown Prince. My mother was also blessedly missing. She hadn't been invited, I knew that much; hers was the only name I had personally struck from any possible list, and thanks to the fact that I'd chosen Simon in the divorce, she couldn't even claim offense at her exclusion. Officially, we no longer had any relation to each other, and she had no right to expect an invitation.

Ginevra, Raj's regent, was also absent. That made sense; with Raj and Tybalt both here, the Court was her responsibility, and it wasn't like we knew each other well enough for her to care one way or the other. Her father, Jolgeir, wasn't there either, probably because, as Portland's King of Cats, travel wasn't really in the cards for him. Dianda wasn't there, but both her husbands and both her sons were.

What mattered more was the people who *were* there. My friends; my family. They filled the seats, a descending series of tiers leading me to the platform at the front, where Tybalt was waiting for me, alone in front of a beautiful, terrible woman I still somehow recognized as the Luidaeg.

She had no illusions left to keep her concealed from our eyes. The tricks she played with her appearance and environment were some of the only lies she had left to her, and so she played them constantly, protean and mercurial even in the presence of the people who loved her. I had never seen her entirely unveiled before. That didn't matter. There was no one else she could have been, and no possible way she could have been concealing herself, not when she was suddenly so much more completely who she'd always been.

She was taller, built less like a gawky human teen and more like the woman that teen could, given time and a series of miraculous wins in the genetic lottery, become. Her hair, still dark and curly, was no longer an indeterminate shade between black and brown, but the bruised blue-black of the deep ocean at midnight, even down to the silvery glints the light struck every time she moved her head. She saw me, and she smiled, her perfect lips stretching back to reveal the serrated shark's assortment of her teeth.

Tybalt was wearing a nicer version of the suit both Quentin and Simon had been dressed in, more perfectly tailored to him, and—here I had to swallow the urge to laugh—with red leather trousers, rather than the heavy linen the others had worn. Well, if you know what makes your bride-to-be happy, why not roll with it? He was tense, his posture oddly anxious, and he didn't seem to have noticed me yet.

No one had. I looked around the gathering again, wondering how I could be standing here in the whitest dress ever known to man or fae, without them noticing my presence. Then I caught the eye of the tall, antlered figure standing behind the rear row of chairs, and I understood.

Oberon looked at me and smiled. Then he nodded, and the moment shattered into shards, raining down around us. Someone moved to my left. I flinched, hand going to the knife that wasn't at my hip.

"It's okay," said August. She was wearing a long, form-fitting gown in the same color as Simon's suit. "No need for stabbings on your wedding night, not from me. I was just told to bring you this." She thrust a mixed bouquet of red roses, white violets, glowing starflowers, and fern fronds into my hands, then winked and dashed away before I could say anything.

Lacking an August to stare at, I settled for blinking at the flowers I was suddenly holding, then pulling them closer to my body, securing the bouquet with both hands. I had the feeling that dropping this one would go poorly for me. The way to the front was clearly delineated, continuing onward from where I was standing. As no one else seemed to have seen me, I stayed still. As I did, August hurried to the front and took the open seat next to Simon, setting her head against his shoulder. That seemed like as good a cue as any, especially since there wasn't any music.

I started walking. There was a strange feeling, like someone was standing on the train of my dress. I looked back over my shoulder. The entire back of the gown was covered in roses, starting at my waist and extending down to the hem. The ones highest up were as snowy white as the fabric around them, but the lower they dipped, the redder they became, until the roses at the bottom were the deep, virulent red of freshly dried blood. Those roses were unraveling endlessly, leaving a carpet of rose petals behind me as I walked.

I smiled and faced forward again, shaking my head. Of course, Tybalt had played stupid tricks with my dress. What's the point of having an enchanted wedding dress if you can't use it as an infinite rose generator? And it wasn't like my dress was even the most ridiculous piece of enchanted clothing on display.

No, that honor went to the Luidaeg, who was wrapped in what looked for all the world like a slice of the sky, taken during the aurora borealis. The colors swirled and danced all around her torso like a living oil slick, never stopping, never stabilizing. It was a gorgeous effect. Her ridiculous dresses generally were.

No one stood as I passed them. That custom was apparently human enough not to have caught on here. I saw a few more people in the red suits and dresses—May and Stacy each had one, as did the man who looked heart-stoppingly like Simon Torquill, but absolutely wasn't. He was sitting alone, and he offered a wan, wavering smile when he saw me, like he wasn't sure I'd want it. I smiled back, as sincerely as I'd ever done anything.

We might not be close right now, but the day I couldn't return a smile from my liege was going to be the day I died.

Tybalt finally glanced in my direction when I was about ten feet away. He froze, the tension leaving his shoulders as his pupils expanded, swallowing his irises completely. He just stared at me.

I stared back, somehow afraid to do anything else, like this was his last chance to realize he'd made a terrible mistake and take steps to correct it. Who in their right mind would want to give up a crown and a kingdom for a changeling with no sense of self-preservation, who needed dozens of stain-repelling charms on her own wedding dress just to keep it from getting drenched in blood?

But I kept walking. If he didn't change his mind soon, I wasn't going to give him the opportunity.

Then I was standing in front of him, and he was reaching tenderly out to take the bouquet I was holding. "These, I believe, are mine," he said, and I let the flowers go, not knowing any better. His smile grew. Letting him have the bouquet was apparently the correct choice. He turned, handing the bouquet to Quentin, who had suddenly materialized beside him.

"My lady's gift to us," he said solemnly. Quentin bowed, to both of us, and disappeared back into the rows of chairs. Tybalt took my hands.

"I knew you'd be a natural at this," he said.

"Convinced many clueless brides to wear a corset for you?" I asked blandly.

"Only you," he said, voice soft. "Only you."

I knew I wasn't his first wife—that honor went to a mortal woman named Anne, who had died long before I was born—but it was somehow nice to know that this was his first formal pureblood wedding. Maybe I have a romantic streak after all.

"If you're ready for me," said the Luidaeg. "We can get started."

We turned to face her. And that was when the archers hidden in the trees opened fire, with a cry of, "For Ash and Oak!" that reverberated around the trees. One arrow hit me in the upper arm, embedding itself deep into the muscle. Three more bounced off the bodice of my wedding dress, not even snagging the fabric in the process.

Tybalt yowled, the angry, animal sound of a tiger unexpectedly injured. I whipped back around to face him. Another arrow was in his shoulder, and he was clutching it, trying to stop the blood that was pumping out between his fingers. "Don't pull it out," I yelled, while ramming the arrow that was sticking out of my own arm the rest of the way through to the other side.

He shot me an irritated look. "I wasn't intending to pull it out," he snarled. "I know how *arrows* work."

"Thank Maeve for that." I winced as the arrowhead broke the skin again, before reaching behind myself and snapping it off, making it easier to yank the arrow out of my arm without ripping the muscle even worse in the process. I crouched slightly, looking around.

The archers had apparently figured out that elf-shot wasn't a great weapon against us, since we just kept waking people up, and had been firing into the crowd with intent to wound. Several of our guests had arrows sticking out of them, although none of them looked more than superficially hurt. Aiming hadn't been high on the priority list when they came to ambush us, making me suspect that half of them—or more—weren't archers at all, but Doppelgangers who had managed to replace members of the guard.

Suddenly, the bad archery at the arrival banquet seemed a lot less inexperience and a lot more the desire not to shoot one of their own. Aethlin needed to take a serious look at his staffing.

The Luidaeg turned, eyes once again solidly black from side to side, hair starting to rise around her head like she was floating in the deep waters of the abyss, where no light could reach and no warmth could penetrate. There was an arrow jutting out of her belly, and as I watched, the dark sky of her dress wrapped around it and pulled it under, and it was gone.

Oh, and she was *pissed*.

"You would dare?" she asked, in a tone that was light, almost philosophical, and completely out of line with her appearance. She raised one hand, almost lazily, and a literal wall of black, brackish water appeared in front of her. She lowered her hand and the wall surged forward, a tidal wave knocking the first row of archers away.

She wasn't the only one reacting with violence. Simon was on his feet, hands working rapidly as the smell of smoke and apple cider rose in the air. One of the archers screamed and collapsed, body convulsing as it twisted into a new shape. Next to him, Patrick was shielding Dean and Peter with his body, keeping his sons away from the fight. Of the four, only Simon was injured, an arrow jutting from his side, and he was using the blood, dipping his fingers into it before gesturing again.

Sylvester, sword in hand, was leading a small group of knights and other physical fighters toward the archers, who were starting to look unsure about their choices. Someone was going to get hurt, worse than many of my guests already had.

As if that thought was an invitation, one of the courtiers blurred and vanished, becoming a vast red-and-white–furred dog that flung itself into the row of archers, snapping his jaws down on the throat of the nearest. Two more dropped their bows and drew their short swords, advancing on him.

I looked toward the back of the crowd. Only a few seconds had passed, and Oberon hadn't moved. He was watching the scene, an expression of deep sorrow on his face. All the rage I used to harbor for the man came rushing back. How dare he leave us alone? How dare he say "just don't kill each other" and walk away, like that was going to be enough to keep his children safe from each other?

He could have stopped so much pain, so much death, so much suffering, and instead, he'd left us to our own devices. And now that he was back, he still wasn't stepping in to protect the people who needed him.

"Well, fuck *that*," I said, and stormed away from the platform, heading for the archers. Two of them managed to notch arrows and fire them at me. They bounced off the fabric of my dress, clattering harmlessly away. I smiled grimly to myself as I kept advancing. Apparently, if something is sufficiently stain-resistant, it's also puncture-resistant. I was going to have some bruises, but those would heal even faster than arrow wounds would have. Bonus: they would keep my blood on the inside of my body, which Tybalt seemed to find reassuring. This was his wedding night as well. He deserved a little reassurance.

Roars and snarls marked the progress of the Cait Sidhe contingent. I kept pressing forward, nearly stumbling over the body of a man in royal livery. A member of the actual guard, then, and not one of the protean imposters. An arrow jutted from his throat at an almost jaunty angle, and his eyes were open, staring at the sky.

"Sorry," I said, bending and pulling the sword from his belt. It was heavy and unfamiliar in my hand, but it was still a weapon, and that made it better than nothing.

Another arrow bounced off my bodice as I straightened. "Oh for the sake of—*stop shooting at us!*" I yelled, glaring at the remaining archers. There were more of them still standing than I would have expected: I could see at least five, begging the question of just how many damn Doppelgangers King Shallcross had been able to sneak into the knowe. I wasn't going to tell them to stop shooting at me in specific: not only was I an obvious target in my pristine white dress and murderous rage, but every arrow sent my way was one not being fired at someone more vulnerable.

"Yo, Toby!"

I looked to my right. There was May, who was apparently angling herself according to the same principle: she was bristling with arrows, at least eight of them sticking out of her chest and stomach, while Jazz and Stacy used her for cover. Etienne was hacking away at a Doppelganger. Chelsea and Bridget were gone, Chelsea having presumably been ordered to get her mother out of there. All the Tuatha de Dannan except for Etienne were gone, in fact, and so were several of the more vulnerable guests. That was nice to see.

"Yes?" I called.

"Nice dress!" May had gotten close enough to one of the archers to punch them soundly in the throat. He went down gasping, and she took his bow away. "Now I have a longbow, motherfuckers, ho, ho, ho," she chortled, and began pulling arrows out of her own torso, using her body as a makeshift quiver.

I resumed my advance. If everyone got to stab someone on my wedding day except for me, I was going to be even more annoyed than I already was.

Two of the archers were still standing when I reached them. "Hi," I said blandly, as one of them tried to shoot me from far too close a distance. The arrow, like the others, bounced harmlessly off my dress. I raised my sword and swung it, hard, at his neck. He failed to duck in time.

I hate blood. I hate ichor more. Doppelgangers, having the bad taste to bleed ichor, are my least favorite thing to stab. He went down hard, as the other archer, panicking, grabbed an arrow and jammed it into the exposed part of my chest. I looked down at it, then up at him.

"Did no one ever teach you any *manners*?" I demanded, raising my sword in a threatening manner. "Stand down, right now, and maybe we let you live."

He dropped his bow.

"Good man. Assuming you are one, which may not be correct. Where are the guards you duplicated?"

"I don't know," he said miserably. "Going about their business, I would guess. We didn't replace them all, we just stole a copy of the duty roster and made sure we were never in the same place at the same time, please don't kill me, please, I'm sorry I shot arrows at your friends . . ."

"You did more than just shoot arrows at my friends. You disrupted my *wedding*. Why did you do that? We already captured your King. This chess game is over."

I could hear a commotion behind me, as several of my friends noticed their runaway bride had one of the bad guys cornered and had somehow acquired a sword. Honestly, with as surprised as they always were to see me armed, you'd think none of them had ever met me before.

"I'm a reasonable person," I said. "You can reason with me. And right now, you can give me a reason not to kill you, or let my fiancé kill you, since he was supposed to be my husband by now, and he's probably pretty annoyed that he's not."

The Doppelganger stared at me in all my blood-drenched, unstained glory, mouth moving soundlessly. Finally, he swallowed. "You're terrifying," he said.

"I've heard that before. Talk."

The Doppelganger took a deep breath. "We're intelligent beings. We have families, we have feelings, we want things, but because we don't have a Firstborn, you treat us like vermin. Like we're *pixies*." He spat the last word with disgusted vehemence. "Shallcross offered us another way. Swore if we helped him take the High Throne, he would grant us the dominion of Ash and Oak and all its ruined glories. We could open our own knowes, live in peace and safety, and stop being used as spies and assassins by every court that needs something done but doesn't want to get their hands dirty. If he stopped checking in, we were supposed to disrupt the wedding. Cause as much chaos and as many deaths as possible."

I stiffened before whipping around. Sylvester and Etienne were closing the distance between us quickly. That was good. I needed a teleporter.

"*May!*"

"Yeah?"

"Come watch this guy, make sure he doesn't try to escape." I looked back to the Doppelganger. "You're not going to try to escape, are you?"

He swallowed hard. "You're terrifying, but the lady in the angry neon dress just hit a bunch of people with the actual ocean, I'm not going *anywhere*."

"Good boy." I turned around again. "Etienne, I need you to take me to the dungeons *right now*."

He blinked. "Why would I—"

"Because there's about to be a jailbreak, and I'd like to stop it." I moved toward them. "*Now*, Etienne."

"Sire, I—"

"You heard Sir Daye," interjected Sylvester. "She would like to go to the dungeons."

"Yes, sire," said Etienne, and waved his hand through the air, leaving the scent of smoke and limes in his wake. A hole appeared, showing a dark, dingy room. I dove through, and they followed me.

"Tybalt is going to kill you," muttered Etienne. "And then he's going to kill me. This had best be worth it."

"The attack on the wedding was planned for if King Shallcross was captured," I said softly. We were standing right at a corner. I inched forward, looking around the edge to the line of cells. They were certainly less palatial than the little mini-apartments where the first Doppelgangers had been tucked away. I didn't have a problem with that.

What I *did* have a problem with was the group of guards standing outside one of the cells, unlocking it at the apparent direction of a very familiar bronze-haired teen who couldn't possibly be here in that form, since he was currently a Banshee, and back at my thoroughly disrupted wedding. How the hell did they even *know* that face, much less steal it? I stepped around the corner, sword up and at the ready.

"That isn't the Crown Prince, and you shouldn't open that door," I said.

The guards turned. Most of them, anyway. One grabbed for the keys, while another moved to put himself in front of their pseudo-Quentin.

"Doppelgangers don't bleed," I said, and ran my hand along the blade of my sword, laying my palm open. I held it up to show the guards that I was bleeding. "Really me, really the visiting hero who's been flushing out Doppelgangers all over the knowe, really telling you that I know for an absolute fact that that is not your Crown Prince."

The guards—who had behaved the way guards were supposed to behave—paused, looking at the pseudo-Quentin and the two guards flanking him. He responded by shooting me a look full of fury and snapping, "Get her!"

"Oh, now, the voice is *all* wrong," I said, bracing myself.

Two charging Doppelgangers pretending to be royal guards were no match for an enraged Duke, the captain of his guard, and a hero who just wanted to get things over with so she could get back to her own damn wedding. They went down hard and slimy, and we advanced on the sole remaining Doppelganger and the actual guards.

"He's not your prince," I said, keeping my tone as light as possible. "He's trying to make you release an enemy of the crown."

"You would listen to this bloody urchin over me?" demanded the Doppelganger. "I'm going to be your King!"

"That's the future, and right now, I represent a much shorter, more painful potential future," I snapped. "Stand *down*."

The guards looked at the Doppelganger, clearly anxious, before stepping away. The Doppelganger snarled and lunged for the closer one, trying to grab his keys. The man reacted without thinking, slapping "Quentin's" hand away. Everyone froze.

Now I had to be right, because otherwise, he had just laid hands on the Crown Prince.

Etienne abruptly appeared behind "Quentin," knife already drawn. He slashed the Doppelganger's shoulder with the blade. Ichor welled forth. The Doppelganger roared, swatting Etienne away. Etienne went sprawling but kept his grip on the knife.

"Well," I said, lowering my sword. I had nowhere to sheath it, and so I just held it. "Guess that's that, then. Etienne, can I get a ride back to the wedding?"

"Of course," he said, picking himself up from the floor and offering me his arm. I took it gratefully.

"I'll remain here to see to the formalities," said Sylvester, with a note of regret. "October . . ."

"Yes?"

He smiled, and it was the best wedding present I could have asked for. "You make a beautiful bride," he said.

Then Etienne waved his hand, and we were gone.

TWENTY

THE COURTYARD WAS STILL in chaos when we returned. Several members of the guard were dead, and several of the guests were hurt, although the worst injury seemed to be Tybalt's shoulder. Someone had helped him remove the arrow, at least. He was pacing back and forth in front of the platform when we arrived, looking like he couldn't decide between furious and distraught.

I dropped my borrowed sword and ran for him, almost slipping in the blood and ichor on the ground. He turned at the sound of my footsteps, relief washing everything else away, and I threw myself into his arms.

"I *love* this dress," I informed him. "Can we do this to all my clothes?"

"Sadly, no," he said, lifting me up and twirling me once around. Then he winced, almost dropping me as the motion pulled on his shoulder. "I see you've managed to get blood in your hair again."

"You knew what you were marrying before we got here," I said. "We *are* still getting married, aren't we?"

"That seems to be up to you," said the Luidaeg. "You chose your path. You stood before me with a willing heart. You came back. So, are you getting married?"

"Assuming my groom's still interested," I said firmly.

Tybalt snarled wordlessly, letting go of all but my hand, which he held onto so tightly it was like he feared I might vanish into mist.

There would be plenty of boring political cleanup after this, which might complicate sneaking away for our honeymoon, but I had plans, and we were going to find the time if I had to stab someone to get it. Right here and now, we were getting married.

"Good," said the Luidaeg, and she whistled, high and long and shrill. All around the clearing, people stopped addressing their wounds and complaining about the blood on their formal clothes, turning to face her instead.

She gave a little wave.

"Hi," she said, and her voice carried through every inch of the space, even though she wasn't yelling. "My name is Antigone of Albany, better known as the sea witch, and as I am the highest-ranking child of Oberon currently awake on this continent, I claim the right to perform this marriage. Does anyone wish to contest me?"

She paused then, longer than it felt like she needed to, and I realized she was looking at her father, still motionless at the back of the crowd, untouched by the blood and chaos. She was waiting to see if he was willing to actually step up and do something.

Oberon didn't move. She sighed. "I thought not. Very well, then. Rand Stratford, better known as Tybalt, King of Dreaming Cats, do you come here of your own free will, with good intentions and the desire to leave with a willing bride?"

"Yes," said Tybalt.

"October Daye, latest of the Dóchas Sidhe, child of Simon Torquill of the Daoine Sidhe, Knight of Lost Words, do you come here of your own free will, with good intentions and the desire to leave with a willing husband?"

"Pretty much," I said. I was fairly sure she'd find a way to drown me if I gave her any other answer.

Instead, she smiled. "You know, I never thought we'd make it this far. I always expected something to get in the way before we could get here. That some disaster or other would step in—and look around, it tried. The world has thrown every obstacle it could think of in your path, and you've just gone over them all, haven't you? Because here we are, the least likely of families, and I can't say we're giving anything away *or* gaining anything today, because you both belong here already. Where we are is your home and has been for a long time. Do you understand how impossible that is?

How ridiculous this all is? This can't have happened, and yet it did, and now we get to see what happens next."

She raised her head and looked around the courtyard, full of bruised, bloody people and the shed ichor of the downed Doppelgangers. "Whatever happens next is probably going to require the services of a dry cleaner."

A few people laughed. The Luidaeg smiled. Guess she wasn't used to people laughing at her jokes anymore. "This is where I'm supposed to talk about how well-suited the couple are to each other, but let's be real here: they're not. This should never have worked. They should never have found enough common ground to be friends, much less fall in love. I wouldn't have been voting for this." She shifted her gaze to me. "If you'd asked me when we met, I wouldn't have placed my bet on today. And that's okay. We live in stories, but we're *not* stories, and sometimes the best endings are the ones no one sees coming. I've already asked if anyone wants to argue with me being the one to perform this wedding. Does anyone want to argue with these people being wed? If you do, now's the time to say it."

So this was another commonality between fae and human marriages, and one I didn't really care for. I looked over my shoulder at the crowd, narrow-eyed, waiting for someone to think it would be funny to object. Sylvester and Etienne were back in their places; seeing them untied a knot around my heart.

About two rows ahead of them, on the other side of August and Patrick Lorden, Gillian met my eyes and gave a very small nod. I tore my gaze away from her and looked back to the Luidaeg, who sighed as she looked at me.

"That's as long as I'm expected to wait, and I'll be honest, if anyone was going to object, I expected it to be the bride." Again, laughter. Somehow, it didn't sting. "All right. My father Oberon, and my mother Maeve, both agreed that their children should have the ability to bind our descendants together, to keep the lines of succession clear. In their name, and in the names of your First-born, Malvic, first King among Cats, and Amandine the Liar, I, Antigone of Albany, better known as the Luidaeg, say you are wed in the eyes of all of Faerie. May the rose and the root shelter you; may the thorn and the oak protect you; may the branch and the tree grant you peace. Your bloodlines are joined, now and always, even if you choose to part."

She stopped then, raising an eyebrow, and waited. When neither of us moved, she shrugged and said, "Well, what are you waiting for? We steal a lot of things from the humans. This is where you kiss your wife."

Tybalt was smiling a smile I'd never seen before as he turned to face me, took my hands, and did as the sea witch said. I returned the kiss with interest, surrounded by the smell of blood and roses, and the sound of what felt like everyone we'd ever known applauding.

We had finally made it here. Despite all the obstacles and all the reasons we'd been given not to succeed, we'd made it.

We were going to make it all the way.

Read on for
a brand-new novella
by Seanan McGuire:

AND WITH REVELING

I woo'd thee with my sword,
And won thy love, doing thee injuries;
But I will wed thee in another key,
With pomp, with triumph, and with reveling.
                    —William Shakespeare, *A Midsummer Night's Dream*

April 14th, 2015

HAVING BEEN GIVEN PERMISSION—or possibly a command, depending on how you wanted to look at it—to kiss his wife for the first time, Tybalt clearly had no interest in breaking off our embrace. He continued kissing me long past the point that should have been appropriate, and I knew if I were able to pull away long enough to look over to Quentin, I'd see my squire approximately the color of the roses still dripping from the train of my dress, all the blood having rushed into his face. The boy is going to have to learn to control his blush reflex before he becomes King of the Westlands, or his head is *actually* going to explode one of these days.

Can Daoine Sidhe suffer from hypertension? Maybe that's something to look into.

But not in the moment, since Tybalt was still kissing me, and when I pulled back—just a little, enough to breathe—he pulled me close again, giving me better things to worry about. And people were still applauding, like we'd done something truly impressive, not just stood in front of a Firstborn daughter of Oberon in a blood-drenched glade and pledged our troth to one another.

No, wait. That *was* reasonably impressive of us. We were reasonably impressive people. Yet I couldn't stop thinking about all those other things we had to worry about, like the fact that we were married now. Divorce is extremely easy in Faerie if you don't have kids, but we had both gone into this intending it would be forever; that made the reality of our marriage feel oddly weighty and permanent, like I'd made a promise that literally couldn't be taken back. We'd been working toward this moment for so long that I didn't know how to feel about it anymore now that it was finally here. Happy, obviously, but also terrified of how the world was going to change. We'd talked about our expectations for our coming lives together, but was there something that hadn't been said? Or something neither of us had realized would be transformed by the simple alchemy of being pronounced husband and wife? Was he sure he was okay with me picking fights with every asshole noble who crossed my path?

He had to be. He knew me well enough to know what I was, and what he'd married. But maybe he was going to realize he didn't actually want to spend the next hundred years sharing a makeshift motel with my Fetch, her girlfriend, and whatever teenagers we had managed to collect that season. Maybe he was going to want everything to change.

I was so distracted by my own whirling thoughts that I almost didn't notice when he pulled away enough to look into my eyes. The feeling of his hand smoothing the hair that had been knocked loose from Stacy's careful twist snapped me back into the present, and I blinked, fighting back the urge to look away from his intently focused gaze.

"There you are," he said, sounding faintly amused. "I lost you for a moment, but now you've returned to me. What horrible concerns now plague your traitorous mind?"

I blinked at him. He still wasn't letting me go.

"Nothing new," I said, somewhat weakly. "Just the sudden worry that you don't really know who you just married, and that when you figure it out, you won't be happy."

"Since falling in love with you, I have been elf-shot multiple times, died repeatedly, been stabbed, slashed, burnt, and betrayed, gotten both feet and fur wet more times than I can count, and learned far more ways than I had ever known possible for getting blood out of fabric. And I didn't fall for you the first time we met, either." He smiled, pulling me a little closer, although not so closely that it hurt. "That took years. Years and years of knowing precisely who and what you were. Calm your worries, little fish. You're stuck with me now, and being so stuck, you get to endure what happens next."

"And what's that, exactly?"

His smile turned feral. "The wedding reception," he said, and dragged me with him as he stepped backward into the shadows.

The Shadow Roads are incredibly cold and unwelcoming to anyone who isn't Cait Sidhe, but they can't be closed to the cats, and with Tybalt carrying me, they couldn't be closed to me either. I held myself as far away from his torso as I could manage when I couldn't breathe or see, trying to be mindful of the injury he'd sustained to his shoulder when King Shallcross's men had attempted to shoot us all to death. They'd mostly failed, succeeding only in shooting us to severe annoyance.

At least one member of the High King's guard had died, but as far as I knew, none of the wedding guests had been more than injured. That wasn't something to celebrate, especially not if the guard had been a friend of yours, but it was better than it could have been. Tybalt had taken an arrow to the shoulder before I ran off to engage the archers in as close to single combat as was feasible when surrounded by people who actively wanted me to keep breathing as long as possible.

I would have been fine even if my wedding dress hadn't been so wreathed in blood-repelling enchantments and cleaning charms as to effectively become magical armor. I heal like there's a global competition and I need to win to be truly happy. Tybalt, on the other hand, heals only somewhat faster than a human man in good health, and was going to be dealing with the repercussions of getting shot on his own wedding day for weeks if not months. So yeah, I was a little concerned.

That wasn't going to stop me from enjoying cake.

Distance is malleable in the shadows, but thankfully usually seems to be compressed from what it would be in the bright world beyond them. We had only been in motion for a short while—less than two minutes, if the ache in my lungs was anything to go by— when Tybalt was emerging from darkness into light, carrying me with him.

As almost always, ice had formed on my eyelashes, effectively gluing my eyes closed. I blew upward out of the side of my mouth as he set me gingerly back on my feet, one more sign that we hadn't gone very far. Long trips tended to strain him more, and could result in me being dropped upon arrival at our destination as his arms gave out and his knees buckled. If he was feeling well enough to let me down gently, he was fine.

I kept blowing, trying to thaw my eyelashes before someone got the bright idea to jump out from behind something and shout "surprise!" really loudly, an action that was likely, under normal circumstances, to result in someone getting stabbed. Not that I currently had a knife, since apparently brides weren't supposed to be armed. I would have been annoyed about that, except Tybalt hadn't been allowed to carry a weapon either.

Then again, he didn't really need one, what with the whole "having claws, fangs, and the reflexes of a hunting cat," but it's the principle of the thing that matters. So there would be no stabbing. Didn't mean I wanted to be startled again. Not when I'd already been shot at on my wedding day.

"Peace, October," he said, almost laughing as he settled a hand on my shoulder. "There is no one here but us. You may take your time at recovery."

I relaxed a little, but kept on blowing, until the warm air thinned the ice enough that it broke and gave way, allowing me to open my eyes and blink into the twilight wonderland around us.

We were in another natural—or curated so flawlessly as to seem natural—amphitheater set into the side of the mountain, surrounded by towering evergreens. Their branches glowed bright with balls of witch light and the tiny, multicolored bodies of pixies, their wings sending faint chimes across the area as they fanned them. Unlike the clearing where the wedding itself had been held, there were no chairs here, no dais. Instead, long tables skirted the outline of the clearing, laden with food. I blinked and glanced at Tybalt, quizzically.

"There is a cake, but at Kerry's request, it has been concealed from view until she can be here to watch your reaction. She's well aware that you can dismantle illusions when you choose to do so, and asks most sweetly that you not dismantle this one, as she would feel compelled to kick you in the ankles and cry if you did. She seemed to think you would find this a very dire threat indeed." Tybalt wrinkled his nose, clearly amused. "As to the rest, Stacy and May were in agreement that you would be happier with finger foods and napkins than with a sit-down dinner, and as Queen Windermere has assured me that a wedding banquet will be awaiting us on our return home, I acquiesced."

I managed, barely, to swallow my groan. I could dodge a formal meal when it was presented to me by my friends. From my Queen, not so much. "That was very kind of you," I said instead, neutrally.

"The modern wedding celebration came after my time. We were fond of feasting when I was a boy, but the feasts were less formal, and less regimented in the components. When Stacy began explaining salad forks to me, I'm afraid my eyes may have glazed over. So this is for the both of us, in truth." He stepped close again, beginning to gather me back into his arms.

Then he winced, hissing between his teeth, and I snapped out of whatever messed-up "new bride" stupor he had been lulling me into.

"Right," I said. "You're going to let me see that shoulder."

"It's nothing," he said.

I fixed him with a steady, disbelieving stare. "You got *shot*. In the shoulder, with an *arrow*, which I seem to remember telling you to leave alone, and which is no longer there, meaning you didn't listen."

"In my defense, I neither pulled it out nor pushed it through," he said, raising his hands appeasingly. It might have been a smarter move if he hadn't winced again in the process, causing me to narrow my eyes and glare. "The Luidaeg said she didn't like watching me pace around with an arrow jutting out of me like some sort of half-slaughtered boar, waved a hand, and transformed it into water. It ran down my arm and washed the wound out in the process." His smile was small, and short-lived. "It wasn't even saltwater. I think she may like me."

"She hasn't killed you yet, so it seems likely." The Luidaeg's magic is tightly bound to the point where she can't do things for other people unless they pay, or unless her motivations are selfish ones. As a consequence, she's gotten very good at coming up with the selfish reason behind absolutely everything she does. Sometimes "I wanted to" can be selfish enough for the geasa that bind her.

"She didn't heal it, though."

"I don't know if she could spin that into being a selfish enough act to allow. We'll have Walther and Galen take a look when they get here." I was fairly sure I'd seen the High King's Ellyllon healer in the crowd at the wedding. Walther was a more familiar face, having traveled here with us from the Mists.

Tybalt wrinkled his nose. "Must we?"

"Well, that depends. If I stopped healing at an unreasonable speed, would you let *me* attend our wedding reception without getting patched up? Be honest."

"That is an unfair comparison to draw and you know it."

"Is it? Because to me it sounds like not wanting your shoulder to get infected and gross before we can make it through the reception." I threw my hands up, stepping away from him.

Tybalt sighed. "If you insist, then, yes, I will allow the healers to look at my injury."

I smiled as brightly as I could. "I insist. And I appreciate it."

He closed the distance between us, leaning close, and murmured, "When we're alone, you can thank me, and I can thank you. For there are no more debts between us."

It says something about the cultural norms of Faerie that he made the option of saying "thank you" sound deliciously obscene. I blushed, not pulling away, and he smirked at me.

Which was, naturally, when the smell of smoke and calla lilies drifted through the air, followed closely by the smell of cedar smoke and lime, and I pulled away, plastering a smile on my face as I turned to face Chelsea and her father.

Chelsea was wearing a red dress a few shades lighter than the ones I'd seen on the members of the bridal party, the hems picked out with darker red embroidery of briars and berries. I glanced back to Tybalt. "Did you choose *all* the wedding colors to show as little blood as possible?"

He shrugged, unrepentant to the end.

Etienne, who was one of the only people I'd seen recently not wearing red, either in cloth or due to bloodstaining, cleared his throat. "We have been sent ahead to inquire as to whether you are done enjoying one another's company and prepared to begin the reception," he said. "Bess has ordered me to tell you that whichever answer you give is the correct one, as today is your wedding day and my lovely lady wife seems to believe the entire Kingdom of Faerie has no manners whatsoever."

"In Mom's defense, she's usually right," said Chelsea. "And I want cake, so I don't care which answer is right, as long as I get the one that feeds me sooner rather than later. Nice job not getting stabbed more than absolutely necessary, Tobes!" She flashed me a thumbs-up.

I returned it discreetly. "I figured it was bad form to give the groom a heart attack before he could put a ring on it. Not that he did, since that's apparently not a pureblood thing."

"Purebloods are weird," Chelsea cheerfully agreed, earning herself a heatless glower from her father, who was as pureblooded as they come. They both are, now, but Chelsea was born half-human, and raised in the mortal world until she was well into her teens, which has made her rather more aware of the oddities of pureblood society than is strictly normal for fae kids in her position. "I'm gonna go get the boys now, okay, byyyyeeeee." And she was gone, stepping through a circular portal in the air through which I caught a glimpse of the clearing where we'd been married. Someone had picked up the fallen chairs and cleared away the bodies, although they hadn't been able to do anything about the blood.

There was so much blood. And ichor, thanks to the Doppelgangers who'd done most of the dying. I looked away, focusing on Etienne instead.

He was watching me with a small, odd smile on his face, looking like he'd never seen me before. I blinked. "What?"

"I know it is an old-fashioned perspective to take, and one that may seem odd to you, young and still mortal as you are, but I am almost of an age with your groom. I saw this county born. I saw my Kingdom founded, flounder, and find new means by which to prosper. I counted my time in decades, for years seemed too brief to make any meaningful measure, and I remember when you were a squalling babe that Amandine didn't want any of us to see. I thought to see you settled in the human world, oblivious to the family you had on this side of the hills, and never sparing us a second thought. I never thought to see you here in all your glory, gowned in red and standing beside a man who was never your better, but only ever intended to be your equal."

He reached forward, seemingly impulsively, and seized my hands in his. "May your nights be long and your days be peaceful," he said. "May you and the heirs of your house always be as well-loved as you deserve."

Then he let me go and stepped through his own portal in the air, leaving me to blink after him as Tybalt chuckled and set a hand on my shoulder.

"I would have expected the first of the formal blessings to come from your liege, or your father," he said. "Not from the man who was so unwillingly your knight. Still, it's good to have it thus delivered, and from an auspicious source."

I turned to look at him, narrow-eyed. He blinked back, the very picture of innocence. "If this is going to be a thing, I need you to warn me about it," I said, poking him in the chest. "We're a team now, and teams don't let their members get ambushed when there's another option. Do you understand me?"

"There are seven formal blessings for a newly-married couple," said Tybalt hurriedly. "They are traditionally delivered by people who have known the pair, or a member thereof, for as long as possible. Most are given to the bride, assuming there is one, but some are intended specifically for the groom, again assuming there is one. We'll receive them all before the night is through, and they'll have been pre-arranged by the ones who carry them."

"Is this one of those traditions where if someone stabs the person who has the seventh blessing, we're magically not married anymore?" I asked suspiciously.

Tybalt laughed. "October, I've told you dozens of times that you're not escaping me now. If there were any tradition, however ancient, that could wrest you away from me after we'd been joined by one of the Firstborn, I would never have allowed it within a hundred miles of our nuptials. You are mine, always and entire, and I'll let no tradition change that."

His pupils expanded as he spoke, blackness growing to swallow the green of his irises, and I shivered, leaning in for a kiss.

A kiss I never got, as the sound of voices raised in conversation, some chattering, some laughing, poured in from the east. Tybalt pulled away as we turned to face our guests.

They poured in like a wave of bodies, more of them dressed in red than not, although only a handful were in the specific combination of wine red and starkest white that graced the wedding party and adjuncts. It should have looked Christmassy, like we were all trying to emulate the mighty candy cane, but somehow it managed to have weight and gravitas and a thousand shades of scarlet all at the same time.

Stacy hit me like a guided missile, wrapping her arms around me and laughing uproariously. Kerry was only half a beat behind, her own embrace hitting me in the midriff and knocking the wind out of me despite the corset I was still wearing under my wedding gown. Not even whalebone can stand up to the enthusiasm of a half-Hob changeling who wants to hug one of her oldest friends with all the strength and enthusiasm granted to her by her hearth spirit heritage.

Julie followed them, substantially more slowly, her hands tucked into the pockets of her pants, which were skin-tight red leather a few shades brighter than Tybalt's, but otherwise almost identical. Cait Sidhe have standards when it comes to fashion, I guess. She met my eyes, lifted her chin in a small nod, and smiled.

"Hey," she said.

"Hey," I replied, trying not to be disappointed that she hadn't joined in the hug. It wasn't that long ago that she'd been doing her best to slaughter me on sight, so this was a big enough improvement to be impressive. I'd had one hug from her today. That was more than enough. "Good job not getting shot or stabbed or anything."

"We checked," she said, and I nodded grave approval.

Shock may seem like an action movie cliché, and it is to some degree, but like most clichés, it got its start in reality. If the trauma is severe enough, sometimes the body will simply refuse to acknowledge it for a while, usually until the danger has passed and the adrenaline starts to go away, creating a situation where it's safe to collapse. It's more common among the fae than it is among humans, because we tend to be somewhat more resilient to start with, but it's not even that uncommon among humans. Pain so big that it fills the world is sometimes easy to leave unacknowledged.

Checking yourself thoroughly for injury after a big fight isn't just a good idea: it's standard procedure for anyone who sees a lot of action. Which wouldn't normally include people like Stacy or Kerry. As a member of the Court of Cats, Julie was a bit more accustomed to playing rough.

"I'm so proud of you," said Stacy, and planted a kiss on my cheek before letting me go. She turned to Tybalt. "You, too, kitty-boy. You got her to hold still long enough to marry her, which I wasn't going to bet on. Now let's see if you can get to the end of the honeymoon with both of you still breathing."

"We're not going on our honeymoon right away," I objected, as Kerry let me go and mumbled an excuse about checking on the cake before darting off across the open space between us and the tables. Interesting. "We have to get home and get settled in, now that Tybalt's officially moving into the house. After that, we'll talk to Arden about when she thinks she can spare me for a few days."

"A few *days*?" asked Stacy, disbelievingly. "Do you honestly think he's letting you out of the bed after a few *days*? I'm not even talking about sex, that's a whole different timeline. He just wants to see you *sleep* for a damn change."

Tybalt didn't argue with her. I glanced at him and frowned. "Hey," I said. "A little support here?"

"The lady speaks no lies," he said. "I do want to watch you sleep. And wake, and shower, and eat balanced meals. I have already spoken to your liege, and to your Queen—our Queen now, I suppose, and that's going to take some adjusting to—and to the Queen Regent of Angels. We are approved by all of them to depart Toronto for the Land of Disney. I would have preferred something with a bit more cultural weight to it, and perhaps a performance of *Romeo and Juliet* on offer, but I am assured the theatrical offerings of Southern California are adequate, and that I will be able to secure us tickets for any performance I can convince you to attend."

I blinked at him. Then I blinked again, and looked to Stacy for confirmation. She was beaming, and nodded enthusiastically when I met her eyes.

"That's right," she said. "October Daye, you are going to Disneyland."

"But . . . I promised the boys I'd take *them* to Disneyland," I said, slightly dazed. "Tybalt, are we taking a flock of teenagers on our honeymoon?"

"Thank Oberon, no, we are not," he said gravely. "Bridget assisted with many of the arrangements, having made this journey herself in days past, and she and Etienne have already agreed that they will take our band of shrieking hellions for their own excursion, after we have returned safely home. The house will never be unattended, the cats will never go unfed, and someone else will take the responsibility for the boys—and, one presumes, Chelsea—while we enjoy a moment's peace."

"Not just Chelsea," said a new voice, as my sister all but materialized at my elbow. Dóchas Sidhe don't have any innate teleportation magic, but purebloods of all kinds move quietly and gracefully, and I'd been distracted enough to let August get the jump on me.

I flinched away, making a small sound of alarm. She sighed, looking disappointed.

"Hey," she said. "You're the one who hit me with a baseball bat and slammed my head into a wall. Do you think maybe you could eventually forgive me for being a little hostile the first time we met?"

I glowered at her, not quite mustering the strength for a full-on glare. "This *is* forgiveness," I said. "I didn't tell them you couldn't come to the wedding, and I didn't ask you to leave when I saw you before."

"Oh." August looked disappointed, and for a moment, I felt almost bad. Then she perked up and beamed at me. "Bridget said there was no way she was going to Disneyland with three teenagers and no help, and then Simon said that if she'd let Dean and Peter come, he'd send me along to help play chaperone."

Because my pureblood, time-displaced sister was absolutely the right choice for helping shepherd a bunch of over-stimulated, over-sugared teenagers around an amusement park. I stared at her.

"You sure you don't want to pick up a few of the Brown kids? Or maybe some of the other teens from the Court of Cats? Raj has a girlfriend who'd probably love to come."

"Helen has agoraphobia and doesn't like to leave her house," said Raj, now standing by my other elbow. This time, I *did* yelp. I'm not proud of that, but I was at my own wedding reception, and thought I had the right to let my guard down a little.

Raj looked at me dispassionately, as if I hadn't just screamed virtually in his ear. "She's seeing a therapist," he said. "Arden assisted us in finding someone whose practice is well-equipped for assisting changelings. But Disneyland would not be Helen's idea of a pleasant vacation, nor would her father allow it. Now, Cal, from the Court, they would probably very much enjoy the opportunity."

"No," said August. "No more random teenagers. Gillian may be coming with us, and if she does, she's the last one."

The thought of my sister taking my daughter to Disneyland was enough to put my hackles up instantly. I scowled, not bothering to hide it. "If you hurt her . . ."

"October. She's my niece. She's *family*. Our mother may not have been kind, to either of us, but she taught me the importance of family, and our father has only done his best to reinforce that lesson, even as he seizes on this pretty opportunity to rid his halls of children for a few pleasant days of peace and plenty." She leaned toward me then, grabbing my hands. "May that same peace and plenty rain down upon you for every day and every night you spend together, and may the hours of your marriage be more than can be counted."

"Two," said Tybalt, sounding faintly impressed, as August dropped my hands and walked away.

I turned my scowl on him. "Will they all be like that? People ambushing me with good wishes and then running away?"

"She appears to be sauntering more than running, and is now soliciting a server for a glass of wine," said Tybalt, eyes following my sister's retreat. "And no, the pattern does not demand an exit, it's merely that it seems the people wishing us well have the good sense to know when they've exhausted your patience. I'm sure some of them will linger, just as some of them will be set to target me."

"I've got one for Uncle Tybalt," said Raj abruptly. We both

turned to look at him, Tybalt making a little "well?" motion with his hand. Raj yawned.

"Not yet," he said. "I don't feel like it. I'll do it in a little while."

"Do you know who the other four people are?" I asked.

"I do."

"And will you tell me?"

"I will not, oh look, there's Cillian, bye!" And he was abruptly a small Abyssinian cat, shrouded by the smell of black pepper and burning leaves, as he turned and ran away across the clearing.

Stacy snorted. Julie didn't bother with even that much discretion. She just laughed out loud, and kept laughing as Stacy backed away from me to stand beside her. Then she grinned at me, widely enough to show the pointed tips of her teeth.

"I don't have a blessing for your house, at least not a formal one," she said. "I sent a wedding gift from your registry—May has it—and I have a promise for you. I'm done being angry and I'm done lashing out. I know we'd started making our peace even before today, but I wanted to reassure you that I understand what happened wasn't your fault, and you've only ever been doing the best you could with what you had. Which, let's be honest, wasn't all that much. I mean, you got screwed pretty hard at the starting line, but you're doing okay as we move toward the finish." She looked at Tybalt, clearly trying to see him like I did, then shook her head. "Just don't expect me to start calling you 'auntie' and we'll be fine."

"Deal," I said, laughing a little.

Julie grabbed me by the shoulders and pulled me in, close enough to plant kisses on both my cheeks. Then she let me go, pushing me away from her, so that I knocked into Tybalt, who steadied me immediately, laughing a little. "No blessing," she said again, "but I promise I won't fight you, and that any kids you have will always know they can run to me for anything they need. You're not my auntie, but I'll be theirs. We were wild kids, and we only turned out as well as we did because we had a full pit crew waiting to fix our engines and get us back on the road when we broke something. I'll be part of that crew for any children you have, forever."

"Weird, but weirdly touching." Over her shoulder, I saw two winged figures walking into the room—the orange sunset shape of the Luidaeg's apprentice, Poppy, and the shorter, slighter form of

High King Aethlin's Ellyllon healer, Galen. "If you'll excuse me, I see a man I need to talk to."

"Of course," she said, still smiling.

I glanced at Tybalt. "Don't go *anywhere*," I said, warningly, and started toward the pair.

The clearing, which had seemed immense when we arrived, was filling up more and more, not only with our friends and wedding guests, but with members of the High King's staff, some in uniform and some out of it. I wondered how well most of them would react if I walked up and asked how they were enjoying crashing my wedding. Not too well, probably. People tend to get twitchy when a kingbreaker approaches them for no apparent reason.

I can't say I've enjoyed the long, slow process of becoming the monster under most of the nobility's beds, but it gives me a lot more sympathy for the Luidaeg. She became the monster under all the beds in Faerie a long, long time ago, and near as I can tell, she deserves it about as much as I do. Maybe less. After all, I've had a choice about most of the things I've done. Not all of them, not by a long shot—I didn't have a choice when I went to Annwn, either the first time or any of the others; I didn't have a choice when I brought my sister home, or when I found our missing communal father-figure—but enough of them that my reputation is at least partially of my own making.

Oddly, that helps me sleep during the day. Knowing I made my own bed makes it easier to lie in it.

The Luidaeg herself had yet to make an appearance. That was fine by me, since her father was also missing, and while it might be my fault he was back, that didn't make me any more comfortable about having Oberon—the actual Oberon, father of us all, first among the fae—at my wedding, however incognito he was keeping himself. It felt . . . mythological, like something that should have happened to one of the great heroes of old, not something that should be happening to ordinary, everyday me. You know what else happened to the great heroes of old? Well, for the most part, they died. And not pleasantly in their beds, surrounded by their grandchildren, either.

Since dying horribly isn't really one of my goals, I'd rather stay as far from becoming one of those sorts of stories as possible. "Galen," I called, once I was close enough not to need to shout. "Do you have a moment?"

"Of course, Sir Daye," he said, looking away from Poppy, who twinkled and offered me a small, quick wave before wandering off into the crowd. "The young lady who accompanied you here from the Mists, were you aware that she's Aes Sidhe?"

"I knew, yes."

"They're a winged breed that hasn't been seen in centuries," he said, clearly warming to his topic. "My grandmother used to talk about having known one of them. He was supposedly a very focused and inventive lover. They all died out, of course, as so many parts of Faerie have. I never thought to see one of her kind."

So someone was smitten, then. I smiled, turning to head back toward Tybalt, Galen now following blithely along.

"She's apprenticed to the Luidaeg, did she mention?" I asked. "It keeps her busy, which I have to assume helps to keep her from getting lonely."

"It must be terrible to be the last of your kind," said Galen.

"It was," I said. I wasn't entirely sure I ever qualified as "the last," since there had only ever been two of us, and I hadn't known August even existed for a very long time. I still wasn't sure I liked her. But one thing I could say for sure was that the time between finding out I wasn't Daoine Sidhe and finding out that I wasn't the only Dóchas Sidhe in the world had been one of the loneliest times in my life, even if I hadn't fully recognized it until it was over.

"Where are we going so hurriedly?"

"Tybalt got shot during the attack on the wedding, and I want someone to take a look at his shoulder before we cut the cake."

Galen blinked at me. "So you want me . . . for my services as a chiurgeon and nothing more?"

"Why? What did you think I wanted you for?"

"To be honest, milady, I hadn't the faintest idea. When a bride who was most recently seen swinging a borrowed sword at attempted revolutionaries demands I go with her, I'm inclined to acquiesce, for my own safety if not to satisfy my curiosity." His wings buzzed as he gave me a sidelong glance. "You travel in the company of legends, after all."

"Yeah, well. One of those legends got himself shot, and I really want him to be able to keep up with me when the morning comes."

Tybalt was waiting where I'd asked him to, now joined by Patrick and Simon, both of whom were toasting him with something I would have called champagne, had it not been a delicate shade of baby blue. Tybalt didn't have a glass. He glanced over as we approached, and since he didn't have the "I am about to gnaw my own leg off to escape" look I knew from so many unwanted diplomatic parties, and normally felt on my own face, I smiled and came closer before I said, "Healer Galen, as promised. Duke Lorden. Count Torquill."

I wasn't actually sure of Simon's title, or of the etiquette of greeting only one part of a married couple by title, but I trusted the two of them to tell me kindly if I'd gaffed, especially since none of the local monarchs were in earshot. And true enough, Simon laughed, and said, "Count Lorden, please, if you must stand so on formality. I have surrendered my surname in favor of my lady wife's, as has my husband, and so we are Lordens all."

"Is that because she has the higher title?" I asked.

"In my case, yes," said Patrick. "That, and the Undersea would have judged her had she changed her name to match mine, being predisposed as they were to disapprove of our marriage. Someone who cannot breathe in the depths is inherently weakened in their eyes."

Thus explaining all over again why Dean had never been in consideration to inherit from his mother, even assuming Dianda ever chose to set her seat aside. By marrying land fae, Dianda had rendered her sons unable to take her place. They couldn't survive the rigors of the position. If there had ever been any question as to whether she'd married for love, that alone was enough to answer it.

"And in my case, I am one man joining an established household. Expecting them to change for me, more than is required by any marriage, would have been unreasonable and arrogant of me—two things I am striving to set aside now that I've been given a second chance at happiness."

"Stop it," said Patrick, and pushed Simon in the shoulder, light, affectionate, and almost playful. "You are an equal partner, and should consider yourself such. If you truly regret the loss of your name—"

"No," said Simon, immediately. "I and my daughter have both chosen to set it aside in favor of less fraught lineages. I loved my parents dearly. I honor them through my continued existence, and by doing my best to finally become the man they hoped I'd be. They don't need me to carry a name that was never truly mine, nor will they care if I disdain it."

I blinked at him. "Oh," I said. "Um, well, sorry if I opened a can of worms there. I just wanted to say it was nice having you both here, and I'm glad you could come. And Simon, I'm glad it was you who led me down the proper path."

"It was only proper because it was yours," he said, glancing down a little.

August was nowhere to be seen. If I was going to hug her father—our father, from Faerie's perspective—this was the time to do it without possibly upsetting my sister. Galen was looking at Tybalt's shoulder, probing the wound gingerly with his fingertips while Tybalt hissed between his teeth; no one needed me for anything.

It seemed like the biggest thing in the world, but it only took a moment to lean over and wrap my arms around Simon's shoulders, squeezing him as closely as I could. He froze immediately, fingers tightening on the fragile stem of his wine glass, which Patrick leaned over and plucked out of his hand without comment.

I held on. After a long, frozen moment, Simon raised his hand and set it against my forearm, fingers curved to cup my skin, not quite tight enough to hold me in place.

"I'm never going to give up my human father," I said. "But he's gone and you're here, and while we have a lot of ground to make up and a lot of learning about each other to do, I'm *glad* you're here. I'm glad we'll have that chance."

"That's all I ever wanted you to say," he said, sounding slightly choked up. I blinked. Across the narrow space we'd made between us, Patrick caught my eye and mouthed 'Thank you,' with exaggerated precision. I blinked again, and let Simon go.

"No, I don't accept that," I said, focusing on Patrick. It was his turn to blink and look bewildered. "Faerie doesn't seem to have the concept of stepparents where changelings are concerned; either we have two fae parents with legal rights in Faerie or we don't. I always thought I didn't, and then for a little while, I did, and now I don't again. And that's okay. I kept the parent I wanted and got away from the one who wasn't good for me. By definition, that means I decided Simon *was* good for me, and if he's good for me, he's family, and there are no debts between family." I turned my attention to Simon, who looked stricken. "Debts between family were how Amandine liked to do things, as if I owed her something for doing the bare minimum to keep me alive when I was a child, and owed her more for mostly leaving me alone as an adult. She wanted credit for what I did right and absolution for what I did wrong. 'Thank you' implies a debt. I don't want any more debts."

Simon blinked again, cheeks pale. Patrick looked pleased, moving to put his hands on his husband's shoulders. Then, without fanfare, Simon burst into tears.

They were quiet tears, almost dignified, as befit a member of the Daoine Sidhe, and I had the thought—as I always did when I saw one of them cry—that it wasn't remotely fair that they could be so pretty when they cried. My eyes got red and my nose ran when I cried. The Daoine Sidhe just wept crystal tears that didn't make them look silly or congested or anything.

"I'm sorry," I said, backing up, until I was just shy of bumping into Galen and Tybalt. I glanced at them, looking for reassurance before this turned into some sort of scene and I had to explain why this was perfectly normal, perfectly fine, the bride always made her father cry at her wedding reception. Why couldn't we have gone with something normal, like the electric slide? At least that was something I would have known how to deal with.

"Don't be," said Patrick firmly. "I know you were probably expecting some things that aren't generally done at pureblood weddings, like gifts on your actual wedding day, instead of arriving at your house over the next few weeks, but this is the greatest gift you could have given your father. Accepting him and his role in your life."

A flash of red across the way caught my eye. I looked at it more closely, then blanched. "Well, unless he wants to explain to his brother why he's crying, this is when the two of you should head somewhere else to finish dealing with all the feelings that were under that rock I just flipped over."

Simon, still crying, looked alarmed. Patrick handed him both wine glasses before taking his arm and saying, hurriedly, "This was meant to be from Simon, but: may your skies be clear and your roads be kind ones, ever leading you toward the destination you desire. Come along, Simon, we have places to be that Sylvester *isn't.*"

And Patrick ushered his crying husband swiftly away, even as my liege bore down on us. I turned to face him, plastering a smile across my face.

"Duke Torquill," I said. "Come to carry glad tidings upon this, my wedding day?"

It was the kind of archaic phrasing that's normally catnip for the pureblooded nobility—although I suppose that's a phrase I should probably be working to strip from my vocabulary, since I'm sure it's offensive to the Cait Sidhe in some way. Keeping my language from turning unintentionally cruel is more and more difficult as I get older and learn how many ways there are to hurt people unintentionally.

And at least it worked. Sylvester stopped, blinking at me in apparent confusion. I had to be at least somewhat disconcerting to look at, since my hair looked the way it usually did—a mess—while my dress remained absolutely impeccable, thanks to the wonders of several dozen cleaning and stain-repellant charms having combined to make incredibly effective and self-cleaning armor. Add in the contrast between my words and hearing them said in my actual voice, and it was no wonder he was a little bit off-balance.

Maybe that was a new way to approach shit I didn't want to deal with. Just pretend I was Tybalt until it got confused and went away.

"Was my brother troubling you?" Sylvester finally managed. He looked past me to Tybalt, acknowledging him with a nod and a terse, "Tybalt."

Tybalt, who was bearing up stoically as Galen rubbed a sparkling white cream into the wound on his shoulder, replied with the faintest sliver of a smile, and no words at all. Given how unhappy I already knew he was with the man, that was probably a blessing. This was one of those situations where the less said, the better.

"No," I said. "My father was simply performing his duty and congratulating me on my wedding day." That was also my liege's duty, and I looked expectantly at Sylvester.

He didn't meet my eyes. "I wish you wouldn't call him that," he said. He was dressed in red, like most of the guests—Stacy and May had really embraced the "if people are going to bleed anyway, let's make it difficult to see" aesthetic with their color scheme—but it was a darker, more subdued red than the wedding party, less fresh blood, more dried. It made for some interesting symbolism, even if there was no way they could have predicted this moment, with me looking at him, waiting for him to say that he was done disappointing me. Finally, finally done.

He didn't. Instead, he finally looked up and met my eyes, his own reflecting weariness and disappointment back at me, so deep and clotted that there was no way I could mistake either emotion for my own. These were feelings he had carried for so long that he no longer had any idea how to go about putting them down, resentments that had festered long enough to turn into weights. If he fell into the sea like this, he'd drown.

Ironic, considering his brother lived there now, but still less than ideal.

"I call him that because that's who he *is*," I said, keeping my voice as steady and measured as possible. "He was married to my mother when she slept with my dad—and yes, I'm distinguishing the two of them on purpose—and the laws in Faerie appear to have been drafted without even glancing at a biologist, much less consulting one, so he's considered my father in all the ways that matter. Sorry, did I say 'laws'? I meant 'traditions.'"

"The man you would call 'father' has *broken* the Law," snarled Sylvester, bafflement fading in the face of a clear path forward. Bully for me. "He killed and stole and cheated, he abducted those I loved and sentenced them to a lightless, airless *hell*. He deserves your disdain at the very best, and better for us all if you denied him even *that*."

"An argument can be made that he did none of those things while he was in his right mind," I said carefully. "He was in the thrall of the First of all his kind, which he entered for the sake of his own loved ones, and we all know how hard it is to set your First aside."

"You did it," said Sylvester fiercely. "If you could—" He seemed to realize, finally, that he was on the verge of saying something truly unforgivable. He stopped himself, taking a half-step back.

I took a deep breath. "I did it, but my First doesn't have quite the same effect on her descendants. Maybe because I've gotten used to her, maybe because I'm just stubborn, I don't know, but I've always been able to tell Amandine 'no,' and from what I've seen, the Daoine Sidhe don't have the same freedom when their First—who I will not name, because I don't want to attract her attention—gets involved. She told him what to do and he did it, or as much of it as he had to do. Some things, he managed to set aside, at least enough to preserve life. She wanted me dead, Sylvester. Because of who my mother was, she wanted me dead. When your brother had the chance to kill me by standing aside and letting Oleander have her way, he intervened. He saved me, because he loved me enough to go against his First."

Not enough to spare me from spending fourteen years as an enchanted fish, but there was asking for salvation and then there was asking for the moon. I shook my head, keeping my eyes on Sylvester's. "He didn't kill Luna or Rayseline when he had the chance. Yes, he left them in a dark and terrible place, and I'm not saying you have to forgive him for that, but unless there's something you're not telling me, I have more blood on my hands than he does on his."

"To be fair, my lady wife seems to view blood as the finest nail varnish available," said Tybalt, stepping up behind me and sliding his arms around my waist. I glanced back at him. The wound in his shoulder was gone, replaced by a swath of smooth new skin that gleamed a bit too slickly in the light, like scar tissue or someone who had just been exfoliated.

Galen was visible behind him. When he saw me looking he smiled, tapped his temple in a salute, and melded backward into the crowd, leaving a faint trail of pixie sweat in his wake. I love Ellyllon. And if his life here was anything like Jin's he had probably been glad to have something small and easily treated to deal with, rather than another ridiculous, life-threatening injury.

On the other hand, that was probably unique to Jin.

Sylvester transferred his gaze to Tybalt. "You've never liked me," he said.

Tybalt nodded. "This is true. To be fair, you were once the man who stood between me and the woman I loved, and then became the man who treated the girl I found fascinating without half the respect that she deserved."

I had known for a long time that Tybalt had been in love with Sylvester's older sister, September, before she married the man who would go on to become my friend January's father. Pure-blooded fae being functionally immortal means there's time to develop the kind of tangled webs of connection and relationship that would make a mortal soap opera seem positively straightforward.

It was interesting that I usually thought of Tybalt as a peer and Sylvester as someone enough older than me to have earned his position of authority, although that may have been partially in self-defense. Not thinking about the age gap between me and my boyfriend-now-husband was a sanity saving measure, and I dare anyone who finds themselves in the same position to do otherwise.

"I have always treated October with respect," said Sylvester. "I fought for her knighthood. I had her properly trained by my own seneschal. Would I have done that if I didn't respect her?"

Tybalt made a small scoffing sound. "By the laws of your own kind, which you hold to so very tightly in all other things, she was your *niece*. Faerie considered her quite literally your own blood. I took in kittens without half the claim to my hearth as she had to yours, and raised them named as niece and nephew to give them some small measure of protection from the cruelty we both know Faerie to be heir to. She was your *blood*, and you let her think herself all but homeless, let her wander the streets until that wild charlatan Devin could claim her as his own, let her think herself unwanted and unloved, and did damage to her foundations that I will be repairing for the next hundred years if not longer, and you would reach to paint that somehow as respect? As if I could ever see past my love for my lady to answer your claims with anything other than scorn? Had September chosen my hand I would have been forced to call you 'brother,' and looking at you now, I am glad in more ways than I ever considered possible that this cruel mockery of fate never came to pass. I know not who holds the remainder of our blessings, but if you are among them, I don't want it. You may keep it, and let it warm you when you grow cold, for you have cast too much family aside to have any other comfort."

Sylvester paled. Then, turning his attention back to me, he said quietly, "You made a beautiful bride," before he turned and walked off into the crowd.

I didn't even have time to move before someone was whistling next to me, long and low. I turned my head to find the Luidaeg standing there, once again back in her overalls and electric tape pigtails, no longer unveiled as the great and terrible sea witch.

"Who knew kitty-boy had that level of epic burn in him?" she asked. "That was rhetorical, by the way. I knew, and I'm sure a lot of other people who've been around for a while would say the same. Still, I am *impressed*. High-five for the once and future King of Cats!" She held up her hand, clearly expecting Tybalt to slap it.

He did, looking faintly bewildered, and she cackled as she tucked both hands into her pocket. Quentin, still disguised as

Cillian the Banshee boy, appeared behind her and rested his chin on her shoulder, blinking pale brown eyes innocently at me.

"How many of you were standing there just now?" I asked.

"Me, the Luidaeg, and Dean," he said. "Chelsea's off with Gilly, trying to convince Kerry to let them have some wedding cake before the official cutting. Ormond told her that when a Hob makes a really *big* cake, they always do tester cupcakes first, to make sure the batter flavors out the way they want it to, so there should be some of those test runs available."

"She's been keeping the cake under a stasis spell," I said, only half-distracted by the thought that my probable next squire was running around the reception with my daughter, who I hadn't even expected to see today. "I don't think the cupcakes would have survived."

"Hearth magic includes a lot of flavors and techniques that wouldn't be strictly possible without it," said Quentin. "I'm pretty sure she'd have put the cupcakes under stasis spells, too, to make sure nothing in the batter counteracted the slowdown or curdled when it was under an enchantment."

I looked at him with blank amusement. "This is your way of saying you support them in their plans to steal my wedding cake."

"Come on, now, October, you don't get to get all possessive and proprietary about it when you don't even know what flavor it is," said the Luidaeg. "Is it even 'your' wedding cake at this point? I think 'the cake for your wedding' would be a better way to describe it."

I fixed her with a flat gaze. "That sounds suspiciously like you're trying to get me to cede my claim to my own wedding cake, which is one of those things that risks getting me drowned in the bay by my new groom."

"Come now, I'll not have these fine people thinking me the kind of man who would even dream to abuse his wife," said Tybalt, snaking an arm around my waist and pulling me into him, so that our hips bumped together.

Quentin laughed. I eyed him, after first glancing around to be sure no one from the royal household was close enough to overhear me.

"Why do you still look like this?" I asked. "I thought your bargain ended once you saw me get married."

"Once I saw you get married, I got the option to end it," he said.

"I can have the counter-agent whenever I want it, because you did what you were supposed to do. I thought it would be better to stay this way until we get home. Avoids a lot of potentially awkward questions."

I nodded. "Good thinking." And it wasn't like this was a mortal wedding, with a photographer running around documenting everything for posterity. I might have been sad not to have pictures with Quentin's real face in them, if that had been the case.

Not sad enough to want to be arrested for treasonous transformation of the Crown Prince, but still sad.

"I do occasionally think things through," he said, sounding stung. I laughed. So did Tybalt and the Luidaeg. Dean, emerging from behind the Luidaeg at last, just smiled.

"I saw our dads," he said, looking straight at me. "Is there a reason you made Simon cry?"

"I told him he was my father, and I wasn't going to let him argue with me about that anymore," I said. Then I shrugged. "Faerie doesn't really seem to understand what the word 'stepparent' means."

"I didn't even hear of the concept until I was old enough to start pilfering human media," said Dean. "Most people don't marry long enough to have kids at all, much less get married again after they get divorced, or marry into a relationship that still has children."

"Hmm." Put that way, it was an unusual enough occurrence that the lack of vocabulary would have made sense, if not for the fact that Faerie really, really likes stealing human language. We're like the anti-French that way. Rather than trying to preserve the language as it is, we want every new shiny thing that comes rolling off the word assembly line.

Taking that into account, you'd expect older fae to talk like a bunch of teenagers hopped up on triple espresso macchiatos with too much whipped cream on top, but instead, they all seemed to settle on whatever era felt the most comfortable to them, resulting in formal Courts where people like Tybalt had to argue with people like Countess January O'Leary, who never met a meme she didn't think belonged in casual conversation, and once had an argument in my presence entirely in Klingon, just to prove she could.

Being fae doesn't make you immune to being a massive nerd. It just gives you more time to really plumb the depths of your potential nerdery.

"If you've decided to accept that Simon Torquill is your father, and he's also Dean's father, does that mean . . ."

"It means Dean gets his own housekey, because it would be hypocritical and a little silly of me to try insisting that he's not my brother at this point," I said, with a small smile. The two boys grinned at each other before high-fiving. I raised my voice and added, "But that doesn't mean I'm suddenly approving hanky-panky under my roof."

"I can't believe you just said 'hanky-panky,'" said Dean. "You are so profoundly uncool, Toby. I have a big sister, and she's *profoundly* uncool."

"Why not?" asked Quentin. "You and Tybalt are committing hanky-panky under your roof. So are May and Jazz. And don't even start with 'we're all adults,' I've seen the way you eat."

"Good nutrition is blessedly not a requirement for adulthood, or the Luidaeg would still be considered a teenager," I said. "We're responsible for you when you're in the house, and that means we need to hold you to rules that your parents would approve of. Now, if you want me to contact them and ask if you can have permission slips for sex, I'm perfectly happy to do that . . ."

I was not, in fact, perfectly happy to do that. Just the thought of talking to Dianda Lorden about her son's sex life was enough to make me suspect that I might not live long enough to ever have sex again.

I was saved from his answer by the Luidaeg bursting into laughter, clapping Quentin and Dean on the shoulders before pulling each of them in for a one-armed hug. It was adorable if I stepped back enough to look at her as the gangly, somewhat unkempt teenage girl she appeared to be. It was absolutely horrifying if I remembered she was one of the most dangerous people alive in Faerie, and could kill them both in an instant if she felt like it was the right thing to do.

I was pretty sure she wouldn't. She genuinely liked Quentin, and while I wasn't sure she was that fond of Dean, she wouldn't want to upset Quentin unnecessarily by killing him. Sometimes with the Firstborn—or any pureblood who's gotten old enough to stop really marking the passage of time the way the rest of us do—the morality of murder matters less than who else it would hurt. As long as I could use that to my advantage, I wasn't going to throw myself against the brick wall of trying to change all of Faerie to suit my own weird standards.

"Both of you go and help the others try to talk Kerry out of cake," she said, pushing the boys away from her again. "The adults need to talk."

"Okay, sorry Luidaeg, bye Toby," said Quentin quickly, and grabbed Dean by the hand, dragging him away into the crowd. I watched them go, suddenly wishing I had a drink.

As if summoned—and maybe they had been—a Silene in the household livery appeared at my elbow, offering me a tray of long-stemmed wine glasses, containing bubbling fluid in a variety of colors. I looked at them for a moment before selecting a peach-tinted one that I hoped would taste like something reasonable. Peaches, maybe.

Nope. Cantaloupe. I squinted at the glass after my first sip. Sparkling cantaloupe wine was a bit outside my experience.

Either misinterpreting or willfully ignoring the cause of my confusion, the Luidaeg said, "Nothing served here today is going to hurt you. All the menus were run through me, as well as through your friends, to be sure that we're not dishing up goblin fruit pie or something equally ridiculous."

"I wasn't worried about that," I said. "This is just a little odd, is all."

"Melon wine used to be a lot more common, before humans refined their palates down to the point where most of them only view grapes as a viable base for wine. Since there were inevitably going to be a bunch of kids here, the wine list was set to have corresponding botanicals, in order to make sure they'd have something to drink."

"Mmm," I said, and took another drink. This really sounded more like a way to make sure the kids could sneak as much wine as they wanted, as long as they didn't actually filch an entire bottle to do their drinking from, but since all of them had parents present, even Quentin, I didn't have to worry about it for once.

All of them except for Gillian. I wasn't sure whether she'd come with the Lordens or at the request of the Luidaeg, but either way, Janet wasn't here, and Cliff couldn't be here, since he had no idea Faerie even existed. If she decided to get hammered, I was going to be the one expected to take responsibility.

I took a larger gulp of melon-flavored wine. It wasn't unpleasant, once you got past the strangeness of it all. The Luidaeg watched, with evident amusement.

"You know, sometimes it feels like I should be able to *see* the gears whirring inside that empty bowl you call a brain," she said. "Did you just think to ask yourself how your wayward daughter got here?"

"Mm-hmm," I said. "I'm sorry, I was a little busy before, what with the whole needing to get married, prevent the overthrow of the rightful government of the Westlands, and oh, right, *not die* in the process."

"As if you've been that easy to kill in years," scoffed the Luidaeg, snagging her own wineglass from a passing server. Its contents were electric yellow rather than peach, and I couldn't for the life of me imagine what she was about to drink.

"If we could not weigh the relative merits of killing my *wife* before I've managed to see her through our honeymoon, that would be an excellent wedding gift," said Tybalt dryly.

The Luidaeg rounded on him. "You say that sort of shit because you know most people will just go 'oh, he's old-fashioned, he talks like he bought a bunch of extra syllables at the vocabulary store, he doesn't mean anything by it,' but I'm older than you are, and I know you didn't just imply that I was going to hurt my niece. You practically worshipped that butcher's boy when he walked the boards in London. You know better than to say such things at a wedding."

Tybalt blinked. "My apologies, lady sea-witch."

"Yeah, yeah, it's always apologies instead of common sense with you people." She grumbled but she sipped her wine, and I knew the moment of danger, if it had been danger and not just the appearance of danger, had passed. She glanced back to me. "You sure you want to keep this one? Might not be the smartest move you ever made."

"Oh, it was," I said firmly. "He's the best choice possible."

"If you say so. As to how the girl got here, which I believe was the question you weren't asking in the first place, Elizabeth felt it would be appropriate for the Roane of Half Moon Bay to send someone to observe the ceremony, and show there were no hard feelings between the colonies and you, since you were responsible in large part for the destruction of their way of life."

"That's a uniquely uncharitable way of putting things," I said, only slightly stung.

She shrugged. "Liz can be a uniquely uncharitable lady when she wants to be. She wasn't always like that, but I guess finding out your lover is secretly the sea witch and will never look at you the same way again after you've draped yourself in the flensed skin of her murdered child has a hardening effect on the psyche."

I frowned. Elizabeth Ryan was the leader of the former Selkies who lived in Half Moon Bay, California, a colony that functioned more like the inevitable, dysfunctional end result of my tendency to bring home every broken doll from the Island of Misfit Toys and give them a bedroom. It was a family as much as anything else, and like any good family, it stuck together.

Most of the Ryans had become Roane during the great binding at the Duchy of Ships, and of the ones who hadn't, most of them had chosen to remain Selkies, preferring the flexibility of mortality. It wouldn't be an option forever, and eventually they'd have to be bound to their skins in order to fulfill the Luidaeg's promise to her descendants. For the moment, though, they were living their lives as they wanted to and believed right.

Elizabeth had been responsible for taking Gillian in and arranging for the bulk of her education when my daughter had first been draped in her own Selkie skin to save her life from the elf-shot that had been in the process of rapidly killing her. The other Selkies hadn't been too thrilled about that. They believed all Selkie skins belonged with the clans by right of blood, time, and suffering, and they hadn't taken kindly to the discovery that the Luidaeg had been in a possession of a certain number of held-back pelts—what they'd referred to as "the Lost Skins," pieces of her own history that she hadn't passed to other hands.

One of those skins had saved my little girl. Gillian had worn the skin belonging to Firtha, the Luidaeg's own youngest daughter, before it had been bound permanently to her flesh, transforming her from Selkie and skinshifter into one of the previously lost, lamented Roane. She and I had barely spoken since then. Partially, I thought, it was because every time I got anywhere near her, Faerie beat the crap out of her and stole her metaphorical lunch money.

If my mother did as much damage to my life just by existing as I've managed to do to Gillian's, I would have found a way to legally divorce myself from her bloodline a long damn time ago, is all I'm saying.

"Why would Liz send *Gilly*?" I asked. "I mean, it's not like I have that many allies among the colony, but sending your newest member seems a little bit like—"

"Acquiescing when the sea witch makes a single reasonable request of you, that you send a specific person as your representative to her niece's wedding, may seem like an onerous burden to some, but other, sensible people understand that it's not so much 'a request' as 'a way to get slightly further into my good graces, which is a place you want to occupy now that you're immortal and technically belong to me.'" The Luidaeg smiled, showing me what felt like every one of her teeth in the process. "Liz is a smart lady who made one massive, life-changing mistake when she was younger. She knew better than to tell me no."

"Did she tell Gilly where she was sending her?" Please don't let my daughter be attending my wedding under false pretenses. Please don't let her hate me even more because the Luidaeg decided that having her here would make me happy.

Please don't let me be a bad person for being happy even if Gillian *had* expected to find herself at some sort of tax summit or property hearing or really anything other than my wedding. At least this way, she got cake. They don't usually have cake at tax summits.

"She knew," said the Luidaeg. "Please credit me with half a sliver of common sense, would you? Now, I need to get going. Dad's been unchaperoned at the buffet for longer than I'm entirely comfortable with, and I'd rather not lose him. But before I go . . ."

She paused and took a deep breath, her eyes shifting colors from green to deepest black. I tensed.

"May you never regret the promises you made today, and may you never have cause, either now or in the future, to recant them," said the Luidaeg solemnly. "That's the formal blessing, and here's the informal one, because this whole 'seven regimented blessings' thing is ridiculous and a little Christian in some ways, which means we shouldn't be insisting on it, as immortal creatures of Faerie, so: when the time comes, may you stand before the Heart of Faerie with no regrets and no remorse for the choices you have made. May you keep each other as close as you can, and never forget who you are."

She turned then and walked away without saying goodbye, leaving us both to blink blankly and bemusedly after her. I looked to Tybalt.

"Not normal?" I guessed.

He shook his head. "Not normal," he confirmed.

"I mean, neither is the part where we've mostly been standing here and letting people come to us," I said. "Not for a mortal wedding, anyway. We're supposed to move around and mingle more than this, and I'd like to hit the buffet before the child swarms clear things out completely."

I didn't necessarily *want* to commit myself to an endless stream of small talk and canapes—although I wouldn't say no to one of the trays of what looked like bacon-wrapped asparagus that I had seen passing by—but I also didn't want to accidentally cause someone offense at my own wedding.

Too much of this was unfamiliar. Fae marriages aren't uncommon; most of the nobility, at least, tends to marry relatively young, to give them as much time as possible to secure an heir and legitimize their claim to whatever position they're insisting is theirs by right. It's just that when people live for centuries and have a glacially slow birth rate, "uncommon" can mean "we have one once every decade, it's been a real bridal boom around here." I couldn't remember Amandine ever taking me to attend a pureblood wedding when I was small.

As if summoned by the turn of my thoughts, May swam through the crowd with Jazz trailing after her and a plate in one hand. "This is all sort of surreal, isn't it?" she asked. Jazz laughed, almost sardonically, and May glanced over her shoulder at her dark-haired girlfriend, unmistakable affection in her eyes. "I've already had to promise a little birdie we both know that when we get married, it won't be anywhere near this big a deal."

"Did she finally say yes?" I asked.

"Okay, one, fae etiquette is as opposed to proposing to your girlfriend at your sister's wedding as human etiquette is, and even though I've asked her several times to marry me, actually *asking* again would count as a proposal, so no, I didn't do that. And two, she was the one who brought it up."

That was encouraging. I handed Tybalt my wine glass and turned, beaming, to sweep May into a hug. "That's wonderful!" Jazz had been remarkably resistant to all May's attempts to propose, of which there had been many. It had been reaching the point of becoming almost comical.

I can't really blame anyone for not wanting to join our increasingly improbable family. But they made each other happy, and if there was one thing I had learned, it was that when something or someone makes you happy, you should do your absolute best to hold onto it for as long as you possibly can, because one day, you're going to blink and it's going to be gone.

Jazz smiled at me as I propped my chin against May's shoulder, the expression sweet and oddly shy, like she wasn't sure how I was going to react to her actually going along with my Fetch's matrimonial dreams. I let May go and transferred the hug to Jazz instead, who squawked before wrapping her arms around me in turn. Unlike most of the guests who were even remotely associated with the bridal party, she wasn't wearing red; instead, she had opted for a pink and gold lehenga embroidered with tiny gold and platinum ravens. The band of feathers that kept her anchored to Faerie was woven into her braid, pulled over one shoulder and fitting perfectly with the rest of her attire.

"I can't wait for you to be my sister," I informed her, and she laughed, voice low and close to my ear.

"I thought you might have filled those slots by now," she said. "What with all the unexpected family you've pulled out of the woodwork."

"What? Never." I let go. "May was unexpected, but an absolute improvement on no sisters at all."

"I feel vaguely as if I should be offended by that," said May.

Tybalt laughed. "If we all got offended by every clumsy thing my lady said, we'd never have any time to sleep."

I stuck my tongue out at him. He snorted.

"Dignified."

"That's why you love me. That, and all the opportunities I give you to learn fun new ways to get blood out of fabric. You'd be bored senseless without me and you know it."

He blinked, then smiled, much more softly. "Yes," he said. "I would be."

I looked back to Jazz. "I still don't really *have* August. I mean, we've met several times, and I know who she is, but I don't know who she *is*. I don't know if I'm going to like that person, ever, or if our mother damaged her so badly that she's never going to be someone I can understand or get along with. Or maybe Simon and the Lordens can help her heal, and she's still not going to be someone I get along with, because no one gets along with everyone. Turns out it's not a requirement that everybody be friends, no matter what the cartoons try to tell us."

May gasped theatrically. "What? You mean the Care Bears *lied* to me?"

I decided to ignore her. "So I really only have one sister you'd be stacked up against, and since she'd get a wife out of the deal, I think she's fine with sharing the title. That's why she keeps proposing."

"All right," said Jazz, and smiled at me as I pushed her out to arm's length. "The next time she proposes, which will *not* be in Toronto, under any circumstances, I'll say yes. But just because you've all worn me down."

"Don't you want to marry me?" asked May.

"I do," said Jazz. "I'm just scared, because I've been waiting for her mother," she gestured to me, "to come charging in and ruin everything again."

"Yeah, well, she doesn't get to do that anymore," I said. "She's not my mother anymore, and this is the end of us discussing her on my wedding night. I'm going to go hit the buffet. Do either of you want anything?"

May was looking at Jazz the way the swarm of teenagers looked at the very concept of cake, and I got the feeling they'd both prefer it if we went away. I grabbed Tybalt by the hand and dragged him away from the pair, heading across the floor at a decent clip. It was easier than I would have expected, given both the fit of my corset and the volume of my skirt, but since I'd already fought a pitched battle and saved a High Kingdom in this dress, I shouldn't have been surprised.

"Sweet Maeve, I love this dress," I muttered.

Tybalt glanced at me, apparently startled. "Really?"

"Well, yeah. I mean, you designed it, right? I'd expect you to have designed it with some concept of what I might actually *like*."

"I did," he said. "But you have not historically liked anything that could be considered formalwear, much less a gown. Stacy and May both warned me, in no uncertain terms, that you were going to object to the corset, and probably to other aspects of the gown."

"So you kept it a secret to keep me from arguing with you about the roses?"

Tybalt's cheeks reddened. "They're traditional," he said. "Not obligatory, but the rose is a symbol of all of Faerie, and shared by all of our Three. I wanted anyone who looked upon you to know, without question, that our union was favored of Faerie, even if I was unable to tell them precisely why."

"It's really important to you that people be cool with us being married, isn't it?"

We had reached the buffet as we walked, a fact which appeared to relieve Tybalt immensely, as it gave him something to do with his hands. He began loading up a plate with small items and rather more vegetables than he, as an obligate carnivore, was usually inclined to eat.

"It is essential," he said, voice low.

"I don't understand why."

"I'm sure Kerry would be able to tell you the nature and provenance of every item on this table," he said, scooping some miniature arancini onto the plate, still not looking at me. "I am not quite so well-versed in the catering menu, nor am I all that acquainted with what you will willingly consume, aside from pizza, cookies, and the occasional burrito. You need to sit down for more proper meals."

"Hey, I also eat frozen waffles and scones," I said. "As long as someone else does the cooking and the dishes, I'm happy with just about anything. And I eat a lot of sandwiches."

He gave me a sidelong look that showed his disapproval with that defense. "The sandwich is a gambler's repast, not a meal fit for a hero who insists on running off and continually getting herself stabbed. But I'll make an effort to cook more often."

"You can cook?"

He turned to face me, thrusting the plate into my hands. "I do realize the times have changed, and that the nobility are not as a rule expected to do for themselves, but I was not always a King, and when I was younger, a man of my station who could not cook was likely to find himself starving more often than not. My recipes may be outdated to your modern sensibilities, but I assure you, they do exist."

"Outdated meaning . . . ?"

"More turnips than modern cuisine seems to focus upon, less tomato."

"European, then. Okay, cool." He still didn't look like he wanted to answer my earlier question. As he started putting together a smaller plate for himself, I picked up one of the arancini and popped it into my mouth. The crust was crisp and still steaming, the interior hot without being scalding. The wonders of hearth magic. No one ever burns their tongue unless they've managed to offend the chef, and when that happens, you generally know what you've done.

"Mushroom and beef stock," I said, after swallowing. "Really nice."

"Kerry will be pleased. She had some concerns, given your famed disregard for the needs of the flesh, that her contribution to the wedding would be less well-regarded than Stacy's. Attempts to reassure her that as she was not the Maid of Honor—a quaint mortal custom which both of them nonetheless seemed to understand intimately—she was not expected to contribute equally did not calm her as much as I had hoped."

"Aw, Kerry." We had never been as close as I was to Stacy, in part because Kerry had been the only one of the four of us with a loving family of her own. I had Mom, who was distant at best and neglectful at worst, seeming to view me as an inconveniently animate houseplant when not sitting me down and drilling me on the finer parts of courtly etiquette—a process that in hindsight seemed more and more baffling as this night went on. What had she been preparing me to become by drilling me on forms of address and types of fae, but not teaching me what were apparently normal elements of a fae wedding?

What had her end goal been?

I shook the question aside and focused on my new husband, who was continuing to add things to his plate. Much more meat than he'd put on mine, and he'd managed to find some sort of scallop thing that hadn't made it into my assortment of offerings. I leaned over and plucked a scallop off his plate, ignoring his wounded expression as I popped it into my mouth.

"Sorry," I said unrepentantly. "We're married now. That means we have to share."

"Does it?" he asked, replacing the scallop with another from the table. "If it means you eat, I suppose I can tolerate thievery."

I took the hint and ate some of the asparagus from my own

plate, swallowing before I said, more gently, "Hey. You still haven't answered my question."

"You ask so many, little fish, I can't be expected to keep track of all of them."

"Come on. It's really important to you that everyone is okay with the fact that we got married. Why? Help me understand. Please."

Tybalt sighed, shoulders slumping, before he turned to face me. "I had thought I was concealing my motivations better than it seems I was."

"You married me because you like me, and part of why you like me is that I pay attention to you," I said. "There's nothing wrong with that. People like it when other people pay attention to them. But it means I'm harder to hide things from than you think I am— especially when you might as well be waving a semaphore and shouting 'I'm unhappy about something, ask me what.'"

"It's unfair to say that I'm unhappy," he objected. "We have managed to be successfully wed, and have already collected four of the seven blessings."

"Is there some sort of etiquette about that?"

"We are not allowed to leave the reception until all seven have been received, or we have verified that the seventh is in the keeping of someone who we do not wish to speak with," he said. "It seems unlikely, however, as that list consists solely of your liege, and he would have been compelled to present his blessing, even after it had been rejected."

"Who was responsible for assigning them? And don't think I haven't noticed you trying to distract me." I ate another rice ball. "I'm a professional detective. I can notice things."

"That was part of the wedding planning that I was not allowed to participate in, so I believe the assignments would have been handled by your sister and your squire."

"Explaining why they managed to rope the Luidaeg in, and why Sylvester wouldn't have made the list."

The crowd was beginning to thin. I glanced around, and realized that small cabaret-style tables had appeared around the edges of the room, leaving the center free to serve as what I was increasingly concerned would eventually become a dance floor. About half of them were occupied, people taking their plates and retreating from the throng.

"Over there," I said, pointing, before I started making my way toward the nearest open table. One nice thing about being in a dress so white that it virtually glowed and kept shedding rose petals everywhere I walked: people could see me coming. They not only got out of my way, but when a few of them saw me heading purposefully toward the table with a plate in my hand, they turned and went looking for someplace else to sit. All four of the table's chairs were still open when we got there.

"Oof," I said, sitting with some difficulty. The dress fit perfectly, and a properly laced corset wasn't actually uncomfortable, but it restricted my ability to bend enough that I was probably going to need Tybalt to help me back up.

He seemed to realize that at the same time I did, because he put his plate down and said, "I'll just go fetch us some drinks before we—"

"No," I said calmly, and gestured to his seat. "I think we're good."

Tybalt looked at my face, sighed, and sat.

"All right. Now will you please, before Kerry brings out the cake or someone starts trying to get us to dance, tell me why it's so important to you that other people approve of me as a bride and you as the man I'm marrying? You know I never cared. As long as I wound up married to you at the end of the day, I was going to be happy."

"I do," he said quietly. "And I know the Luidaeg explained to you why it couldn't work the way you wanted it to. I would have been happy to avoid all of this pomp and circumstance, if the decision had been solely mine. But I've seen what happens when parts of Faerie turn against themselves, and I understand the consequences that can follow on from even the simplest and most innocent of actions. I was first a King of Cats in Londinium, my father's Kingdom, where my sister and I lived in peace for many decades. There, I watched a family tear itself apart because the idea that a child might live whose veins contained the blood of both the Cait Sidhe and the Daoine Sidhe was too much for them to bear."

I'd heard some of this before, in bits and pieces over the nearly three years we'd spent as an official couple, and the four years before that that we'd spent as increasingly close friends. It was still unusual for him to string it all together into a coherent whole, and so I nodded, and said nothing, letting him work his way through whatever he needed me to hear.

"After that, I went to a Kingdom called Armorica in what you would probably recognize as the Brittany region of France. It still endures, both Brittany and Armorica itself; Kingdoms rise overnight and fall to the tune of centuries, when they fall at all. Even when the people who control them change, the common element tends to insist on a certain amount of continuity."

"Shallcross would have had his work cut out for him if he'd somehow managed to overthrow the High King," I agreed.

"Shallcross would have cast the entirety of the Westlands into war," said Tybalt, tone dark. "The other High Kingdoms would have taken his claim of illegitimacy on the part of the Sollys line as a sign that we could not be trusted to govern ourselves, and invaded before his heralds could return home. Especially since I doubt they would have had such an accommodating assemblage of Tuatha de Dannan and neighboring monarchs to assist them in reaching their destinations."

"Yeah, probably not so much."

"You haven't seen Faerie go to war, October. I have, more than once, and it's never a sweet story for the survivors. In Armorica, I learned what it was to build a kingdom on the foundations set by war." His gaze was very far away. "Their founders had slain one of the Firstborn, and been cursed for their actions. The shifting kinds, Cait Sidhe and Cu Sidhe and Selkies and all the rest, we had been scoured from the land, put to death to preserve the sensibilities of the Daoine Sidhe who held the throne."

I blinked at him, utterly horrified. "They *killed* them?"

"Yes."

"Not during a declared war or anything else that they could use to justify it to themselves? Just *killed* them?"

"Again, yes." Tybalt took a sip from his wine glass and grimaced. "They hunted them down like beasts, not to be too flippant about it, for beasts they were and beasts they were regarded, and the fact that they were thinking children of Faerie mattered not at all to the ones who held the swords. We were collateral damage in a curse that had been meant to punish only a few, and I will never know how many lines and lives were ended, how many stopped their dancing."

He gazed at something beyond me, something I suspected only

he could see. "I went to many lands after Armorica, but those were the Kingdoms that showed me how cruel the Divided Courts could be to the shifting kind, who dared to take more after Oberon than his pretty, static queens."

The thought of someone calling Maeve, who was supposedly the most protean of the Three, static, would have been funny under any other circumstances. I didn't laugh.

"In Ash and Oak, I thought I had found a Kingdom that would not punish me for my beginnings. They allowed and accepted those of us who danced between forms, and they did so without question or challenge. Before the iron came, New York seemed set to be a paradise. I was not a part of the convocation which seated the High Kingdom, but had I been, I would have argued for Shallcross's side. I am not ashamed of that, even now that we know I would have been wrong. I thought it might be my home forever. I even considered sending word to my sister in Londinium, asking her to set her crown aside and follow me across the ocean for the sake of her freedom, and our family."

I blinked, and still said nothing. This was something he needed to finish on his own.

"I met my Anne in Ash and Oak. It may seem odd to sit at my own wedding supper, odd as it is to my remembrance of tradition, and think fondly of my first wife, but she was a glory, and I continue to say that you would have liked her."

"From what I've seen of her in your memories, I think you're probably right," I agreed. "She seemed like my kind of lady. No common sense or sense of self-preservation."

"I like my women attracted to danger and my men eminently practical," said Tybalt, with his first real flicker of humor since we'd settled at our table. "And of course, I now prefer you to either, as you are my singular and forever wife."

"Good save," I said, with a wide smile.

"Anne and I met in the mortal world, courted in the twilight of the Court of Cats, wed with the full acceptance and understanding of my people, and had no congress with the Divided Courts. They were disinterested in my comings and goings as one of the Cait Sidhe, having judged us to be beneath and below them in their own assessment, and because we had nothing to gain from their company, I did not question it, or attempt to change the situation."

A slow dread was beginning to gather in my stomach. "Was King Shallcross the one . . ."

"No." Tybalt shook his head. "I was not a King in Ash and Oak, merely a Prince without a crown, and so I lacked the authority to speak to the King of the Divided Courts. My suit never reached so far as his attention. But when it became clear that my Anne's pregnancy was going poorly and she would not survive the birth, when I understood that I would have to be the beggar at the gate if I wanted any hope of saving her, I went to his Court. To the Baron who claimed ownership of the borough where we lived, with the full intent to go to the Duke above him if necessary, to continue pressing forward until I was able to save her."

"And they told you no."

"The Baron laughed at me for even attempting to ask." Tybalt still sounded wounded by this, even centuries after the fact. Some wounds never fully heal, even if they stop being quite so visible as they used to be. "He said there was no reason for him to intervene on behalf of beasts who lay down with beasts, and if we wanted to rut, we should be prepared to pay the consequences. He said some other things that were even less flattering, in their own cruel way, and refused to arrange an audience for me with his superior. When I attempted to speak to the man on my own, I was rebuffed in no uncertain terms, and by the time I had found a way to enter his Court without being stopped, it was too late. Anne's condition was too pronounced. In the end, I was given the choice that was no choice: I could either stay with her as she suffered in her labors, and hope we might have a better outcome than all logic said was coming, or I could continue in my quest to change the unchangeable. I stayed with my wife."

"I'm sorry."

"It was long ago. Even if she had lived, she was mortal. No matter what, she'd be gone by now, and I like to think that in that better world, you and I would still have found each other. More swiftly, perhaps, as I would have been so much less damaged, and less inclined to project that damage onto changeling shoulders that never deserved to carry it. But all I have just said, all that I have lived through, is the reason I've been so set upon our wedding being a spectacle that could not be overlooked. Even aside from the Luidaeg's reasons, which were excellent, and I agreed with her when she expressed them to me, I wanted this so no one could ever look at you and think you were lesser for marrying a beast."

I leaned across the table and put my hand over his, folding down my fingers so that he would have to pull if he wanted to be free of me. He met the motion with a fragile smile.

"You're not a beast; you're a part of Faerie, same as I am," I said. "No matter what shape you are, you're the man I love, the man I married, and the man I'm planning to be married to for the rest of my life."

"Which will be very, very long," he said.

I smiled back at him. "Yes. Very, very long. Long enough for us to learn every frustrating truth about each other, and figure out all the reasons they don't matter. I'm in this for keeps, Tybalt. Or whatever I'm supposed to call you now." I scowled and poked one of my remaining rice balls with the tip of a finger. "I don't approve of changing names just because you got married."

To my relief, Tybalt laughed. "Well, I changed names the first time I became a King, and Raj will do the same when he makes the crown his own, and not merely a borrowed ornamentation. It is a way to differentiate between someone who will one day carry the burden and responsibility of the crown, and someone who already has those things upon their shoulders. It's meant to tell those who knew us as children, subject to the whims and wills of our parents, that we have grown beyond the coddling of the cradle."

"So what *is* your name now?"

"Technically, unless I choose another, Rand. The name I was given as a kitten, by my mother, who I never knew."

I frowned. "That seems contradictory."

"You know it was unusual for me to allow Raj's parents to remain with him in my Court?"

"I do." And he'd been poorly rewarded for that allowance, with Raj's mother dying at the hands of Oleander de Merelands, and Raj's father using our relationship as a lever by which to raise up a rebellion against him. Some Cait Sidhe didn't care for the idea of a King who loved a member of the Divided Courts, and were happy to follow a man who could never be King if he promised to return them to a world where they could know, for a fact, that they were in charge.

"My father . . ." He grimaced. "My father was a poor bearer of the title. My own children will not be raised in such a manner."

"You've told me this before," I said quickly, trying to suppress the little thrill of delight I felt every time he reminded me he wanted to have children of his own. I wanted that too, more than anything. Being here in Toronto had been one long reminder that the boy who was my son in all but blood would eventually need to go back to his actual parents, the woman who bore him and the man who'd never been afforded the opportunity to raise him. Call me selfish, but I wanted a kid I didn't have to give back to anyone else. I loved Gillian. Thanks to the combination of Evening, Simon, and Janet, she'd grown up thinking I was a heartless deadbeat who'd abandoned her as soon as I'd realized motherhood wasn't always easy or fun, and I'd only been her mom for a few years before that happened.

Much like Quentin with Maida, I was always going to be her mother, but another woman was always going to be her mom. It was too late for me to win that title back. So yeah, I wanted kids of my own, kids I could stay with and be there for and find entirely different ways of screwing up with.

"They won't," I said, as reassuringly as I could. "For one thing, with the way my bloodline seems to behave, your kids are going to be more Dóchas Sidhe than anything else."

His smile was brief but utterly sincere. "I can't wait to meet them."

"I can. I know we both want kids, but I'd like to wait to get anyone else involved in our lives until things have calmed down a little bit, and I'm not spending quite so much time nearly getting myself killed."

"Oh, look," said Tybalt, deadpan. "Who's that over at the buffet? Is that the sea witch and her father? And have they managed to call the Firstborn of the Merrow out of the tide to help them raid the shrimp cocktail?"

There was a shriek from the other side of the room, high and giddy and surprised, like a teenage girl getting home from school to discover that the new car in the driveway is for her to keep, no kidding, no strings attached. I twisted to look over my shoulder. Pete and the Luidaeg were in fact standing by the buffet, and Pete had her arms locked around Oberon's shoulders and her face buried against his collarbone, her own shoulders shaking with what could have been either laughter or tears. A plate of what looked like spaghetti was spread across the floor at Oberon's feet, having apparently been knocked out of his hands when his daughter embraced him.

Everyone around them was ignoring them, as if this weren't happening. The Luidaeg was standing back and watching the pair, a tolerant expression on her face.

"You know, I can't decide whether the Luidaeg put the whammy on all our wedding guests, or whether they're just smart enough not to stare at one of the Firstborn when she's having a moment." I turned back to my husband and my plate, picking up another rice ball. It was still hot. The stasis charms on the food really were top-notch. "How did she get here, anyway? I didn't see her at the wedding."

"Judging by the number of people in this clearing, some of our guests skipped the ceremony in favor of the reception."

"Smart." If I hadn't been the one getting married, I would have been perfectly willing to skip the ceremony in favor of the reception. Especially given how much of the buffet I had yet to investigate. I popped the rice ball into my mouth, chewed, swallowed, and asked, "So was that meant to distract me, or to remind me that our lives are always going to be ridiculous?"

"Primarily the latter," said Tybalt. "However much we might wish differently, you, my love, are a hero, and that's a title as much earned as given; stop chasing down danger, try to stay home and live a peaceful life, and heroism will still come sniffing around the rafters, looking for a way into the house. If you would make me wait until you feel the possibility of danger has passed before I experience fatherhood, then we will be waiting until your essential nature has changed, and I would prefer not to."

"Mmm," I said. "You still haven't told me how it is that your mother named you, but you never met her."

"I didn't say we never met, only that I never knew her," he said. "She sold my sister and I to our father when we were still new, mewling babes whose eyes had yet to open. He was always searching for possible heirs to the Court of Fogbound Cats, which was the largest and most powerful Court of Cats in all of Albion. Our father, Ainmire, was a powerful man. A great man, in his own manner, but never, not for one instant in the long days of his life, a good man. He gathered children to set against each other as pawns. Our mother had no way of knowing that when he came to her to make his purchase; she knew only she lacked the power to refuse him, and that one of us might inherit someday, and find ourselves placed such that no one and nothing could harm us. So she sold us to Ainmire, with only our names and each other to carry with us into the future. I don't know whether my sister was allowed to keep her name."

I blinked. "I thought—"

"I was raised with three sisters. Jill, Colleen, and Cailin."

I blinked again, more slowly this time. "All three of those names mean 'girl,'" I said.

"Yes. My brothers were Carr and Arlis. I fear our father allowed the boys to keep the names we were bought with, and changed the names of the girls to remind us always what their role was in his Court."

I didn't want to ask. I had to ask. "What was their role?"

"They were guarantees against our good behavior. If we challenged and lost, they were killed to remind us of our place in the Court. My brother Carr challenged, and his hostage was killed. My other brother, Arlis, walked away rather than risk his dear Colleen in such a manner, and left me with both her and my own hostage, Jill, as guarantors of my manners. I was a flippant, foolish boy, because I could not play games with the lives of my sisters."

I looked at him in absolute horror, suddenly glad that I hadn't been drinking anything.

"So my mother named me, for all that she may not have named my sister, and if I am not a King of Cats, my name will be Rand, as it was when I was but a boy." He shrugged. "Your name is October, and yet you reject it as much and as often as you can."

"Not that you ever listen," I said, lips gone numb.

"No, for 'Toby' is no name for a woman of your grace and value," he said. "I would grant you 'Tobias,' if that were the name you had chosen, or 'Toviah,' but 'Toby' is a step too far for me to swallow. And yet you deny that 'October' is your name, and I deny that 'Toby' is."

I frowned. "All right, I accept your premise. What are you saying?"

"Some people change their names for reasons of personal identity, or to reject a name that fails to fit them. Neither of us has done such a thing. We both possess multiple names by which we can pass, and choose the one that suits our situation. When two people disagree about a name, it can sometimes be appropriate to disregard their instructions and call them as you wish."

"So you're saying . . ."

"I'm saying that when my nephew takes his throne, it would be a profound insult to call him 'Rajiv,' for he will set that name aside, and that to call Walther by the name his parents once gave him would be a disgrace to your house, as well as a denial of the man himself, but that you may call me 'Tybalt' for as long as it pleases you. You do not belong to the Court of Cats. It is the name by which you have long known me, and our customs are not your own, nor is it common for a King to slip back into Princehood. It may do me a favor, to use a name other than the one to which I truly belong."

"It might." I took a breath, intending to chase the topic of my own given name further, and stopped as a hand landed on my shoulder. I looked back, and there was Amphitrite, standing behind me in all her vaguely nautical finery, although she had at least ditched the pirate look for something a little more "untouchable goddess of the infinite sea." Fine scales speckled her cheeks like extremely expensive body glitter, and there were tears shining in her oceanic eyes.

"My sister told me you were to be wed within sight of the sea, so of course I knew myself invited," she said, as if this were a logically constructed sentence and not some weird kind of pureblood word salad. She grabbed a chair from the nearest open table and dragged it over to ours, plopping herself into it without so much as a by-your-leave. "I mean, she also told me what you'd gone and dredged up from the bottom of the sea, and I didn't believe her about *that*, so I guess the joke's on me if you didn't want me here."

"I didn't know you were speaking to each other," I said.

"Eh, Annie's banished from my domain for seven years. That doesn't mean I'm barred from the land. She'd need more power than even she has to accomplish that, and since neither of our moms has decided to put in an unwanted appearance, there's not much of a risk of me getting locked into the watery deep any time soon." She leaned over the table, claiming my wine glass and taking a deep sip before setting it down again. "She sends me messages in bottles. It's quaint and a little old-fashioned, but we're old-fashioned girls."

"Yeah, and that's why I expected you to be over there for a little longer." I waved a hand, vaguely indicating the point by the buffet where the Luidaeg and Oberon were still standing. He was filling a fresh plate. She appeared to be scolding him, brows knit and hands waving wildly. Everyone around them was studiously pretending they weren't there, which showed a remarkable amount of common sense, for the fae; even if they thought Oberon was just another random wedding guest—which seemed strange to me only because I knew the truth, and would probably have seemed much more realistic than what was actually happening if I hadn't—they knew better than to interfere with the target of one of the Firstborn's ire.

If the Luidaeg started yelling, they would probably stampede for the doors and leave us alone with the buffet, the cake, and the small army of desensitized teenagers who no longer had the common sense to be afraid of the sea witch.

Really, I was going to *have* to be Chelsea's knight when the time came. No one else would have any idea how to deal with her.

"Eh. Big sis has a way different relationship to her parents than I do to mine." Pete shrugged fluidly. The motion took a while. There was a lot of Pete to shrug. As mother of the Merrow, Pete took her role as first ship's figurehead in the world very seriously. Her full name was Amphitrite, after one of the better-known Greek goddesses of the sea, and she lived up to it gloriously. "Kinda like I have a way different relationship to my descendants than most of my sibs, and that brings us, my sweet little rosebud, to you." She leaned forward, resting her elbow on the table and her chin on her knuckles, and fixed me with a steady, shark-eyed gaze.

I did my best not to squirm. I have more practice standing up to the attention of the Firstborn than most people, but that doesn't mean I *like* it, exactly, just that it no longer feels like fire ants crawling over every inch of my skin, looking for tender places to burrow into my flesh.

"You know, not all of our children have liked their parents. Strange, really, when we're all such sweet, attentive, loving parents." Pete smiled as if daring me to argue with her.

Tybalt reached across the table and put his hand over mine. Well, at least if I was about to be turned into a sea turtle or something, he'd be with me on the way down. I kept my eyes on Pete, all too aware that dealing with the Firstborn is like dealing with any sort of charismatic megafauna: don't show fear. It never ends well.

"Sorry," I said. "I've met too many of your sisters to believe that."

"Not my brothers?"

"I've only met one of those, and since he was a literal monster, I'm not sure you want him included in the count."

"Mmm," she said, noncommittally. "But as I was saying, we haven't always gotten along with our kids. My descendants, for example, tend to attack me on sight."

"You do rub some people the wrong way," I agreed.

"But you, rosebud, you are the first among all our children not to choose their First during a divorce. Not that we usually marry our lovers; even our children are short-lived compared to us, being so much easier to kill than we are, and so it seems a little pointless, as a rule, to marry. Some of my sisters do it for sport, but only when they intend no issue from a union. At least one of my brothers did it as a sort of bad habit; he would disappear on us for a decade or so and come back with a bride he scarce remembered getting, usually some pampered princess he'd abducted from her bower and wed with blood and with weeping, but on the main, we don't bother."

"Yeah, well, I'm not Firstborn."

"I noticed. And neither is your handsome husband." Pete winked at Tybalt, who tightened his hand on mine. "Don't worry, kitty. Even if I were in the market for a lover, I don't steal from ships unless I plan to sink them, and I'm not in the mood for piracy tonight. I came here to see my sister, and see whether she was telling me the truth, and to lay my own blessing upon the happy household—not one of your seven. Such a quaint little custom! I wonder if Dobrinya knew that little custom, out of all the customs he tried to define, would be the one that lingered. He would have been very pleased if he had. But no, I brought you a blessing of my own, and you'd do well not to refuse it."

I wasn't sure refusing a gift from one of the First was even possible. I forced a smile instead, and said, somewhat insincerely, "We look forward to hearing it."

"I know enough of your past to know that you fear death by water, daughter of Simon, who dwells in the deeps now with a daughter of my line, and whose loyalty would be mine to claim, if only I wanted it."

"Please don't," I said hurriedly, realizing only after the words were out that I'd just cut off one of the Firstborn, and that might not go well for me. I cleared my throat and continued, as carefully as I could, "Simon has suffered enough at the hands of the Firstborn, and while I trust you to be kinder than many of your siblings, the Lordens took him into Saltmist so he'd have a chance to rest for a while before anything else could happen to him."

"Do I look like the sort of thing that happens to people?"

"Please don't be offended, but that's exactly what you look like," I said, and shrugged. "You're like a very busty natural disaster. You happen to whatever gets in your way, and you may or may not mean it, and you definitely aren't malicious, but I need my father to get better, because it seems he's the only parent I'm going to have for a while, so if you could not please break him again, that would be cool."

To my immense relief, Pete threw her head back and laughed. Across the floor, both Oberon and the Luidaeg looked in our direction. I flashed them a wan smile, keeping most of my attention on the immediate threat.

It says something about my life that the King of all Faerie didn't register as the biggest threat in the room, but at the moment, the woman who could fill my lungs with water with a wave of her hand seemed like a much more immediate and pressing concern.

"I will not break your father," said Pete, still laughing a little. "I should probably be offended that you even felt the need to tell me you didn't want me to, but I've met you and I've met him and I've met your mom, and asking was the right thing to do, absolutely. Back to the blessing. I know you fear death by water. I know it's largely due to the man you just asked me not to harm, so good job there, your loyalties aren't confusing at *all*."

"You know, talking to the Luidaeg is easier, because she's not allowed to lie to me, which makes sarcasm a lot less useful for her," I said direly.

"Yeah, well, I'm more fun, so it balances. Anyway, as long as I make my home in the peaceful sea, her waters will not claim you. No undertow will take you or your spouse or children from the shore, no depth will see you drowned. If you're to suffer death by water, it will be at someone else's doorstep. Sorry it's not a dinette set." She stood, offering us a small wave. "That was all. You can go back to gazing into each other's eyes and trading wine glasses now."

"That's not what we were doing," I began to object, but she had already lost interest and was walking away, heading across the room toward points unknown. I sighed and looked back to Tybalt. "Well, I think the lady who kind of owns the Pacific Ocean just gave us a 'get out of drowning free' card. That's a pretty nice wedding gift."

"I knew when I proposed that I was marrying into madness," he said, a bit unsteadily. "It is possible I underestimated the degree."

"Too late now," I said cheerfully, and beamed at him.

After only a beat, he beamed back. "It's been too late for ages," he said.

"Good man." I leaned across the table, intending to kiss him.

I didn't quite make it before Stacy grabbed my arm and halfway yanked me out of my seat, pulling me away from both table and Tybalt. "*There* you are," she said, in a tone that implied I'd been hiding all night, and not wandering openly through my own reception in the whitest dress anyone had ever seen.

"I've been right here," I said. "How could you miss me?"

"No one could see you," she said. "Notice-me-not illusions at your reception are dirty pool, and I'm going to make you pay for this later, when I won't get in trouble for beating up the bride." She continued to haul me across the floor, heading back toward the buffet.

I glanced back. Tybalt was following, not looking nearly bothered enough about the fact that I was being abducted. 'Help me,' I mouthed exaggeratedly. He shrugged, a small smile on his face.

'No,' he mouthed back.

I settled for pouting at him. If he couldn't save me from my soccer mom best friend, what good was he really?

Stacy didn't seem to have noticed any of this. She was intent on getting me to her destination, whatever that happened to be. "Have you at least been circulating enough to collect your blessings?" she asked.

"Four of them, plus a bonus from the Duchess of Ships," I said.

"We don't shut this party down until you have all seven," she said. "In case you thought you could keep avoiding the rest of us forever."

The rest of . . . "Stacy, do you have one of the remaining bless-ings?" I asked, keeping my tone light.

She looked back over her shoulder at me. "Oh, and here I thought you were having so much fun avoiding me that you'd for-gotten I might be asked to be one of your seven."

"Stacy . . ."

"No, no, it's fine." She waved her free hand like she was batting away a moth. "Did you get a blessing from Raj?"

"Not yet."

"Then here you are: may you and yours always have full bellies, solid roofs, and money enough to do whatever must be done, plus a little left over at the end, for tomorrow's bread."

"Oh, that's a nice one, I like that one," I said. "They should all be that reasonable. I'm down with the practical blessings. Much nicer than the ones I don't completely understand."

"There are like ninety classical ones on the list," said Stacy, thawing slightly. "We picked the seven that seemed most applica-ble to your life, and split them up between people we knew you'd be happy to talk to, and ones who might need an excuse if they actually wanted to talk to you."

"That explains August," I said.

To my surprise, Stacy actually looked hurt at that. "You really *were* hiding from me, weren't you?"

"What? No! No, Tybalt and I have been here the whole time, right over there at that table where no one could miss us. I'm sorry if you couldn't find us for some reason. Maybe one of the kids was playing some sort of silly game or something."

"I doubt it, since it's been delaying cake." She thawed a bit as she kept hauling me onward. "She telling the truth, Tybalt?"

"As my heart knows it," he said. "We have had no privacy since well before we were wed."

"Huh. Then I apologize for the rational assumption that the two of you had slunk off somewhere for a quickie."

"No need to apologize," said Tybalt. "Had I believed we might be successful without arousing your wrath, or perhaps that of the sea witch, I would absolutely have absconded with my new bride. This whole process of blessing and milling about takes up so much time, and when one is dealing with October, moments of peace must be seized while they exist."

"Hey," I protested, without heat.

"Say he's wrong without telling a lie and I'll tell you where to find your last two blessings so you can go to bed," said Stacy, releasing my wrist as we reached the seemingly empty buffet table. "I dare you."

"And you know I can't," I said.

"Yes, I do," she agreed. Then she clapped her hands three times, briskly. The conversation around us, which had not flagged when she came dragging the bride like a runaway puppy and trailed by the faintly amused groom, stopped, and the illusion that had been concealing the final banquet table dropped away.

There was Kerry, in the same red as the rest of the wedding party, her riotous hair tamed into a crown braid and streaks of flour on her cheeks. There were my missing teenagers, plus Gillian, and Diva, Liz's daughter, who I hadn't noticed in the crowd before. It was quite the little swarm, and it was almost inconsequential in the face of the cake they were doing their best to surround, like an army preparing to lay siege to a well-defended castle.

"Oak and ash . . ." I breathed.

Kerry had promised me the wedding cake of my dreams when we were both children young enough that dreaming about wedding cakes took up a surprising amount of our time. We didn't know if we were ever going to get married, or ever going to *want* to get married, but we knew we liked cake, and we knew a wedding was basically like the biggest birthday party ever, and you could have as many frosting roses as you wanted. Well, Kerry had managed to grow at least somewhat beyond that decorating aesthetic as she got older, but frosting roses still featured fairly heavily.

The cake she had constructed—and "constructed" was really the only word that came even halfway near describing the work that must have gone into that monstrosity—was ten tiers high and looked like someone had decided to cut it before we got there, using an axe rather than an ordinary knife. A vast gash had been sculpted into one side of the otherwise impeccably-frosted cake, and the interior gleamed with massive sugar crystals, each one a perfect pale pink rose quartz, and bled in a river of red and white roses that mirrored the train of my gown. They looked perfectly real, like she had been gathering them from one of Luna's gardens the moment before we approached, but I knew Kerry well enough to know that they would be completely edible, even down to their spun-sugar thorns.

The cake wasn't white. Under the roses it was the deep, earthy brown of semisweet dark chocolate. Tybalt stepped up next to me, joining me in silent, wide-eyed staring.

In case the cake hadn't been enough, there were two trays of cupcakes with matching roses atop them, although they were frosted in a variety of colors, and a shorter tower of stacked cheese and sliced fruits, which poured down the side of the cheese in a river effect similar to the roses on the cake.

Kerry stepped forward, smiling shyly, hands buried in the skirt of her dress. "Do you like it?" she asked.

"What flavor is it?" I asked, sounding overwhelmed even to myself.

"Which part?"

I slowly turned to blink at her. "Kerry, if this is where you tell me that every tier is a different flavor, this is where I pass out, and also get a little huffy because I can't possibly eat ten pieces of cake, and I can't *not* taste my entire wedding cake."

"That's why I made you cupcakes for later," she said, in a tone that implied it was the only reasonable thing she could possibly have done. "Cake flavors were way different when Tybalt was our age. Less chocolate, more rum, less sweet, more savory, all that sort of thing. So making a cake you'd both recognize as dessert took some doing."

"I promise, I am well acquainted with modern culinary trends," said Tybalt, sounding only faintly affronted. "I know what butter-cream is, and consider the invention of chocolate cake to be—"

"Which is why," continued Kerry blithely, "the base level is a dark ginger cake with a boiled frosting center, while the level above is vanilla cake with extra vanilla, and a strawberry rose center, to suit your ridiculous sweet tooth, which hasn't gotten any less disturbing since we were children. Next layer up is chai with a raspberry jam filling, and above that is almond and honey and why is Tybalt staring at me like he thinks I might be on the menu?"

"I rescind anything I may have said to offend you, oh most beauteous of bakers," said Tybalt, sounding slightly stunned.

"Thought you might," said Kerry smugly.

"Do all those flavors get along with chocolate icing?" I asked.

"Hush," said Kerry. "It's magic."

Sometimes "it's magic" is the most annoying answer in the world. Other times, you're being stared at by a cluster of hungry teens who desperately want cake, and arguing is not a plan that keeps things peaceful. I smiled and shook my head. "Cool," I agreed. "It's magic."

Kerry stepped forward and grabbed my hands, a comforting scent of sugar and grated ginger surrounding her. "May you never hunger, never thirst, and never want for more than you deserve, which is more than you can possibly believe," she said. "I love you, Toby. I'm so glad to be a part of this."

"Of course," I said, and pulled her in for a hug. "You were always going to be a part of this, no matter how it happened."

I meant that. Kerry and Julie and Stacy were my first friends. They were there for me when no one else was, when I couldn't imagine anyone else ever wanting to be. We could fight and fall out and come back together, the way we always had and always would. Through births and deaths and breakups and marriages, we were meant to be together. It was the way the world worked. So I embraced Kerry, and she hugged me back, and Tybalt put a hand on my shoulder as he stared at the monumental undertaking that was our wedding cake, and everything was perfect, despite all the damn roses. Everything was exactly the way it was supposed to be.

"April asked me to save her a piece of wedding cake, but since it comes in ten different *kinds* of cake, I can bring her a piece of each, right?" asked Quentin in his unfamiliar Banshee voice, right next to my elbow. Tybalt snorted, and somehow that was perfect, too. My life wasn't supposed to be peace and Hallmark Hollywood perfect. It needed the little disruptions, or it wouldn't really be *mine.*

"There aren't ten flavors," said Kerry, sounding stung, as she pulled away from me. "There are fifteen. Do you think I'm an amateur or something?"

"Fifteen?" I demanded. "What the hell, Kerry?"

She smiled as she looked at me and shrugged. "You inspire me to do ridiculous things. And some of the tiers are actually multiple tiers of cake that are almost the same size. It was necessary if I wanted to have enough height to really stabilize the roses. Which are all made from either candied sugar or frosting, depending on the size and how far down the cake they are—the frosting ones are heavier, so they needed to be closer to the bottom if I wanted them to adhere properly."

"Have you never heard of fondant?" asked Tybalt.

Kerry gave him a look that could have been used to etch glass. "Unlike some people, I have *standards*," she said.

Tybalt roared with laughter. Kerry stopped glaring and giggled. I turned my attention back to the cake, and the throng of teenagers lurking around it, including Quentin, who was still waiting hopefully for my response.

"You can take some cake to April, after everyone who's actually here has had whatever they want," I said. Then I paused. "So, um, how does this work?"

Quentin frowned. "What do you mean?"

"The cake. If we were in the mortal world, doing this the human way, I'd be expected to make the first cut."

"Okay . . ."

"And then Tybalt and I would feed each other some cake, because reasons. I don't know what they are, and I can't explain them to you without understanding them myself. I think it's supposed to be a sign that we trust each other enough to be hand-fed, but I'm just guessing. Anyway, that's part of why human wedding cakes are almost always white, so when they wind up all over the bride, they won't stain her dress." I looked down at my own dress, which remained so white as to be pristine, and had turned away several arrows without so much as snagging a thread, as well as refusing a wide assortment bloods and ichors. "Not a problem for me."

I looked up again. Quentin and Tybalt were staring at me in horror. Kerry, who worked part-time for a human bakery while not working in the kitchens at Shadowed Hills, simply looked disgusted.

"What?"

"That is *barbaric*," said Tybalt. "And I say this as a man who has passed time among barbarians. Literally barbaric. I will not be smearing cake on you in front of an *audience*." He lowered his voice. "Now, if you wish to have a food fight of sorts in private, we could perhaps come to some arrangement . . ."

"Later," I said. "So feeding the bride cake is not a thing in Faerie?"

"No," said Quentin. "And also, ew."

"Okay, well. There would also be toppers on the cake that were supposed to look vaguely like the bride and groom, but which wouldn't look anything like us to anyone but the most charitable, and we'd take those home as souvenirs after the wedding was over."

"I suggested cake toppers," said Kerry. "For some reason, no one thought it was funny."

"Is *that* why you wanted to put a plastic figurine of a cat on top of the cake?" asked Tybalt. "I thought you were joking."

"Nope," said Kerry. "Humans are weird as hell. Before you ask about any more cake customs, Tobes, you *do* want to take some cake home, I've already prepped you a platter with sample-size slices of all the different flavors, under a long-term stasis spell that should hold up just fine as long as you don't leave it in direct sunlight. It would hold up better in a knowe, but." She shrugged broadly. "We work with what we have, and what you have is a pantry with a door that closes. Still pretty good, given where you started."

"You mean an enchanted tower under the hill, owned by a woman who usually forgot to feed me?"

"That's the one! You do make the first cut, though, and you use my knife to do it, since yours is probably covered with something unspeakable that would despoil my beautiful creation."

"Or she can use mine," said a male voice, from behind me.

I turned.

There was Oberon, still in his mostly-unassuming guise, the antlers on his brow small enough not to attract more attention than he wanted. He was wearing red, which was a little odd, since he wasn't part of the official wedding party, but he was also *Oberon*, which meant absolutely no one, not even his daughters, was going to tell him "no."

And he was holding a knife by the blade, offering it to me hilt-first. I blinked, first at the blade, then at him. "Sire?" I asked.

This was one of those things that probably held some great meaning and import no one had ever bothered to explain to me, assuming it wouldn't be important enough to matter. Mom's continuous drilling in the rules and etiquette of Faerie had been suspiciously absent on the topic of wedding traditions, probably because she couldn't imagine a world in which I would have any reason to get married to someone who actually cared about them. For her, the world where I married Cliff and settled into a mostly-mortal existence was the best I could ever have hoped for.

And for a long time, that world was the best I could imagine myself deserving.

Thank the root and the tree that sometimes we get more than we deserve. "I would be honored," I said, and took the knife from Oberon's hand, turning to face the cake.

It was a monument to the baker's art, and it seemed like it should be some sort of minor crime to cut it, much less consume it. Tybalt put his hand over mine, seeming to pick up on the direction of my thoughts, and guided the knife toward the bottom layer. "Once we make the first cuts, the baker will take over distribution," he said, in what I'm sure was meant to be a reassuring tone. "All you have to do is cut, and she'll handle the rest. You're good at cutting things." He took his hand away. "As with so much else in your life, this begins with a stabbing."

"Guess so," I said, and slid Oberon's knife into the cake.

There were no fireworks, just the mingled smell of chocolate and gingerbread, and then Kerry was bustling us out of the way, me still holding the cake-covered knife as she went to work with a knife of her own, dividing and sub-dividing the mountain of cake with incredible speed and precision. Hobs put all their magic into hearthwork, including the construction and, it seems, deconstruction of cakes. She knew what she was doing.

Oberon was gone when I turned around, leaving me holding his knife. I tightened my grip on the handle. I wasn't putting this one down until I could return it to its owner.

In very short order, Tybalt and I had been herded back to another of those little cabaret tables with plates of cake and glasses of sparkling wine, these ones pale yellow and ordinary, even down to the bite of the alcohol when I finally took a drink. No unexpected Firstborn appeared to steal my drink this time, and I sipped gratefully as I looked at the plate in front of me.

The cake was pale in its shell of dark chocolate, topped with three of Kerry's sugar roses, one each in red, white, and pink. Tybalt's slice was darker, with a distinctive scent of spiciness. He had the same number of roses, though.

"No one gets to eat their cake until you do," announced Quentin, sitting down next to me. Dean and Raj were next, dragging chairs to the table and settling like they'd been invited, only leaving enough space for one more person to join us.

Gillian pulled her chair over a moment later.

I stared at her, mouth gone completely dry. I had never felt less like I could eat, or care about, a slice of cake in my life. "Um, hi," I said.

"Hey," she said.

Quentin elbowed me. "Didn't you hear me? I said no one gets to eat their cake until you start eating yours. We're sitting here with *plates of cake* in front of us—cake baked by a Hob who had really good reason to be doing her best work, even—and we can't *eat* it."

I said nothing, but kept staring at my daughter.

Quentin groaned. "I take back every nice thing I've ever said about having you as my knight. You're the worst knight. You torture hungry teenagers for fun. You're heartless and cruel."

Dean poked him with his fork. Quentin yelped and jumped in his seat, turning to glare at his boyfriend with exaggerated dignity while he rubbed the site of the poking with one hand. "Hey!"

"Hey yourself," said Dean. "Be nice to her, she's had a long day."

"We've all had a long day," grumbled Quentin.

"It's nice to see you," I said, having managed to summon the vague thought that if I didn't talk, Gilly might decide I didn't want her here and walk away. If I was the reason she left this time, I didn't know if I'd be able to stand it.

"Yeah," she said. "It's nice to see you, too." She waved a hand at my dress. "You look really . . ."

"Nice?" I guessed.

She smiled, halfway smirking. It was a familiar enough expression to make my heart lurch. "Clean," she said. "From the way everyone talks about you, I figured you'd be covered in blood by this point, not sitting there all white and shiny."

"Stain repellant charms," I said. "Look." I dragged my finger through the frosting on my cake, then wiped it against the bodice of my dress. The act left a thick trail of chocolate on the fabric, until I pulled my hand away. Then the frosting fell off like my dress was somehow frictionless, landing on the table where I could sweep it into my napkin.

"Smart," said Gillian.

Quentin pressed a fork into my hand, trying to urge me to get on with it.

"I can't take credit," I said. "None of this is my doing. Stacy and May handled just about everything."

"I know," she said. "The sea witch explained last week when she came to tell me and Liz that she wanted me to attend. Part of me agreeing to come was her sitting down and spending an hour answering all my questions."

So my daughter had known more about my wedding than I did when we all got to Toronto. Somehow, that didn't bother me the way it would have before the ceremony. It was pretty standard for the rest of my experience here, and if it meant she'd been willing to come, I wasn't going to argue with it. Anything that got her here was fine by me.

"Cool," I said.

"Yeah. Firtha really wanted me to come. She misses her mom." Gillian tucked her hair carelessly back behind her ear. The gesture revealed the dull point of her ear, which wasn't as sharp as it would have been if she'd remained Dóchas Sidhe, like me, but was far too sharp to be mortal, and called attention to the webs between her fingers. Between those, her glass green eyes, and the silver streaks in her hair, she looked less like me all the time.

That was probably a good thing. Children are supposed to look less like their parents as they get older. Unlike me, who just keeps looking more and more like Amandine as I shift my blood away from humanity and toward the fae.

The thought made a knot rise in my throat. Mechanically, I used the fork to cut off my first bite of cake. "So you just came because Firtha wanted you to?"

"Would you be angry if I said yes?"

Gillian looked at me with what seemed like honest curiosity, and so I forced myself to slow down and consider her question, sticking the fork in my mouth as I did. Kerry's cake, which I knew was excellent because she never bakes anything that isn't excellent, tasted like sand. Well, we'd have that sampling platter for later.

Quentin made a small, barking sound of approval and tore into his own cake with enough gusto that everyone around us could see. Some people laughed. Others just glanced up long enough to verify that someone at the bride's table was eating, then began eating their own cake. For the first time since we'd arrived at the reception, near-silence fell across the room, broken by the clank of cutlery against silver plates.

"No," I said finally. "Sad, a little, and disappointed, but no. Firtha deserves to see her mother when she has the chance. I know your relationship with her is special, and a little odd to the rest of the colony. We weren't sure she'd still be able to talk to you after the binding."

"She doesn't talk much," said Gillian. "She sleeps more than she used to, and we both think she's going to go to sleep for good one of these days, the way the rest of the Roane did. But she wanted to stay long enough to see the binding done, and then I asked her not to go if she didn't have to. So she's here because I didn't want to be alone." She looked down at her plate, sounding faintly ashamed of her own admission.

Firtha was the youngest of the Luidaeg's daughters, and when she died, her killer flensed the skin from her body and used it to create a line of Selkies. At some point not too long after that, the skin passed back into the Luidaeg's keeping, and she'd kept it tucked away until my own daughter, who'd been human at the time, had needed it to save her life.

Because Firtha's skin had been unworn for so long, she'd remained trapped inside it in a sense, haunting her own remains. I wasn't entirely clear on how it worked, and neither were May or the Luidaeg, who would have known if anyone did, but she'd been there for Gillian since the moment the skin of the Luidaeg's daughter was draped around my daughter's shoulders.

"I would have been deeply gratified if, in my darker days, someone else could have been with me," said Tybalt, and took a bite of cake. "I've never much cared for being alone."

"I thought cats were solitary," said Gillian.

"A foul untruth," said Tybalt. "The domestic cat is a social creature, preferring to live in large colonies and family groups. This has made your mother, with her fondness for bringing home every stray that crosses her path, absolutely perfect for me. Wherever October goes, she builds a colony around herself, and I am privileged to benefit from her labors."

Gillian looked directly at him for what felt like the first time, and I realized I couldn't remember whether the two of them had ever actually been able to sit down and have a conversation before.

"You're not my stepdad, you know," she said.

Okay, guess not.

"Perhaps not," said Tybalt. "And I hope you will not be angry if I say I don't mind that fact."

She blinked at him, then scowled. "Why? You one of those guys who thinks that when he marries a woman who has a kid, the kid should just magically disappear?"

"Cake is nice," said Quentin. "I sure do like cake. Yay for cake."

"No," said Tybalt. "I appreciate your presence at my wedding more than I can possibly say. You are very important to your mother, and your absence would have been a small but marked blemish upon a day intended to be perfect."

"Armed insurrectionists attacked your wedding!" protested Chelsea, having wandered over with her cake to stand behind Raj's chair.

"And I know the woman I've married," said Tybalt. "Had I not been confident the world would provide some sort of chaotic complication, I might have felt compelled to synthesize one, simply to guarantee her comfort."

"He's not wrong," I said, still watching Gillian closely. "I do better when formal events involve a certain amount of screaming."

"If you say so," said Gillian. She kept her eyes on Tybalt. "I've already got a father, and a mother, and an October, and then there's Liz and Firtha. I'm all full up on people telling me what to do."

"Understood," he said. "Still, for your mother's sake, it would be pleasant if there were space in your life for our branch of your family, strange and convoluted as it seems to be. We would welcome your presence in our home."

"I don't know if I'm ready for that," she said, looking down at her cake. The admission sounded like it pained her.

"What you were told about your mother's motivations—"

"Was untrue, yeah, I know that." She glanced up again. "The woman who raised me is a big ol' liar who told me lots of things that weren't true because she thought she could 'protect' me from Faerie if she just made sure I didn't know it existed. I get that. I still *love* her. She *raised* me. When I had the flu in third grade so bad I couldn't get out of bed for a week, she's the one who held my hair and brought me soup. When I had my first crush, she's the one who told me it was going to be okay. You don't get over that because someone you've spent your whole life hating says 'whoops, sorry, she lied, she's the villain and I'm the good guy.'"

Since that was almost poetically relevant to my own relationship with Simon and Sylvester Torquill, I didn't say anything, just swallowed the contents of my wine glass in one swift gulp. Gillian finally switched her gaze to me.

"But I guess maybe it's time I find out why she was so determined to keep me away from you. So if you really want me to try, I'll try."

I blinked, suddenly finding it difficult to breathe, much less speak or swallow. My daughter being willing to have a relationship with me again, however tenuous, was more important than all the wedding gifts in the world. When the words refused to come, I nodded vigorously, aware of Tybalt setting a hand on my shoulder.

"I think we would all appreciate that," he said.

The sound of someone whacking a spoon against a piece of stemware dragged the entire table's attention back to the buffet, where High King Aethlin Sollys, the second most important man in the room, was holding his wine glass aloft, waiting for the room to focus on him and quiet down.

Bit by bit, it did, with everyone watching him. And to his credit, he bore up under the attention of two of the Firstborn, as well as Oberon himself, remarkably well. It probably helped that he didn't *know* Oberon was looking at him.

"Seven blessings for a bride," he said. "Seven blessings for a new household formed in love and revelry. Sir October Daye, Knight of Lost Words, sworn to Shadowed Hills, Hero in the Mists, do you attend upon me?"

The knot was still in my throat, stopping up my words. I nodded again, and Quentin called, with the strength that only a Banshee could, "She does."

"Then if you've been attending to your guests as you should, you'll have received your first six blessings already, and here is mine," he said. "May you always have open roads and kind fires, and all the winds to guide you. May the fires of the hearth only warm, never scorch, and the waters of the well soothe your thirst, but never steal your breath away. May you be happy."

Tybalt put his arm around me, pulling me close. My daughter was willing to try again, and my squire was by my side, and all my family was nearby.

"May you be healthy."

This wasn't an ending, and it didn't feel like one, but it was a culmination in many ways. It was a homecoming. And it was time, finally, to let myself be happy.

"May all of Faerie welcome you wherever you go."

I turned to Tybalt, smiling, and kept smiling as he leaned in and kissed me.

Happiness didn't sound so bad.